'A tender, powerful and richly embroidered novel from a courageous st...teller... Bhutto's new novel will move you with its profound wisdom and sharp grasp of our ...times'

ELIF SHAFAK, AUTHOR OF *10 MINUTES 38 SECONDS IN THIS STRANGE WORLD*

—

'A shocking, moving and deeply compassionate novel'

VOGUE

—

'Highly topical . . . an involving and satisfying novel'

FINANCIAL TIMES

—

'This is a bold and probing novel, from a writer strikingly alert to something small and true: the disquietude of youth, the vulnerability and the foolishness – and how catastrophically it can be exploited'

GUARDIAN

—

'Every page of this is priceless. I can't think of a better guide through the world we live in. I've never used the word "transformative" before, but I just did now'

GARY SHTEYNGART, AUTHOR OF *SUPER SAD TRUE LOVE STORY*

—

'As compassionate as it is trenchant, this rare fiction is an illuminating guide through the great disorder of our times'

PANKAJ MISHRA, AUTHOR OF *AGE OF ANGER*

—

ABOUT THE AUTHOR

Fatima Bhutto was born in Kabul, Afghanistan in 1982. She grew up
in Syria and Pakistan. She is the author of six books of fiction and
non-fiction. Her debut novel, the highly acclaimed *The Shadow of the
Crescent Moon*, was longlisted in 2014 for the Bailey's Women's Prize
for Fiction.

The Runaways

FATIMA BHUTTO

PENGUIN BOOKS

PENGUIN BOOKS

UK | USA | Canada | Ireland | Australia
India | New Zealand | South Africa

Penguin Books is part of the Penguin Random House group of companies
whose addresses can be found at global.penguinrandomhouse.com.

First published by Viking 2019
Published in Penguin Books 2020
001

Set in 12.5/14.75 pt Garamond MT Std
Typeset by Jouve (UK), Milton Keynes
Printed and bound in Great Britain by Clays Ltd, Elcograf S.p.A.

A CIP catalogue record for this book is available from the British Library

ISBN: 978–0–241–34701–0

www.greenpenguin.co.uk

For the brave and the defiant are never forgotten:
Shaheed Aitzaz Hasan Bangash (1998–2014)
Shaheed Mashal Khan (1994–2017)

And always, forever, for the Beloved

And I was lost in Rita for two years
And for two years she slept on my arm
And we made promises
Over the most beautiful of cups
And we burned in the wine on our lips
And we were born again.

Mahmoud Darwish

Anita Rose

Karachi, April 2016

The moon hangs low in the night.

Anita Rose Joseph closes her eyes. She opens them.

The stars are drowned by Karachi's endless curls of dirt and smog, the glow of the terminal, and the floodlights mounted to blind the road leading towards Jinnah International Airport.

Anita Rose keeps her gaze down, away from the towering billboards advertising Gulf Airlines and skin-lightening creams. 'Max Fairness for Max Confidence,' a purple-and-black advertisement promises over the smiling face of a famously fair cricketer. She walks alongside the queued-up Pajeros and Toyotas, impatiently and pointlessly honking, climbing the long slope to the departure terminal.

Under the cover of darkness, before the floodlights bleed into dawn, a mynah bird, with its yellow bandit-beak and orange eyes cut through its coarse black plumage, sings.

Anita lifts her eyes for a moment, looking for the lonely bird. But in the early hours of the morning she can see nothing in the dark, empty sky, not even the dacoit dressed up as a mynah bird. The moon carries only the heaviness of the city, suspended in the charcoal sky.

Anita pulls her *dupatta* tighter around her face. She

closes her eyes, irritated by the blinding floodlights, and opens them, breathing slowly, reminding herself of what she must do.

She holds her passport and red notebook tight against her chest and exhales deeply. Aside from a small bag with a necessary change of clothing and some make-up, she has no other luggage.

Ahead, a Pajero inches forward; it brakes at the checkpoint manned by armed commandos. A Ranger with a submachine gun strapped to his chest walks towards the Pajero, but no one gets out of the car. The front window rolls down, letting out a blast of English pop music as a driver relays the name of a VIP. Anita moves slowly, not wanting to draw attention to herself. She stops just before she reaches the jeep and waits for it to pass.

Even with the loud music, the rumble of the running engine and the sound of the commandos circling the car, lifting the bonnet, opening the back, searching it for explosives, Anita Rose can still hear the mynah bird.

On Netty Jetty, overlooking the mangroves that crawl thin just before the Arabian Sea, kites swarm the sky like a thick cover of clouds, waiting for lovers to throw chunks of meat to them – or if the lovers cannot afford the bloody parcels sold on the bridge, then small doughy balls of bread. In the chaos of Karachi's congested traffic, surrounded by barefoot boys promising in their high-pitched voices that your dreams will come true if you feed the hungry, Anita always felt protected by the soar of kites. And though she is almost certain that the mynah she hears so late at night is all alone, she is also almost certain that it has come to walk her safely through the airport, with its yellow feet and bandit-beak, and out of this city forever.

The Pajero's engine is still running and the fumes from its exhaust choke the air around Anita. Coughing into her palm, she doesn't hear the VIP's name, but she can see the silhouette of a young woman, voluminous hair held back by sunglasses, perched on the crown of her head. The VIP presses a button and her window begins to open. No one lowers the music; it plays at full volume, percussion and thumping bass. As the VIP moves, a piece of jewellery reflects everywhere, a thousand rays of iridescent light.

The Ranger with the Heckler & Koch cranes his neck to see through the narrow slit. *As salam alaikum,* he salutes the VIP briskly.

Anita looks behind her, there's no one there. No one has followed her here.

As the Pajero raises its windows, muffling the music, and begins its climb towards the terminal, and before airport security can see her, Anita traces the shadow of a cross along the hollow of her clavicle. No one has noticed she has gone. No one except the birds.

Anita Rose lifts the thumb that drew the sign of the holy cross to her lips and closes her eyes for a kiss.

This city will take your heart, Osama had told her. You don't know what Karachi does to people like us. Take your heart, do you hear?

Anita had not understood the rage in his voice then. She had not understood that he was angry for her, long before anyone had hurt her. Anita didn't like it when she didn't

3

understand Osama. No matter her age, those moments made her feel just as puny and small as she had been the first time she knocked on his gunmetal door, all those years ago.

It was late at night and Anita had snuck out of her mother's suffocating home to be with him, with Osama comrade *sahib*. Her only ally. Her one true friend. The evening was perfumed by *champa* flowers that bloomed amongst the garbage in Machar Colony and that summer, just before the monsoons, the scent of the white flowers was so strong Anita could no longer smell the sea.

'How do I protect myself?' she had asked him.

Osama ran his hand through his dishevelled silver hair. He lifted his spirit and drank the medicinal liquid slowly, before placing the glass smudged with his fingerprints on his knee and leaning forward, so close that Anita could count the fine grooves of his iris, the lines that cut and coloured the warm brown of his eyes.

'You take *their* heart,' he whispered, even though no one could hear them on the roof – not the trees that wilted in the summer heat, not the constellation of yellow-and-white flowers that bloomed in the rain. 'Anita Rose,' Osama caught himself on her name, 'promise me: you take theirs *first*.'

Anita blinks quickly as her sandals hit the asphalt this cool, starless Karachi night. Above her, over the flood-lights, around the Rangers in their camouflage uniforms, past the armed man who holds his dry palm out for Anita's passport, overlooking Karachi – a city so tired it can be overpowered by the fragrance of monsoon flowers, a city so beautiful Anita cannot bear to look back at it, now that she knows she is leaving – the moon hangs low in the sky.

Anita places her bag gently on the ground, freeing a hand to pull the fabric of her polyester *dupatta* tighter around her face, so the commando cannot see her properly.

The Ranger lifts his eyes from Anita's passport, its faint green pages crisp and relatively unstamped, and looks at the girl in the yellow *shalwar kameez* standing before him. He runs his finger along the photo, scratching the laminated page with his nail.

Anita watches the young Ranger. The hair on his face is light brown, though his stubble is flecked with white on his chin and near his sideburns. Without the worry lines pinching the space between his eyebrows and the frown deepening along his forehead, he would be handsome.

His walkie-talkie cackles with static and Anita drops her gaze to the scuffed black of the commando's boots. She holds her breath and waits for him to recognize her.

Does he?

Anita looks behind her once more. No one. No one has thought to check the airport. No one has noticed she's gone.

The commando reads the name in Anita's passport, almost to himself, and flips through the pages once more, in case he missed something, turning it round in his hands before handing it back to her.

'Are you travelling alone?' the Ranger asks Anita softly, stepping closer to her, a note of concern in his voice. 'It's not safe here,' he gestures at the empty, floodlit tarmac before them. The air smells of cigarette smoke and sleep, heavy and sweet. 'Not for a young girl.'

Anita instinctively takes a step backwards and wipes the corner of her eye with a finger, using her notebook for cover. In ten minutes she will clear this checkpoint, collect her boarding pass, float through security and be gone. Forever.

She thought once more of comrade *sahib*'s words; she never lost anything he taught her. Every line, every word, every poem is in that notebook of hers. If you let it, this city will shatter you. It will take your heart like a trophy, like Salome receiving the Baptist's head. But Anita Rose, tall and slender in *champa* yellow, standing alone before Jinnah International at four in the morning, was not like everyone.

One day, the city would burn and someone would ask her: Karachi? Wasn't that your home? And she would shake her head slowly, *no*. Even smiling, *not at all*.

'*Beta?*'

Anita Rose lifts her eyes and looks at the young commando, not old enough to call her *beta*. Maybe the rough stubble on his chin wasn't white; maybe it had only been lightened by the harsh glare of Karachi's sun.

'Thank you, Uncle,' she picks up her bag. 'I'll be safe soon.'

PART ONE

They Call Me the Lion

2014–16

Anita Rose

Karachi, 2014

In the small, grey cement room lit by a solitary naked bulb, Zenobia dragged her hands, glistening with silvery coconut oil, through her daughter's long hair. Anita Rose closed her eyes and tried to imagine herself as one of the women she had seen in the dramas on TV who sat in pink chairs and had their beautiful light-brown hair washed and dried in salons.

'Anita . . .' Zenobia shook a slim glass bottle of *sarson ke tayl*, splashing her palm with the bitter-smelling liquid. She rubbed her hands together, warming the oil before continuing. 'We don't have any gas left, nothing to cook with.'

Her mother yanked her fingers through the tangles in Anita's hair, jerking her head backwards and her mind away from her floating dreams. Anita squeezed her eyes shut and concentrated harder, resisting the damp cold in their bare room. She pictured her mother's sad voice getting lost in the knots of her hair.

'Baby?'

Zenobia's brown oval face had rounded out over the past few years. The small pouches under her eyes seemed heavier and her already-swollen lips bulged slightly, the way a face looks when it cries and cries and cries.

'We need some gas to cook with.'

Anita shook her head. Her hair smelled sweet and bitter like the coconut and mustard oils.

'Anita.' Her mother's voice was tighter, angrier.

Anita Rose closed her eyes again and imagined herself wearing a plush pink towel, sitting in one of those pink chairs, being perfumed and pampered and offered tea thick with milk, and sugar that came in little cubes. The kind you picked up with a silver tong. She had seen it on one of the shows, long ago. A man used it to pick up ice from a metal bucket.

'I don't want to,' Anita said the words softly so her mother would not shout at her for being *batameez*. She said it softly because she wanted her mama to know that it made her stomach hurt to go there and ask.

The first time she went to Osama Shah's flat as a young girl, Anita tiptoed up the stairs to the old man's house shyly, trying to make as little noise as possible. She passed a boy in the stairwell playing football against the wall, all by himself. He was a few years older than she was then and, with his dark eyes furrowed and his face frowning, kicking the ball angrily and then stopping it with his chest, he didn't even notice Anita climbing past him. 'Hello, my dear,' their neighbour, Osama, opened his gunmetal door, looking down sweetly at Anita, who had come to ask for rice. No one had ever called her 'dear' before.

Since then, Zenobia had treated the old Marxist across the *gully* as her own supply shop. She knew Osama lived alone. She knew the man had no family and a robust pension from his days with Pakistan Railways. She knew also that he was fond of her daughter, though Anita seemed almost desperate to avoid asking for things, from anyone. She didn't like asking for water, no matter how dry her throat; she didn't want to beg the use of his cooker or ask to borrow oil or sugar – she especially hated asking for that.

Anita felt uneasy disturbing their old neighbour, who was always – no matter what time she knocked on the gunmetal door – alone. She could smell the emptiness of his life, the dust of books, strewn all over his simple home and gathered on yellowing pages and cracked spines, the smell of food spoiling in plastic bags and ageing in containers and, worst of all, the odour of his *sharab*, a clear liquid he poured into a tall glass, cradling it in his palm as though hiding it from her, which lingered in the air like sweat and paint, curdled together.

After Osama Shah opened the door, Anita lowered her eyes, so he would not see the indignity of her return, back to ask for more. She would relay her mother's request and Osama would say nothing, shuffling towards the kitchen shelves to retrieve what she had asked for.

Anita was grateful for that kindness, she was grateful that he never looked surprised or annoyed at her presence. He never pretended an interest in her circumstance, never burdened her with small talk or meaningless chit-chat about her studies or the weather.

But still, she wrapped her thin arms around her stomach. She didn't want to go there. Anita never knew what to say to the old man, not even now that she was older, almost sixteen.

'The man likes you. You have to go.'

*

When they were children, Ezra had told Anita that the man in the drama with the silver tongs was drinking wine with his ice from the metal bucket. Why do people drink wine? Anita had asked her brother. She had never seen any before. Was it sweet?

Because, Ezra answered, smirking, people drink *sharab* because it tastes of heaven. Even though he was only a measly six years older than his sister, he lorded his age and infinite experience over her. Because it makes you forget all your sorrows.

He told her the man next door, their neighbour, he drank wine every day. Even though he was poor.

At that time, when she was in class four, Anita had her own troubles. She didn't have time to worry about being poor. At school, the girls sharing her bench would kick at her heels. Anita learned to cross her legs, wrapping one over the other, protecting the narrow tendons of her ankles with her chunky black school shoes. But the girls found other, less ambiguous ways of letting Anita Rose know how they felt about her. 'Go home,' Mira would hiss as she knocked Anita's copybook off the desk.

At the front of the Lady Girls' English Medium College, Prep to Matric classroom, a teacher with a slight stoop and long, unvarnished nails recited sums out loud: *two twos are four, three threes are nine, four fours are sixteen, five fives are twenty-five*. With every set, the teacher slapped a ruler against her palm. *Six sixes are thirty-six, seven sevens are foh-ty-nine*.

The girls on the bench would crowd together, squeezing Anita between them. Anita used to try to defend her space, pushing them back with her elbows, but when they

12

kept pressing against her, she invariably moved forward, sitting with her bottom on the edge of the hard wooden seat. In new, improvised moves, someone would flick a nail against her neck or spit down her shirt collar. But usually Mira pulled her hair. Without turning round, Anita would collect the hair she had tied in a ponytail that morning and wind it into a snail's shell at the top of her head, adjusting a taut rubber band around the bun.

'*Kutee ke bachi*,' Mira would whisper, her voice buried under the drone of the teacher's sums. Her breath always smelled like onions and *achar* early in the morning. 'No one wants you here.'

On cue, one of the other girls sitting on the bench would lift her knee straight up to her chest and bring it hard against Anita's back, pushing her to the ground. And Anita would slip easily off her seat, knocking her cheek against the desk on her way down.

'Anita!' Zenobia slapped her greasy hand on the thin cotton of her thighs. Her *kameez* was a delicate green like the stalks of mustard flowers. Anita stood to her feet and swept her eyes around the room. In the corner were the three *rallies* they rolled out every night to sleep on, her mother's worn plastic bag of oils, their small cooker, a stack of plates that her mother wrapped in a torn *dupatta*. On the wall, on top of a small cupboard where they kept their clothes and school books, was a piece of glossy paper the size of a damaged, wrinkled photograph. In the middle of his blue robes, Jesus's heart burned. With one hand he pointed to the flames, with the other he sheltered it from the world.

Sunny

Portsmouth, 2015

Cricket had been the early love of Sunny's life. It was a gentleman's game, a slow, elegant sport that cultivated not only stamina in a player, but also subtle perception. But when his modest athletic scholarship to the University of Portsmouth came in, it was on the strength of his boxing, not his fast bowling, that Sunny had been selected.

Whatever his own personal failures, Sulaiman Jamil had always cheered his son's successes. Sunny's victories couldn't come fast enough. First, a Bachelor's degree from a marvellous university, next a beautiful job in a booming industry, then an office in the city, a Jaguar, a warm and loving wife, some children. Mixed-race, Hindu, Muslim, Sulaiman Jamil didn't mind.

That was all Sunny ever heard at home.

Be someone else. Do something else. Be better. Fit in more, try more, work hard. Don't get stuck in a dead-end job, don't marry the first lady who comes your way, don't be a slave all your life. Pa repeated his mantras, smoothing down his soft brown hair, its colour fading with age, absenting himself from his life's own failures, transmuting his personal traumas into general advice.

I only want you to be happy, he told his son repeatedly. What father can rest until he sees his boy settled?

It made Sunny laugh, coming home from running in the park to see his pa sitting at the kitchen table, the acceptance letter with the second-class stamp propped up before him. The first time that he'd done right by him, it felt like. He would major in business studies for Pa too; he would have preferred Islamic history or even sports therapy, but there was no money in that, no future, Pa said. And a future was all a man really ever had.

'My boy,' his widowed pa, Sulaiman Jamil, sang softly when he held the thin acceptance letter in his hands. Sunny had left the envelope with the second-class stamp on the kitchen counter for his father to see. It was one of the few times he had sought his approval. 'What a thing you've done . . . what a marvellous thing you've done . . .' As though Pa knew all about the place, as if he'd got in himself. He hadn't gone to university, only a polytechnic back in the old country, but his parents couldn't afford it and, after a year, Pa was forced to drop out. It was a story he told Sunny over and over, embellishing the drama of his life with extra details in every telling.

It had been the first of his life's tragedies.

Sulaiman Jamil had not studied and so was denied the life he deserved. As a young man, he had seen and re-seen all the great James Bond films of his time – *Moonraker*, *Live and Let Die*, *Octopussy* – in cinemas clouded with the honeyed smell of *beedi*, masala chai and potato samosas, and had devotedly checked out all the Ian Fleming books from the circulating library.

It was with Nur Muhammad, his long-lost best friend, that Sulaiman Jamil had seen his first James Bond. Folded into the torn leather cinema seats, together they watched car chase after ski chase, instantly disrobing women, and saw 007 disobey one superior after another as he flirted with a revolving rota of secretaries, all the time taking careful note of the gleaming, elegant MI6 offices. As the dense *beedi* smoke rose up around them, obscuring the light of the projector, the two friends gripped the arms of their seats and didn't utter a word. Only after the film had ended to a rousing Shirley Bassey number and they lurched out through a dingy corridor into the cinema's courtyard, their eyes adjusting to the harsh afternoon sunlight, did Nur Muhammad break their awestruck silence.

'*Bhai*, those offices,' he blurted out. 'They were so neat and clean . . .'

After polytechnic in Lucknow, but before Portsmouth and the journey there by plane, before the travel agent at Janpath in Delhi who had cheated him, a suffocating Air India flight staffed by superior but inept sari-clad stewardesses, filled with the shrieks of bawling babies and the smell of the air sick-bags being used, and which Sulaiman Jamil could not imagine being strong enough to transport the burden of his expectations across the black waters of exile; before he packed away his life into a single brown cloth suitcase, Sulaiman Jamil had been struck by his life's second tragedy: marriage.

His second cousin, a thin crane of a girl – in her slippers, she stood a head taller than Sulaiman – had been un-marriageable. Safiya Begum was too dark-skinned, too severe, too aloof to have found a match among her peers. Her poor Muslim family had gifted her a name befitting a Mughal princess in the hope of brightening the stars in her favour. But they needn't have bothered. A question of debt and settling an unpaid loan had been enough to change her fortune. You don't have to love her, Sulaiman Jamil's father told his son on his wedding night. It is not a promise expected of you, Jamil senior counselled his son.

But Sulaiman Jamil wanted to love his wife flamboyantly, with panache, the way he had seen James Bond court Miss Moneypenny and all those lithe gymnasts and glamorous villains. He sat next to her on their bed, the first night they were husband and wife, and cleared his throat. Safiya Begum's hair was perfumed with sandalwood and her hands were stained orange with henna – a smell he instinctively recoiled from, but still he wanted to try. When Sulaiman Jamil reached for his bride's hand, she pulled it away.

Tragedy number two: he did not have to love the woman he married.

Tragedy number three: she did not have to love him, either.

Sulaiman Jamil had never been in the right place at the right time. That was the alchemy of life, he always believed – timing. But if only it had been that simple. After all, what sort of Indian believed in time?

Even this Indian, escaping the hour of his birth, his family home, his polytechnic college, flying off to England, even he didn't have the heart to fool himself entirely about the powers of time.

Nur Muhammad insisted his friend was making the wrong decision. 'Cent per cent, *bhai*, you are wrong,' he said, shaking his head as Sulaiman Jamil recounted his plans to settle in England. 'They don't have anything to offer the world now,' Nur Muhammad argued. 'They don't grow cotton, don't plant tobacco, not even a stalk of basmati grows in that frigid English countryside.'

Nur Muhammad, like Sulaiman Jamil, didn't know England. He didn't know anything except the isolation of India. But Nur Muhammad was staying; he had made up his mind and would not be persuaded by Sulaiman Jamil. He saw the future as eastwards-facing. India, finally free, unshackled, had its arms open to the world.

'But, Nur Muhammad,' Sulaiman gently warned, the last time he tried to convince his dearest friend to accompany him, 'if you don't leave now, you might not have another chance.'

'Why would I want to leave later?' Nur Muhammad replied innocently. He was working on an idea, a top business plan. He had been speaking to elders who would loan him a lakh here, ten thousand there, and he was going to take their money and move to Varanasi, setting up a tour company catering exclusively to foreign travellers. No matter what Sulaiman Jamil told Nur Muhammad, he would not budge. It was a top business plan, Nur Muhammad promised. He would not leave.

Sulaiman Jamil embraced his friend when they met for the last time, exiting a brightly lit cinema after having watched *Licence to Kill*, a startlingly dazzling Bond starring Timothy Dalton. Even though he understood that the grandeur of cinema existed in the lies, Sulaiman Jamil still imagined that the world that would meet him, post-exile, would bear some resemblance to the glamour and excitement of (preferably) Roger Moore's movie life. He was not naïve, but he had hoped that if roulette tables, tuxedos, Aston Martins and stylish gadgets were not nearby, they would be at least in the vicinity of his new neat and clean existence.

At the very least, Sulaiman Jamil would dress in tweed, smoke refined cigarettes out of an engraved silver case and live in a sleek house with all the latest mod cons. It was a shame Nur Muhammad did not feel he deserved the same things; even more shameful that he was not prepared to sacrifice for them.

'*Khuda hafiz*,' Sulaiman Jamil wished Nur Muhammad affectionately as they parted, holding his worries deep in his heart. Who would look after his friend, now that Sulaiman Jamil was gone? Who would pick him up and encourage him after his business collapsed?

Sulaiman Jamil pressed 5,000 rupees into Nur Muhammad's palm. It was nothing, all he could afford to give, taken out of the enveloped gifts given to him and Safiya Begum at their wedding. 'Something small,' he mumbled, embarrassed, patting his friend's hand, which he noted did not resist the donation. Nur Muhammad didn't do the polite thing and pretend to refuse the present. This surprised Sulaiman Jamil, but also made him sad. Even before he began to work on his 'top business' venture, Nur Muhammad seemed to acknowledge that it would be a failure. Sulaiman Jamil left Lucknow even more certain that a good life awaited only those who dared.

But from the moment he landed at Heathrow one autumn morning, immediately pierced by the chill in his gabardine suit tailored at K.P. Shahani & Sons, it was as though he had never left India. He heard the sweepers in the airport loo speaking Punjabi, was rudely and roughly interrogated by a Hindu lady officer at immigration, who still seemed to blame the Partition of India on educated Muslims like himself, and suffered the long train ride south, missing his connections, which were delayed to the point of absurdity, forcing Sulaiman Jamil and his new bride (even less amused at this tragic series of déjà vu) to sleep in a cold train station, curled over their cloth suitcases like the nearby hobos, smelling of the musky, rotting-wood odour of unwashed hair, their arms lovingly embracing black bin-bags of belongings, shopping trolleys parked at their sides.

His brother-in-law had found him a job at Fratton Station, Sulaiman Jamil whispered to his wife as she pulled her lambswool cardigan tighter over her belly to protect herself from the falling night temperature. He would be an announcer, but he said the word with less pride than he would have done a day before. An Announcer. He had taken elocution lessons at the British Council in Lucknow. He would do it right, Sulaiman promised, shaking his head with determination – that he would, all right.

But all that met Sulaiman Jamil in Portsmouth were replicas of home: kitchens smelling of curry, the toxic scent of *methi* clinging to the walls, everyone – his sister, all his Lucknow expatriated friends and neighbours, but most of all him – keeping their heads down and holding their breath in the dreadful anticipation of something greater, that neat and clean life, that never seemed to come.

Tragedies four (or five, depending on his mood) through seven encompassed the humiliations of travel, migration, perfecting the new accents and intonations of a language that, although familiar, seemed foreign in Portsmouth, and the continued alienation of his wife.

In order to make their new house a home, Sulaiman Jamil brought his wife flowers every Sunday morning. A few daisies picked from the park, nothing extravagant, but the gesture went by unnoticed all the same. He left *The News* open on the horoscope page so that she could read her sign, but aside from cutting out and collecting articles on Princess Di, Safiya Begum only used the paper to soak up the oil of freshly fried onions.

Sulaiman Jamil was encouraged by Safiya Begum's fascination with the glamorous English royal, relieved that she was finally taking an interest in her new country. He had hoped, deep down, that this would result in his wife loosening up, and imagined that she would begin to act a bit like the liberated women in his favourite films.

Sitting on the foot of the bed as she slept one morning, before they had figured out how the heating worked, Sulaiman Jamil took Safiya Begum's feet in his hands. Cupping his fingers around her heel, he pressed down and tried to warm and soothe his wife's skin with his own. For a few minutes, Safiya Begum didn't stir. She lay on the bed, her knees bent into her chest, and let her husband massage her feet. Do you see, Sulaiman said softly, how much we need each other here? It's only us, Safiya Begum. We have no one else.

He had never massaged anyone's legs before, only his mother's, and he pushed his thumb gently against Safiya Begum's ankle, just as he had done as a child. Sulaiman Jamil bent his body and brought his lips down to the finely criss-crossed skin above his wife's arches, but before he could kiss her feet, Safiya Begum pulled her legs away. Don't be disgusting, she snapped with irritation, sitting up quickly and removing herself from the bed. She shoved her feet into her house slippers and pulled her robe tight against her body. I'm not Fergie, she shouted, slamming their bedroom door behind her.

England, she later complained to her husband, had made him a pervert.

Portsmouth was not grand; it was definitely not London. But it was still a step up from Varanasi.

Sulaiman Jamil wrote to Nur Muhammad of the neat and clean life he was slowly but steadily building, folding a ten-pound note in a sheet of white paper so it wouldn't show through the gauzy blue airmail envelope. These were lies Nur Muhammad would never catch, because he could never have imagined how poor England was, often bewilderingly so. With its small houses, sunless harbour and streets coated with the yeasty smell of beer, even in the early morning, it failed to conjure up the new beginnings of life that Sulaiman Jamil had imagined.

Loneliness had a scent that Sulaiman Jamil came to associate with Portsmouth – it was the dour smell of the roads after a football match, of rain, of pensioners who stank of cat hair or the feline smell of urine, pungent and overpowering as you stood behind their mottled bodies, spotted with the blue-and-purple bruises of old age, at the supermarket or post office.

He loathed this poverty of England's, more so than India's – the poverty of takeaway boxes strewn on the roads, festering in unheated homes and the waiting rooms of betting shops, jeans exposing pale buttock cleavage, women slack under clingfilm skies, foolishly burning their great advantages over the futilely toiling masses of the Subcontinent.

He hoped that one day his newborn son would avoid this dismal fate – the poverty of the educated and overfed, which was so much more fearful than the rag-and-bone destitution of India.

But Portsmouth was what Sulaiman Jamil could afford. It was where he knew people, others who had escaped Lucknow and had called him here, assuring him that he would all but be given the keys to a brave new life. But England was cold and grey and quiet – the worst was the quiet, both in his loveless house and in the streets where mothers shushed their children and men spoke loudly to each other, but never to a passing stranger.

There were no animals, no bullock carts, no dung fires with their smoky mesquite smell, no children screaming as they swam in the canals – nothing. A deathly silence welcomed every day, the long lonely hours between day and night broken only by dolorous church bells.

Emerging from those *beedi*-perfumed cinemas and James Bond films of long ago, Sulaiman Jamil had yearned for adventure and beauty, but instead he had found in England a cold power that destroyed all possibility of love and intimacy. It made him secretly long for, despite himself, the grit and the grime, the broken pavements and dusty roads that he had sought to escape, the squalor in which it was never possible, even for the powerful, to forget that one was human and frail.

It's not what I expected, Sulaiman Jamil confessed to

his wife, her back turned to him as she stood at the kitchen counter, stretching dough with her gaunt hands. The small curve of her shoulder moved sensuously as she pulled and massaged the *atta*, but Safiya Begum said nothing. She did not turn to comfort her husband, her only friend in this strange, foreign land. And you? Sulaiman Jamil had asked, longingly, seeking commiseration, friendship, even just a suggestion of casual solidarity.

Safiya Begum leaned her pelvis against the kitchen counter, rolling the dough as far as she could. I didn't expect anything, she finally replied, without turning round to face her husband, whose skin was pale and ashy in the English winter.

Sulaiman Jamil's loneliness was only removed by the grief that flooded his heart in a way he did not expect, when Safiya Begum died suddenly from a vicious and decisive strain of breast cancer, leaving him behind to care for a two-year-old child.

Even in sickness, even after the cancer spread and ate away her body, even then Safiya Begum hadn't turned to her husband and taken his hand. She said she was ashamed by the sight of her metastasized breasts, the smell of death that surrounded her, the soft tufts of hair that fell on her shoulders like dandruff, so she distanced herself even more. Finally, in death, she had managed to be free of her husband. Let me die in peace, Safiya Begum begged Sulaiman Jamil. For once, won't you just leave me be?

'Look at you now,' Sulaiman Jamil smiled at his young son. This was the moral of the story: Sulaiman Jamil had fought the karma of his life to build something new, something better for his precious child, his only boy. 'We did all right, didn't we?'

Sunny nodded at his pa.

'You and me, the two of us? We did good, didn't we?'

Standing at the kitchen counter, Sunny watched his father's eyes fill with tears. He bowed his head and nodded once more.

'You have a home, you have a city, a country even – a place in the world.' Sulaiman Jamil's voice broke with emotion. 'You have a father who loves you. What more could your poor papa have given you?'

Just a moment ago, holding his University of Portsmouth John Doe acceptance letter, they were happy. Sunny was happy. He felt it. But it was gone now. Happiness didn't hold. Nothing lasted very long for Sunny Jamil.

'Nothing,' Sunny mumbled, reaching out his arm to squeeze his old pa's shoulder, massaging him for a moment, before leaning forward to embrace him. His pa. His protector, his defender. 'I've got everything I need.'

Monty

London, 2015

The English capital was cool in the evenings. With a fine mist of pollen in the air, July in London felt like Karachi in winter. They had dinner plans at Novikov, and Papa had called a taxi from his phone, insisting on using Addison Lee instead of Uber. Akbar Ahmed said he didn't come all the way here just to sit in a Prius, have his identity known to the driver – nearly always called Mohammad – and then have to endure long harangues about fasting in the summertime.

It was just the one time, Monty pointed out, but Papa was still annoyed. Two days ago, arriving via Emirates from Dubai, they had sat in the heavily perfumed car of a cockney-accented Uber driver with two gold teeth and a toothpick dangling from the corner of his lips, which he flicked around with his tongue; he was from, it turned out, Multan.

As salam alaikum, this Mohammad in ripped jeans and a Juve jersey said in a voice dripping with sanctimony as soon as they had shut the doors. *Salam*, Monty mumbled, while Mummy nodded and Papa rolled his eyes.

The driver watched the Ahmeds in the rear-view mirror, taking his eyes off the road to turn round and look at them as he pulled the car out of the Heathrow parking

26

lot. Khadija, their maid, sat in the front seat, Zahra's carry-on bag pressed against her knees, holding the family's four permissible duty-free bottles of Laphroaig in her lap. A plastic silver-painted الله اكبر hung from the mirror, twirling slowly, as they made their way onto the M4. *Bismillah*, Khadija whispered, reassured, pulling her hijab tighter around her face while trying to stop the bottles from clanking noisily against each other. Mohammad clocked the duty-free bags out of the corner of his eye and exhaled deeply. '*Astaghfirallah*,' he muttered, as though complaining about the traffic.

Monty had taken a sip of coffee, bought at Caffè Nero while Papa was changing money, and the driver, biting his tongue after hearing the clank-clank of the bottles in the front seat, lifted his toothpick from his lips and shook his head. 'Only the first week of *Ramzan*, mate, couldn't you wait till *iftar*?'

Monty laughed nervously. It was a long flight, he replied – you didn't have to fast while travelling, he thought, not that he kept any *rosas* anyway. Zahra, who was fasting, flight or not, patted her son's knee and looked out at the overcast skies, ignoring the young driver.

'It's not for everyone,' the Uber driver continued in his thick accent, glancing sideways at the maid and then back at the Ahmeds, before sliding the toothpick behind his ear. 'Needs real commitment, real understanding of the faith, you know?'

Monty was glad that Khadija couldn't speak English and would miss this dig at his impious family. Papa rolled down the window, muttering that his suit would smell like a rose-petal factory, but Mohammad carried on.

'Took me mam for *Umrah* last year,' he smiled in the rear-view mirror. 'I work seven days a week, drive an Uber on me off-time. Can't afford to travel for *vay-cay-shun*, just to faff around shopping and looking at sights, you know? Took me just five days off last summer and went with the family to Mecca Medina, *subhanallah*.'

He turned to Khadija, nodding his head, but she wouldn't understand anything the driver said, especially not the Arabic words mispronounced in his cockney drawl.

'Could you put the radio on?' Papa snapped at the driver, but Mohammad shook his head. 'Sorry, mate,' he spoke coldly, '*haram* to listen to music during *Ramzan*.' He clicked his tongue against the roof of his mouth, reaching for his wet toothpick and returning it to his lips. 'Thought, from your tags, you'd know better, coming from Pakistan and all.'

Akbar Ahmed thought of complaining to Uber and asking for his money back, but settled for a single-star review of the BBCD driver. British-Born Confused *Desi*, Papa typed simply, as the justification for his low rating. They may have been civilians here, but Akbar Ahmed's position, his social standing, required a certain respect. He would not be spoken down to and lectured on religion by some second-generation immigrant from Multan. Not here, not in London.

Papa wanted to be chauffeured by white men, suited and booted, not in ripped jeans. Addison Lee was not ideal, frankly, they used Romanians almost exclusively, but they would do.

The family had been subjected to Papa's sour lectures on Brexit and the failures of British transport since that first taxi ride – two days of complaints and unhelpful suggestions on hospitality and urban planning. It wasn't so complicated, Papa said. He wanted to be called 'sir', respectfully be handed a selection of financial newspapers and have his door opened for him. Most of all, though, he wanted an executive car with a driver who would zip him through Knightsbridge and Park Lane without any *bak bak* on the way to dinner. 'How would you like us to go to The Connaught, Mr Ahmed, sir?' his favourite driver, Aleksander, once asked him. 'Silently,' Akbar Ahmed replied.

Back home in Pakistan, the Ahmeds never had to struggle for anything. Our people made this country, Akbar Ahmed had told Monty since he was a child. Our people embroidered the dream of Pakistan. We wove it out of the clouds, out of thin air. It was a sacrifice, the Ahmeds believed, that forever insured them against difficulty or hardship of any kind. We birthed a country – our very own – moving millions across this ancient soil, shifting land like mah-jong tiles across a board.

As the fires of Partition swept from *gully* to *gully* and neighbours plundered each other's homes, hacking women and children to death, Monty's grandfather walked off his Deccan army base with nothing in his pocket but his cigarettes and matches, his service pistol holstered to his hip. He walked across Hyderabad and, as the family legend had it, all the way to Bombay, where he boarded a steamer for Karachi.

We are *nawabs*, Akbar Ahmed often told his scion, his only son. In the draughty haveli that once was the Ahmed abode, thirteen gun salutes met the princes every dawn. In the morning, at a more civilized hour, soldiers and

29

boiled eggs, presented in ruby-encrusted cups, were served on the verandah. Armando, the family Borzoi, lay on the freshly cut grass and waited for breakfast to be over. The dog was nearly one and a half metres tall and wore a shaggy brindle coat. Every morning he sat patiently, resting his long, elegant snout on your grandfather's polished dress shoes. Every day Armando the Borzoi's wet shadow had to be wiped off the English leather by one of the Ahmed valets. Some days Nawab Ahmed didn't even bother, that's how close master and dog were.

But your grandfather, the romantic, gave up his monogrammed Rolls-Royce and bespoke Cartier leopards. He gave up the shoe-shiners, the egg-boilers, and even, sadly, Armando, who was too old to make the journey to a new country – all for the very idea of Pakistan. He re-joined the military in his new country and fought India. These were the foundation stones of Ahmed family lore.

Monty's father, Akbar, continued the Ahmed tradition: glorifying and protecting the dream of Pakistan. He did not enlist, but made his money divvying up parcels of the country's promised land. He had a fine eye for disaster capitalism and, post-Partition, he made a fortune convincing the citizens of the new country to give their land away for a song. *Bath Island? No, not a good investment. Place is too near the water. Plus, difficult being a Parsi, now that we're all Muslims, no?* In his Lawrencepur tailored suits and Grammarian drawl, young Akbar Ahmed preyed on old ladies who set their hair in curlers and wore long, pleated skirts. *Looks patriotic, one has to admit, being Muslim. Never know when people will turn on you in your, uh, situation. Do you have a plan regarding your property, if you have to leave in a hurry?*

Once the Parsis had packed up and moved out of prime real estate, Akbar set to work fudging the papers of abandoned Hindu homes, one of which he settled his own family into. Next came the business of growing and expanding the Defence Housing Authority, a brainchild of his father's old chums, who pinched and pocketed land for the Armed Forces until they owned most, if not all, of Karachi's reclaimed land. Eventually Akbar Ahmed went into high-rise development, Dubai-style. Soon, the Ahmeds would own the sea.

In London they owned only one plot of land, but with its view of Harvey Nichols and its elegant courtyard sheltered from the tourists prowling Knightsbridge, one could argue it was the best possible address. Their neighbours were arms dealers and senators, Akbar Ahmed told everyone, and those were just the other Pakistanis.

Monty sat on the sofa in the living room of their Sloane Street apartment that evening while Papa held a phone in each hand, one on hold with Addison Lee and the other dialling Novikov, to add another four seats to their dinner reservation. Monty flipped channels on their Sky-satellite remote, jumping from one reality show of English teenagers binge-drinking in Spain to another reality show of chinless heirs drinking in Chelsea.

'Mummy,' he called out, not lifting his eyes from the screen as he heard the front door open – there had to be some actual TV somewhere – 'are you ready?'

'Madam abi toh tayar nahi hai,' Khadija slipped into the living room, her arms weighed down with Waitrose shopping bags and her *dupatta* hanging loosely from her shoulders.

Khadija's thick hair reached the back of her knees, and although she tucked it under a *dupatta*, you could still see the tail of a plait peeking out. Madam was in her room, still getting dressed, Khadija said, smiling nervously. She set the bags down in the kitchen and returned to lean against the doorframe, briskly rubbing her shoulders. She had never been so cold in her life; she even felt it in her teeth. Madam mustn't get a chill, Khadija bobbed her head with concern at the ominous British weather; she would tell Madam to wear a coat.

Teek hai, teek hai, Monty nodded glumly, trying to get rid of her.

His parents had insisted on bringing Khadija with them to clean the flat and look after the laundry and the housekeeping. Monty had tried to tell them that it was embarrassing, Khadija wasn't even eighteen, she looked like an indentured labourer. What if someone saw her trailing after them on Oxford Street and reported them to the authorities?

'Don't be ridiculous,' Papa had snapped, 'what makes you think Britishers care about indentured labour? Don't you know what they did to us for four hundred years?'

'She's not indentured,' Zahra Ahmed swatted her son on the shoulder. 'She's very happy to be here.'

Monty tried to argue with his parents that it just didn't look right, that it would seem weird, that Khadija would be uncomfortable; she looked unlike the rest of them, with her sun-blotched skin and elevated cheekbones, and more like a hostage, always seated at a separate table in restaurants. Why did she have to come? Couldn't they bring the new Filipina Mummy had just hired, who at least spoke English and was Western, or whatever? London would be too big a shock for Khadija, she would stick out with her cheap slippers and ratty *shalwar kameez* and covered hair.

But unless Monty wanted to take the rubbish out himself every day, and cook omelettes with chillies and tomatoes every morning, the maid was coming, Papa said. The Filipina would run away, Papa explained; with her passport and her fluency in English, she would get it into her head that she could survive in London. Filis were bloody hard to find in Pakistan these days, why take the risk of losing her? And besides, Khadija wouldn't be so *chalak* as to assume the same. 'Our people are much simpler,' Monty's mother agreed, 'more innocent.'

But still, Monty didn't like what bringing Khadija here, on a month-long summer holiday to London, said about the Ahmeds.

'Turns sixteen, thinks he knows everything,' Akbar Ahmed shook his head.

'I'm seventeen, Papa,' Monty reminded him. His birthday had only been the month before, in June. They cut a cake at Fujiyama, it wasn't that long ago.

'Sixteen, seventeen,' Akbar Ahmed draped a thin cashmere scarf over his neck to ward against the evening's summer breeze. 'What's the difference?'

Anita Rose

When Anita thought of her mother, she could still smell her, a warm scent of sweat and sweet oils – clove, apricot, mustard, almond.

Zenobia liked to tell her how when she was a baby, colicky and crying night and day, Anita Rose nearly got them thrown out of the squat they lived in near Railway Lines, a much smaller room than they had now, with walls built of collapsing wood and surrounded by tired migrant labourers as their neighbours. Anita Rose kept her older brother awake night after night as she screamed and howled until the sun rose, till her frail blue body exhausted itself.

Zenobia realized after a week of the neighbours pounding and swearing at her door that it was Anita's teeth, poking through her red, swollen gums. She rubbed clove oil all along the pink-and-white ridges of her baby's mouth.

She had a cure for everything – they were not rich, she said, but only fools paid doctor's fees when they could mine the earth for medicine. Sweet *tulsi* oil mixed with scentless sesame was a balm that settled all her children's coughs, when rubbed against their brittle chests by their mother's strong hands. A drop of cinnamon oil, *dalchini*, peppery and warm, cleaned even the murky, unfiltered water in Railway Lines – though now, in Machar Colony, they filled their drinking water in jerrycans at the local tap, waiting in line behind fifty people every morning. And for her hands, her aching, tired hands, Zenobia visited a homeopath in Empress Market's sunless corridors, who sat on a block of wood dressed in blue tarpaulin in the spice section. The old Hindu never told Zenobia what was in the concoction he sold her in the small, brown glass bottles. There was a trust between healers; she did not need to know.

Anita's mother worked as a *maalish wali*, massaging the tired bones of rich women with her scented oils, pressing their backs with her old body, rubbing coconut oil in their hair and massaging their tense, knotted shoulders until she could barely feel her own fingers. But the house in Clifton was Anita's favourite, with the large living room covered in paint that looked as though someone had run their fingernails through it, white streaks through burnt orange, and the wall-sized windows that reflected beams of light everywhere, like Christmas sparklers. The boy who lived there was the same age as Anita. His name was Rahim, but Anita heard his mother, when she waddled out of her bedroom after her *maalish*, call him Baby. Just like her own mother called her sometimes.

But unlike Anita, Rahim/Baby was round and wide and groaned when the cook placed only three different bowls of lunch before him. When they were children, he had all kinds of things Anita had never seen before: video games, guns that shot out jets of water, and a machine that looked like a piano but also made the sound of trumpets and drums. He had a new toy every Sunday. She used to hide, watching him play, from behind the laundry-room door.

He had an older sister, Rima, who looked nothing like him. She was as tall as he was stumpy and as slim as he was chubby. Rima was an artist and she carried around a stub of charcoal and a big notebook the size of her fat brother's belly. It was red, a deep beautiful colour that seemed to catch and hold the rays of light that filtered in through the windows, shining as Rima held the notebook in her hands. She had hair that was – Anita had counted – four glamorous kinds of brown, and she smoked cigarettes, even though she was not a grown-up.

Anita Rose had seen beautiful women on her travels around Karachi, but no one nearly as elegant as Rima. She floated through the big living room as though she could have been anywhere. As though the world existed only when she touched her feet down on its streets and paths. Rima sat down at lunch late and often had a mobile – a small, bright-pink phone that flipped open – on her ear. Every Sunday, Anita went home and stood in front of her mother's hand-mirror, its corner cracked and its cheap glass scratched with black veins, and mimicked Rima's deep, languorous inhales, pressing her lips down on a pencil.

Once, long ago, Rima took out a camera shaped like something strange, a plastic box or an old telephone, like the kind they had at the PCO office. She sat down next to her brother and held her arm out in front of them. *Say cheese*, Rima said as she leaned her head against her fat brother's. *Cheeeeeese*, he said and the camera spat out a picture. Rima picked it up and flapped it in front of Rahim's face for a few seconds, before looking at it and laughing. *You look like a toad*, she said and held out her arm to take another one, and another one and another one.

36

Later, when brother and sister had run down the stairs to go to the cinema and there was still ten minutes before her mother would come out of Madam's bedroom, cracking her tired knuckles and tucking 700 rupees into her high brassiere, young Anita tiptoed into the living room and picked up one of the discarded photos. She ran her finger over the glossy paper. The colours were faded, as though the picture had been taken a long time ago. *Say cheese*, Anita Rose whispered to herself.

Her heart had ached with a longing she didn't understand. She wanted to be in the photo, she wanted to be the one answering Rima, sitting with her at the round table to eat. She wanted to smell of Rima's perfume, a delicate jasmine, not of the heavy oils that her mother slathered all over her. She wanted Rahim to talk to her and to call her Baby. I am also called Baby sometimes, Anita wanted to tell him. Rahim would like that, she thought. But my real name is Anita Rose, like an actress.

She wondered if he had watched the old Bollywood films that had starlets with names like hers, Helen and Violet and Margaret.

My name is Anita Rose, she wished Rahim could have known, Anita like an actress, Rose like a flower.

Anita slipped the photo into the elastic band of her *shalwar*. *I love you*, she whispered to the picture, pressing it against her skin. She had heard Rima say that on the telephone.

Sunny

What is it? Pa asked, thinking of himself. Is it a girl? Are you lonely?

Safiya Begum remained a distant, morose figure in the house on Britannia Road, long after her death. Sulaiman kept a photo of her as a stern-looking bride on the mantelpiece, a heavy *dupatta* weighing down the crown of her head, but not large or heavy enough to obscure her forbidding gaze and her thin lips, locked in a worried frown. Every other week or so Pa sat down in their small living room and covered a side table with old newspapers and polished the frame, marked with a rubber stamp from the Lucknow studio on the back, with an old rag that left the smell of metal on his fingers for hours afterwards.

This was your mother, he would say out loud, speaking to his son, whose feet were propped up carelessly on the newspapered table, his arms crossed behind his head, watching the Premier League on TV.

Sunny had no memory of Safiya Begum, no sense of motherly love, no feeling for what it was like to have had a mother.

Underneath Pa's shoeboxes in his narrow cupboard, filled with crisp, old airmail letters, Sunny had found a stack of self-help books: *Love after Loss: Kick-Start Your Emotional Life in 10 Steps*, *Alone and Unafraid*, *The Widow's Guide to Dating and Sex*.

And sex?

A further search resulted in a pile of men's magazines, including *GQ*, of all things, underlined and dog-eared for future reference, buried at the back of the cupboard.

How to Dress like a Quintessential English Gentleman: The A to Z of Savile Row was one of the pages Pa had marked. Sunny could just see his father, smoothing down the page as he studied it, so it wouldn't crease. He had even written in the margins, copying the instructions on how to tie the perfect ascot. Who was ever going to invite Sulaiman Jamil anywhere he'd have to wear an ascot? Sunny didn't even want to think about it.

He pushed the magazines back, replaced the boxes and closed the door.

Why do we always ape the West? Sunny wrote on his Face-book wall that night, thinking of the words of the Pakistani playboy-cricketer-turned-politician, Imran Khan.

Why we strong Muslim men always gotta go around in jeans and suits and ties like we don't got a PROUD culture of our own? Why read Shakespeare when we have our own holy book – worth a thousand pages of English classics? Why we follow their laws, their democracy, their ideas when we have the hadiths, the Shariah, the purest guidance to a virtuous, Islamic life?

But even then, even echoing the opinions of a like-minded, world-famous soul, Sunny was alone, like his pa, speaking into a void.

Sulaiman Jamil first cleaned the glass over Safiya Begum's face with a tissue, wetting it with the tip of his tongue, then running his hands over his wife's cheeks, the colour of burnt toffee.

But Sulaiman Jamil never found a second love.

The indignities of loneliness were too many to catalogue and count. Though Sulaiman Jamil had joined senior singles' Latin-dance classes, diverse voices of colour book clubs and yoga ('ancient de-stressing exercise!'), he had so far failed to meet anyone special.

But Pa had no idea how easy it was for Sunny to get girls in sad, small Portsmouth. Ever since he was eleven or twelve, since his first erection, Sunny got girls all the time. There was no shortage of them: white girls who wanted to piss off their parents by sleeping with Indian, Muslim, brown, boxing Sunny. Foreign girls, reckless and easy.

The headscarf girls were the wildest. Put a hijab on a sister, Micky said, and see what kind of antics she got up to then. And it was true: the Maryams and the Aishas and Kareenas stalked Sunny at the clubs something relentless – pressing their tits up against him and asking if he had any weed, if he wanted to drive them home, if he knew somewhere quiet they could go to and hang out, their acrylic nails running up the inside of his thigh. Sunny couldn't shake the *Desis* even if he tried.

Since he had started growing a beard, though, the God Squad were falling over themselves to get with him. Didn't matter that Sunny didn't have but a basic debit card, no car, no flex, no flash job at a London bank; that lot didn't care about that, once they assumed there was a righteous, God-fearing brother at hand. The brown girls didn't tart it up on Facebook or Instagram. They posted pictures of religious sayings raining down on sunflower fields, cat memes and portraits of their nail art. The *Desis* didn't advertise, they got right to business.

Romina, a plump little Bangladeshi, her hair tucked so tight under her hijab that it pulled her eyes back, making her look a little Mongoloid, took Sunny to the cinema and sat on his lap, grinding against him right there, where everyone could see. Reshma got off on messing around in public, too, always in the park. Afterwards, she used to make Sunny take her to Nandos, her breath smelling of peri-peri, her oily fingers clasped tight around his own.

By the time Sunny turned nineteen he had had enough fooling around. He didn't want any of those girls, brown or white. He was done with all that.

He started to spend more and more time online, sitting at the desk in his room that Pa had carried home from a charity shop, smelling of pine freshener and old women's powdery perfume, his blinds drawn and Frank Ocean streaming out of his phone, watching the world through Facebook and Twitter.

Sunny spent hours on Instagram, scrolling through strangers' lives, looking at photo after photo, until his eyes ached from the dull light of Photoshopped colours. He shopped for cheap designer gear on eBay, looking for brands of sweaters and kicks that his favourite rappers wore. But it was on YouTube one night that Sunny came across a video of Muhammad Ali. Sitting on a stage in front of thousands of people, the boxer formerly known as Cassius Clay spoke of his Muslim faith. 'All the angels in the Christian religion are white,' Ali said of his Baptist past. 'Why come we never get to go to heaven? Why come Mexicans never get to go to heaven?'

Ali, in his elegant blue blazer and black turtleneck, spoke of being turned away from white churches, but finding love everywhere in Islam. 'You say *as salam alai-kum* you got a home, you got a brother anywhere in the world.'

He was never good enough, the boxer said, but in Islam he was always striving to change, to be better.

From there Sunny discovered Malcolm X, another strong man persecuted and put down, finding the light of solidarity only in Islam. And it was then that Sunny began to devote himself full-time to looking at the heritage of his people, educating himself on the struggles of Islam and the centuries of battles fought over people's souls.

Fiqh, Sunny posted on his Facebook page one day:

> *What does it mean in the modern world? Yo, fiqh is the key. You know any other people who have so much study, so much pro-fun-dity in their world? Deep knowledge, deep deep comprehension. This is the illumination of Islam, it seeks answers to all questions and guides its followers exactly towards the right path.*

Sunny spent hours googling Arabic translations, reading blog posts about jurisprudence, collating and collecting fables and histories. And then he shared his learning, waiting hopefully for someone to appreciate all his proud knowledge and analysis.

But no one responded to Sunny's posts.

One day, a stranger liked his offering on gambling. There it was, a thumbs-up. The first validation of his investigations. But when Sunny logged back into his page later that afternoon, the like was gone. What had he done? Why had someone bothered to go back, find his post and un-like it?

What lessons can we learn from the kingdom of jahiliya? Plenty! Look around you, brothers. Our lives are thick with jahiliya – or 'ignorance of God's divine guidance' in Arabic – and we shelter our lives with lies and falsities instead of looking that ignorance head-on and defeating it. This was the desperate state of our forefathers before Islam, but we are still shrouded in its wicked darkness.

Sunny linked his Facebook to his Twitter account, thinking he would receive greater traction in a universe built on trading information, but everything Sunny tweeted landed soundlessly, as if he had not written anything at all.

He waited patiently, sitting at his old lady's desk, his knees bent up against the wood until his skin went red and his legs cramped, listening to *Channel Orange* on repeat, feeling personally, acutely, like a diamond in a rocky, rocky world. It felt like all his life Sunny had been waiting until the moment when someone would see him. When someone would know him – would meet him at the intersection of his confusion and emptiness – and, in seeing him, would lift him from his troubled self.

At the same time, at the exact, concurrent second, sitting at his desk alone, Sunny bumped against the disorder of his room. Reaching down to look for the fallen bottle-cap of his Diet Coke, he hit his head on the legs of the old lady's desk, still smelling faintly of lavender perfume. Feeling the carbonated, chemical water of the Coke bloat his stomach against his jeans, Sunny thought: *I have too much. I hate it all. I want nothing. A minimum of things, a skeletal frame of belongings.*

And then, as he lifted his head and saw the scratches all along the frame of the desk, carved out of the wood by a hand not his own, and raised himself up on his sneakers, scuffed and old, Sunny looked at his portable speakers, busted so that only one of the cones played any music at all, and the second thought collided with the first: *I wish I had more.*

But the recognition, the reckoning, the being seen that Sunny so desperately wanted, never came.

He spent more time out of the house, evading his father's heavy mood and lectures on world capitalism and Asian Tigers yet to claim their space among the pantheon of the great. If only Sunny knew, if only he would try harder to fit in, to assimilate, his pa promised he would take his place among Britain's rising Asians. This is why they had come here, to Britain, to be a part of a rising tide. Sulaiman Jamil knew history was on his side and he hounded his son with his unflagging hope in global capitalism's ability to absorb all men, no matter how peripheral.

At first, Pa was happy thinking Sunny had finally gone and ingratiated himself in some internship or was bettering his interview and management skills on a training course, but Sunny had started leaving his classes early and going straight to the gym, a small box on Dickinson Road, open twenty-four hours, the kind of place you went to train, to destroy your body so you could build it up again, to be alone in the company of others who were also hiding, transforming, beating their flesh for their sins.

Where are you all day? Pa badgered Sunny, returning his efforts to safeguarding the stability of his only son. Only at the gym? Are you sure?

What could Sunny tell him? Sorry, Pa, I wasn't at a finance internship. Sorry, Pa, I wasn't with a girl. Sorry, Pa, haven't been to uni in ages, bunked half my classes last term. Ain't been in the ring boxing neither, no heart, no energy to be beat down no longer. Sorry, Pa, I was at the gym, with Stefan actually, a mate, feeling more alive than ever actually. More certain, more inspired, more connected than I've been in a long, long time. He's given me peace, a bit of relief, some solace, a way of being.

Sulaiman Jamil would worry anyway, no matter what Sunny said.

But there was nothing to worry about, nothing! Sunny was fine, he was totally, totally fine. There had been a moment once, but it had passed. It had passed and Sunny had worked hard to forget it.

There had been a trainer at Sunny's gym, Stefan. He helped Sunny sometimes, spotting him, throwing him a bit of technical guidance here and there. Stefan was from Berlin and he had come down to England to study nutrition and make a bit of money. He never asked Sunny for anything, never needed anything from him. When they hung out at the gym, Stefan never talked about the news or how migration was ruining Europe, like every other Whitey did. Stefan never advised Sunny to tell the millions of moderate Muslims he knew personally to speak out more, and never asked questions about suicide bombers and grooming gangs in Birmingham. He never treated Sunny like a spokesman; he just spoke to Sunny as Sunny.

They chatted about whatever random things they felt like, and sometimes, after working out, they went and had a pint.

Stefan understood, without Sunny having to say anything, that alcohol was tricky for a brother, so he'd suggest hitting up a juice bar or going for a coffee. But Sunny liked the way Stefan's face flushed when he'd had a few drinks, he liked how he laughed, how he ran his hands nervously through his pale-blond hair, his voice heavy with beer.

One night, after they did legs and back, Stefan told Sunny he wanted to take him to a different pub. A new place. Sunny didn't think anything of it, no big deal. Why not try a new pub? Most of the *Desi* uncles did the respectable thing and drank secretly at home, so he wouldn't run into anyone he knew.

But it was a big deal.

'The fuck is this?' Sunny asked, stopping in his tracks as they reached Hampshire Boulevard, lit up in purple lights with a squad of men in fishnet vests, skinny jeans and guy-liner smoking outside. 'The music is something painful, Stef,' Sunny said, wincing as they walked towards the door. 'Camp as hell, plus.'

But Stefan just laughed and took Sunny's hand in his. 'You'll like it, promise.'

He led Sunny inside, past a throng of people, all dancing with their eyes closed to the throbbing music, their arms glowing with sweat and, though he couldn't be sure, glitter. Sunny pulled his hand out of Stefan's and jammed his hands in his pockets, keeping his head down till they made it to the bar. Stefan was saying hello to friends, laughing and waving across the crowded floor.

Sunny stood at the corner of the bar, his elbows resting on the surprisingly clean counter. 'Why are we here?'

It smelled like dishwashing liquid, which Sunny assumed was why the bar was spotless, but then he noticed the machine blowing enormous bubbles out over the dance floor. The bartender wore no shirt and platform sneakers.

There were only men there. It was then that Sunny took a proper look around; he couldn't see a woman anywhere.

'What?' Stefan was moving his shoulders to the music, and it disconcerted Sunny as Stefan brought his face closer to his, shimmying and dancing as though they were at any old club, leaning into Sunny, touching his hand on his back.

Sunny felt his body go warm and slack. He spoke into Stefan's ear. 'Why did you bring me here?'

'It's good, no?' Stefan smiled. And just like that, misunderstanding the question, misunderstanding the colour in Sunny's face, he moved away, dancing and pushing his body hard against the music.

Sunny leaned across the bar, beating the heel of his palm against the counter, tapping his fingers along to the drumbeats in the music. He hadn't had a drink in almost a year, but if he had to listen to Gloria Estefan, then he was going to need a vodka. And as he leaned across the counter, he saw Uncle Haroon's kid, Ibrahim. Uncle Haroon ran a big construction company, a proper Portsmouth business. He was from the fatherland, same city, same neighbourhood, same *gully* as Pa.

It was on his door that Sunny's ma had knocked that cold morning after the night spent sleeping on the floor of the train station. It was at Aunty Tina and Uncle Haroon's home that Safiya Begum, her face furrowed with concern at the immediate difficulties of English life, first arrived, clutching the fabric of her lambswool cardigan close to her chest. Pa had told Sunny the story a hundred times. Your ma was shivering and annoyed. Aunty Tina made her chai. Uncle Haroon laughed at our story of the bums at the

47

station and said that now we were true *Angrez*, having camped out in the rough.

Sunny spun round from the bar at the double and turned towards the door, moving as fast as he could through the press of bodies. He tried not to touch anyone, pulling his sweater over his hands and digging his chin into his chest to avoid eye contact with the crowd. What would he tell Pa, if he found out his only son was here? Here, in a gay bar, with a handsome German man.

Just as Sunny neared the bouncer, a heaving big body dressed in smart velvet, he felt someone's hand on his waist, pressing a thumb into his hip.

'What happened?' Stefan shouted into Sunny's ear. 'You want to leave?'

'I have to go,' Sunny said, keeping his hand inside the sleeve of his sweater because he wanted, in a way he didn't understand, to place his fingers through Stefan's, resting protectively on his waist. But Ibrahim was at the bar and he was a fag, and Sunny wasn't. He was just there with a friend. A friend.

Sunny couldn't turn round to face Stefan.

'Baby, I'll come with you,' Stefan said into Sunny's ear, his lips grazing his neck as he kissed him lightly.

Sunny felt his body flash hot and cold and then Gloria Estefan was screeching in her high-pitched, tuneless voice and Sunny's eyes were burning, even though no one was smoking, and his throat constricted and he couldn't feel his tongue against the wet corners of his mouth and, for the briefest moment, Sunny wanted to cry. He turned round and with all his force pushed Stefan away from him.

Stefan was a big guy, he stumbled backwards, spilling

the gin and tonic in his hand, but didn't fall, buoyed by the sea of dancing men around him. No one even noticed what had happened. Sunny's eyes scanned the bar for Ibrahim, but he couldn't see him, not from the edge of the dance floor.

'Stay the fuck away from me,' Sunny shouted, trembling. His hands hurt, his fingers, his joints, even somehow his knuckles, from touching Stefan like that, from hurting him. But Stefan didn't fight back, he didn't grab onto him or smash Sunny's face into his knee, like Sunny knew he could. He just looked at him sadly and smiled. He had been smiling the whole evening.

Sunny walked home feeling ashamed and so, so stupid.

He should have known from Stefan's tattoo – two thick black stripes, the equals sign, coloured into his forearm. He should have known from the way he looked at him, the way he seemed genuinely curious about everything Sunny thought of the world. He should have known from the way Stefan listened to his stories, the way he asked about his childhood, about his dead mother, like it mattered. Like he cared.

Why would anyone care about Sunny without wanting something from him, like those girls – the *Desis*, especially the *Desis*?

Sunny closed himself in his room, drew the dirty yellow curtains over his already dark blinds and sank into his bed. He stayed awake all night watching episodes of *The Wire* on a pirate site, studying Omar not like a spectator but like a thief, five episodes a night, committing to memory the sharpest lines – *You come at the king, you best not*

49

miss – and wondering when, in his small life, he'd ever have the chance to use power like that.

When Pa knocked on his door, letting air into the sealed chamber of Sunny's depression, he found his son curled into a foetal position, holding a pillow – weeks in need of a wash – against his stomach.

Darling?

But Sunny couldn't hear him. He wore his earphones tight against his ears. All Sunny could hear, all he could bear to hear, was the fluid poetry of Frank Ocean.

At moments, when the pain rolled against Sunny's every thought and every breath, it felt as though the lyrics had been written only for him.

At his lowest moments, Sunny played Russian roulette with the world. If the dog barks, I'll walk in front of the next passing bus. If it rains, I'll set fire to the yellow curtains. If the next man who enters the library is wearing gloves – it was winter after all – I'll bleed it out in the bath.

But whether through fate or God's direct intervention, the dog stayed quiet, nuzzling its owner's heel. The sun fought through the clouds. The next person to walk through the open doors of the library was a woman in a headscarf, the skin on her knuckles cold and pink. So he would live, though he could not understand why.

Maybe it wasn't Sunny, maybe he was not the source of his own depression. Maybe the quality of the women he was coming across was below par. He needed to meet someone who shared his values, who lived their life according to a certain purity of tradition and ideals. Someone with culture and knowledge.

But where was Sunny supposed to find that? Where

was he supposed to find a true companion, a comrade of the soul?

Sunny went for long walks, circling Portsmouth, trying to find refuge in what appeared to him to be only a wasteland, a town of forgotten people. Why hadn't Pa stayed in India, with his people, where they would have belonged? Why hadn't he stayed with that friend of his, Nur Muhammad, whom Sunny had to hear about all the time, instead of coming here, where they were nobodies? Sunny walked everywhere, kilometres along the muggy Southsea sea front, around the modern glass university buildings betrayed by the shabbiness of their designs, and even around Fratton Park where the Islamic-looking Pompey flag, star and crescent moon, was pasted confidently from every windowpane and shop.

After a home game, the streets around the stadium were littered with greasy tissues dropped from burger trucks, and cans of 1664 lager spilled out of the bins, like teenage bedroom drawers stuffed too quickly and shut. Cops in bright-yellow fluoro vests walked the closed streets, the clip-clop of their horses not far behind. Men with pot-bellies and closely cropped salt-and-pepper hair, aquamarine tattoos fuzzy and out of focus, the ink bleeding into their sun-grizzled skin, leaned into you as you walked by. 'Extra tickets?' they both solicited and offered. 'Extra tickets. Extra tickets?'

Sunny dug his hands into his jacket pocket and kept his eyes on the tarmac, the tingling at the back of his throat itching for a fight, the anxiety in his chest desperate to avoid it. How long must a man walk through this city with no armour? His body was a naked wound in those days, his heart beat ferociously beneath his breast, so aware was he of being unprotected, so alone and afraid. On the kerb, yellow-and-orange clumps of vomit clung to the grass.

It was around then, six months before leaving, that Sunny set up a Tinder account. Sunny J, he called himself, putting an old, pre-beard picture up. When Tinder asked Sunny whether he was looking to meet men or women, Sunny paused. Both, he clicked.

After a couple of left swipes over girls posing in group photos (a classic ugly move) and far-away scenic shots (fat), Sunny went back to his settings and un-clicked women. He widened his search distance to sixty kilometres and spent a few hours looking at the men. Most of them seemed like guys Sunny knew – young, athletic, well dressed, their clothes and swagger carefully calculated. Like Stefan.

Sunny didn't see him there, even though he narrowed the search radius to the neighbourhood around their old gym, which he had since quit. He worked out in the park now, as far away from Stefan's old box as possible. It was a relief; Sunny didn't ever want to see him again. He wished Stefan would just vanish, as though removed from the earth, scrubbed from humanity, dead, erased.

Sunny cruised through his matches, but none of them looked like anyone Sunny had seen at that pub. They didn't wear make-up, they weren't pierced. They were so ordinary-looking, so masculine. He could have been any of those men on Tinder.

Sunny spent hours on the app, his finger hovering over the Like button. But in the end, he did nothing. He lurked and hesitated, swiping left all the time.

Monty

During the summer, Papa spent about two weeks with the family in their Sloane Street flat, before work called and he had to return to Pakistan or China or Saudi Arabia for meetings. Even though he spent his evenings having drinks with business associates or else on conference calls, pacing through the park with his earphones connected to his phone, disturbing the birds, it was the most time Monty and his father spent together in any given year.

When Monty was ten, Papa had taken him to Windsor Park and driven through the animals with the radio on Kiss FM, humming along to all the summer hits while Monty cowered in the back seat as lions and baboons circled the car. 'Sit up, Monty,' his father ordered, 'look at the beasts! It's like being on safari in Africa!'

Monty could see them just fine from where he sat, glued against the door of their rented car so that the animals couldn't see his head in the window, but he would attempt a straightening-up, first making sure that his seatbelt was secure.

'Can you see the lions? Can you see them from there?'

Yes, Monty would assure Papa, yes – you could see them a mile away, you could smell their muddy, earthy, dirty-skin scent even with the windows closed.

'Be brave, *beta*,' his father eventually snapped, ruining their father–son day without stopping to consider that

Monty *was* being brave. He had been using his reserve tank of brave to get through the safari park where animals roamed free all day.

The next summer they didn't go back to Windsor, but to Centre Court at Wimbledon. Monty watched Roger Federer play. He had nurtured a feverish crush on Anna Kournikova, with her short white skirts and tanned, endless legs, but she no longer played, not at Wimbledon at least. The sun – rare for London – had given Monty a migraine and he spent the day trying to hide it from his parents, who drank Pimm's – even Mummy, because Papa told her there was no alcohol in it – and ate strawberries and cream like real English people.

Everything Monty knew about culture he had learned in London. Watching plays in the West End, eating fine food in Mayfair, watching his father buy tailored suits on Savile Row and feeling not pride, but confidence, when he saw his father step out of a dressing room in expensive cloth cut to his precise measurements. Akbar Ahmed stood with his arms spread akimbo, like the Rio Jesus, while a white-haired English tailor adjusted his cuffs, stepping back admiringly, before bending to his knees to attend to the fall of the elegant charcoal-black silk trousers.

When he was eighteen, Papa said, he would bring Monty to Anderson & Sheppard for his first bespoke suit. Until then, Monty had to study and work hard and make his father proud. The rewards would follow – nothing could be denied to a man who faced his responsibilities head-on. Nothing could be denied to a man who upheld the honour of his family's name.

This summer, the summer Monty turned seventeen,

Akbar Ahmed couldn't find the time to spend with his son. There was no boating in Regent's Park, no steaks at The Wolseley, no strawberries and no Pimm's. I'm busy, was all Papa said, can't make it. Tomorrow, day after, at the weekend.

But Monty had walked by Ladurée, behind Harrods, and seen Papa sitting outside under a pale-green umbrella, sipping an espresso by himself, just watching the world go by. He hadn't looked very busy then. Monty paused, standing on Brompton Road, and wondered whether he should approach his father, whether he should walk across the street and join him, sitting down for a coffee, but Papa looked so happy, so content, sitting at his table alone that Monty bowed his head so his father wouldn't see him and walked back home without saying anything.

Since Monty had been born, since the day he had been delivered by Karachi's most respected Parsi obstetrician a full eight days early, his skin pink and wet, glistening like a polished pearl, Zahra Ahmed had made a promise to God: she would love her son like no other. More than any other future children (which God did not see fit to grant), more than her husband, more than her own siblings or parents.

'You're going to spoil the boy, ruin him,' her husband warned, his irritation with her seeping into how he began to see the child born of his own flesh and blood. 'He needs to learn how to be a man, for heaven's sake.'

Monty was not supposed to have heard the conversation, late at night as his parents argued in the guest bedroom. He had gone out to the Trocadero with a bunch of kids from school – everyone was in London that year. After the Trocadero, Danial Hoodbhoy messaged saying he'd booked a table at Loulou's and did they want to come? Everyone else went off, but Monty didn't really know Danial, who had graduated that May and was a few years older. There was something strange about him, something obnoxious. He wore blue nail polish and claimed to party in Miami and Nice with celebrities, always offering a selfie as proof: Danial flashing a peace sign with his arm draped around a glassy-eyed Leonardo DiCaprio or a barely upright Lindsay Lohan.

Monty had hay fever, always awful at this time of year in London, and he used his watery eyes and itchy throat as an excuse to go home, instead of joining the sausage-fest congregating around Danial Hoodbhoy.

Monty walked down Park Lane instead of calling an Uber and strolled home through Green Park. When he opened the door to the flat, he saw Khadija sitting on the carpeted floor of the living room, knees bent and remote in hand, her brown hair and warm face lit by the glow of the television screen. She was watching Fashion TV, Monty recognized the catwalk music.

He went to the bathroom and had a shower, making sure to wash off all traces of smoke and beer, brushed his teeth and was heading to his bedroom when he noticed that the light in the guest bedroom was on. As he walked towards the room, he saw Papa sitting on the bed, his tie undone and his head in his hands. Mummy was in her too-big bathrobe, pacing the room and shouting.

'He's my son. He's my only son! I'm allowed to love him. Who else am I going to love, Akbar? You tell me. What crime am I committing?'

Akbar Ahmed didn't rise to his wife's volume. He spoke bitterly, but softly. 'He can hardly get through a sentence without fumbling and looking back at you for help. He doesn't know the first thing about standing up for himself, and he's got no bloody sense of who he is, Zahra.' Papa stood up and unbuttoned his shirt, hanging it in the cupboard. 'Let the boy breathe, for heaven's sake, stop terrorizing him with "don't drink" and "don't be a bad boy" and "don't smoke" and "where are you going?" The child can't tell left from right. Is that what you want?'

Zahra snorted. '*Acha*, so I should raise him to have no morals, like you?'

'I want a son,' Akbar Ahmed hissed, holding his wife's arm as he brought his face close to hers, 'but you're raising a sissy.'

Monty noticed, when the sting of the words had subsided, that all his father's shoes were lined up outside the cupboard in the guest room. His tan Barbour jacket was draped across his chair and his iPad was charging on the bedside table. Had Papa been sleeping in the guest room? Monty felt dizzy: what was happening? What had he done to upset his father? Is this why Mummy slept all day in the dark? Was it him?

'I'm not going to turn him into a thug like you,' Zahra clenched her teeth as she enunciated every word. 'I'm going to raise a good man, you understand? Much better, much softer, my son.' She ran her hands through her hair, breathing deeply. 'He's my son.'

On a grim cloudy day, Monty went to a new coffee place that had opened up on the King's Road. It was nearly the end of their holidays. School was starting in a week and they would be leaving soon. He sat at the counter by himself, drinking a too-sweet matcha latte, looking out onto the street as a brunette and her boyfriend kissed in the middle of the busy pavement. Monty watched them achingly as the man moved the girl's hair from her face when they parted from their kiss. For all his school flirtations, late-night calls with girls in his class and meaningless hook-ups at after-parties, he'd never had a real girlfriend. Maybe it was true what his father said: maybe he didn't know how to be a man, how to command the world around him.

Monty watched the man closely, observing how he laughed and smiled, pulling the girl's face towards his. As they stood on the street, their arms entwined and their breath on each other's skin, an old city cleaner in a bright-orange jumpsuit shuffled past them, pushing his bin. He wore a turban, the same colour as his uniform, over his white hair. He kept his eyes downcast, away from the couple, adjusting himself around them. But as the Sikh passed, the girl pulled herself away from her boyfriend and lobbed her coffee cup from the trendy new shop into the cleaner's bin. It missed. She giggled as the lid came off and a milky latte dripped down the bin and dirtied the road. The boyfriend buried his nose in her hair and pulled the girl back to him for a kiss, ignoring the old Sikh as he bent to the kerb, exposing a small bald patch that his turban had failed to cover, and cleaned up their garbage. And at that moment Monty felt his heart burn with shame.

He left his matcha latte on the counter and went out into the street, crouching down to try and help the old man, but the cleaner waved him away. 'Don't worry, don't worry,' he said, avoiding Monty's eyes. 'Don't worry, please.'

Anita Rose

'Ezra?'

Anita lay on the cold floor with her hands folded underneath her cheek. The first time she said his name, her brother pretended not to hear her. He sighed deeply and his eyelashes fluttered lightly, like a trapped butterfly beating its wings. Anita knew when Ezra was pretending, she knew all his mischief and lies.

'Ezra?'

He opened one eye slowly, theatrically, like he had been summoned from a dream.

For a moment they just stared at each other and then Ezra smiled, easing the tension between them. '*Kya hai yaar?*' He rolled over onto his back, breaking the line of seeing and knowing between the siblings. He folded his elbows behind his head and made a pillow out of his palms. 'EzraEzraEzra – all night long. What do you want?'

Anita moved her mother's heavy thigh (which Zenobia draped suffocatingly over her daughter's small body every night) off her cramped legs and scuttled her bottom away from Zenobia and closer to the patch of floor that Ezra occupied. She inched her way towards her older brother and lay flat on her back, raising a knee to copy his pose, arms crooked and head pointed up at the distant, distant stars.

Ezra turned his face and looked at Anita, rolling his

eyes. She could see him do it, even in the dark. 'What?' he moaned, exasperated.

'I don't want to worry you, *bhaiya*, but,' Anita took a deep breath, 'I'm running out of birdseed.'

When they were children, Ezra hated going to the big Clifton house. He didn't care if they had a big garden or an aviary of birds that the *mali* with the shaggy dyed black moustache supervised, walking the chickens around the big garden, like soldiers on patrol, a thin bamboo stick in his hand. He carried birdseed in his grey *shalwar kameez*, holding the hem of his old tunic as though it were a bowl, as he made clucking noises to call the hoopoes with their striped brown bottoms and the koels that met every morning with a plaintive, urgent song.

The *mali* gave Ezra and Anita some of his birdseed on Ezra's last visit to the house, and invited the Joseph children to join his march-past of chickens and hoopoes and singing koels. Anita delighted in being included, tossing the seeds in the air like rice at a wedding, but even though Ezra seemed to enjoy the Clifton family's aviary, eventually his small pinched face clouded over and he threw the birdseed into the bushes, frightening the fat stray cats that lounged in the shade by the boundary wall. *I don't work for them*, Ezra shouted at his mother on the rickshaw ride back to Machar Colony, *I'm not their servant*.

'Come on, *baba*,' Zenobia prodded him as she packed her plastic bags of oils, a full week after the incident, 'you don't have to play in the garden. You can sit by the gate and do your school work.' She didn't want to leave Ezra at home. He was becoming distant and – perhaps only his mother could see this – meaner too, and it was at this angry, fragile age that boys joined gangs and found themselves running errands for local gangsters, a fate Zenobia refused to entertain for her only son. Ezra had already started talking about quitting school and working, and was picking up odd jobs after 3 p.m., staying out through the night.

The *chowkidar* always gave Zenobia a cup of sweet tea before she left the house, sometimes even two cups if she arrived early for her appointment. 'Maybe Allahditta will give you some tea while you study,' she suggested, but as soon as she said it, she knew it had been a mistake.

Anita Rose had listened quietly as her mother and brother argued. She stood near the metal door of their small home, a thin purple fabric hanging weakly as *pardah* between the Josephs and the outside world. She dug her fingers into the pocket of her school uniform and fingered the bird-feed she had kept, an extra palmful taken when the *mali* with the shaggy moustache wasn't looking.

She wished Ezra wouldn't make a scene; she wanted so much to play in the birdcage in the garden, flush with plump, purple bougainvilleas. The *mali* couldn't play with Anita alone. It wouldn't be right, her mother said. Anita was a growing girl and her brother needed to be there. Men made very bad mistakes if they were alone with young girls, Zenobia said. If Ezra wouldn't come, then Anita would have to sit at the gate and wait (though there was a man, Allahditta the *chowkidar*, there too). Zenobia didn't know Anita had discovered the stairway in the servant quarters that led right up to the laundry room, into the heart of the beautiful Clifton home.

'I don't want anything from those people,' Ezra glowered at his mother. He closed his school book and stood up angrily. 'I don't want to play with their birds and I don't want to drink their tea.'

So from then on, Anita alone accompanied Zenobia. And every Sunday before she left the Clifton house, Anita walked through the kitchen and the servants' quarters holding her *chappals* in her hand, stepping quickly across the hot tiles. In the back of their garden, near the boundary wall, was the prison for birds. In the morning, the old *mali* with the shaggy black moustache (almost certainly dyed) opened the padlock, twisting a finger of twine that he had fashioned as a key, freed the jungle-green parakeets, mynahs and assorted other jailbirds. He filled large terracotta bowls with cool water and sprinkled seeds across the floor of their cage. At night, the birds returned to eat, and the *mali* faithfully locked them back in.

Anita Rose stood in the garden, her toes in the warm mud, and set out a trail of birdseed, dotting the earth with a pattern away from their cage – an anti-trap designed for liberty. But the birds always landed back inside their chicken-wire cell, no matter how elaborate her sneaky trail. Anita always left the Clifton house with a reserve palmful of seeds in her pocket, dropping them further and further away from the metal jail at the back of the garden, but had yet to see any results.

Even now, as a teenager, Anita Rose walked home from school along the rotting rubbish of the colony, careful not to dirty her black school shoes in the waste that seeped out from the open gutters, a slick brown slime of sewage and the ash of burnt garbage that congealed with a ferocious stench, dropping a seed of stolen bird-feed here and there, leaving a trail of manna for the birds.

A sugarcane seller wheeled his cart slowly, careful not to be hit by speeding motorcycles racing through the slum's cramped lanes. The long yellow canes, green only at the top where their stalks met the sun, were balanced along the edge of the cart. In the twilight, the sugarcane man called out to the children playing with dice by the dim gas lamps of the *paanwalla* in a soft Afghan accent.

Anita placed a hand in her pocket now and silently counted her stock of seeds.

Her back hurt from the heavy bag she carried across her bones, filled with school books that she took home every night, so the other girls wouldn't rip her pages and graffiti her property with bad names and curses.

It was evening and the electricity was gone. There were no lights in the colony, nothing to guide Anita's way except the weak gleam of motorcycle headlights as they rumbled through the knitted, unpaved alleyways of the slum.

As she reached home, a blue pickup truck was being loaded outside their neighbour's house. It was weighed down with furniture – a set of dining chairs, a cane loveseat, a wooden table, an old white fridge and a pair of tall floor lamps. It was more furniture than the Josephs could fit into their single room. Anita had never really been all the way inside Osama Shah's home before, only to his doorstep. The old man must have had a much bigger home than theirs.

In the middle of everything, the chairs stacked two on top of each other and the lamps tugged together by their black wires, the boy she had once seen kicking a football against the wall stood in the open back of the pickup truck, balancing himself next to a steel trunk, holding a cloth suitcase in his arms. He still looked older and was much taller now. His hair was thick and black, curling at the nape of his neck, and his body was still muscular and lean.

Anita looked at him trying not to fall, as the truck slowly pulled away from the Marxist's home. He had the same kind eyes as the old man and she couldn't be sure in the dark gloom of the evening, but she thought, as the truck rattled down the road, that the boy was screaming.

No matter how serious she sounded, Anita Rose could never convince her grumpy brother to return to the Clifton house with her. She spent her childhood worrying about the hungry birds, and even more years with her school pockets lined with the crumbs of old feed, before deciding she would have to look after the imprisoned birds herself.

Recently, hiding in the laundry room and wishing that Rahim cared about the birds that lived a stone's throw from his home – the jungle of mynahs and kites and tailor birds, with their pointed tails and patterned bodies, that he and his family sheltered without knowing or caring – Anita finally decided to take matters into her own hands. She snuck into Rahim Baby's room, emboldened by her crisis concerning birdseed, to see if he kept his own private stash.

But slipping through his door, she found only a boy's room, a messy bed strewn with jeans, posters of racing cars, a litter of balled-up socks on the floor and crumpled Kentucky Fried Chicken boxes that gave the room a greasy, oily smell.

Anita lifted one of the black-and-red takeaway boxes and brought it to her nose, inhaling the scent of fried bird, and thought this was not a boy who knew anything about seeds. With her fingernail she scraped the bottom of the KFC box and lifted a slick of orange goo, but before she could taste it, she heard Madam's bedroom door open and the sound of what could only be her mother's torn slippers slapping loudly on the tiled floor.

'Anita?' her mother called, somehow sensing she was there.

Anita dropped the soggy box and slid out of the room, eyes downcast, ready for a shouting. She wasn't supposed to be inside, she knew that Madam had very strict rules about what sort of people were allowed in the elegant Clifton house. On the table in the living room, just sitting there alone and unattended, was Rima's red notebook, its cover shining softly in the sunlight. Anita Rose moved towards it, reaching her hand out to touch it, but before she could, her mother saw her.

'Come,' Zenobia said, grabbing her daughter's hand, not stopping to ask what Anita was doing upstairs. She paused only to adjust Anita's hair, smoothing down a small strand and tucking it behind her ears, before hurrying her into Madam's dark bedroom.

The room was warm, the curtains drawn and although she could see her mother's plastic *thela* of oils already packed, Anita could smell the perfume of coconut, glistening on Rahim and Rima's mother's bare shoulders.

Their mother was fat, like Rahim, and she sat on the edge of her bed, wearing only a towel, the nape of her neck and back curved like a heron, her bad posture accentuating the soft flesh under her arms and the roll of skin underneath her chin.

'*Yeh meri beti hai*, Madam,' Zenobia spoke in a high-pitched voice that Anita had never heard her use before. With one hand she pressed her daughter's body close, and with the other she ran her hand proudly down Anita's arm, as though all of her was somehow untucked and Zenobia's smoothing was required to keep her in place.

'Fifteen years, Madam, *takreeban*. Anita Rose.'

Madam rubbed her palms together briefly, the metal of her rings chiming as the bands on her fingers came into slippery contact, before wiping her hands on her towel, which seemed dangerously close to unravelling. 'How old are you, Anita?' She hadn't been listening to Zenobia.

'Sixteen,' Anita replied, correcting her mother, 'sixteen years old.' She could see Zenobia smiling and nodding in confirmation. It was exciting being brought into this beautiful home to meet the family, whom she had watched from afar for so long.

God bless, God bless, Zenobia muttered.

Like her mama, Anita forgot the panic of her own discovery in Rahim's room and relaxed slightly, smiling at the broad lady in the fuzzy towel on the bed.

'Are you hard-working, like your mother?' Madam spoke to Anita but looked at Zenobia, so it took Anita a second to answer, unsure if the question was actually directed at her, but before she could answer and say that yes, she was a very hard worker, she was a topper at school, her teachers said if she did well this year she could apply to any A-levels college in the city, Madam continued.

'Would you like to work here?' Madam spoke in what

Anita understood to be a friendly tone, even though the question came out of the dark like a knife, glinting and dangerous. 'I need a girl to clean upstairs and look after the family rooms.'

Anita looked at her mother. Zenobia was beaming, her face bright and luminous. She was sweating from the heat in the warm room and lifted the end of her *dupatta* to wipe her brow. Was this why her mother called her here? So that Madam could give Anita a job?

'No,' Anita spoke clearly, hoping that she, on the other hand, did not sound friendly.

'*Arre*,' Zenobia pinched her daughter's shoulder and shook her. 'What kind of answer is that?' She hissed at Anita as though Madam couldn't hear her.

'I am in school,' Anita replied through clenched teeth, feeling her face burn.

'Sorry, Madam . . .' Zenobia began speaking in that fake voice again, but Anita couldn't follow what she was saying.

'I am in school,' Anita repeated, talking over her mother's protestations, humiliated, her voice breaking. She understood now why Ezra had been so angry that day, so many years ago, when he threw his seeds at the cat. She understood why he kept away, but she didn't want to stay away. Anita Rose didn't want to fight with these people, she didn't want to be rude to them, she liked them so much, but still, she understood.

She wasn't going to be their servant.

Monty

'Monty, sir?'

A small crack of light filled his dark bedroom. Monty pulled the covers over his head and turned away from the door.

'Monty, sir, time to wake up . . .'

Monty hadn't been sleeping properly since they got back from London. Jetlag kept him awake till three in the morning; last night he only managed to fall asleep with the *azan*, his eyes closing as the muezzin's voice tumbled out of the minaret and across the roofs of the neighbourhood.

The Filipina his mother had hired just before the summer stood by the open door, rapping her knuckles softly against it. 'Monty, sir,' her voice sang across the darkness. 'You have school today.'

Monty groaned and sank deeper into his duvet, curling his legs into his chest. 'I'm not going,' he spoke into the warm bed sheets. He couldn't remember the girl's name, he'd only really spoken to her for the first time the day before, when she came to empty his suitcases and sat barefoot and cross-legged on his carpet, folding T-shirts and sorting through his dirty clothes. Angela maybe. Angelina?

Monty had already skipped the first day of school, missing out on senior-year orientation. What was the point of being a senior, without these liberties? Kashif had FaceTimed him from school yesterday, turning the camera out to face three girls, walking up the ramp from the library. They all had long hair, platform sandals and tight jeans, fitted snugly across their hips.

'*Bhainchod*, where are you?' Kashif had zoomed the camera in to focus on three bottoms, climbing the slope towards the high school. He moved his phone left and right, left and right, left and right.

Monty's hair was a mess, falling in front of his face. He sat up in bed, in his boxers, and rubbed his eyes. Who is that? he asked. He couldn't recognize any of the girls. Kashif's camera narrowed in on the one in the middle, scanning the back of her long legs and ass.

'Fresh meat, son. Fresher than your average.'

Monty could hear Shavez laughing, but he couldn't see either of his friends, as the lens concentrated on the slender girl in the middle.

'You coming to school or what?' Shavez shouted, offside.

'Jetlag, bro.' Monty lay back in bed. Papa was in Shanghai and Mummy had gone on a package trip to Umrah with her friends. Why Umrah, of all things? Monty had asked as he watched his mother put on a white smock, its sleeves long around her wrists and billowing at the ankles. Zahra Ahmed draped a white cloth over her hair, letting it fall to cover what showed of her neck, and examined herself in the mirror. Does this look right? his mother murmured, unpinning the hijab and re-draping it. She looked so unlike herself – uncertain, lost in all that ghostly white.

Zahra fumbled with the fabric, calling over her shoulder for the new maid to come and help her, as though

Monty wasn't there, as though she were alone at her dresser, pinning and unpinning the cloth around her anxious face.

It had been a strange summer; something had changed in the chemistry of the family, of Monty himself even, but he wasn't sure what. Mummy was off on this new tangent, which made dealing with Papa – against whom she usually acted as a buffer, her sweet mood softening all his distance and disappointment – all the more confusing, and although he'd hung out in London, shopping and eating and chilling with friends, Monty felt off-kilter, drained, bone-tired.

Where was he going to go to college? Where would he get in? He was going to have to join some sort of extracurriculars for his college transcript, which was embarrassingly thin at this late stage. SATs, applications, graduation – it was all too much to think about.

'Get off your backside and come to school,' Kashif shouted, bringing the phone to his mouth. 'You think you're the only one who went on summer holidays?'

'Wish my parents didn't give a shit what I did.' Shavez grabbed the phone as Monty felt the surprise sting of his words. He considered telling them about his mother's Umrah trip; she did care, she cared a lot. She was going to Umrah for him, too, she had said, to ask God for the strongest protection and blessings for her only son. But before he could say anything, Shavez passed the phone back to Kashif, laughing, 'It's not like you flew the fucking plane, Monty', and they clicked off.

Monty settled back against his pillows and slept till the afternoon, his dreams interrupted only by the shaky camera vision of the girl in the low-waisted black jeans with the long, long legs.

'Sir?' The delicate rapping of the maid's small hands on the door.

Angelise. That was her name.

'I'm awake, I'm awake.' Monty threw the duvet off his face and reached for his phone, charging at his bedside. Three texts, all from Mummy: a picture of the holy *Kaaba*; another of sunrise in Medina, painted in golden yellows; and one of her, sitting on a marble floor alone, her hands folded in prayer. Monty zoomed into the picture, into the radiant calm of his mother's face. He almost didn't recognize her.

Angelise leaned against the doorframe, watching him, her voice floating patiently like a song. 'Monty, sir, the car is waiting for you.'

Sunny

'My son,' the imam asked Sunny in his thick accent, 'what you are doing here?'

Sunny sat on the thinning red carpet of the Jami Masjid, in front of the small Bangladeshi man with no moustache connected to his thick white beard, and tried to tell him that he was lost. His father – the same father who taught him how to do his *namaz* as a kid in the years after his mother's death, replicating the exact punishments his own father had meted out to him as a child, smacking Sunny and pinching his ears when he didn't remember to stand or bow down – didn't pray any more.

Pa refused religion, though he had even fewer answers than Sunny did. Sunny saw Pa strike out, had seen him come home from his Rumba class alone, his socks in need of darning. He watched him at the park, waving to a friend from his book club, but the old lady in a bright-pink cardigan looked at Pa as though she couldn't place him. 'Tough read, this *Cloud Atlas*, isn't it?' Pa said as he approached her.

Still nothing.

'I'm in your book club,' Pa carried on, oblivious, waving the book at her, trying to jog her memory of him, trying to be someone worth remembering. And the woman cocked her head and scrunched her narrow, dry lips, thinking. 'The one that meets on Fridays?'

Sunny didn't know where to look.

And even though Pa didn't know about Stefan, or about how the mosque was an empty, hollow place, or about how Binyamin – or Ben, as Sunny's childhood friend insisted on calling himself – had put him down, like he was nothing, he continued to hassle Sunny.

'Why don't you get up and do something with yourself? Why don't you go see some friends? Aren't you worried about your future, darling?'

But Sunny couldn't see any future. The walls around Portsmouth had never felt so high, he never imagined he could scale them.

The kids he had grown up with – white boys like Shane and Ben – didn't want anything to do with him. They still hung out with the Asians, with Mickey and Raj and those guys, but not with the Muslims any more.

Ben wasn't even white. His dad was a proper Pakistani, a real corrupt sort of uncle, with money hidden away in offshore accounts and an English wife whose passport kept him from getting deported back to Peshawar or wherever he came from. Ben and his family had an attitude more royal than the queen.

Sunny and Ben had never got along. As kids, they had been the only Asians at St Thomas's, the fancy school Pa had scrounged and saved to send Sunny to. But Ben started to rebel early, pulling crazy stunts to distract from his brownness, to erase what memory people had of his *Desi* dad, rolling up in a customized Rover, his accent as thick as curry, mispronouncing all the teachers' names.

Ben started wearing a crucifix, a big gold one. His mum was Christian, he said. 'So what?' Sunny replied, immediately humiliated and defensive, 'you're half Muslim

73

too.' But Ben wheeled round and slapped him, a move out of nowhere. Sunny was stunned, his face burning.

'I'm not half nothing!' Ben had shouted, tears in his eyes.

It got worse as they got older. Ben picked on him in front of the whole school; he gunned for Sunny and this other kid, David. David, the Jewish kid a year below them. Ben called David vicious things, forced him to do the Hitler *Heil*, bashed him up plenty.

But outside St Thomas's – which Ben was always at pains to remind Sunny his family couldn't afford – they'd see each other at Eid parties and Holi celebrations with all the other *Desi* families. The Khattaks had no idea Ben was an Islamophobe and racist, and so Ben would put on an act and be civil, even friendly, to Sunny. It went on like this, half enemy, half community member, until Sunny nearly broke Ben's jaw, slamming his face against the art table for drawing a swastika on David's bag. 'Fucking anti-Semite!' Sunny had cried, fifteen years old and so wounded that he felt not sympathy but communion with David, over having to suffer a century of slurs in one small lifetime.

Years after the jaw incident, a sort of peace had been established between him and Ben. Ben tiptoed around him and Sunny, for his part, never overcame his curiosity and attraction for Ben, who both excited and repelled him.

It's been ages, Sunny texted him in those low months when nothing seemed to give him any peace. He wanted it to sound like it was nothing, like being with Ben and the boys for a couple of hours would be no big deal.

Hey, homo, thought u had gone underground with your sleeper cell, Ben replied. Laughing emoticon, bearded-man-with-turban emoji. Exploding-bomb emoji.

Why did they even make a bomb emoji?

Sunny didn't answer. His phone pinged a minute later. Ben was up to hang and smoke later, if Sunny wanted? *Nah*, Sunny texted, *I don't do that shit any more.* He never liked it, especially not then, when it made him even sadder. *Let's go out, catch a film, eat some Nandos.*

You bringing your Taliban pals?

Sunny didn't reply. He just deleted Ben's number.

Around that time, Sunny ran into Ben's sister. She was fourteen, maybe fifteen, and a skinny little thing with dimples and curly red hair the colour of sunburnt skin. He saw her at the pick'n'mix, filling a bag with sour cherries. Naya, that was her name.

Naya came over and said hi, she didn't look like she was fifteen. She wore heavy mascara and lined her lips, so they looked plumper. Ben might not have wanted anything to do with Sunny, calling him a sand nigger, a Taliban, whatever they called any proud man of colour. But Naya couldn't get enough of him.

'Listen, darling,' Sunny said as they sat in a cool, dark corner of Southsea Castle, their voices echoing in the empty old fort, 'either you're a grown-up or not. Which is it?'

Naya looked around, making sure there were no Chinese tourists clutching selfie-sticks and walking through on guided tours. She didn't play it as white as her brother, was still scared to be spotted, terrified of getting caught by her parents. But it was a turn-on, being with an older guy like Sunny, he could see it in her eyes.

I've been coming here for years, Sunny assured her, I know all the blind spots. And Naya, embarrassed little

Naya, said she was a grown-up, wasn't afraid or anything, and brought her head back down to Sunny's lap. Wasn't her first time or nothing, she'd done it plenty of times before.

'That's right, sexy,' Sunny said, stroking her hair as he pushed her head back down. 'I bet you have.'

Sunny watched Naya going down on him, struggling to move her curly hair out of her face. He pulled her up, looking at her, at her colouring – just like Ben's – and kissed her neck. Sunny kissed the tracery of blue veins that ran all along the crease of her elbow, up her arm, into her soft, white neck.

He opened his eyes and really looked at her, taking her in. She and Ben had the same light rust-coloured hair, the same transparent skin, the same thin eyelashes, so fair they were almost not there. He moved closer to Naya; she even smelled like Ben, like mint body-wash, but she jerked away before he could kiss her lips.

'Don't be disgusting,' she squealed, her brow furrowed. 'I've just had you in my mouth.'

Naya took a stick of gum out of her pocket and smiled, her teeth too big for her mouth, sticking out and biting down on her lips, which sparkled a light-pink shade. That was the mint, Sunny realized. It wasn't the body-wash Ben used, it was her lip gloss. Naya was ready to kiss after a minute of intense, belaboured chewing, but Sunny wasn't in the mood any more.

Did I do something wrong? Naya asked Sunny, texting him for days afterwards. *I'm sorry . . .*

But he hadn't felt right for months. Most mornings, Sunny woke up and found it hard to breathe. He wanted so much to be seen, to be known – a wanting so bad it was an ache, stitched across his skin so tightly if he acted rashly, he felt he would be torn apart. *It's not you, darling*, he texted back. *You're a beautiful girl.*

Really? Naya replied, a text message brimming with hope.

The most beautiful. I'm just messed up right now.

He went back to the mosque then, after that.

'I don't know why I'm here,' Sunny said to the imam, close to tears.

The imam looked at him blankly. 'The mosque?'

Sunny shook his head. 'No, Uncle, I mean here.' He pointed to the floor, the red carpet, worn and fraying. Along the corners of the mosque a man in a white *shalwar* suit walked barefoot, collecting pamphlets printed with prayers, organizing them into little piles.

'Here?' The imam looked down at their feet.

Sunny had been coming to the mosque every day. He hung around before prayers and sat on the old red carpet reading the Koran after *namaz* was over. He taught Friday school and volunteered in the office, but everyone here was from another generation. The uncles wore their mobile phones on their heavily stretched belts, their wives donated Tupperware biryani in plastic Poundland bags. They never had to fight for anything. They never had to draw battle lines.

The imam's English was accented and Sunny didn't speak Bengali. He didn't get it. He got it as much as Pa did. As much as Ben, Naya and millions of other invisibles did. No one could help Sunny. Not here.

'It's okay,' Sunny said, feeling embarrassed. 'It's okay, thank you.'

'May Allah bless you.' The imam bobbed his chin from side to side. 'Thanks for your coming.'

So Sunny kept his head down. He prayed at home, rising and falling to meet the patterns of his small *jahnamaz*. He read, he questioned, isolating himself to his four thin walls, and spent hours on YouTube watching sermons from Nairobi to Srinagar.

Anita Rose

When Ezra turned fifteen, he finally did drop out of school to start earning. He worked three jobs at first, coming home to Machar Colony in the darkest early-morning light to rest for two hours, stepping over his sister and mother, bodies curled against each other on the floor, rolling out his *ralli* for the briefest of sleeps.

He hustled every angle he could, printing cheap business cards with his phone number on them and handing them out liberally. No job was too small or too humiliating – Ezra did everything. He delivered DVDs, worked errands for busy bootleggers, balancing their books while they enjoyed the perks of their trade; he even made a bit of money here and there helping the police bribe drunk rich kids, pretending to be hit by their fancy cars and putting on a big show, so nearby officers could come and shake the *burgers* down.

Running all over the city on one errand or another, Ezra hung off the doors of multicoloured buses, crammed against the tired bodies of other passengers who, failing to find a seat inside or on the crowded roof, stood in the open doorway, like the ticket collector, perched half inside the moving vehicle and half outside, feet dangling in Karachi's air polluted with diesel smoke. Ezra had lost a shoe that way once and had to spend the rest of the day hobbling all over the filthy city, careful not to step in broken glass and shit with his bare foot.

Now, almost twenty-one, his hard work was finally bearing fruit. Ezra brought home the remains of his salary, at last free of the suffocating loans and debts that had clung to his family. After he had paid the rent on their small room for three full months, he told Anita he could afford to get her only one thing. Nothing too big; they still had her school expenses and Mama's doctor's bills. Zenobia's hands had started to freeze and her joints throbbed with a pain that made her cry out with rage. The oils, even the mysterious Ayurvedic potion from Empress Market, no longer worked. Now all Zenobia could do was stuff her large hands into her mouth and bite down on her fingers, the dull pressure of her teeth the only way to soothe the agony of her tired hands.

Gas was expensive, and who could afford rice any more? But because she was a proper girl, a good girl, who listened to and respected her older brother, Ezra told Anita Rose that she could have one thing. She asked for a red copybook immediately.

He took her to Saddar, after Friday prayers when the shops reopened, and Anita stood in front of a shelf of notebooks, trying to find the deepest red there was. Ezra dropped her at the shop and told her to hurry; he had to meet some people and would pick her up in ten minutes. But none of the notebooks seemed quite like Rima's. They were either not red enough or too matte, unable to pick up shards of sunlight.

Even after Ezra returned and paced impatiently behind her, suspicious at the way the shopkeeper had positioned his mobile phone, just so, almost as though he were snapping photos of Anita as she stood on her tiptoes, her *kameez* lifting slightly and exposing a peek of skin as she reached across the shelves, Anita lifted notebook after notebook and held them in her hands. She studied them judiciously: the number of pages, the size, the texture of the cover. It had to be perfect. 'Come on, Anita,' Ezra sighed, tapping his new plastic watch. But it had to be right; it had to be just right.

She had started learning English now, real English, not the gibberish they taught at school, *rutofied* expressions and mispronounced words. She was learning from the dramas on TV.

At night, Anita draped her mother's heavy black *chador* over her shoulders, crept out of the house and walked to the nearby *hotal* and sat on the corner of the *chaiwalla*'s block, listening to the way the actresses spoke. She heard a talkshow host interview one of the ladies from one of her favourite serials. *It's such a blessing, you know,* Shela Kazmi said in English that sounded like velvet felt against the skin, smooth and luxurious and unaffordable, *to be able to follow my dreams and do what I love.*

Until she could stand it, until her eyes became lazy with sleep, Anita Rose sat on the corner of the street, cockroaches scurrying in and out of the garbage tickling her feet, and wrote down all the words the actresses said in her own shiny red notebook. She repeated her favourite lines to herself as she walked through the alleyways piled high with rotting banana peel and mulch, lit only by the milky white of the distant stars, committing them to memory before she went to sleep.

*

'What's a prostitute's daughter like you doing with a fancy notebook like this?' Mira taunted Anita Rose at school. Anita didn't answer her. She had learned a long time ago to ignore the girls who hounded her. Mira's mother was actually a prostitute; Anita had seen her standing in the window of their home, wearing only a *choli*, pressing her breasts against the metal bars and calling down to the men in rickshaws and scooters below. It was why Mira hated Anita, why she teased her and bullied her. Because she knew Anita's mother never sold her body, even though the Josephs were infinitely poorer than her mother with the *choli*, standing at the window grilles.

'Leave it,' Anita said. She had filled three pages already, selecting only the most precious words. She had even started watching the news, where she learned an entirely new vocabulary. *Corruption, fraud, hypocrite, fundamentalist, Zionist.*

She could not afford to lose the notebook now. *Conspiracy*, she had learned that only yesterday.

Mira's eyes flickered with doubt as Anita refused to relinquish the notebook, and Anita saw her panic in front of the other girls. If Anita defeated this one bully, the rest would see Mira for what she truly was, an empty threat, defused of all her power. Anita saw it – all that pride and anxiety – in the way Mira's eyes swelled and then contracted. But before Anita understood that she would never have the chance to exact any kind of retribution, the game was already so skewed against her, Mira sank her ragged fingernails into the veins of Anita's hands.

Anita tried to release herself from Mira's grip, but Mira only dug in harder until her nails had left a scratching of demilunes, burning into the back of Anita's hand.

She had not let Mira see how much she had hurt her. Anita would not give those girls the pleasure of knowing how their cruelty had marked her. She walked back home from school with her head held high, as though she were carrying a book on the centre of her crown.

As she walked, stopping only to pet the stray dogs resting in the shade of the billowing banyan trees, Anita bit her lip to keep the tears from falling down her face. As soon as she opened the door of their single cement room, which Ezra promised he would soon upgrade, now that he was earning real money, Zenobia wailed that they were out of matches. Not a stick anywhere in the house. Anita would have to go to their neighbour and ask to borrow some.

Without speaking or setting down her heavy school bag, black like her uniform shoes, Anita walked to Osama Shah's home, holding her breath against the rubbish of rotting bones and innards from the butcher that lined the *gully* to his door and being extra-careful not to step in pools of fetid water, radioactive slicks of green and orange. She massaged the bruised back of her hand in her palm, soothing her wounds, and knocked on the old man's gunmetal door.

When Osama appeared at the door, Anita, her eyes glazing with the promise of tears, sniffled and asked for matches. He reached into the pocket of his fraying *shalwar kameez*, its Mao collar buttoned at the neck, and, handing his last box to Anita, asked: *Who dares make a lion cry?*

And Anita, no lion, began to weep.

Soap. Salt. Paper. Eggs. Candles. There was no end to what her mother borrowed from their neighbour next door. 'Baby,' Zenobia would announce as soon as her daughter lay down to read or, having freshly washed her hair at the tap behind the *mandi*, was shaking it out to dry, 'we need thread.'

Thread. Chillies. *Dawai*. Pencils. Somehow, the old man had everything.

Anita would knock, Osama would answer. Anita would ask, he would grant. Soap, salt, paper. Anita would mumble her thanks and Osama would – at most – nod. It was a routine rehearsed over years – she was a child when she had first knocked on his door – and never broken. Until the day her red notebook was almost snatched away and she appeared, rapping on the gunmetal door, close to tears.

Who dares make a lion cry?

When Anita stopped weeping, wiping her eyes on her cap sleeve, and accepted a cup of creamy chai to which she added three spoons of uncubed sugar, Osama invited her to sit down on a *charpai* he had covered with round cushions and a faded maroon-and-black block-printed *ajrak*. There were only two seats in the sitting room crowded with dust and books: the *charpai* and a wooden chair, which Osama lowered himself into carefully.

'Do you know about poetry?'

Anita shook her head, careful to hide under her bottom her hand bearing the crescent moons of Mira's nails.

'Do you want to learn?'

Anita thought for a moment. She nodded. Yes, she did. She liked learning.

He read her the lines of a poem he said was like a weapon, devastating and fatal. *Rise like lions after slumber in unvanquishable number.* Osama recited it to Anita in both Urdu and English.

'I know English,' Anita said, somewhat proudly. She would write the line down in her red notebook later. It was filled with new words, translations and, now, maybe even poetry.

'*Acha?*'

'Yes, from the TV.'

Osama smiled. Correct me then, if I make any mistakes? he asked.

Okay, Anita agreed.

As he read her the poem, he swore it was an exception. Those *goras* didn't know anything about love and the tragedy of true intimacy, not like our poets did. Not like Hafiz and Ghalib and Faiz, O *lal salam* comrade Faiz. However, this time a *gora* poem was allowed because it was a poem of a lion for a lion, read by one.

But Anita didn't understand most of the words.

'I don't speak proper English,' she admitted, shaking her head so he would understand that this was a sad confession and that her earlier boast had not been a lie.

I will teach you, Osama promised. Together we will shake your chains to the earth like dew. Together we will make sure no more such things fall upon you.

Monty

'Have you seen the new girl?' Monty's friend Kashif asked him as they walked down the hallway. She was the girl in the FaceTime video, the one with the ass like a peach. 'What a body,' Kashif fanned his hand in front of his face, his fingers snapping lightly against each other, 'what a body!' He swore he saw Layla's nipples through her see-through man's shirt, and said she wore that shit on purpose – it was some cheap-quality Juma Bazaar cotton, the kind peons wore. Plus, Shavez said, she had blow-job lips, all pink and puffy and rosy.

Nothing about Layla at the city's most elite private school, the American School of Karachi, made sense. She came to school on her first day in a small grey Suzuki Mehran, wearing a polyester *dupatta* over her hair and shoulders and her long black hair smelling of tobacco. No one at ASK covered their hair – not the sweepers, not even the Urdu teacher – no one. It was her brother, the guys said, who sometimes took her to school on his way to work. Apparently, her brother – or her father, Kashif wasn't sure which – insisted she wore the *dupatta*, and she made sure to yank it off as soon as his dinky car with a broken tail light turned round. When he didn't drop Layla at school, she turned up in a rickshaw.

No one knew what school Layla transferred from; she had neither the resting-bitch face of a Grammarian nor the accent. She could have been a scholarship case, but the school never said. She came the year that all the teachers had been airlifted out of the city due to terrorism threats, so the school was taking anyone that applied.

She was the daughter of a substitute teacher in the elementary school, one of the mean girls in their class insisted (Zara: younger sister of a famously beautiful graduate. Ergo: easy, insecure).

Her father was an Indian drug lord, Karachi's most famous fugitive.

She was a plant from the American Embassy. What seventeen-year-old talked the way Layla did? Possibly, she was CIA.

Layla never confirmed or denied the stories. Karachi was swimming with conspiracy theories and the American School was no exception. In truth, she liked the legends that surrounded her. She sat in the high-school lounge, drinking a full-sugar Coke, biting the straw with her teeth, and encouraged people to speak. What did she care what they thought? This was part of Layla's power, her privacy and mystery.

In the middle of the day, during class time, Layla sat outside the school gates and smoked cigarettes under the shade of the bowing banyan trees. The guards never reported her and so, when the mood struck her, Layla strolled out of geometry and rested her back against the ravaged bark of the ancient trees, blowing smoke rings and reading Mir Taqi Mir.

On what must have been her third day at school, Layla had raised her hand as Mr Alter introduced the Holocaust by writing #neverforget on the whiteboard. Mr Alter, the history teacher with his tie-dye shirts and love-beads on his wrist, was everyone's favourite teacher at the American School of Karachi. 'Mr Alter?' she asked, mispronouncing his name.

Awl-ter, he corrected, nodding his head for her to go on.

'Who decided that only some historical events were forbidden to forget?' Layla asked accusingly. 'Because surely the point of history is to remember? And remember all of it, not just selective chapters?'

Before Mr Alter could explain to Layla that he regularly hashtagged and tweeted their history lessons, offering questions for the students to ponder at home and creating a free space for them to continue their discussions after class ended *(#eatcakeoreatchaos? #industrialEVOlution? #sufferingsuffragettes #POCrock!)*, Layla leaned forward in her chair till she was sitting on the edge of her seat.

'What about Partition? Millions killed in the course of weeks? What about the Dirty Wars in Latin America, tens of thousands disappeared and murdered in football stadiums? #theywereallbrownsowedontcare?'

Mr Alter tried to answer, backing away from the whiteboard and sitting down to adopt a less authoritative posture, but Layla only grew more hostile. 'What about the *Nakba*? Seven hundred thousand people thrown out of their own country? Does that count?'

The whole class listened in stunned silence.

'What's next?' Layla snarled, springing out of her chair. 'All lives matter? Well, they don't, Mr Awl-ter. History isn't stagnant; you're judged by your present as well as your past, and those who oppress don't get to hashtag themselves as the victims just because you've got a Twitter account and want to feel important.'

That night Monty stood in the shower and tried to jerk off to Layla. As the hot water fogged up all the mirrors and Monty rested his back against the tiled walls, he thought of Layla's tight jeans, her nipples hardening under her transparent shirt, the peek of her stomach that he had seen when she jumped out of her chair, her blow-job lips. But after a while, as the water grew tepid and his wrist strained, Monty stepped out of the shower and, quickly laying a towel over the toilet-seat cover, sat down and reached for his iPad.

Careful not to wet the screen too much, he typed in a proxy site and waited patiently for YouPorn to open, scouring the site for the highest-rated amateur clips. But the Wi-Fi was weak and not even the GIFs of the videos would load. Monty opened proxy page after proxy page and struggled against his slow connectivity. Depleted, he sat on the soggy towel over the toilet seat for a while, pondering his failure. Layla couldn't fit into his pornographic imagination, no matter how hard he tried. What kind of power did she have over him? One that seemed to un-man him.

He had seen how other guys struck out with Layla. She smoked their imported Marlboros and walked off with their engraved Zippos and flavoured e-cigarettes in her pocket, not bothering with them again till she needed lighter fluid or menthol e-liquid for her e-smokes. He watched how Layla sang to herself as she walked out of the lounge at lunchtime, pausing to sing a line directly to someone every now and then – walking right up to them, resting her hands across the birdcage skeletons of their skinny chests, holding their eyes as though she meant every word – and then laughing as she turned away towards class.

Everyone wanted Layla. Because she was beautiful, because she was a tease, because she flirted absent-mindedly, easily, the way other people dreamed. But Monty wanted her because she was fearless. And he was – and had always been – afraid.

But still, even after they got together, Layla's self-conscious sexuality always unsettled Monty – who was she trying to excite with all that? It was jarring, this dangerous knowledge set upon the delicate innocence of her face and the soft nobility of her eyes. Layla always knew she was being watched and she made no secret of enjoying the attention. She moved slowly when she walked, when she entered a room, when she sat down, crossing her legs and lighting a cigarette, making sure you witnessed every rising curve, every feline stride that her long legs made.

Monty had never known anyone like Layla, ever. Everyone at their high school could be summed up in one small, pithy line. Sarya: *Lahori*. Jealous because even though she was cute, she was nowhere in the universe of pretty, not even with that ass of hers. Shavez: Accommodating. Broken family. Never kissed a girl, loves Federer. Rabia: Husband-hunting, *Memon*. This high-school ESP was not unique to Monty, most teenagers had a similarly functioning radar that worked on everyone – everyone except Layla.

What do you know about the world? Layla asked Monty the first time he dared talk to her.

Layla was wearing a man's shirt that day, several sizes too large and untucked. Monty couldn't see a line of her body, which made him think of it even more. He stood in front of her as she crumbled a pinch of *charas* into a palm-ful of tobacco leaves – right there, in the middle of school.

'Do you think you should be doing that?' Monty asked, more out of awe than anything else. He couldn't believe the guts of the girl. With her full lips and that mole above her chin, she looked like something Monty had only seen in the hazy borders of his dreams.

Layla lifted her head and glanced at the boy with the large doe-eyes in front of her. He wore an expensive shirt and designer jeans. His hair had been freshly cut and his cologne was a warm, cinnamon scent. When he spoke to her, she noticed that his pupils dilated, like coffee spilling in slow motion, until you could no longer see the light brown of his eyes.

'What do you know about the world?' Layla shot back, running her tongue along the seam of the cigarette. 'What gives you the right to have an opinion about anything?'

And without meaning to, Monty gave the only answer someone like Layla would respect.

Nothing, he replied. I don't know anything.

Anita Rose

Anita hadn't heard of *Soviet Life* before. Whatever book Osama asked her if she'd read, she always replied no, because then he would wander over to his bookshelf and extract the volume for her, giving her a mountain of books to read. It was the only time Anita received gifts from anyone besides her brother. She wrote down the name of every book comrade *sahib* gave her, and a line or two summarizing the heart of each in her red notebook.

'Oh ho, the poetry women used to write in the golden days of Moorish Spain,' Osama comrade sighed. Did Anita know Aisha bint Ahmad al-Qurtubiyya? A noble-woman of Cordoba, where the great mosque still calls the ghosts of its bricklayers to prayer, Aisha wrote poems to Andalusian kings. One day, when a court poet asked her to marry him, she sent him a little gift in reply. Comrade *sahib* folded the book, breaking its spine, and held it out for Anita to read:

I am a lioness and I will never be a man's woman.

She copied the line in her red notebook. Cordoba, she wrote alongside it. قرطبة – the only word she could read in the original Arabic. Anita ran her finger over the text; all the Arabic words were embellished with accents, decorating each letter like jewellery.

What about *Discovery of India*, have you read that? No. *Wretched of the Earth*? No. Yevgeny Yevtushenko? No.

Anita now had a pile of *Soviet Life* magazines, which she kept under her *ralli* in the corner of her small cement room. She read them the same way she pored over school books, carefully turning the pages as though they might tear with force, memorizing every word and expression, the way a map-reader traces lines, fearful of getting lost.

Standing at his bookshelves – he had built them himself, picking discarded planks of wood in the dumps behind the port – Osama, comrade *sahib* ('Don't add *sahib*, you silly girl. Don't you see how wrong that is?') sighed mournfully. 'What do they teach children in this country nowadays?'

I'm not a child, Anita reminded him. I'm sixteen.

Her neighbour waved his hand in the air, swatting away her age as he carried back a bound book, the fabric ripped from its cover, exposing a lattice of dusty white thread.

I'm almost a woman, Anita insisted, and soon poets will send me marriage proposals, and I, like the noble-woman of Cordoba, will tell them I'd rather marry a dog.

Osama smiled at Anita Rose, who likely had no sense how many marriage proposals had already floated her way.

'*Acha*, please tell me you know Habib Jalib?' Osama asked the question wincing, the corner of his eyes disintegrating into a spider's web of fine, delicate lines. 'No, don't answer,' he lifted his hand in the air before Anita could speak.

Anita leaned against the old wooden chair as comrade *sahib* bent to his knees and ran his finger along the titles on the last shelf, coughing as particles of dust floated up into the air.

'*What is the meaning of Pakistan, there is no God but God, the rab al alameen . . .*' Osama held the volume of Urdu poems and touched the open pages lovingly as he recited, speaking directly to Anita, '*Hold on to freedom, do not cave in* . . .

'Young comrade, learn these lines, carry them in your heart, okay?' Osama waited for her to agree before continuing.

I will, Anita promised.

'*Pukee baat?*'

She nodded.

'Finger-promise?' He held out his pinkie finger, curled into a hook. Anita smiled and linked her little finger with his.

Pinkie-promise, she said. He had taught her the expression.

Anita sat on the wooden bench with her posture straight and repeated the teacher's recitation of more complicated sums exactly as she said them; though older and wiser now, Anita knew that the teacher was wrong. It was nearly the end of the school year. Anita closed her eyes and reminded herself how soon this would all be over.

'Filthy pig,' Mira, her eyebrows knitting together and the hair of her sideburns growing longer and darker, snarled at Anita.

The girls on the bench giggled, but Anita paid them no mind. She thought of Rima, how she would never be bullied by these sorts of girls. Hiding behind the laundry-room door, Anita Rose had recently watched Rima fighting with a man on the telephone. Anita had heard Rima speaking to him for months now. Sometimes Rima giggled suggestively, sometimes she whispered dangerous things to him – naughty things, things girls never said out loud – but for the past four Sundays they had only been fighting.

'You think I need you?' Rima blasted the man on the phone. 'You think I need anyone?' She paused to light a cigarette from an elegant golden box. 'Well, let me tell you something,' she spoke slowly as she exhaled a long plume of smoke, 'when I put down this phone, you'll be gone. I won't even remember you in a week.'

Anita listened, rapt. That was who she wanted to be, the kind of girl who could forget someone in a week. Who didn't need anyone, who wasn't afraid, who was brave and free. A lioness who was not, and would never be, a man's woman.

Anita was transforming, she felt it. Things were going to happen for her. Her life was changing. She could easily become the kind of woman Rima was.

She had begun to develop breasts, real breasts, you could see them through her clothes now: small, puckered buds of soft brown skin. The acne that dotted her forehead, a small constellation of spots, had started to fade and, in the span of a few months, she had grown at least five centimetres.

Mira leaned even closer to Anita. '*Sewar*,' she repeated, aiming the words straight into Anita's ear. But Anita couldn't hear Mira, she couldn't hear any of them any more.

Sunny

'You're looking everywhere but the right place,' Sunny's cousin Oz told him, when he came back from Syria. Oz's face was tanned and his normally bleached-blond hair had lightened even more from the sun. Sunny hadn't seen him in at least a year, and they had never really been close as kids, either, but Oz no longer wore what had once been his uniform of tank tops and sweat pants. Now, Oz covered up his muscular body and had begun to grow out a beard, shaving his moustache every morning. 'You're looking for everything but the truth.'

Women, Oz told Sunny, were distractions from the self. They pulled you away from investigating and understanding God's truth. Women, since Eve and her poisoned fruit, were out to dirty the message. Sunny thought of Naya going down on him, of Romina making him come in the cinema, and shifted uneasily. He had given them up, Oz said. Never felt clearer or more balanced. He sat back in his chair, folded his hands in his lap and smiled beatifically.

Oz spoke with a confidence Sunny had never seen before.

When Oz went travelling, his parents had been relieved. He'd gone to volunteer in the refugee camps around Syria, Aunty Shaista, Sunny's dad's sister, said. 'Thank God, *beta*,' wiping her forehead with her *dupatta*. 'Thank God he found a calling in life.' Oz's parents were relieved he was doing something, anything; they didn't really ask where and what. And no one else, to tell the truth, ever really noticed Oz was gone. And then he was back – and there was something different about him.

He met Sunny and Sulaiman Jamil at the door the day they came for Eid lunch. *'As salam alaikum*, Uncle,' Oz stressed all the Arabic words hard, like he'd always spoken his *salams* with the right accents, and enveloped his uncle in a bear hug. He looked serene, smiling broadly and wearing a starched *shalwar* suit. The tattoo of his name in Arabic was still curled around the nape of his neck, but Oz had taken out the eyebrow-ring that once pierced his left brow. The gold chains he used to wear around his neck were gone and he smelled distinctly, heavily, like *oudh*. Sulaiman raised an eyebrow and patted his nephew on the back. 'Muscles, shuscles, Oz,' Sulaiman Jamil said, impressed. 'Looking good, my boy.'

'Subhanallah,' Oz replied, pointing a finger up to the sky. 'Feeling good too, Uncle.'

Sunny watched his cousin that day, how he spoke to everyone over lunch, how all the relatives were captivated by what Oz had to say. How glorious Syria had been, a country of people who wanted for nothing. The seat of Islam's most divine caliphate, a kingdom that ruled over centuries and commanded respect from Europe and the world. When it was time for *namaz*, Oz stood at the front of the drawing room and led the men in prayers. He had learned how to call the *azan* in Aleppo, he said. It was sung like music there, the most beautiful sound you ever heard.

As Sunny and his dad were leaving, Oz walked them to their car. Standing by Sunny's door, Oz bent down and rested his arm on the window. 'Come and see me, my brother,' he said. 'I have a world to share with you.'

Sunny nodded and promised he would, shaking his cousin's hand before he rolled up the window.

'*Voh sala kya bakwas bolraha tha?*' Pa asked as they drove off. 'God this, thanks God that,' Sulaiman Jamil shook his head sadly. 'I thought the boy had grown up a bit.'

'Nothing,' Sunny turned away from his father. 'He wasn't saying anything.'

'Refugee camp, my bottom.' Sulaiman Jamil sniffed.

But Sunny couldn't stop thinking about his cousin. He had never seen a man that strong before, that at peace. There was something new about Oz, Sunny didn't know what exactly, but there was something radiant, even beautiful, about him.

That night, Sunny couldn't sleep. He lay in bed, feeling agitated and restless, thinking about Oz. He walked around his room, watched some TV, had a shower, but he was humming, literally thrumming with excitement. At two in the morning Sunny texted his cousin and asked if he wanted to hang out the next day. He suggested meeting at the mosque, thinking Oz would appreciate the venue, but Oz replied – he replied! – and said nah, better to go somewhere where they could talk freely, somewhere real.

What was freer than the mosque? What could be more real?

Oz just smiled when Sunny asked him the following day. 'Bro, they are so last century.' They sat at a kebab shop on Albert Road, waiting for some pals of Ozair's to arrive. 'These imams been here so long, they don't even know what's *haq* any more. They're so busy assimilating, bowing to the white man and his "prevent extremism" agenda, they forgot we the ones *others* should be assimilating to. They forgot the glory of Islam! They're so busy believing all the lies we get fed night and day in the *Daily Mail*, they lost themselves polluting our message and leading good brothers like you astray.'

The shop was empty. There wasn't anyone behind the counter, only some fellows in *shalwar* suits and beards talking to each other in low voices. An old woman with a handkerchief tied tight under her chin and pushing a canvas trolley opened the door. 'Sorry, love,' the beard behind the counter said, 'we're closed.'

The old woman looked around the shop, her eyes falling on the men sitting at various tables.

'In-house work today,' the beard smiled, apologizing. When she closed the door, he came out from behind the counter and locked the floor-jamb. 'Keep an eye on it,' he said to Oz, resting his hand on his shoulder for a second.

What lies? Sunny asked his cousin. He had his issues with the mosque; the imam was soft and didn't really inspire anyone with his *tooty-pooty* sermons in bad English. But they were good folk. It calmed Sunny to be there. They were all right.

Oz shook his head. 'Oh, brother,' he said sadly. 'Where do I start?'

Sunny spent days at the kebab shop with Oz.

The West had gone mad, Oz explained. It had lost sight

of the path to truth, letting gays have parades, bringing women out of the home, out of where they nurtured life, and into the market place like prostitutes. Women have no righteousness any more, bro, they get abortions when they're bored with a man, they have zero respect for the family. There's birth-control chemicals floating in the water supply, making good sisters sterile and turning men into women. Why else were sex-change operations on the rise? Only these people were shameless enough to over-turn God's design. Why we got to code ourselves *all* the time – People of Colour, Asian descent, cis-male WTF! Just to make these *chutias* feel more comfortable, dealing with a world that don't look like them no more, that ain't *white*. The West was finished; it was corrupted beyond repair. It wasn't the place for real men any more – not men like them.

Sunny nodded, rapt. 'The elites are eating up the world,' Oz explained. 'And at the same time, they are casting *you* out.' Oz placed his hand on Sunny's chest, right above his heart. 'Because you and me, Cuz, they'll never accept us. We're the periphery, we'll never be the centre. We're not like them. We come from a different culture. They don't understand our people, our struggles.'

As they sat at Starbucks, watching Guildhall Walk from their stools at the window counter, Oz sprinkled vanilla powder over a coconut-milk latte and explained to Sunny that that was how capitalism worked. It made you want all kinds of shit – Xboxes, Yeezy Boost Triple White V2 sneakers, Bose surround-sound – always adding more things to the list of what you needed. But you could never catch up. No matter how much they had, men like him and Oz would always be left out. Because they weren't white, because they were Muslim, because they were *different*.

It was true. It made sense. All his life, Sunny never felt he belonged in Portsmouth. Ben and those guys, they never understood him. Underneath all their banter, Sunny knew one thing: no one had ever seen through all the fog he put up around himself, no one had ever touched upon the heart of it all – the pain, the loneliness, the confusion. No one until Oz.

No matter how intelligent he was, Oz said, he would never be famous. He'd never be the face on the BBC screen, he'd never be sat on a morning-show couch, never be the man on the cover of a magazine. And why not? Didn't he deserve it? Didn't he see things? Know things? But this mediocre world of theirs was bent on destroying men like Oz. It was why they had to fight it.

Sunny deleted all the numbers of the random girls who called up late at night – Naya, Romina, Reshma – he was done with all that. Whatever time Sunny had now, he spent with Oz.

'You're not becoming a fruit, are you?' Pa asked after Oz had come and spent the weekend at their place on Britannia Road. Sulaiman Jamil sat at the kitchen counter eyeing his son for the telltale signs that he had become a gay, too, like that muscle-building fundo Oz. 'I didn't leave Lucknow and come all the way to Britain just so you could fall in love with your cousin, you know.'

But Pa didn't get it. It was being with Oz that made

Sunny feel more like a man than he ever had before. 'He's not a poof,' Sunny replied, irritated.

Sulaiman Jamil rolled his eyes. '*Acha*, he just has bleached-blond hair and tattoos for style, is it?'

'He's not, Pa.' Sunny didn't know why the suggestion bothered him so much. Oz was returning Sunny to his ancestral beliefs, guiding him through the teachings and study of their forefathers, helping him find his way on the road to their promised past, the land of milk and honey, the glory of their original selves. He had nothing to do with the corruption of the West, nothing to do with the vulgarity of those people. Didn't Pa see that? Didn't he see his son amputating himself from the rot of this-here life, from everything British, belonging to this alien country and culture? Didn't he see Sunny returning to something pure?

He was just bitter. That was all. Pa was just a sad, old man the world had spat out. Sunny was going to be different – people would respect him. They would remember him. Recognize him. Already, Sunny was happier than he had been in months. Oz lifted his grief, only he had the power to do that. His cousin, his friend, his brother in arms, for a while his everything.

Before he went away to Syria and was saved, Oz mainly hung around gaming with his friends and doing little else. As far as Sunny remembered, Oz didn't even go to uni, just milled around the student athletic centre, using the machines for free, chatting to the trainers and selling dime bags of weed to make ends meet.

He was different now, Sunny promised Pa. Truly different. Oz had a foot in the future – in truth – since Syria. He had seen the horizon and come back to sing the gospel. Pa saw how confident and certain Oz was, how fluent in politics and current affairs. But it wasn't what he wished for his only son, spending all his time in the company of his older, tattooed cousin.

'All I'm saying is, I didn't raise you with modern, British values so you could act like you still lived in a village. I didn't spend my life working just so you could break my heart with this nonsense.' I didn't, I didn't, I didn't.

Sunny ignored his father. He didn't need him, not any more. He had his music, which had always been a refuge for him. But Sunny had a place in the world now, too, thanks to his cousin, and for the first time in his life he felt that sanctuary expanding, opening up into the light. Pa didn't know anything about Oz. Pa didn't know anything about the struggles of being a man with the force of the world against you.

Monty

They spent lunchtime every day at school together, Layla
sitting on Monty's lap. He kissed her hands, her eyelids,
the mole below her lip. Every time his lips touched her,
Monty thanked whatever God existed for Layla and the
impossible, miraculous fate that had brought her into his
life. He kissed her eyes, left and right, and knew that no
man on earth would ever know the joy he felt as her eyelashes, thick with mascara, curled against his lips.

When they weren't together, when she was sitting with
her girlfriends and Monty was at the other end of the
lounge, hanging out at the foosball table, or else when
they were seated separately in class, sometimes Layla
caught Monty looking at her.

Layla, always in her own world, slouched down in her
seat, her neck bent in such a way that you assumed she
was sleeping, so close that her chin almost touched her
chest. Sometimes she looked up, lifting only her eyes, to
see Monty watching her. When she saw him, how he
looked at her, full of love and trust, Layla's heart swelled
with something close to pain.

Monty, elated to have caught her eye, would smile. And
Layla, who did nothing false, would not smile back. She
would lift her chin and say only his name: Monty, quietly
rounding out the letters with her mouth. Monty.

Just that:

Monty.

And his face would light up with joy.

It cost Layla so little to make Monty happy.

She took one of his shirts, a black pinstriped dress shirt that his father brought him back from a business trip to China. Layla had ears like a hawk and she made sure to listen to all the information Monty sweetly, innocently, telegraphed. Akbar Ahmed was always travelling, every month he flew to Guangzhou, Dubai and Jeddah. He spent a few days at home with wife and son and then took off again.

Layla wore Monty's Guangzhou shirt loose over her skinny jeans, bought with defects at Zainab Bazaar, black nail polish always chipped and scratched on her nails. It looked so good on her, the loose shirt, the tight jeans. 'I love it when you wear that,' Monty whispered to her from his seat behind her in chemistry class.

'Get me more shirts,' Layla said, 'and I'll wear them all the time.'

She didn't like to talk about her father or mother, she never said anything about her brother, either. Nothing about her family at all, only that she had really been raised by her best friend, her grandfather Monty thought it was, an elderly man whom she adored. She owed everything to him, she said. I'd love to meet him sometime, Monty said, but Layla never offered, never suggested that she might like the same.

The girls Monty had grown up knowing were neither bookish nor confrontational. They wore pretty tops to school, accessorized with their mother's jewellery, and spoke of who did what which weekend, and what party was coming up next. Layla, on the other hand, read constantly. She sat on the floor at lunchtime, resting used books of poetry scoured at Urdu Bazaar on her knees. She was reading Mir when they first met. Mir's poetry made her feel less alone in the world, Layla said. One day, she hoped to be sent into exile, like Faiz.

Who? Monty had asked, embarrassed.

Faiz Ahmed Faiz, Layla replied. He fought for something beautiful once, how can you not know his name?

Chastened, Monty went to Liberty Books to buy some Mir Taqi Mir and Faiz Ahmed Faiz, but they didn't have anything of the poets in English. Did he want some Isabel Allende or Paulo Coelho? Monty bought a couple of books for Layla, the bookseller said they were so popular, but she made him return them.

She sat for hours in the school library and read everything in the slim Urdu section, her back leaning against the metal bookshelves, her long black hair falling across her eyes. Layla said she didn't consider European books classics, because they spoke to no part of her experience. She read in Urdu because it was the language she suffered in, a language that encompassed all her sorrows.

Don't you feel strange, speaking a language every day that's not your own? Layla asked Monty. But Monty had never spoken anything besides English.

Monty bought tickets to the Karachi Festival of Literature and took Layla to a session on the exclusion of American novelists from the Nobel. As they sat in a conference room at the Beach Luxury Hotel, overlooking murky mangrove swamps and steel cranes dramatically suspended over Karachi's port, Layla held Monty's hand and rolled her eyes at everything the panellists said.

A visiting self-published American novelist with corkscrew hair, wrapped up in a sweater ragged with pilling, to guard against the chill of the air-conditioned room, made sure to interject and add her two cents to every question. 'This nobody is the least likely of all to get any prize,' Layla whispered, smiling. Monty rolled his eyes too, *chamcha*-ing along, without really understanding why.

On Kashif's birthday, the group went to K's parents' French Beach hut. The full moon hung low, eventually it would disappear into the water. There was a DJ and a bartender, and even food catered from Flo. As Monty walked through the hut, touching the sofa cushions, checking for sogginess and finding that the muggy humidity of the beach had sunk into all the furniture, he saw Kashif and Sarya standing on the patio. Sarya was leaning into Kashif, listening to him. As he spoke, whispering into Sarya's ear, Kashif's hand travelled down her back, settling on the small curve at the base of her spine. Monty stood still and watched them.

Sarya wasn't even Kashif's girlfriend; they'd only hooked up once or twice. But Kashif held an authority over Sarya that was effortless and confident. He dropped his hand down the waistband of her long skirt, squeezing her flesh and pulling her closer into him.

Monty looked for Layla, for his actual, official girlfriend, but she wasn't there. He stepped carefully around Kashif and Sarya, embarrassed, and walked out onto the beach, lit up by the white moonlight. Someone said it was nesting season. If you watched for them, after sunset you could see small sea turtles, their winged flippers burrowing in and out of the seashore.

Monty walked away from the hut, following the scratches of the tracks the turtles laid in the sand, until he had walked to the shore, away from the music and the smoke of the barbecue. And there was Layla, lying on her back in the sand, her hair splayed all around her, closing her eyes and waiting for the tide to rise, to rush up and submerge her.

Anita Rose

They sat on the roof of Osama's small building. There had been no lights in the colony for two days. She spent most days at her neighbour's, knocking softly on his gunmetal door when she had finished her school work, running away from the new home her brother had leased and from her mother who, Anita suspected, had begun to hate the world. Zenobia took her illness, her tired hands, as a personal affront from God. He was trying to destroy her, crippling her like this.

So Anita went to see Osama, no matter the distance to his gunmetal door, and sat on his old wooden chair, a thin shawl draped over its seat to disguise its discomfort, and listened to comrade *sahib* speak of fighters, men he had known who believed in something great, of writers who opposed oppression and injustice.

But this evening, with the colony draped in darkness, Osama hailed a rickshaw and took Anita to the Press Club. From the moment they walked through the white gate, comrade *sahib* saluted and shook hands with important-looking men. 'These used to be my people,' he whispered to Anita Rose. For an hour, they sat in front of a television on a comfortable sofa, drinking sugary milk tea and listening to the news drowned in the hum of a generator.

During every advertisement break, someone would come and say hello and someone else would pass comrade *sahib* a phone, which he would lift gingerly to his ear. *Ji janaab?* he began every phone call, his face relaxing into a smile as the caller's voice became familiar.

At the end of the news, their bellies full with tea and buttered biscuits offered by the canteen, Anita and Osama walked to the road to stop a rickshaw. There was a crowd of people gathered on the pavement, lit by a sea of oil lamps. Some of the protestors attending the evening vigil carried posters and banners, but all of them wore black armbands. As they exited the Press Club, a young man stood up from sitting cross-legged in the crowd and watched them. He was tall and broad-shouldered and wore a white *shalwar kameez*. He waved to Osama, calling out to him from across the road.

'Wait for me,' comrade *sahib* said softly, patting Anita's arm. He signalled to a rickshaw on the kerb and the driver picked his bare foot off the street, slipping it into his sandal as he started the engine.

Osama walked towards the protestors illuminated by small, earthen *diyas* and embraced the young man warmly. Anita Rose watched as they sat down on the kerb to speak. As he lowered himself, Osama placed a hand on the man's shoulder. At that moment the rickshaw driver pulled up and stopped in front of Anita. 'Are we going or what?' he asked, his cheek swollen with *paan*. Anita Rose climbed into the rickshaw and watched Osama through the open side, craning her neck to see him.

The young man had placed a hand over comrade *sahib*'s and he held onto him in an intimate, affectionate way. He looked like someone Anita had seen before. He had thick black hair that fell in front of his face. With his free hand, the young man pushed his hair out of his eyes and, from where she sat, Anita could see that he looked at the old man with something resembling love.

'*Mohtarma*,' the rickshaw driver turned in his seat and addressed Anita sarcastically. 'Are we going or what?'

Anita Rose ignored him, watching the way Osama's face softened as he stood up slowly, saying goodbye to the young man. Suddenly he looked frail, old. Much older than he was.

'Madam!' the rickshaw-walla shouted at Anita, exasperated.

'*Ji, sahin*,' Osama answered as he limped slowly towards them. He held onto the metal handle as he climbed into the rickshaw, exhaling with the effort, and patted the driver on his back, '*Chalo*.'

'Who was that?' Anita asked, once they were moving, but Osama's eyes were far away.

'How dark this city looks without its jewellery,' he sighed, ignoring her.

Anita didn't want to push too hard and upset her comrade. The more her life evolved, growing towards a new future, a better future, the more she felt tensions open up between them. The only time Osama had shut his door to Anita was the month before, when she had asked if she too could have a glass of his antiseptic-smelling *sharab*.

He always drank from the same glass, wetting his lips till his words tumbled out with a dreamy slowness. He offered Anita only tea, with plenty of sugar, but nothing else. Can I have some, too? Anita Rose, growing more confident in their companionship, had asked.

Like a switch had been tripped, Osama stood shakily

to his feet and, smoothing down his frayed white *shalwar kameez*, asked her to leave. Surprised by the sudden end in their conversation, but attributing his mood to the alcohol, Anita got up and picked up the volume of Faiz Ahmed Faiz they had been discussing. 'Leave the book, please,' Osama had said, looking away from her. 'This will kill me, Anita,' he said, before closing the gunmetal door in her face, 'I won't have it touch you, too.'

Osama didn't answer the light rapping of her knuckles on the metal door the day after, or the next. He hadn't answered Anita, who stood outside his home as a delicate summer drizzle dirtied the staircase, open to the elements. Osama didn't welcome Anita back into his home, didn't call her his lion again until, a week of silence later, she slipped under his door an apology written on the faded cover of a magazine.

It was a discoloured *Soviet Life*. *I'm sorry*, Anita Rose had written over the features of a smiling Afghan man, tracing the letters again and again over his weathered, dignified face.

She stood outside Osama's door and waited. The mynahs flew in circles, dipping in and out of the light shower. Soon they would settle on the earth and seek shelter under the wheels of parked motorcycles, hopping along the scattered rubbish, scavenging for food.

But just when Anita turned to climb down the steps of Osama's first-floor home to sit among the orphaned birds, he opened the door.

'Keep my words close to you,' Osama said, speaking to the young girl's back.

'Always,' Anita replied, not turning round. She wrote down everything he said to her in her notebook. *I am a lioness*, she had even written on the first page, over her earlier, less confident scrawls.

'One day I will be gone,' he spoke tenderly, like the harmless patter of the falling rain. 'You must promise me.'

Anita turned to face Osama, his wild white hair growing around his face like a mane. 'I promise.'

Sitting in the rickshaw on their way back to Machar Colony, Anita had wanted to ask why they didn't come to the Press Club every time the lights cut, but she understood that the young man was part of the reason why. And now that they had seen him, she knew that they wouldn't be coming back.

'Did you know him a long time ago?'

Osama nodded slowly, his eyes still cast out into the darkness, away from her. 'A very long time ago.'

'Was he a student of yours?'

Osama faced Anita then and smiled, his eyebrows arching. 'A student?'

'Like me,' she replied, a little embarrassed at the way he repeated the word. 'Someone you taught things to – you know, poetry and writing and politics.'

Osama lifted his arm and draped it over Anita's shoulder, squeezing her gently. 'You, my dear, are my comrade. My rogue associate and friend.'

Anita smiled. But he hadn't answered her question. 'And him?'

'Laith.'

Laith? It was a name Anita knew. She had seen it scribbled in some of the books Osama gave her, in a brittle, clumsy hand.

'My son.' Osama withdrew his arm and brought it to his lap, leaning his head back against the plastic cover of the rickshaw.

Anita fell quiet. She had seen him before. Kicking a deflated football against a wall. Screaming, his handsome face howling, at the back of a pickup truck. She knew Osama's family had left him; Ezra had said it was because of his drinking. But that was before Anita knew him. She had since grown up assuming that Osama Shah belonged only to her. And why not? She took care of him, visiting him every day, bringing him news of the outside world as he grew older and more frail, listening attentively to all his stories and lectures, keeping him company while he drank late into the night.

Anita had assumed that his first family, whoever they were, belonged to another life and, as such, had been erased from the dusty flat lined with old books, from Machar Colony, from Karachi and from the world. She assumed they had been part of the unfeeling, cruel city Osama often spoke of, teaching her how to navigate its unkindness. They were abandoners, deserters. They didn't understand Osama like she did, one outsider to another.

Osama looked out onto the road. His eyes were glittering with tears.

'He seemed brave.' Anita didn't know what else to say. She hadn't even read the signs Laith and the protestors had been holding, she had been so focused on his face, how he looked at his father with tenderness.

Comrade *sahib* nodded absently. 'Laith,' he repeated sadly, pronouncing it dreamily. 'The only boy in all of Karachi with that name.'

'How do you know?' Anita asked, though she had never seen anyone with the name anywhere, not even on TV, before.

'I named him.' Osama closed his eyes again. 'Have you ever heard such a beautiful name?'

No, Anita Rose shook her head, feeling a little jealous, never. 'What does it mean?'

Comrade *sahib* sighed. 'Lion. It means lion in Arabic.'

Sunny

He slept over at his cousin's place, the two of them alone, waiting by the computer for calls to come in from Hama, from Tikrit, from Ain al Arab. He watched the faces of those men, younger than him, light up on Skype as they spoke about the Ummah Movement's jihad and how blessed they were to finally be in a place where the strict law of Shariah was followed.

'You see, Cuz,' Oz said to Sunny, 'these *mujahid* aren't sitting at home, doing nothing and complaining over their artisanal lagers, while their children sleep comfortably in their bunk beds and *our* children, *our* sons and daughters, are being massacred.' His lips curled with disgust. 'We are fighting to protect Islam.' It is your duty to fight for Islam, to die for it, Oz told Sunny. Why else do you think God put you here? What else is your life for, but God?

'Syria is a laboratory, Cuz, you don't know what we're building out there.' Oz's face glowed with pride. 'You know the Kouachi brothers?'

Sunny nodded – everyone knew those brothers. Shop owners on Albert Road plastered their windows with *Je suis Charlie* posters, and EDL thugs threw Molotov cocktails at the mosque for weeks after that attack.

'I trained with them.'

Sunny's eyes widened.

Oz nodded slowly, proudly. He snapped his fingers against his thighs. 'You say shit, you get hit.'

It was France's money and guns, their support for the rebels in Syria, that trained those brothers, Oz said. It was a circle of energy, of karmic retribution. You give, you get. You sow, you reap. You say shit, you get hit. No, *Je ne suis pas fucking Charlie*. 'Oh no,' Oz said, his eyes dancing. *'Je suis* something else altogether.'

Oz showed him videos of the Iraqi army chanting slogans: No god but Saddam, they said, over and over like robots. He showed him clips of Shia militias. Clips of women walking around Damascus in miniskirts and high heels before the war started. Those people were not Muslims. Infidels were not Muslims. Men who whored around, outside of marriage, corrupting their sisters in Islam, those were not Muslims. Women who didn't cover their bodies, they were loose and dirty. They were not Muslims. Men who drowned in pleasure, who sang and danced and listened to music, not prayers, they were not Muslims. Men who went to mosque but not to war, those were not Muslims.

'I done all that shit too, Cuz,' Sunny confessed to Oz one day, feeling the shards of his depression return. He rolled his fingertips on the Formica table nervously, turning his hands over and drumming percussion with his knuckles. 'I've done all that shit and more,' Sunny admitted, his heart heavy with worry.

But Oz just pulled into the booth next to him, looking over his shoulder to make sure no one was in the kebab shop, and laid an arm round his cousin. 'But you're finished with all that, aren't you?' Oz said gently, covering

Sunny's hand tapping out music with his own. 'You're not going to see any of those girls again, are you?'

He was so close, Sunny could smell his Lynx body spray. How had Oz forgiven him? Sunny kept his eyes down, afraid to look at Oz. He knew he didn't deserve his cousin's amnesty, knew he had lived a life of lapses and transgressions.

'God's got a plan for you, a destiny.' Oz's breath was warm against Sunny's ear. 'He's watching you, Sunny. He sent you to me.'

And just like that, Sunny felt lifted. Once again, he felt liberated. All the weight he carried in the dark recesses of his soul was freed; all the stones that bore down upon him were gone. Just from the comfort of Oz and his words. And just like that, when Oz was distant and didn't have time for Sunny, or their long nights spent talking and watching videos, it came crashing back.

'You're not a Sunni,' Oz told Sunny after two weeks. 'You're not a Sunni because a real believer wouldn't be sitting here; he would be out there, defending his people from infidels and moral collapse. You just want to sit here feeling sorry for yourself.'

I am, Sunny insisted. I am a Muslim.

'I said Sunni,' Oz replied. '*He who lives by the sunna.*'

I am, Sunny promised. I do.

'Then?' Oz suddenly became angry. Sunny didn't notice it when his cousin first arrived, but the more time he spent in the closed-down kebab shop on Albert Road, the more he saw how angry his cousin was. For a moment Sunny wondered if there was something he wasn't doing, if he had let Oz down in some way. There was an uneasy tension between them, like Oz was always waiting for something, like Sunny hadn't yet proved himself to be the kind of man Oz knew he could be. And in truth, Sunny felt it, too.

'Cuz, Muslims fighting Muslims . . .' Sunny demurred, trying to voice a part of what had bothered him from the start. 'Isn't it wrong? How can it be a revolution, if all we do is kill each other?' To be honest, he didn't really know many Shias anyhow. He just didn't want to find himself on the wrong side, once again. He didn't want to leave one life full of lies, only to walk right into another.

But Oz just laughed. 'This is jihad, my brother. Islam is at stake here. It's that mosque of yours, brainwashing you. Having you pray alongside them, thinking we all the same. Thinking that all men are brothers. They are *Wajib ul Qatal*,' Oz said to his cousin. 'We have a *right* to kill them.'

'I was just asking,' Sunny replied softly. He didn't need Oz to translate for him. He didn't understand the Arabic or whatever, but he knew that '*a'ridh anil jahilin*' meant ignore the ignorant. He knew from previous conversations with Oz that those marked for death included a growing list of infidels: Ahmedis, activists, Americans, seculars, blasphemers, drinkers, dancers, bloggers, romance novelists, pornographers, women's magazine writers, writers at large, polytheists, apostates, Valentine's Day celebrators, Syrian/Iraqi soldiers, Kurds, Russians, cartoonists, illustrators, actresses, women who didn't cover their hair, women who showed their skin, women who smoked, women who drank, women who drove, immodest women, women in general and now Shias.

But what about men who were close to other men? What about them? Sunny wanted, but was too afraid, to ask. Was there something wrong with that?

For real, though, Sunny had never heard of any of this before his cousin. It was in none of his readings, none of the books he studied at the Jami Masjid, and certainly not in any of Muhammad Ali or Malcolm X's videos. All he had known of Islam before Oz had gone off to fight in Syria was mercy. He had known Islam only for its refuge, its tolerance. It was submission, not violence. It made no distinction between sons, neither Sunni nor Shia. They were all one – all Muslims, all connected. But Sunny didn't want Oz to be angry with him. He didn't want to lose the one thread he had ever found that led somewhere.

'I believe.' Sunny stood up, facing his cousin, who looked like a stranger to him at that moment. What Sunny felt for Oz, a closeness that tightened in the pit of his stomach when he thought of him, a warm burn at the back of his neck, it confused him. And he knew, he understood, that his cousin didn't feel the same. He saw something in Sunny that he didn't recognize, something that wasn't right and it disturbed him.

Sunny could feel Oz pulling away. He had become so distant, always testing, always antsy, constantly threatening to leave. The longer Oz stayed in Portsmouth, the edgier he was.

'You don't understand me,' Oz explained, by way of apologizing for snapping at Sunny – which he had started to do more and more. 'I'm not being recognized for my efforts, for what I do for you. You don't get me. It brings a brother down, you know?'

I do, Sunny promised, close to tears at the idea of hurting Oz. I do understand you. Oz had changed something in the world for Sunny; he had opened up hope where there had been nothing. 'What do I do next?' he asked Oz. 'I'm ready, tell me what's the next step.'

'Oh, Cuz, it's so beautiful there,' Oz said, smiling. He embraced Sunny and held him in his arms. 'You're going to feel things you never have before.'

Sunny didn't speak. He just let himself breathe in Oz, his happiness, his acceptance. 'You're going to be a different man now,' Oz said, still holding his younger cousin. 'It's so beautiful there, *wallahi*, you'll see.'

It was spring. Sunny ran along the edges of the small park near Britannia Road, his feet pounding against the earth. He ran longer than he had in years, breathing in the crisp April air, perfumed with the damp scent of wildflowers. A couple of kids kicked a football around. 'Hey,' Sunny called, 'pass it here.' The youngest boy kicked it to Sunny, who caught the ball with the width of his chest, stopping it mid-air. With a choreography so delicate it could only be natural, he balanced the ball against his body, shoulder to ankle, knee to air, almost as though he were dancing. The boys watched in awe as Sunny shuffled against the light breeze of a spring morning, moving the ball along his body and the young grass coated with dew.

Monty

Monty's phone beeped. He covered it discreetly with his palm, shielding it from his mother. Rami Nayar's show had been on for the last hour, as the cleric sang tunelessly alongside a choir of *madrassa* children.

Ever since Zahra Ahmed started practising Islam, covering her head and praying five times a day, she had become a different woman. Zahra, unlike her husband Akbar, had nothing to do with the seeds of nation-building, but she came from a good Islamabad family of civil servants, old gin-and-tonic-drinking, moustachioed ICS. And she had been lucky all her life – good marriage, good son, good home, good fortune. But there had to be something more, she reasoned, and as such she ought to give thanks to the Almighty, in order to make sure the good never gave way.

A newly divorced friend of hers introduced her to Rami Nayar, a slight man with a Yusuf Islam beard, who wore a crisp burgundy suit and wire-rimmed glasses and pros-elytized on TV. Nayar spoke with a pronounced lisp, but was otherwise impeccably turned out as he lectured a stu-dio audience on the tenets of Islam. His hair was neatly buzzed at the sides, his long spiky fringe glistening with gel, his camera make-up thick and pasted across his angu-lar face, round circles of blush swept around his bearded cheeks. Over the course of Nayar's four-hour lectures, he sang religious *naaths*, recited hadiths and cured audience members of degeneracy.

For a donation to his evangelical ministry, Nayar met wealthy supporters from time to time, offering private prayers and consultation for their troubles. Zahra Ahmed met him only once – *Begum Sahiba*, Nayar had said, placing his palm on the top of her head. *I have seen you in my dreams. You are a great woman. It is time you do great things.* He advised Mrs Ahmed to remove her nail polish, for it contained alcohol, and asked if she employed any Filipina staff at home. It was wrong to have attractive young Christians in such close proximity to husbands and sons. They vexed the hearts of innocent men.

Indonesian maids, on the other hand, were fine. The world's biggest Islamic country, Nayar concluded approvingly.

Superstitious and afraid of losing the advantages that God had blessed the Ahmeds with, above all their peers, Zahra no longer indulged in the comforts of her old life. She wore ordinary slippers now, no more black-and-beige Chanels looted at the Selfridges summer sale, she plucked all her jewellery off her ears and collarbones, like weeds, and rendered them to a safe-deposit box.

Now, Monty's mother spent her vacations in Karachi, teaching the cooks to memorize the Koran. She used the remainder of her designer scarves to cover her head at home, a practice she continued long after firing all their male servants.

Zahra spent every evening in front of the family plasma-screen TV, a notebook in her lap, writing down Nayar's pronouncements and mouthing along silently to all his mispronounced prayers. Monty sat on the sofa, next to his mother in the living room, his phone in his hand and his legs stretched out across the table in front of him.

Monty.

Yes, Laylee? He added a red heart after his beloved's name and watched the screen as she typed a reply. He gave her his older iPhone, after making sure to wipe it clean of the amateur porn sites he sometimes surfed, so she could email him when she was at home in Gulshan, a good hour and a half away from him in Clifton. Only her brother had a computer, Layla said, and he was always on it, networking apparently.

Pick me up. She never used emojis.

Now?

No, next month, duffer.

Zahra closed her eyes as she swayed softly in a dreamy trance. Papa stood at the door to the living room, a crystal glass cupped in his palm, watching his wife. 'How long is this hocus-pocus going to last?' He took a sip of his whisky. 'Some of us want to watch the actual news.'

The cleric never seemed to breathe, he sang non-stop, overpowering the soft voices of the children. Monty looked between his parents; he couldn't remember the last time they'd sat together in front of the TV. Even with Papa's illicit evening drink and Mummy ignoring him, it was nice this, being together.

Monty hesitated, he wanted to tell Layla that he would pick her up in front of the blast wall, a squat row of beige blocks obscuring their school's perimeter, in fifteen minutes, but he didn't want to leave just yet, not as Papa sat down on the sofa next to him, swatting his son's feet off the table and placing his glass of Laphroaig in front of him.

Zahra opened one eye, just a peek, enough to see that Akbar had not had the manners to use a coaster.

'*Nazreen!*' Nayar threw his gaze at the camera, glancing over his wire-rimmed glasses. 'Join me tomorrow in my latest programme . . .'

Loud groan from Papa. 'How many shows does this fraud have?'

'. . . where we will visit my new foundation for young ladies learning the Koran.' A phone number materialized at the bottom of the screen, as Nayar adjusted his glasses and sang the digits, advising all faithful members of his audience wishing to donate to do so immediately.

1 hour? Monty typed.

No.

Her answer came immediately.

Now.

Monty smiled; she must have been sitting there waiting for him to reply.

'Who are you texting? *Tik tik tik* all day?' Papa leaned across the table and picked up the remote, clicking the channel to the BBC before Zahra wrote down the phone number and pulled out her credit card.

A still image of General Pervez Musharraf flashed across the screen. *Arrest warrant issued for fmr Pakistani Pres*, the red breaking-news ticker read. Papa slapped his hand on his thigh angrily.

'Damn shame,' Papa said, shaking his head. 'Damn shame we didn't support that brave chap.' Akbar Ahmed frowned, the ice cubes in his highball of Laphroaig clinking against the glass. General Pervez Musharraf was an old friend of the family, a fellow single-malt connoisseur and Muhajir from India. Papa raised the volume another three decibels.

Monty's phone emitted a little gulp, the sound of a video being uploaded onto iMessage. He switched the sound off with his thumb and tapped on the clip. And there she was, Layla, lying on her back, holding her new iPhone up above her and wearing a thin camisole that lifted just enough to show her stomach, saying his name and blowing him a kiss.

The words of an Irish BBC anchor filled the emptiness of the living room, as Layla's video flickered in Monty's hands.

Monty, kiss.

Kiss, Monty.

It was a boomerang video and Monty let it play soundlessly, again and again, holding the phone in his lap.

'Bloody nonsense.' Papa placed his glass down hard on the table. 'Only man brave enough to set off a war against these crazies coming out of the woodworks' – he looked sideways at Zahra, her eyes still closed, mumbling the *naaths* that Nayar had sung all evening – 'and look how they treat him.'

Zahra didn't answer her husband. She kept her eyes shut as her lips moved softly through the memory of prayer.

Monty didn't quite understand how Uncle P had set off a war or who exactly should have supported him more and, in truth, it didn't matter. The Ahmeds, like many of their wealthy peers with flats in Kensington and Knightsbridge who genuinely believed fashion shows were a way of resisting the Taliban, had very little to lament about Pakistan. It had been kind to them. Not since Partition had they lifted a hand or shed a tear or sweated unseasonably for their country. 1965 came and went. The humiliations of 1971 and 1999, too. Monty was a child when Kargil happened, too young to be moved by a war fought over glaciers and kilometres of barren Kashmiri mountaintop.

Not until Layla – until brave, beautiful Layla – did Monty care to ask any questions about his life. Before Layla, Monty floated through the world; only after Layla did he begin to occupy it.

Coming, Monty texted.

Good boy, Layla replied.

Anita Rose

Ezra rarely said where he went to work. He had a new job and though he had always been secretive – you won't understand, he said to Anita; you don't know that part of the city, he told his mother – he assured his family things were different now. He was done shuttling all over Karachi, scrounging for work here and there, picking up part-time shifts and running small cons. Ezra promised his mother and sister that those lean years were far behind them.

He was working for big men now. Important men. English-speaking, foreign businessmen. Powerful people. They were fantastic, he told Zenobia, they had such class. Anything they desired, they got. They could force the wheels of Karachi to spin this way and that. With their money they could jerk the city to a halt. And he was learning from them, yes, he told his mother, he was. Soon he too would be a Don.

Ezra brought home more and more money and told Anita, in confidence, that in a year, maybe two, he was going to move them to a real home, a bungalow. One with more than three rooms, with windows that weren't cut so high near the bloody ceiling, so you could feel the sunlight on your face, maybe even with a small garden. He was looking at a few places now, talking to landlords in Malir. Maybe after that they could upgrade to Nazimabad.

Upgrade, it was Ezra's favourite English word.

He had already upgraded their small home, but there would soon be further rental upgradation, upgraded education, their mother could upgrade her clients, he would re-upgrade his bicycle to a scooter and then, *janaab*, to a car.

One night, just as Anita Rose was lying down to sleep, her mother already snoring softly, her hands tucked underneath her dark, round cheeks, Ezra came home. It was just before midnight, early. He pushed open the door as softly as he could and smiled when he saw his younger sister, now nearly as tall as him, sitting upright, awake.

Shhh, Ezra lifted a finger to his lips.

He was holding a brown box between his hand and the crook of his elbow, like a disc, the warm smell of dough wafting into their small home.

Ezra kicked off his boots, pointy in the front with a slight heel, before lowering himself down to the cold floor. He wore black socks and they looked thin and old under his brand-new distressed jeans. Ezra opened the brown box and lifted a triangle of the thinnest *roti* and cheese, dropping the greasy slice into Anita's palm. 'It's pizza,' he whispered, pronouncing the word softly, like the name of the city.

There were only three slices in the big box, all of them collected soggily around a red wheel.

'I know what pizza is,' Anita whispered back as she took a bite of stringy cheese, even though it didn't look or taste like any pizza she had ever seen before. It had small green petals, perfumed leaves, bruised into the dough, and unsweetened white cheese that tasted like warm milk.

'This is the best kind, original pizza.' Ezra leaned closer

to his sister; he had a slick of oil on his chin that the moonlight, streaming in from the high window near the ceiling, caught. 'From Clifton, a place called Xanders.' With his mouth full of food, he dug his hand into his jeans pocket and took out his phone.

He had recently bought a Samsung, a stylish make from Korea, he said, a country Anita had to look up on a map. Its best feature, the most original one, was its sharp colour camera. Careful not to dirty the screen, still protected by a thin, transparent plastic sticker, Ezra opened up the photo album and turned the phone towards Anita, so she could see the fairy lights strung up around a cloistered garden, tables filled with women in sleeveless tops and red lipstick. There were men in baggy shorts and others with thick moustaches smoking cigars.

'Everyone talks in English, even the waiters. There's music all night long. They make the pizza right there, in the garden, in a brick oven in the wall.'

Anita wiped her hand on her *kameez* and clicked through the pictures. How big was the garden? She tried to count all the glamorous women; in one photo there was a table of several girls, her age, all by themselves, their big purses resting on the tabletop, instead of food. She had made it up to six when the phone started to vibrate in her hand.

Anita looked at her brother, now leaning back against the wall, seemingly unbothered by the noise that might wake up their sleeping mother.

'*Bhai*,' she whispered, pushing the phone towards Ezra, 'answer it.'

'You answer it,' Ezra smiled.

Anita Rose clicked the green button and lifted the

phone to her ear, looking back to check if Zenobia had stirred. 'Hello?'

'Hello, Feroze?' The voice on the phone spoke in a pinched English accent. Hell-ew, Fer-uze?

Anita frowned. 'No,' she replied carefully in English. 'This is not him.'

Ezra was watching her intently, a smile crawling over his tired face.

'Oh, I see . . . Well, please tell Feroze Hameed called, when he's uh . . . free again . . .'

Euh, ahsee. Weeel, pliz tell Fer-uze Ham-eed cwaled, when he's uhhhhh freh ahgain. Even with the strange way the man spoke, there was something dirty in his voice.

Anita lowered the phone from her face. She was still holding the slice of Clifton pizza in her left land. 'Feroze?' she mouthed.

Ezra nodded slowly.

Anita looked at the screen of the Korean Samsung phone. The ID of the caller was saved as CEO HAMEED RINGOLA VIP. 'Okay, sir, thank you,' she replied shyly into the mouthpiece, but the line had already cut.

Ezra stood up and walked to the cupboard. With his back towards Anita, he unclipped his watch and placed it in a drawer, unbuttoned his shirt and hung it on a wire. Anita watched her brother's back, the white of his *banyan* almost glowing in the dark.

'Why did he call you Feroze?' She spoke loudly, uncon- cerned with the tired, sleeping woman between her and her brother.

Ezra peeled off his socks and stood quietly for a moment. 'It's the only way,' he finally replied, his back still towards his sister. Anita thought she saw his shoulders fall. 'There's only so far our people can go in this city.'

'But, don't they know where you live? What Mama does? How little we have?'

Ezra unbuckled his belt. G, the brass buckle said. G for *goonda*, he laughed when he brought it home from the shop with his distressed jeans. He rolled the leather in his hands silently as though winding a rope.

'It's not your name.' Anita held the cold phone in her lap.

Zenobia groaned and rolled over on the floor.

Ezra shrugged, slowly turning to look at his sister in the dark, grey room. 'What has my name ever done for me?'

Sunny

Before he left, Sunny and Oz had stood together, shoulder-to-shoulder on Oxford Street. It was Sunny's first trip to London. He had always wondered why he hadn't been before, why it had taken him so long to get there. Sunny picked out his best clothes the night before, a black *Yeezus* sweatshirt, the text printed in dull gold – he'd bought it off the Internet, but no one would know it wasn't concert merch – a pair of fitted black jeans, torn at the knees, spotless white sneakers. He threw on a nylon bomber jacket and stood in front of the full-length mirror hanging on the bathroom door. He'd filled out lately, since he had started training, firing up his already demanding exercise routine. But with the jacket and its thin parachute material, you couldn't tell that the *Yeezus* sweatshirt was snug around his broadening shoulders.

Sunny woke up early in the morning to iron the sleeves of the jacket, just a touch, to get it right. Oz, meanwhile, rolled up in a shirt stained with toothpaste, a ribbon of white goo along his breastbone. 'Bro,' Sunny had said, eyeing the stain, 'you gotta wear that?'

And Oz, who had one hand on the steering wheel of his beat-up Skoda, and the other stuffing a sausage roll into his mouth, laughed. 'Put it on specially, Cuz.'

But even that couldn't ruin Sunny's first trip to the big city. Here the promise of Portsmouth's Commercial Road – belied by the homeless sleeping rough on benches, and the girls in torn denim hot pants barely covering their cheeks – seemed real. Sunny saw cars he'd only heard about in Frank Ocean songs: BMWs, Bugattis, he saw a white Ferrari.

The young women strolling down Oxford Street were dressed like he had only seen in posters back in Portsmouth. Their hair was mannequin-sleek and their clothes perfectly coordinated and styled, just like in the life-size French Connection posters peeling off on bus stands and red double-deckers. Their skirts didn't ride up their crotches, and their blouses didn't rustle and crackle with movement.

Sunny watched the hectic parade of shoppers. Petite Japanese girls who, with their long black coats and hooded eyes, holding onto each other and whispering their secret, unguessable language, reminded him of ravens hopping delicately across the branches of shaded trees. Even their platform boots hit the pavement soundlessly. He saw an olive-skinned beauty with long wavy hair, the ends dipped in faded green dye the colour of Fairy washing-up liquid. A quarter of her head was shaved off, exposing a grizzly patch of skull. She carried a designer handbag and wore John Lennon sunglasses. He didn't see one man like the old geezers who walked around Kingston Park in canvas sneakers falling apart, shouting at the birds and throwing punches at the air.

Sunny watched Arab sisters piling out of chauffeured cars, their lips and eyes painted in pinks and blues so sharp, so tight, it might as well have been graffiti. If they covered at all, it wasn't behind loose shapeless cloth, like back home; here, in London, they used silk turbans and cashmere bands stretched across their luminous, silky hair. He thought he spotted the Pakistani weather girl from Channel 4.

She wore a pleated leather skirt with snakeskin boots that stopped at her ankles. As she walked by, up close, he could see slight bags under her eyes, not camouflaged in make-up. He wondered if she had been crying. But as she passed him and Oz, her phone on her ear, Sunny heard her dissolve into giggles. Was she laughing at him?

Among all those exalted creatures gliding effortlessly there was no anxiety. The air was thick with money, with all the endless possibility and frictionless ease that wealth can buy.

But Oz didn't even look like he noticed the women in fur-lined capes, the men – who in Portsmouth exclusively wore funereal black – in patterned pinks and burgundy business suits, and the whitened teeth that shone like diamonds in the early afternoon. Oz kept his phone in his hands and checked his Twitter obsessively. *If I can't breathe, neither can U #Londonwillfall* @Ozmatic tweeted. In the hour since they'd hit the capital, it had garnered only one like.

Oz eyed the road contemptuously, with his jacket of imitation leather peeling away across his collar, like old paint, his legs akimbo, shoulders spread wide, his chest with the toothpaste stain thrust out against the street. 'Straighten up, Cuz,' he barked at Sunny, who slunk behind him as they made their way down the crowded street. 'Who you hiding from?'

Sunny's *Yeezus* sweater felt cheap now, too soft, sewed all wrong, cutting off the circulation under his arms, stretched too tightly across his shoulders. 'No one,' Sunny mumbled, zipping up his bomber jacket.

Sunny hoped that his cousin hadn't noticed his

inability to negotiate the turnstile at Waterloo when they rode the Tube into town. He hoped Oz hadn't seen the flicker of panic in his eyes as commuters bumped against him in the tightly packed subway, everyone straining to get out fast, ahead of their fellow travellers. 'Come on!' an already tall blonde, made uselessly taller by high heels, grumbled at Sunny in what he thought was a Slavic accent, when the doors failed to open at a stop because he did not press the button. Sunny innocently thought the doors opened automatically.

Women didn't notice Sunny here, they ignored him. Unlike in Portsmouth, where they gazed at him hungrily, whistling when he jogged around the Common, finding all kinds of excuses to come up and talk to him ('cuse me, but like, wot ethnicity you? You look Puer'o Rican but swee'er'); here they pushed him out of their way, mumbling angrily under their breath as he stood on the wrong side of the escalator.

Oz and Sunny were slouched against a big black Adidas window, counting pedestrians. It was Oz's idea. Oz counted one side of the street, Sunny the other. Within five minutes they were up to 500. 'You see, Sun?' Oz held a small paper bag of caramelized peanuts in the palm of his hand. Sunny kept his head down, trying to keep track of his numbers and hoping that no one would notice his weak threads and thin jacket, but Oz was cool, eating his peanuts, surveying London Town.

He bought the nuts off a brother, fresh blood, just arrived, the pink flesh of his lips smeared bloody red with betel juice. Oz tipped him a pound. 'You see how much damage some righteousness could cause? One man, ten kilos.'

Oz had paid the thirty-quid return fare for the both of them, said he wanted to show Sunny London before he set him loose on the world.

Oz licked the sticky burnt sugar off his fingers and pointed at the crowds, heaving luggage and shopping bags, faces lost in their phones. 'You think they see anything?' His voice was thin and angry. 'You think they see us standing here, you think they know anything of our pain? Of what they done to us without even *feeling* it, Sunny?' But our eyes are open, Oz swore, and together he and Sunny counted them: 500, 700, 1,000.

As they rode the escalator down to the Tube, back to Waterloo, Oz rested his hands on his cousin's shoulders, massaging the tight knots of muscle braided under his skin, digging his fingers into Sunny's bones. 'Ride or die, Sunny.' Oz's breath smelled of caramel, and Sunny heard his teeth click against each other as he stressed the words. 'Ride or die.'

Two armed coppers, black truncheons and Glock 17s holstered to their bodies, bulletproof vests strapped tight against their chests, climbed the stairs parallel to Sunny and Oz. They were chatting away to each other, watching the station out of the corner of their eyes as they bounded up the steps. These weren't the coppers from the recruitment posters, one Sikh, one woman, one Chinese. These two were chalk-white, dirty blonds. One of them had the bluest eyes, blue like the colour of plastic, so bright. The other had a goatee, shaved that morning, he'd nicked the skin on his cheek.

'Officers!' Oz called out, releasing Sunny's shoulders and straightening up into a salute. The policemen looked at the two men, floating down the escalator beside them. 'Thank you for your service!' Oz shouted at them in his plummiest accent, and raised his hand briskly to his temple. The cops smiled and nodded, but just as they were level with them, just as Oz and Sunny met the blues of their eyes, Oz curled the ring and pinkie finger of his salute, turning his hand into a pistol, and aimed it at the officers.

Only the cop with the goatee, closest to the boys, noticed Oz pointing his hand at them, pulsing his fingers as though firing the pistol. The officer frowned and stopped, turning to look at them, but the escalator reached the ground and Oz had dropped his hand back to Sunny's shoulder. 'God bless!' he shouted at the coppers with a wink. 'You see, Cuz?'

Sunny saw. And he felt his heart pound.

'Walking corpses,' Oz whispered into Sunny's ear. 'Don't even know it yet. They don't even see us, hiding in plain sight.'

Point a gun at a pig, Sunny noticed Oz had tweeted as soon as they were out of the Tube, back in service range. *Beg 4 yr life bitch.*

Sunny sat on the train out of Waterloo, back to Fratton Station, drumming his fingers along the window, his buds in his ears the entire two hours back to Portsmouth, Frank on full blast, but hearing nothing at all.

How do I tell my pa? Sunny asked Oz. He hadn't booked his ticket to Turkey yet, but had started giving his things away to the mosque collection box. He donated his Xbox, his boxing gloves, his DVDs and all of his sneakers, except the ones on his feet.

What is there to tell him, Oz asked, doesn't he see what's happening out there? They're setting fire to the Muslim world. 'Why don't we do anything? We're British, aren't we, don't we have a role? It's about humanity, isn't it, Cuz? That's what we're doing – saving humanity from collapse. Trump's trying to stop Muslims from travelling, like we ain't even people, like they done to the Jews back in '39. You just going to allow that?' Right-wing governments were building up in Europe, Oz said – look at Brexit – won on propaganda posters of Muslims flooding in from Calais.

Oz had his Instagram suspended, for posting a picture of Nigel Farage's face in a gun-sight. *Fuck UKIP*, he tweeted in response, *I aint even begun yet #shootback*. Look at France, the Netherlands, Poland holding anti-Muslim rallies by the hour, Swedes and Swiss, the two most boring Euros, burning mosques down to the ground. They're not going to help us, Cuz.

Oz told Sunny it didn't matter, it didn't matter because all that right-wing hate just made their cause stronger, it drove more people to jihad. 'So let's go home, Sun, let's go to where we belong, where they need us.'

Sunny had started shaving his moustache and pressing his forehead into a tablet of mud as he prayed, marking his body with as many signs of his devotion as he could. But he couldn't drop the music, not that. The girls, the thoughts that hurt his stomach, that knotted his throat, even those he could control. But he still sat up late at night on his computer, listening to Pyramids till he fell asleep.

Pa watched his son transform, moving away from the

139

life he had built for him out of perpetual sacrifice. At night, as they sat in the living room, the glow of the television illuminating Safiya Begum's sepia-toned face, Sulaiman Jamil muttered to himself, 'This is not my son,' shaking his head at the stranger in his living room. 'What kind of son is this? Only thinking of himself, so selfish. No thought for me, for everything I've done for you. Me, me, me. This is not my son, not my son.'

Sunny lifted the remote and raised the TV's volume, before popping his Beats back in his ears.

One day Sunny stood on the bus, licking a smear of honey off the lifelines of his palm as he chewed a piece of toast and watched the people he had known all his life, every single one of them oblivious to his knowing, oblivious to him, to Sunny who had learned to see. This strength, the ability to truly observe, had been building in him for years now, a by-product of spending life without ever being seen.

White people were so sluggish, so slow. They had no drive in them, they hungered for nothing. All that easy success and comfort, brought on by colonizing and occupying other people's countries, had fattened them up good. But Sunny, angry, hungry Sunny, had eyes like lasers now. Sunny could see everything, all of it, everywhere.

He watched the young Arab mother who loaded two young boys in school uniforms onto the bus, pushing a crying third in a pram. The baby was mewing as hard as he could, but like broken machinery all that came out of him was a sputtering, gasping sound. The older boys sat down together and the mum, lifting the newborn out of its pram, fell into a seat next to a large white-haired woman, her face curled in distaste at the family speaking a foreign tongue.

Sunny knew from watching, from sitting outside society, that the drunk who climbed onto the bus clutching a plastic bag was not, as she looked, sixty-five, but closer to forty. Her face was pruned, like fingers wrinkled in a warm bath. Sunny could tell she was a pack-a-day smoker – drunks always were. He knew, when he saw her smile at the lady with a dog standing at the back of the bus, that she drank because of love, because of being – or feeling – unloved. He knew that the fear that drove her to drink, reducing her to smelling of hot, oaky whisky at eleven in the morning, came from a desperation that quieted all sentient parts of her: who will love me? How can anyone love this?

Sunny knew, rubbing his fists against his fatigued eyes, that tomorrow the same cast of loners and unloved would be on the bus again. And the day after that, and the day after and the day after. He would never escape them, not if he stayed in Portsmouth. Even with Oz and the world he had introduced him to, even then Sunny couldn't escape his sadness at being a part of nothing, of being unseen.

The girl with the dog droned on, as girls on phones do, 'Yeah ... yeah ... I know ... yeah ... I dunno ... you think so?' Always seeking confirmation, validation – why was it always girls who were never anyone, unless evaluated and approved by girlfriends on telephone lines? 'Yeah ... yeah ... Paid thirty quid for them ...' She touched her eyelashes with her fingers nervously, her nails as fake as the lashes. 'You think so? You think he'll notice?' Again she squeezed her eyelashes, their seams dotted with glistening glue.

No, he won't notice. What man would notice a bunch of infinitesimal hairs glued onto other microscopic hairs?

'Yeah . . . really? You think . . . ?'

It was too late for Sunny to join them. He had seen them. He could never be one of them now.

It was too much, the solitary passage of life. Even with Oz's reassurance that wrongs would be violently and finally righted, Sunny was under no illusions: he was alone.

He would suffocate under the weight of his father's dreams, women crying into telephones, the sadness steaming off the floors of coffee shops. Where could Sunny go to escape the mourning of this-here life? Where could Sunny go to find relief from the nothingness of it all? Not the pubs, not the gyms, not even to God – who was everywhere and nowhere, all at once – not the mosque, not the kebab shop. And then, just like that, he found it.

He opened his eyes, and in return he had been seen.

Aloush was a test. A moment Sunny was not sure he would survive. It came right at the end, right when Oz began preparations for Sunny's travel, right when Sunny imagined he had finally made peace with his life. His time with Aloush lasted just over a month. But the weeks passed before him like hours, as though in his twenty-two years it had been only those moments in which he was truly alive.

One evening Sunny had walked down to Apollo, a small basement dive on Guildhall Walk. They didn't serve in there, so there was nothing wrong with him going, there was no need to mention it to Oz. Sunny just slung his earbuds around his neck and stepped down the stairs, lit up in a red glow of bar lights. Around midnight, they brought the drums out. They cut the lights and the DJ started spinning. While boys in baggy harem pants and T-shirts stained with deodorant patches flung plates of soggy falafels to club kids crawling in for a bite, Sunny sat on the DJ's tiny stage, his feet resting against the delicate legs of a wooden stool, and balanced a *darbuka* against his thigh.

Apollo was dark then, except for the red fairy lights. As the DJ – Aloush – raised the bass, Sunny ran his fingers against the tight skin of the drum. He closed his eyes and played, guided only by the throbbing in his chest. Sunny had no real knowledge of drums, and had never taken lessons before. Arabic music wasn't what he had grown up listening to, he had no history with its rolling blows, its sharp snaps and the sliding percussion that mimicked the heart's adrenaline, but he felt it. Sunny felt the music swim through him.

The drums in the caf beat against him in exactly the way his body felt when he was running, when he was turned on, when he was happy in a way that was fully his own.

'*Habibi*,' Aloush shouted, throwing an arm around Sunny, 'break me a beat.'

And Sunny, sweat falling across his brow, his pulse racing to keep time with the music Aloush spun, would crouch over the curved drum and play with his life.

'*Habibi*, where did you learn to play like that?' Aloush asked him later, a burning cigarette in the corner of his lips, the first night Sunny stepped onto his stage.

'God gave me the gift,' Sunny shouted over the techno thrum of a remixed Fairuz number.

Allah allah, Aloush fanned his fingers against the air, dense with sweet-smelling smoke. *Allah allah*.

Sunny closed his eyes as Aloush praised God for his skill. He would miss this most of all when he was gone, he knew that the very first night he played at Apollo. He knew somehow that if anything held him back, it would be this, whatever it was.

Since Oz, Sunny had been prepared to end his life: to journey, to fight, to die. Nothing threatened to stop him from detonating himself against the world. There was nothing in his life worth preserving, nothing he wished to hold onto. Until this.

Sunny who had never been seen, who had never been known, found it impossible to speak of what happened then.

But those nights, on the small stage in the underground café, Sunny let himself go, throwing his knuckles and calloused fingertips over the drums as fast as they would go. *Cleopatra, Cleopatra.*

Sunny couldn't speak to Oz about this secret thing, so he confided to him about his father. About how Sulaiman Jamil spoke badly about religion, how he called it a man-made disease, a way to control the weak. Sunny told Oz how his pa brought home cider on the weekends and no longer observed halal, even bragging that he ate bacon with his work colleagues, who called him Sal. One of us – our Sal, they said. It had made Pa so proud. 'They thought I was born here, darling. Imagine, I speak better English than most of their children.'

As Oz considered this embarrassing moral decadence in his own family, Sunny held his breath. He didn't want to disappoint Oz. But his cousin ran his hand through his spiky blond hair and mulled over the information quietly for a minute. 'Just leave, brother,' Oz said finally, placing an arm around his younger cousin. 'Just leave him.'

The British *kataa'ib* of the Ummah Movement would welcome him, Oz promised. He had Skyped with his brothers in the brigade and told them he was sending over a true warrior. 'Normally *tazkiyeh* takes ages,' Oz warned. 'They don't let just anyone fight for UM. They have to make sure you're not a spy, that you're not a collaborator, an infiltrator.'

Sunny shook his head – no, never. None of those things.

'But they also gotta check that you're not a tourist, you know? One of those kids who thinks jihad is a gap year or a place to cruise hunks.'

Sunny frowned. It was a weird thing to say.

Oz laughed and leaned into him, patting his knee. 'Not you, Cuz. But you know, those girls who run away from home, thinking they can hack our war. Those sisters aren't prepared to be the companions of true warriors. They're not of the calibre of our women, our leader.' Oz had shown Sunny the videos of this straight-up Muslimah out of Pakistan, who posted these crazy calls to arms on Twitter. Since she joined the Ummah Movement, she had her own LiveLeak channel dedicated to exposing the hypocrisy of so-called liberal Muslims.

Why were all those Asians – rich Pakistani socialites, Indian cricketers and Bangladeshi writers – holding up 'Bring back our girls' signs, but not saying a word about Arab sisters getting raped by American soldiers out in Iraq? Why did no one question how the Qataris planned to pay for a World Cup, when children all over the Muslim world were dropping like flies to hunger? Where was Red Nose Day for the Muslim world? Where was our 'We Are the World'? Where were the hashtags and Kickstarter funds for us, dying out of your field of vision, crippled by your wars? Our sister, posting the videos, she was the first Muslim to force those questions out into the open on social media.

Oz said she was a genuine fighter, a renegade, and that she alone was responsible for a 20 per cent increase in media attention to the cause, sounding even a little bit jealous. She had hundreds of thousands of followers, gaining them by the second, every single day. Twitter couldn't shut her down, didn't even understand the level at which her calls to jihad were reverberating. She was a warrior, a lone wolf. 'But the others,' Oz warned, 'they just come out for a bit of a story to tell their friends, panic and run back home.'

They vetted the Euros extra-rigorously, they had to be vouched for by an existing member, but Oz had already put in his recommendation. It was going to be fine, he reassured his cousin. He'd asked a couple of his pals who had spoken to Sunny on Skype to do the same. 'You're in, Cuz,' Oz told him, holding Sunny's face and laughing, fragrant with Lynx body spray. 'All you got to do is get there.'

Oz wouldn't travel with him. It was best that Sunny go alone. 'I might be on their radar,' Oz said. He was going to lie low in England for a while, raise some funds, recruit some more soldiers. 'But Imma meet you there,' he promised. 'We'll fight together, don't you worry.'

Monty

Monty moved the hair out of Layla's face, tucking the long, lank strand of wavy hair behind her ear. She breathed softly, saying nothing, watching him as he bent down, his back stooping slightly, and pressed his tongue against the seam of her lips.

Layla let Monty, whose kisses were hungry and sweet, into her mouth. She leaned against the cold brick wall of the stairwell behind the psychology classroom, until she felt the jagged edges of the red stone cut into the small of her back. She didn't close her eyes.

He kissed her as though he knew she was watching him. It was October, a hot, humid month in Karachi. Only when he moved his face away from Layla, who tasted of chocolate, did Monty realize that she was breathing deeply. A thin film of perspiration coated the bridge of her nose.

Monty listened to the sound of sneakers on the cement, the bell had rung five minutes ago. Everyone should be in class already. But he didn't care who saw them hiding in the dark stairwell. He didn't care if they got into trouble. Monty grazed his lips against the curl of Layla's ear, her neck and the soft, pale skin of her collarbone, holding her hand tight in his own.

'Slowly, Monty,' Layla instructed him. 'Don't be in a hurry.'

She dropped her head gently against Monty's chest,

breathing in his warm cologne. His heart was beating quickly, as though he was afraid, and she listened for a moment.

'Monty,' Layla asked, her mouth buried between the buttons of his shirt, 'are you scared?'

He was quiet, but she heard his trembling heart, a pace faster than before. Monty lifted Layla's face off his chest and raised her chin towards him, kissing her slowly, just like she had asked.

No one had ever kissed Layla like that, so tenderly, so adoringly. Monty touched her cheek, softly, moving her hair away from her face, just the way she had seen in the serials on TV, like he loved her. She looked into his eyes, watching her hopefully, and it occurred to Layla that was why his heart beat so fast.

Out of love, not fear.

Layla de-tangled herself from Monty, stepping back slightly, pressing her head against the cool bricks of the empty stairwell, closing her mouth, pulling her hand out of his clasp. But Monty stepped closer, drawing his hands against the small of Layla's back, breaching the space she had created between them.

'Layla, where you going?' He kissed her neck, her cheek, her temple, the crown of her head, her hair, long and messy and scented of tobacco. 'Always running,' Monty murmured as he pressed himself against her, 'always trying to get away.'

Layla could feel his heartbeat, loud and drumming against her own. She hesitated for a moment, a fatal second, and before she could move, Monty reached for her hand again, weaving his fingers into hers.

'Don't go,' he whispered into her hair between kisses, 'don't go, Layla.'

Anita Rose

In no time, the Josephs were enjoying a genuine upgradation in their lives. Ezra bought their mother *golian* from Kausar Medico, the best in the city. The pharmacist said if she took the expensive pills every day, her arthritic joints would no longer pain her. He travelled not on public transport now, but on his own scooter, a modern make from China. And at the end of her first term at the new school, after she brought home good marks – the best in her class; the fancy principal said Anita had real potential, she could apply to any college she wanted, with results like that – Ezra took Anita Rose to Seaview.

I told you, he said as he hugged his sister, her long hair freshly washed and smelling of lemons. I told you, Anita Rose, we deserve better and we're going to get it.

Anita squeezed her brother, euphoric with the promise of a better life. Really, *bhai?*

I promise you, Ezra's voice broke, I promise we will have everything, *everything* we want. New school, new home, new future. He told his sister to dress up nicely. 'Wear your best *jora,*' he said, seizing the initiative to pull out a black net *kameez* with the straight black trousers that Anita had had copied from a magazine. 'Wear something nice on your face also,' Ezra advised, in a jolly mood. 'And leave down your hair.'

Like this, Ezra *bhai?* she had asked, parting her hair

carefully down the middle and brushing it down. He looked at her for a moment, before walking behind his sister, examining her carefully.

'No, make it more casual, more relaxed,' he drew his fingers like a comb through her hair, shaking it free around her shoulders. 'And it's Feroze, Anita. You know that.'

Anita stood still in front of the cracked mirror while 'Feroze' put his keys and wallet in his pocket. It wasn't the time to argue with her brother. She saw how things had changed, how they had picked up for him, now that he had been reborn as another man. Suddenly there was more of everything, more time, more gifts, more food. He told her if she behaved, he would find a way for her to work like him too, to make some money, real money, on the side while she studied. Anita wanted to know how, when, what kind of amount was *real money*, but she didn't want to upset Feroze, especially not now when he seemed intent on bestowing his generosity upon her over everyone else. 'Thank you, *bhaiya*,' she said instead, still unable to bring herself to say his new name out loud.

Their mother was happy. She worked less now, taking Sundays off for church. Sundays, which had been her busiest day, were now only reserved for special clients whom she saw every other week. Anita missed those Sundays at the Clifton house, she hated sitting on rock-hard pews in the back of church.

But for every loss these days, there was a gain. Anita had never been to the beach before and she screamed with delight when, sitting on the back of Feroze's new Chinese motorbike, she smelled the approaching salt air as it rushed through her hair. 'The beach, *bhaiya*?' she asked, clapping her hands in delight.

'The very beach,' he replied happily.

Feroze bought his sister a soft drink, with a bendy green straw, and an ice cream from a Wall's cart. It was Chocolate Crunch, she had seen it on the *chaiwalla*'s TV late at night. After she ate, Feroze treated Anita to a horse ride. After a little negotiation, the man with the long black moustache who held the horse's beaded reins agreed to let Anita ride for free.

He helped Anita Rose mount the horse, gripping her hips tightly with his wide hands, leaning close to her, his body pressing against her as he lifted her onto the saddle. The man smoothed down his oiled moustache and stood beside Feroze, watching Anita as she rode the skinny Arabian horse, bouncing softly across bitten cobs of corn, hollow cigarette boxes and hundreds of torn plastic bags, whipped by the strong breeze and spread all across the dark-brown sand.

They never took their eyes off her. The man held his hands in front of his crotch as he looked at her. When Anita tried to ride away from them, her brother called out to her, 'Circle back, Anita.' When Anita tried to lead her horse down the long stretch of empty beach, as far away from them as she could see, 'Circle back here,' Feroze shouted. 'This part has the softest, cleanest sand.'

Sunny

In the end, Sunny said nothing to his pa.

He connected his pa's bank details to his phone's direct debit and increased his O2 data package from one to five GB. He went to the cemetery where his mother was buried and laid daffodils on her moss-covered grave. Sunny never had a mother, and now his pa had washed his hands clean of him, too.

His last night in Portsmouth, Sunny walked over to Oz's and stood outside his house in the dark, unsure why he had come. He wanted to say something to Oz, he wanted Oz to know how hard it was to leave, how much his cousin had given him, even after the thing, the secret thing, had almost turned it upside down. He wanted to ask if it was so bad what he was doing, if it was wrong. Deep down, Sunny wanted to tell his cousin that he had made a mistake, that he wanted to stay now.

But after an hour of pacing up and down outside Oz's parents' place, Sunny left. He couldn't think of the right words, the right way to tell Oz what he felt. Even he didn't understand what he felt.

This was the sacrifice. This was the hardship. Not leaving a place that meant nothing, but forgoing something you wanted, something you might have loved, for a higher purpose, to fight for a beautiful cause.

Sunny walked quickly to Kofi's, a loud, dark reggae bar

where none of the Asians hung out, and sat on a stool, feeling embarrassed.

What was he doing, lurking outside Oz's like that? What if Aunty and Uncle saw him? What was he supposed to say – Oh, sorry, Uncle, I just wanted to come round and look through Oz's window and tell him how confused I am. Sorry, Uncle, is Oz in? Just wanted to tell him how all my life I wished I could leave, but now I found someone who makes me want to stay and I can't bear to leave him.

But he couldn't say any of that. There was so much Sunny couldn't say that he could barely allow himself to think, to feel, blinking it back like a dream because it was too incredible to be true.

Sunny went out to Kofi's that last Saturday, looking to hook up with someone – anyone. It was coiled up in him something ferocious, something urgent. He blinked back all the thoughts as they came, blinking them back hard while he scanned the dance floor, sipping his Diet Coke. And then he saw her, Naya, with her tight little body, slumped against a wall. She was wearing a short dress, green and sequinned, a sleeve falling off her shoulder.

'Hey, Naya,' Sunny said, walking over and squatting down in front of her. 'Hey.'

But her head just rolled from side to side and she mumbled some rubbish about the music, which was Jamaican trance anyway and didn't have any lyrics. He looked around, but Naya was alone and wasted, like he'd never seen her. Sunny stood up and scanned the club for the pack of mean girls she was usually out with, but he couldn't spot any of her friends. Checking one last time, he slipped his arm round Naya's waist and carried her out of the smoke-filled club.

He thought about taking her home, about the look on his pa's face when he woke up in the morning and saw Mr Khattak's young daughter in the kitchen in her underwear.

But he was going to break the old man's heart soon enough. So Sunny took Naya as far as the parking lot and held her against the cold brick wall. He put his hand up her dress, pulling at her underwear. He thought of Oz; the light in his bedroom had been on. Why hadn't Sunny just rung the bell and gone inside? Maybe Oz would have understood. Maybe Oz had been in love once and confused, too.

Sunny pressed Naya against the wall with his body, biting her neck, her shoulders, pushing his fingers roughly inside her. Sunny ran his tongue along the nape of Naya's neck and even though he could taste the bitter alcohol of her perfume mingled with sweat, he thought of Oz's thick, tanned neck and wished he was tracing the letters of his tattoo with his tongue. He thought of Ben and wanted to fuck Naya right there, in the parking lot, he wanted to fuck her hard, until she screamed and begged him to stop.

He couldn't think of Him, he couldn't think about what had happened with Aloush, which was beautiful and pure. The harder Sunny blinked all those feelings back, the angrier he became.

An ugliness rose at the back of his throat. He pushed his teeth down, biting Naya, pulling at her skin. Just then Naya's eyes flickered open and she moaned, her back cut against the stone. 'What are you doing?' she mumbled.

She was so out of it, she didn't even recognize Sunny. And just like that, Sunny saw Naya for what she really was: empty, useless, a pathetic substitute for something real. He lowered her to the floor – where she crumbled into a shapeless rag, her green dress pulled up to her crotch – and walked away.

The next morning Oz dropped Sunny at the train station, the sunlight reflected on his light hair. Sunny looked at his cousin, his skin pale except for a dash of freckles across the bridge of his nose, and felt his heart would break with tenderness. 'You know, Cuz,' Oz said as he drove him to Fratton Station, Sunny sitting in the front seat with his bag on his lap, 'brothers don't come back. They go to die there.'

'*Inshallah*,' Sunny said, holding his bag to his chest. How would Sunny face his life now, with no Oz, no Pa, no Aloush to define himself for? What would he do, with no man to define himself against?

Sunny had been unable to tell his cousin how much he would miss him. '*Inshallah*,' he prayed when Oz spoke of young men becoming martyrs, wishing for his own death.

And it only got worse from there. It all went wrong the moment he left British soil, the words of the flirta-tious easyJet check-in woman ringing in his ears. 'Drink responsibly,' she leaned in to whisper to Sunny, her rancid coffee-breath smelling of death, 'my nephew went out there and came back sick as a dog.'

Sunny walked all the way to his gate, before being told he was in the wrong terminal and had to run, his lungs burst-ing, to make it to the North Terminal in time for his flight.

He breezed through security, no one looked at him twice. A white security officer with a paunch took away Sunny's bottle of water. 'Over a hundred ml,' he shrugged as he tossed it into a bin. Sunny had to stop himself from smiling. *Took the bottle, let the bomb thru*, he tweeted, it was the only light moment his journey had thus far. On the aeroplane a heavy-set stewardess with dyed blonde hair moved him from his emergency-exit seat with the extra legroom, because he had looked confused at her garbled explanation of emergency procedures. 'Don't worry, darlin',' the plump stewardess said, scanning the seats around Sunny, 'let's just find some-one else who's up to it, and put you somewhere simpler.'

He landed in Antalya and was detained at the airport for four hours. Airport guards placed Sunny in a small room that smelled of stale cigarettes and sweet tea, and asked him the same questions over and over again.

Why have beard?

Who you meet?

Come from Talibani?

'I am a British citizen,' Sunny repeated, like Oz had coached him. 'You have no right to hold me, I am a British citizen.'

But the guards just laughed. Salman Khan not British. Salman Khan *Moslem*. One of the guards knew the Indian actor. Salman Khan Indian Bollywood, he laughed, his breath sour and his teeth stained by nicotine.

'My name is Salman Jamil and I am a British citizen,' Sunny repeated, but nothing. Twice they threatened to take him to jail if he didn't speak.

'You know what happen in Turkeesh jail?' the one with the breath sneered. 'You have seen fillum?'

The guards searched his beach bag, and Sunny was thankful that although he had ignored Oz's advice to shave off his beard before travelling, he had at least managed to travel light. Two T-shirts, one pair of track pants, Eno because the brothers on Skype said the water out there was funny sometimes, his charger and adaptors.

'Why no money? Why no condom? Why no girlfriend?'

It was as though he had never left home.

But Sunny insisted, winding the wires of his earphones against his fingers so tight, it cut the blood off, 'I am a British citizen, I am here on a stag-do. I am going to the beach resort of Antalya.'

After four hours, during which they didn't allow him a bathroom break or give him a glass of water, the guards opened the door and let Sunny go. His iPhone battery was almost depleted and, as he was leaving, Sunny stopped near the glass doors of the airport and considered charging his phone, but figured there'd be plenty of opportunities later.

It was a twenty-hour bus journey from there. He had to change buses in Adana, in Viranşehir, even in Al Qamishli in Syria, before he reached Mosul. No one spoke English, no one spoke anything other than Turkish. Before boarding the first bus, Sunny called Oz, his battery life at 10 per cent.

'The fuck?' he found himself shouting on the phone, all the exasperation and tension of the past hours ragged in his voice. Oz answered, sounding drowsy with sleep, though it was the middle of the afternoon. It was normal, Oz said; they had to do that kind of stuff to make it look like they were tough on the brothers. But you'll see, Oz promised, they'll all but escort you to our camps.

But they didn't. They didn't.

It was a journey of insults and wrong turns from start to finish. Wiping his eyes with the back of his hand in Icel during a short stopover, Sunny got trachoma. The bacterial disease spread by flies was eradicated in most of the world, even India, but was still knocking around in Turkey, apparently. His eyes burned and teared up, turning red until finally his left eye swelled up and shut.

Everyone stayed clear of Sunny on the bus. Even as he asked the driver, please, to stop at a pharmacy so he could buy some antibiotic eye drops and charge his phone for five minutes, the driver leaned away from Sunny and his infectious eye and shook his head. No, thank you. He waved Sunny away with his fat hand. No, thank you.

On the bus to Gaziantep someone finally took pity on him and wrote directions to the pharmacy at the next stop. Problem was, Sunny was allergic to the medicine. He didn't find *that* out until another two stops later.

At the bus depot in Kiziltepe, his eyes burning and his feet bleeding from his plastic slippers and the heat, Sunny considered going home. Trachoma – what he had, the pharmacist signed, blinded a brother out here. The pharmacist covered his eyes with his palm until Sunny nodded, signalling that he understood. I know, Sunny tried to mime back, using a combination of sign language and whispers. I feel like utter crap.

Standing in the dusty Turkish pharmacy, his eyes burning and watering, Sunny caught himself. He was supposed to be his true self out here, empowered and free. But he was as sick as a dog, feeling alone and slightly humiliated for believing in Oz so easily.

Had he made a mistake? Had he been misled? Out of loneliness and wanting, had he come out here all on his own, thinking someone would make him feel like that time with Aloush had? He hadn't found a socket anywhere, not on the ramshackle buses, not in the bus depots, not even in the pharmacy. His phone was dead. He couldn't call anyone or google the stinging eye drops. Sunny didn't have any money. He carried only enough with him for food and transport. He had left his debit card at home, just as Oz had instructed. 'You won't need money when you reach the Ummah Movement,' his cousin promised. 'Everything is taken care of there.'

What did Sunny even know about the Ummah Movement? All he'd seen were some YouTube videos of a Pakistani girl in a burqa. A couple of brothers called him up on a bad Skype line. That was it. That was what he left everything – his home, his pa, his comforts – for? How far had he come to lose himself?

It went on and on.

Reaching Mosul, fifty-two instead of twenty hours later, Sunny was not welcomed by his cousin's comrades. Instead, there too he was locked away in a room for a day. No one believed him, just like the Turkish immigration officers. Because of security concerns, he carried no one's phone number, no reference. 'How do we know who you are?' a brother with a German accent asked, a mousy blond whose hair had lightened in the desert sun. 'How do we know who sent you?'

'I'm here for you,' Sunny said, his throat burning and his eyes welling with tears. 'What else would I be doing here?' He was dirty, he was tired. His eyes were swollen and puffy from the incorrect eye drops he had administered and the bacterial fly disease he had carried since Turkey.

He spent a night in that room, alone, holding his bladder and thinking of the hot chocolate he had not drunk at Costa Coffee at Gatwick, because three pounds ten pence seemed too much to hand over for a hot drink. What he wouldn't give for a hot chocolate now, in this filthy room. He thought of that day in London, how easy it had all seemed, counting civilians and pointing imaginary guns at policemen. How brave Oz was, how much Sunny wanted his belief, his confidence. How much he missed his father's daily offer of guilt and the *Financial Times* at breakfast time. How much the music and the drums, and the DJ who spoke to him in Arabic and met all his messy melodies with a hand in the air, *allah allah*.

'You'll be far from home,' Oz had told him as he dropped him off at the station where his father once worked, 'but close to *jannah*.' You'll be close to so many other men, just like you. You will be welcomed and embraced. Sunny remembered the words now and wished he had not been so needy.

He thought about how that idea had kept him going, how it had made him skip past all the things he didn't realize he loved as he left the only home he had ever known – the piping hot chocolate with chocolate shavings and cream, the prawn salad at Pret A Manger, the gym and clubs – all those things that had been a comfort to him replaced by the idea that a gang of men would like him, basically. And for that night, Sunny felt like a fool.

He woke up the next day as the door slammed and the

footsteps of a heavily built man walked towards him. Sunny wiped his mouth with the back of his sleeve, hoping he had not drooled in his sleep.

'Why have you come here?' Abu Khalid stood in front of Sunny, his knuckles on the table as though he were preparing to climb it. The faint chime of a phone rang in the commander's pocket. Sunny looked at the man, his nose bashed and bent as though it had recently been broken, his long hair wiry and unclean. In his exhaustion and confusion, Sunny even thought he smelled a whiff of alcohol on the man's breath. He wore a long tunic and baggy trousers, black boots and a vest weighed down with ammunition. He had a beautiful calm in his eyes. Sunny stared at him.

'Because I believe,' Sunny said.

PART TWO
And We Were Born Again
2017

Monty

Abu Khalid stood in the shadow of the bonfire and looked at the eager boys gathered before him. He had been on the phone to Baghdad for the last hour. He pressed his hands into his temples. It had been like this for months. He dreaded phoning home, dreaded hearing the drippy Iraqi pop that Lubna, his wife, had downloaded as her ringtone – she was always texting him lyrics from Kadim al Saher's songs – and dreaded the click of the dial as Lubna answered. As the flames warmed his tired face, the commander of the Ummah Movement gathered the words he had spoken so many times before.

The boys who crossed oceans, betrayed families and abandoned comfortable lives, much of them spent behind iPad screens and video consoles, to come to Mosul and fight were not much younger than Abu Khalid, but they gazed upon him in quiet reverence. Unsure of what he would say, but excited for the meaning he would bestow upon their simple lives, the men averted their eyes respectfully as Abu Khalid, who walked with a slight limp, heaved his body to the side, standing at a tilt for a second, before bringing his lame leg down. In a few steps the commander had successfully positioned himself in the centre of his followers.

'Who among you is courageous enough to sacrifice long days and nights for the glory of the brotherhood?' Abu Khalid intoned before the recruits, casting his eyes across the forty sunburnt faces illuminated by the glow of the night fire.

The commander spoke to the boys in the desolate training camp on the outskirts of Mosul as they ate a dinner of rice and stale Arabic bread, using the hard bread to shovel pockets of rice into their mouths with a greedy but shy hunger. Lubna had been upset, as usual. She couldn't keep doing it on her own, she cried on the phone from Baghdad. Is this why she got married? Is this why she chose him above all other men?

Monty chewed quietly so he didn't miss anything important. The brothers said Abu Khalid had been drafted into Saddam's army just before the Americans invaded. He defected as soon as the statues of the dictator were pulled off their pedestals, and became an interpreter for a well-respected American journalist. Monty had never heard of Mother Jones before, he didn't know who she was or why she had come to Iraq, but the brothers said she had worn a 'No Blood for Oil' badge the whole time she had been out here. That was why Abu Khalid knew how to fight the Americans, because he had been one of them once.

'Who here has the courage of a million men? Who will walk through the desert to Ninawa tomorrow?' The commander steadied himself, massaging his palm against his rotten bones, and searched the eyes of the boys, all of whom wore black, the colour of mourning, the colour of those who were not soldiers yet, but who came to northern Iraq eager to realize the promise of death. Only Abu

Khalid wore the warm green and brown of khaki, only he wore the comportment of a man promised something greater than the hereafter.

Calm down, Lubna, Abu Khalid had told his wife. But Lubna didn't understand the world, she didn't understand this filthy world, and she howled on the telephone, ignoring his words. The commander had had no respite. He fought, and was fought, on every front.

'Every army must have its sentinels,' the commander's voice softened as he struggled to meet all the men's eyes, and they, hurriedly chewing their rice and stale bread, struggled to meet his. He lifted his phone in the air, opened to a LiveLeak page and summoned a brother to set up the projector.

The night that Abu Khalid asked his men to walk 150 kilometres to Nineveh, under the eyes of their enemies who were everywhere – hiding in the dark earth, gliding soundlessly through the skies – he spoke to them of military strategy. Mosul was a command centre, but the Ummah Movement's work here was done. War depended on a certain kinetic energy, a constant and merciless momentum that never slowed. The forces of the young rebel army would soon converge in the ancient Assyrian town, but first brave souls must scout the passage ahead.

Monty had zoned in and out of the lecture, exhausted from the day's training and exercises, but more so from the total heaviness in his heart. He wasn't suited for this, not for any of it. Not the shooting, not the starving, not any of the drills. As he wondered whether he would survive the battle to claim a new town, and whether the bargain he had made with fate was too grand – he was a city boy, a child of comfort and privilege, not a warrior; what had he been thinking? – Abu Khalid played the men a video.

And there she was, ethereally beautiful, cloaked in black. There was Layla, standing proudly on the fertile banks of the mighty Tigris.

Did she remember sitting in his car, her hands holding the brown leather of the seat as her body strained against it, singing to Strings at the top of her lungs? Did Layla remember how Monty drove her all over Karachi, up and down the wet tarmac of Seaview, past the green fairy lights protecting the saint's shrine of Abdullah Shah Ghazi, past sandstone colonial army bases, past the truck stops in Malir – where the city became hers, not his – just so she could sing backup to her favourite band? Layla always held Monty's hand in hers, using it as a microphone, raising his fingers to her lips as she sang. Even though Layla sang with her eyes squeezed tight, she always opened them and turned to Monty when she sang, never dropping his gaze.

Monty sat on his haunches in the cooling desert sand and closed his eyes in gratitude, offering whatever God existed a silent prayer of thanks. It had only been three months, just about, since he had been out here in this dry, miserable wasteland. He always knew he would find Layla, love of his life, beautiful Layla, but in his wildest dreams he hadn't thought they would be reunited this easily, not this fast.

As they drove around Karachi, Monty bought Layla

wilting roses from the orphans begging at traffic lights, and jasmine garlands to wear in her hair. In Khadda Market, she ordered onion chicken rolls from the window of Monty's silver Audi. In Boat Basin, she whistled at the skinny boys in baggy red T-shirts to bring her Baloch ice cream in a cup, always pistachio. In between songs, they drove through unlit residential lanes, stopping in Defence's deserted plots to kiss; Monty leaning across the driver's seat to taste the salt of Karachi's sea air on Layla's lips. But this Layla he had followed out to the desert was a different Layla altogether.

> *'We will not spare the liars of Ninawa,'* Layla declared in the video, her voice soft and controlled. *'We will spare no man, no child, who dares stand in our way. Truly they speak, only those who have seen the truth. Know that the moment to fight has come. You who did nothing, who abandoned your people, we will not forgive you. You who compromised everything for your comfort, remember this, my promise to you: one day our soldiers will fight you, too.'*

The camera panned away from her and swept across the sacred river, across the landscape that would soon fall to bloody battle, carrying Layla's sweet, melodious voice along the holy water:

> *'Say it now and be saved: There is no God but God. Those who follow the last prophet serve in the army of the lord. Declare the truth and be heard: there is no God but God. There is no God but God.'*

She pronounced the Arabic as though she had been speaking their accents all her life. In the Ummah Movement's modest training camp – two cement barracks where the recruits slept, built on either side of an obstacle course made up of pits and rope climbs and targets on the outskirts of Mosul – Monty watched Layla's LiveLeak video projected onto a dirty wall and was transfixed. He had been googling Layla obsessively since she'd left:

Layla + Iraq + where
Layla + Mosul
Layla + Ummah + Movement + danger
Layla + danger
Layla + past
Layla + Karachi
Layla + American School of Karachi + video
Layla + fighting + jihad
Layla + dead

Monty had searched for Layla everywhere. He looked through old Arabic newspapers scattered around the Mosul camp, combing the thin pages for a photo of her face, reading the text letter by letter, looking for the Ls that made up her name. He listened to the rumours that floated between the men, sifting through shreds of gossip as he lay down to sleep, meditating on each hopeful piece of news. The brothers said it was Layla, and that first video of hers, that inspired the birth of the Ummah Movement. But Monty didn't believe any of that. He was there! He was witness to the mythology that crept around Layla, he didn't buy any of the legends. He knew the old Layla – the original Layla.

Monty watched all of Layla's videos on YouTube and LiveLeak, scanning the scenery, studying her, searching for clues, trying to glean her ever-shifting mood. Even with the shapeless black *abaya* shrouding her long neck and the hijab wrapped tight around her heart-shaped face, her eyes wiped clean of the eyeliner that she smudged like charcoal along her lash line, even then Layla was unnaturally beautiful.

Monty noticed that even here in Mosul, even in the middle of all this terror and war, there was a glint of that same power he had seen in Layla's eyes when she kissed him in the cold stairwell.

When Abu Khalid asked the men: Who is ready to fight?

Who among you possesses a heart empty of fear?

Who will cross the desert on foot, armed only with what weapons they can carry and protected solely by the Almighty?

The brothers shouted praises and fired their Kalashnikovs in the air. But as Abu Khalid stood still on his good leg, only two hands were offered, Monty's and Sunny's.

'Where have you come from?' Abu Khalid ran his hand along his brow, wiping the sweat from his weary face. 'Who did you leave to join our struggle here?'

The world, Monty wanted to say, I left it all to come here. 'Pakistan,' he replied instead. All the other men had returned to their barracks, only Monty and Sunny stood to attention in front of the commander.

Abu Khalid nodded sombrely. 'A true country.' The commander spoke without the fatigue that washed over his face. 'This is how guerrilla wars are fought, on the backs of foot soldiers, ground troops with an intimate knowledge of the terrain. It's a long journey,' he warned the boys, 'but three kilometres an hour, two shifts in a day – early morning and under the cover of night – you should be there in a week.' Monty tried hard to remember everything Abu Khalid said, without writing it down. All they had to do was watch, observe, see. A courier would meet them before Nineveh – the commander called it by its Arabic name, Ninawa – and anything essential would be passed on to the brothers before they began their assault.

They would leave first thing in the morning. As they surveyed the land, provided they sent no word that the roads were compromised, Abu Khalid and the rest of the rebels would follow in technicals armed with Soviet ZPU-4 anti-aircraft cannons, recently looted from Fallujah. Some would travel in soft-skin Humvees and BMPs, and others in KrAZ-6322 trucks. Only Monty and Sunny, Abu Khalid assured them, would move as the early warriors had once done – their earthly bodies as shields and their eyes scanning the stars.

The commander paused, warming his hands over the open fire and signalling to one of his deputies at the same time – by curling his fingers before the flames – that more wood was needed. A brother ran in the direction of darkness to search for kindling in the middle of the night.

'Your name?'

Monty must have told Abu Khalid his name ten times since the start of training, and each time the commander remembered it only long enough to reprimand him. *Ya* Mustafa, Abu Khalid wailed as he corrected Monty's shooting stance and bemoaned his aim, *ya* Mustafa, you have to keep your eyes open when you shoot. *Ya* Mustafa,

I wish you fought for the other side. *Ya* Mustafa, have you never used a gun before? Even as a child?

But every time they spoke, the commander looked at Monty as though he were almost sure of him – almost, but not quite.

'Mustafa,' Monty replied. 'My name is Mustafa.'

He didn't like using his real name in Iraq. Everyone, even his mother, called him Monty and he clung to the name now, using it as a barrier between these men and himself.

What was the weight of a secret?

Some days Monty struggled under its heaviness, as though a look, a sigh, an answer incorrectly given to a seemingly unrelated question would betray him. Other days he held it in the palm of his hand, like open fruit, and waited confidently, sure that no one would come close to touching the truth. Like the jewels of a pomegranate, no one would ever pluck enough seeds to fully taste the tart, peculiar juice. But still, he had to be careful.

'One day, you will return, Mustafa. One day you will carry our movement back to lead our people in Khorasan.'

He could hear the commander's phone buzzing, on silent, in his pocket.

Monty hadn't thought of going home, not after burning his Pakistani passport, its jungle-green cover curling in a bonfire, when he finally passed his *tazkiyeh* in Turkey. 'You belong to the Ummah Movement now,' Abu Khalid, who choppered in that day, congratulated the new recruits as they flung their passports one by one into a smouldering pile of documents, burning slowly in the sand. 'You are the first sons of our new world. This is your home now,' Abu Khalid said, holding his fist tight against his heart. Monty remembered the brothers saying that Sunny hadn't tossed his passport in the fire, he said he'd burned it long ago, the very day he arrived on Iraqi soil.

'This here is the only sanctuary you will have now, your only safety from the ravages of the outside world. Nothing matters now.' It had seemed to Monty as though Abu Khalid was holding back tears. 'Nothing matters now, nothing' – the fist hard against his chest – 'but this.' At that moment Monty understood how it was possible to die of a broken heart.

He hadn't burned his American passport. He had left that at home, in his father's safe, just in case. He wished he had been brave enough to burn that, too, but Monty lacked real courage, true courage, and he knew that was why he had lost Layla in the first place.

He remembered one of the first times they spoke late into the night. Monty was lying on the black sheets in his room. His air conditioner was on fan, sweeping cool air around his tidy, polished room; and the Bose speakers, bought in Dubai, were on high, so his mother wouldn't hear his voice on the phone past midnight. 'If you had any guts,' Layla had teased in a low voice, 'you'd be here with me now, not halfway across the city, hiding behind a telephone in your bedroom.'

Monty had laughed, what else could he do?

Outside his French windows, the night watchman who circled their Clifton neighbourhood on an old creaky bicycle from dusk to dawn whistled. Monty counted the twilight hours spent with Layla by those whistles – one hour, two hours, three. He laughed, but he knew it was true: he had no guts. And Layla, unfortunately, had known it too. 'A man stays awake all night, pedalling in circles, just so you can feel safe?' Monty couldn't tell whether the rise in Layla's voice came from being impressed or hurt. It wasn't such a big deal; he got paid and everything, Monty replied, every neighbourhood had one of these guys. Layla fell quiet for a moment. 'Not mine,' she had said.

'Abu Khalid?' Sunny interrupted. He had been standing there the whole time, his hands clasped behind his back, watching the commander. 'About tomorrow?'

'What about it, Sunny?'

Sunny? How did Abu Khalid remember his name? Did they know each other already?

Monty hadn't spoken to Sunny yet, and Sunny said nothing to him about the long march they would be embarking on together. Sunny kept to himself, hardly mixing with any of the other recruits. He didn't seem like any of the BBCDs Monty had come across in London. When the camp cook set up two filthy folding tables near the bonfire every evening to serve the evening meal of gruel and old flatbread, Monty noticed Sunny never ran to be served first. He walked slowly, casually, unburdened by hunger. Sunny didn't have any of the desperation that marked most British-Born and Confused *Desis* – he had no apparent interest in being recognized or liked.

Monty had watched him during training and seen the cold determination with which Sunny prowled through low crawls in the grenade range, earning top marks everyday in target practice. And he watched with particular envy as Sunny overcame the humiliating physical-fitness obstacle course on his very first try.

For a moment, Monty worried how he would keep up with a soldier as self-possessed, as sure as Sunny. But he shook the thought from his head. It didn't matter. As afraid as Monty was, he would have walked to Nineveh alone if it meant finding Layla.

As they stood there in front of the commander, Monty felt uneasy at how eagerly Sunny had waved his arms in the air, volunteering for the march. Why did he want to go so badly?

Karimov, a lanky brother from Ingushetia, walked past them and threw a stack of logs into the waning fire. He ran off again and returned balancing a tray filled with foil-covered boxes, bottled water and soft drinks. The smell of lamb wafted behind the Ingush, hanging sweetly in the air, even after he ducked into the commander's tent.

'Any further instructions, Commander?' Sunny asked.

'Don't get killed,' Abu Khalid sighed, taking out his phone. It had been buzzing the entire time they had been standing by the bonfire. The commander read his messages with a sad flush spreading across his face.

Another brother, holding a pack of tissues scented with the perfume of rose petals, spoke quietly into the commander's ear. Monty saw him slip Abu Khalid something from his pocket. The commander took it and moved towards his tent, limping slowly until he disappeared inside.

Monty looked at Sunny, noticing the way his clothes – the same ones he seemed to wear every day – didn't fit him properly. His shirt looked a size too small and his cargo trousers were ripped and fraying at the cuffs.

Monty pulled at his own shirt uncomfortably, brand-new and thermally lined for the cold of the desert night.

He moved to speak to Sunny. It made sense that they should exchange a few words at least and discuss how they were going to proceed, but as Monty tried to formulate what to say, Sunny nodded briskly at him and, shoving his hands in the pockets of his cargo trousers, made to leave.

'Sunny?' Monty ventured brightly, speaking to his back. Sunny stopped and turned to look at him. 'Should we figure out tomorrow?'

Sunny watched him for a minute, running his gaze carefully up and down Monty, studying him suspiciously. 'Yeah.' Sunny didn't come closer, didn't take his hands out of his pockets. When he spoke, he didn't look Monty in the eyes. 'Tomorrow.'

Sunny slipped his phone out of his back pocket and carried on walking.

Monty moved towards the barracks, where he would sleep for a few hours on a hard cot before they set off early in the morning. He had wanted to thank Abu Khalid for his faith in him and for selecting him for this mission. He wanted to ask about Layla. Would she meet him and Sunny at the gates of Nineveh? Was there a special message he was to pass on to her? Monty had so many questions – How was she? Did she know he was coming to her? Had she asked for him?

But what would Monty have called Layla? He couldn't bring himself to use any of her nicknames – Bride of Damascus, Daughter of Jihad, Pride of the Martyrs, Niece of Struggle. He didn't quite understand how Layla, who had been so cool, allowed these ridiculous names to circulate. But he would have called her any of those names over the prospect of having to call her 'sister'.

Ibn Usman told Monty that Layla was the only 'sister' out here who didn't have to cover her face. Sam was Jordanian, Jordanian-Australian as he insisted, never forgetting the hyphen. The same age as most of the brothers – twenty, twenty-one – but he'd been out here longer, almost a year, and took a serious pride in this seniority. Abu Khalid wanted the world to see Layla, Sam said. He wanted the world to see the quality of women joining their movement. It wasn't just dumpy British schoolgirls running away from home, not just sad, lonely girls looking for husbands, but real women, free women. True fighters.

Sunny

In the cold, dark quiet – so cold and so dark it falls heavily on the soul, heavy like a fever that won't break – Sunny turns on his phone. He rubs his hands together, trying to keep warm as he waits for the glow of his iPhone to light up like a halo before him. The eerie stillness of the desert night is unbroken.

His eyes adjust to the dark slowly, blinking back the cold he feels deep inside, snapping at his bones.

Password, 786.

Volume, off.

It's 5 a.m., time for them to start walking, but Monty's still asleep; he was moaning a girl's name in his sleep. All night long – Layla, Layla, Layla.

Who the fuck is Layla?

Sunny rolls over onto his side and brings his knees up to his chest, digging his toes into the sand, trying to conserve his body's fading warmth. His bag is under his head. This – what he's wearing – is all he has. Sunny Jamil carries nothing to blanket himself against the early-morning chill, nothing to keep him till the sun comes up.

He checks his mail, pulling the page down, trying to refresh it while he waits for his phone's data to activate. *2G*, it says, before vanishing and returning as *EDGE*. Sunny refreshes the page again, waiting for the emails to download, though the only thing writing to him since he's been out here is a computer, spitting out blasts for jobs in the City. Today's offerings: an HR position at HSBC, five low-end High Street banking positions – teller, advisor, diversity officer (whatever that means). The emails stink of all his father's hopes and fears, that precious cargo of dreams.

But no matter how his pa bullied him and blackmailed him, Sunny never fought for his place in that world, which he had the confidence to judge as hollow and empty.

Oz taught him that.

Monty snores lightly across from him, sleeping on the barren sand, his mouth slack. He hasn't shaved in weeks, but his face is still smooth, a few wisps of hair curling along the border of his jaw; that's all he's managed to cultivate on that baby face of his. He lifts a soft, manicured hand to wipe away a vein of drool sliding down his cheek, and turns away from Sunny, moaning warmly to himself.

The sun will be up soon, rising slowly. They'd walked late into the night yesterday, and today was their first full day of the march to Ninawa. They have to get moving for the first part of their schedule, walking 5 a.m. to 10 a.m. Then they rest and pick up again at dusk, moving late into nightfall. It's only their first proper day, but at this rate the whole thing should take five days, a week tops. They should already be on the move, but a bit of peace and quiet, a bit of *khamoshi* from Monty's incessant questioning, isn't going to kill anyone.

Sunny double-clicks away from his email and looks through his apps. It takes a moment of scrolling through folders before he finds it. He opens Tinder and heads to his profile page. Sunny's jail-broken iPhone allows him to keep Portsmouth as his location, even though he's miles away from home.

But his data isn't connecting. Sunny sighs and goes into Settings. He puts his phone on flight mode for a second and then switches it off. His apps load painstakingly.

He leaves Discovery on for this, so when he's up early in the morning or in the small hours of the night, when the world is still, nothing racing, nothing rising, just quiet – like movie-quiet, with only the air whistling through the waves of the desert sand, actually *whistling* – Sunny can be wherever he wants.

He logs on only for a minute, just to look for Aloush. But he's not there. He wouldn't be.

'Was I talking?' Monty lifts his head from his bag and slurs, his voice heavy with sleep. He runs a hand through his long hair, the same hand he'd coated with drool and then dug into the sand a moment ago, the fool. He props himself up on his elbow. 'How come you're up so early?'

'Why do you think, boss?'

Monty groans and sits up properly. 'I'm sorry, Sunny,' he mutters. 'I have a hard time sleeping out here.' A light breeze moves through the desert dunes the way a stone cuts through water, disturbing it.

Sunny nods, fishes his Beats earbuds out of his bag and puts them in, muting Monty. Just woke up and off he goes, like gunfire.

He steps out of Tinder and into Scruff, moving it into a folder within a folder, double-glazing it so it's well out of sight. Scruff's multi-culti vibe means he can cruise through a whole bunch of cities before the stars die and the birds begin their morning patrol of the sky. London, Paris, Beirut, Nairobi. But Aloush isn't in any of those cities. Sunny knows that before he checks.

Monty stands up and stretches, pulling a stick of *miswak* out of his bag. He clamps it between his teeth like a cigarillo, chewing while he puts on his boots.

Sunny opens Facebook and then, just as he scrolls down his wall, a calico of smiling, bronzed, filter-heavy faces from around the world, he sees Oz. Clear as day, he sees Oz's face.

'The fuck?' He jerks up.

'Everything okay?' Monty stands with his back towards Sunny, urinating into some anaemic shrubbery. The orange of the sun is slowly bleeding into the sky. 'Something happen?'

It's a mistake. It has to be. An old post recycled, someone breaking into his account. Sunny has been writing to Oz for months now, since he got out here – texting, emailing, the works – but his cousin had dropped off the face of the earth. Vanished. Gone.

Oz's Twitter was shut down, Facebook cleaned out, no sign of life anywhere. As though Sunny had imagined him, his own flesh and blood, the only man he knew brave enough to point a finger curled into a gun at not one, but two coppers in London.

Sunny even wrote home after five weeks had gone by with no word from Oz, panicked, just to make sure nothing had happened, but Pa wasn't speaking to him.

Salman Jamil, Pa wrote in his last email, *for so long as you are out there, I will not talk to you. For so long as you defy me, you are dead to me.*

Imagine the ice in a parent like that – so arctic. Wishing your kid dead over disobedient.

Pa didn't write to Sunny on his birthday. Didn't even say thank you when he wrote to him on his.

Sunny stares at his phone. Oz is back.

He clicks on his cousin's face. His page is freshened up, new background, new bio, new albums, new photos, new Oz. Ozair Shafi, he's going by now. No more Oz, no Ozzy.

Sunny sweeps through Oz's page. There's just one new post. And at the top, some heavy-duty *Desi* bio data:

24 years old
175 cm
British
Single
Currently looking for chats, dating, real relationships

Relationships? British? Sunny feels his heart burn.

He had been waiting months – literally months – for Oz, who promised he was coming back, that he was just biding his time, getting some shit together and then he'd be back here, where he belonged. With the lads, with him. But he just disappeared.

Like he didn't know Sunny no more, like he done something wrong to him.

And now, like nothing's happened, he's back.

'Sunny.' Monty stands over him, his bag on his shoulder and an anxious look on his face. 'We should get going.'

Sunny hadn't seen much of Monty before they left camp. He was a new kid from the old country, an OG out of Pakistan, a rich boy, like that weather girl he thinks laughed at him. Monty left his parents, his home, his car, his friends, his life to come out here, Sam had said, sounding impressed. Same as the rest of us, Sunny told Sam, annoyed. Same as the rest of us, my brother.

'Give me a minute.' Sunny holds the phone against his chest so Monty can't see the screen.

But Monty doesn't hear what Sunny is saying. He hovers in front of him, stepping into Sunny's light.

Sunny looks up. 'What you doing, Monty?'

Monty moves away quickly, walking backwards. 'Five minutes, Sunny,' he says, trying to sound tough.

Yeah, Sunny nods. I'll show you five minutes.

He opens his email, deleting the latest monster.co.uk letter without even looking at it, and opens a new message.

Hey, what the fuck, Oz?

Delete, delete, delete.

Hey, where you been, 'Ozair'?

Delete.

OZZZ!

Not even Uncle calls him Ozair, not even when he's mad. Sunny bites the rough skin around his thumb, spitting out the chewy bits of debris that taste of sweat and sand. Monty sits on top of his enormous backpack, chin in hand, just watching him.

Oz, you know how many messages I sent you?

You just leave me? After what I done?

Sunny deletes every line.

Where you at, bro? I'm here, Oz, here where you sent me.

'Sunny? 'Don't you think we should get moving?' Monty says gently, trying to be as unobtrusive as possible. 'The sun will be strong soon, and we'll have to stop . . .'

Sunny focuses on his phone, on the blank email to ozmatic99@gmail.com, struggling to find the words that have been lost between them. Last he'd seen Oz, he was preaching fire, singing the gospel, calling lost brothers to arms, all fury and rage.

Monty hooks his bag and his gear over his shoulder and pulls out the map on his phone, jabbing the screen with his finger as he adjusts the weight on his back with one hand. 'We only walked about fifteen kilometres so far.' He pinches his fingers together, zooming in on his iPhone, squinting for a moment before releasing his hand. 'I think we'll have to double that today, at the very least. Right?'

Sunny keeps his head down, staring at the white of the empty email till his eyes hurt.

'I don't think it looks right for us to be behind schedule, not so early in the day. They're watching, and I don't know about you – but me? I didn't come out here to make a bad impression . . .'

Sunny exhales slowly.

Monty kicks at the sand with his boots, shaking his head. 'I mean, I know you didn't. I just don't want anyone to get that impression. They wouldn't . . .' Monty's voice trails off and he tugs uncertainly on his bag's straps.

The sun, the moon, the stars – Sunny would have told Ozzy everything, if only he hadn't been afraid. He was the first brother who understood him. Whatever he saw of Sunny, whatever he wasn't too scared to show, Oz saw – the anger, the lies, all his fear. And Oz, unlike everyone else, never looked away.

'Sunny? You're not upset, are you? I didn't mean it like that. You didn't take it the wrong way?'

Oz, Sunny types, *you ok? I'm out here, bro. Waiting for you. Where you at? This shit ain't the same without you.*

Monty

Monty stared out at the wide expanse of naked desert that surrounded them. There was no way they were going to cross it in time. If they made some real progress today, at least another twenty kilometres, they would be at the Mosul dam by tomorrow, maybe the day after.

Sunny had chosen all the offline maps they would download for their journey, before leaving Mosul. He said TomTom did the best app, but it was expensive – forty dollars. 'Too rich for my blood,' he confessed sadly, shaking his head.

Monty had bought the app anyway; he didn't trust the free ones that Sunny vetted, which redirected them every time they paused for a bathroom break. After they'd got lost for the third time that morning, Sunny conceded graciously that he might have been wrong about the maps. 'Sorry, bro,' he said with a faint, tired smile. 'Maybe you should have bought that TomTom one.'

But Monty didn't want to tell Sunny that he had bought it and had been using it discreetly all this time, not now when they'd had their first moment of connection. He had no data on his phone, his father had cut him off since he'd left Karachi. Monty asked Sunny, who was always on his iPhone – religiously so – if he could use it or link up to his hotspot or whatever, just for five minutes. He wanted to check on Layla; since they'd left Mosul he had no access to her videos. He mumbled some excuse to Sunny about family.

All Monty needed was five minutes, three even, to enter his searches into the browser. He knew exactly what to search for: he alone knew how to look for Layla, how to read her hidden moods, how to find the truth behind the cover of all her words.

But Sunny, holding his phone before him, the light of the desert sun reflecting off its shiny metallic back, shook his head.

'I'm on a budget,' he replied gruffly.

Course, course, Monty shook off his disappointment. Me too, don't worry.

So he didn't want to tell Sunny about the TomTom, not now when, after Sunny had apologized, slapping Monty genially on the back, it looked like they might even be friends.

Monty scanned the app quickly while Sunny charged his phone at a deserted petrol pump, rivulets of green along the quiet yellow of the desert indicating the fastest route to Nineveh. The dam was the halfway point of their journey; the sooner they reached it, the better. Sunny had seemed preoccupied since they left Mosul, never speaking beyond what was needed, always distant, his mind somewhere far away. Monty was relieved for this slight shift in his mood. It would bode well for their march. They were going to make it to Nineveh, things were going to be all right.

'Coming in two,' Sunny called out, winding his wires tightly around his plugs.

Monty didn't like the idea of stopping so often, but Sunny said it was important that his phone was charged, so they could stay on top of the news. No point fighting blind, he said.

'Take your time!' Monty waved, holding his hand out. He wanted Sunny to know that he could be gracious, too.

So far, Sunny had taken the lead on pretty much everything. He decided where they would camp for the night, poring over the earth, tracking the landscape, making sure they were safe. Sunny slept with his Kalashnikov right beside him, always ready, he said. He had looked at Monty strangely when he, on the other hand, had sheepishly put the weapon's safety on before he slept, laying it down at some distance.

There had been gunfire in the distance the previous night, a low-intensity firefight that carried on for hours.

I'm not used to these things, Monty laughed twitchily, but Sunny didn't laugh back. He drummed his fingers along the cold, grey metal of the gun as though it were a musical instrument and rolled over to sleep.

Abu Khalid hadn't told them what they were to do if they were stopped or taken. Monty assumed the worst – they would be tortured, held prisoner, deported or killed. They were guerrilla fighters, rebels, and this was the least-dangerous assignment they would have – it was just walking, just observation, like Abu Khalid said, intelligence-gathering. That was all. He steadied his breathing. But he wasn't afraid to die, not any more.

Monty only wanted to be the kind of man Layla could be proud of. A real man, not a reflection. Not the small, frightened man he had been when she left him.

He smiled at the symmetry of it all. He was a totally different person since arriving in Mosul. Maybe Layla had to break his heart. It led him here, where he was rebuilding himself, reimagining what it meant to be a man.

When the brothers in the camp gathered to watch Layla's videos on YouTube, Monty held himself apart from their congress. Seeing her on the screen, he always felt himself harden; was she talking to him in those videos?

No one could know about him and Layla. No one could know about her past. But unlike Layla, Monty had no courage for secrets.

It was at night that Monty gave himself fully up to Layla. Regardless of how long he slept or how anxious his mood, he always saw her. Beautiful, beautiful Layla, slipping away from him, her hair rising up around her like smoke. He could never hear what she was saying in the dreams. Every time he tried to move closer, she fell apart, her head moving one way, her body and her limbs another. And Monty would jerk awake, his chest pounding, his ears throbbing and his throat burning, as though he had been screaming.

When he closed his eyes again, still shaking from the terror of his nightmares, Monty tried only to remember the beginning of the dream: beautiful Layla.

For Monty, everything began and ended with Layla.

Sunny

Sunny lies down against his bag, using it as a pillow. Rita is lying next to him and he strokes her gently for a moment. 'What a beautiful little thing you are,' he sings to his Kalashnikov softly. After checking that he has enough battery, Sunny clicks on a picture of Rita and uploads it as his WhatsApp status. *Never tire of looking at her, of touching her, of knowing she's mine*, he types in purple.

He adjusts his body against Rita, who is especially cold this afternoon, since they paused their walking to rest before the second shift, and makes himself comfortable. Sunny opens Gmail, calculating ten, maybe fifteen minutes online before they started walking again. In the afternoon, as the sun drifted out of the sky, deep in the desert when they moved away from the roads for cover, so as not to be spotted by passing cars, the only sound for kilometres was the wail of birds, calling to each other as they flew through the empty, cloudless sky. Sunny lifted his phone to snap a picture of the birds – from their strangled calls, he thought they might be vultures – but they were gone already.

He lowers the iPhone back to the desert floor. Sunny needs this time, a bit of meditation before the night march. It is only the second day of the march to Nineveh, but already it is something brutal, *boring*. Hours of walking across deserted highways and no-man's-land, broken only by even more monotonous hours waiting for the sun to fall so they can resume their regime. The endless landscape never lessens, never relents and allows some sense that they are breaching distance and cutting across time.

Sunny looks at his phone battery. Ten minutes of cruising will leave him with 60/65 per cent battery left – perfect. He'll charge his phone when they stop to get food later today. Might be the middle of nowhere, but every joker out here has a mobile phone, trust.

Sunny checks his mail: in-box heaving with corporates, non-stop. For years his pa had been at him – business this, business that. Did Sunny know Uncle Haroon's kid earned 70K his first year out of uni? Did he know starting bonuses in the City hit fifteen, sometimes twenty grand? Pa was convinced wealth was only a matter of will, said he had seen it happen himself, heard his friend Nur Muhammad back in the old country make a fortune out of thin air. Did Sunny know Forbes had a list of the 100 richest Asians – including women – now? And, like, a good percentage of them were Indian?

I'm not Indian, Pa.

But he'd just wave his hand at his son. 'If that *sala chutia* Donald Trump can be President off the back of that crap TV show, who are you to sniff at the power and prestige of the financial world?'

Heard you, loud and clear, Pa. I'm not good enough, I ain't real. I'm nothing, invisible. Remake me then, remake me into something beautiful. Something you can believe in.

But no one was going to fix what was broken. That was down to Sunny. Only Sunny could take himself apart and build something new, something strong and fierce, fresh, from scratch. And when he did, the moment he acted on all his pa's counsel, then he was all – no, Sunny Salman Khan, I didn't mean *that*. Don't go off and do something crazy, don't throw your life away, don't ruin everything you have here, don't you know what you're getting yourself into?

What life?

Pa never did hear Sunny, never could listen to the truth. Not when it was coming from him.

What life, Pa?

If there were any justice in things, if the world was attuned to the struggling, to those who fought and strived to be free, Pa would be proud of his only son. But there isn't and he ain't.

Doesn't matter what Pa feels; Sunny deletes the emails, all six of them. No one matters to him any more. *Imma wear my name*, Sunny taps into a tweet, watching the characters count downwards from 140, *and wear it proud*.

Pa must have uploaded his CV somewhere – after writing it first – and clicked every box going. In the five months since Sunny left home, he'd got emails from Barclays, Credit Suisse and HSBC on the regular. They never left a brother alone for more than a week.

Pa should know he don't believe in all that no more, it was *haram*, too – all that interest. He should know Sunny wasn't going back, no point jazzing up a CV on his behalf – languages: top-class Hindi, A-star in Latin. Hobbies: travelling, behaving well, Islamic history, cricket, etc., etc.

Here Sunny is, right where Oz sent him. Here, following his cousin. Living as he wanted Sunny to. No drums, no music, no girls, nothing between him and his saviour above. But since Sunny got here, Oz's been gone. Nearly five months of silence, nothing – not a peep – until last night.

With his eyes half shut, Sunny logs into Facebook. Ozair Shafi has uploaded ten photos in an album called 'Freedom', of all things. There was Oz at home, Oz reclining on his bed pretending to sleep (if you're sleeping, who took the selfie?); Oz at the gym, fronting like he was about to lift a crazy set of weights Sunny knew he couldn't bench; Oz at the beach, his defined body dark and tanned against a cloudy sky, his trunks slung low on his hips, so a brother could see the trail of fine, sun-kissed hair snaking down from his navel; Oz in the park; Oz at Starbucks holding some stupid creation of his, a half-caf caramel coconut mint rip-off-acino; Oz cooking 'vegan lentils' (i.e. daal, you poser); Oz stepping out of the shower, holding the towel around his waist in a tight fist, his hand even lower this time, his eyes gazing over the camera like he don't even know it's there.

The shower, Oz?

What's he doing back in Portsmouth? How's he had the time to nano-surgery his Facebook; but not to reply to the hundreds of emails, texts and WhatsApps Sunny sent him?

'We should get going,' Monty says, breaking into his thoughts.

Sunny clicks back onto Oz's profile. Sure enough, he's written a ridiculous post, to boot. Sunny doesn't know this Oz, doesn't know the visuals, doesn't recognize the words:

Been a long time. A life time! But time's been good to me. I rose from the ashes of something ferocious: I am Reborn. Holla at me! I'm back and I'm free. **What I do now**: *work out, guns out. You heard me! Like the life I live, 'cause I went from negative to positive.* **What I'm looking for**: *Someone I can be me with and share my soul. No true believers, sorry.* **Activities and interests**: *Fifa 17, GTA, travel, truth, public speaking, debate, being me. Any enquiries, please see my updated contact info.*

No *what*? Brother was brown like no one else. Had his name inked in Arabic round his neck, like a fallen crown, ate only halal *kaana*, the fuck did he mean: no true believers? *I'm free? Enquiries?* You were offline, Oz, you didn't win an Oscar.

Share my soul, my arse, Sunny shakes his head. This one time they were at the cinema, Oz had bought two cans of Diet Coke at the Poundland and stuffed them into his jacket, and as the cousins were walking through to pick up their tickets, they saw this girl standing there, anxious like, looking at her phone. She was Kashmiri maybe, real fair, light-green eyes, but *Desi* for sure, polyester blouse, whiff of coconut in her hair. She was just standing there, all dolled up, waiting for her man. Oz paused a second, looking at her.

'Hey, baby,' he said, rolling up to the girl, 'what kinda brother makes a lady like you wait?' She smiled nervously, thinking the same thing. Oz stepped in a little closer to her, shaking his head, real sad like. She didn't move away from him, didn't push him back, didn't cut him outta entering her space. It was Oz's signature move, always did it to see how much further he could go. He leaned even

194

closer to her then, almost grazing her cheek with his own. 'He ain't doing you right, darling.'

And just then her man stepped up. A Jamaican, big guy, no joke, coiled muscles trapped under his tight shirt and all. 'You wanna move on?' he says to Oz, frowning at his girl.

Oz gave him the once-over and smiled, throwing his arm around the Kashmiri. 'I was just telling your girl here she oughta find herself a real man.' For a second it looked like she was trying to move away from Oz, but it was just her hair – it had got caught under the crease of Oz's elbow, and she turned her head left and right to free it.

The boyfriend was crazy enraged and went for Oz, but Oz, in some wild ju-jitsu move, grabbed the Jamaican by the shoulder and *groin*, lifted him like a plank of wood and slammed him to the ground, tossing him like rubbish. The Jamaican was on the floor howling, his girl looking at him with something like shame – and Oz? Oz was holding his stomach and laughing. He picked up one of the Diet Cokes that fell out of his jacket and threw his arm around Sunny, just like he did around the girl, who was bending reluctantly to lift her guy off the scuzzy cinema carpet, and said, 'Lesson number one, Cuz: you don't throw down unless you're ready to beat the king.'

Sunny thought he'd come up with that on the spot, mesmerized with how Oz had floored the Jamaican in one move flat. He thought Oz was a genius, a magician lifting lines like that out of his hat. An original, a renegade.

Sunny swipes out of Facebook and refreshes his in-box. Nothing. He looks at his iMessages, not a blue box in sight. Not a line. Nothing from Oz. He drums his fingers along his thigh, it doesn't matter.

He don't care.

No one writes to Sunny, no one hears any of his calls. He doesn't let it smoke him no more. He's fighting a bigger battle now, speaking another kind of language, elevating the discourse.

He's grown since his days sitting in front of the computer on Britannia Road, blinds drawn, Frank Ocean's soft voice slipping through his beat-up speakers, walls so thin he could hear Pa snore at night. So thin, he could hear Sunny cry.

Sunny opens WhatsApp and scrolls through his favourites. Oz's profile picture is different – it's no longer the white and green of Saudi Arabia's flag, the sword of Islam curved upwards like the arc of a dying moon. Now, it's a selfie of Oz and some white guy Sunny doesn't recognize, really high shirt collars and ridiculously good hair, black and flowing wingwards past his ears. Underneath the picture 'Out to war' has been replaced with 'I am writing in the age of barbarism, which is already, silently, remaking the world of men.'

The fuck?

Sunny still has a line from one of Frank's songs under his picture, an old Polaroid of Pa and him. Pa's holding Sunny over a birthday cake, his face illuminated by the candles. His father's soft brown hair is slicked down, his face obscured by the shadow of his smile. Sunny has one eye open, the other closed in a wink. He still has a line from 'Pink Matter' under the photo, even though he knows he should change it, his heart still sings *Cleopatra,*

Cleopatra. Then and now, Frank still speaks to Sunny when he's alone.

Sunny bites the inside of his check, wondering if Oz is on his phone now, thinking of him, too.

Ozzy baby, he types. *What's the low low? You don't write, you don't call?*

Sunny hits Send. One tick. And then, though he doesn't expect it, two. And then they're blue.

Oz is online. Right now.

Oh oh oh. Don't tell me! Back from the dead, my man Ozzistan!
Where you at!
Ozzzzzzieeee!
I knew it was some kind of error, here he is, my boy!!
I was so worried, bro.
What's the word??

And again, in seconds, Oz has read Sunny's messages.

You been watching the news? @Ozmatic is dead and I ain't seen u tweet about our movement since I been out here, not since u up and disappeared.

Sunny watches the screen for some proof of life, waiting for the little italics that'll tell him Oz is typing back. But it never comes.

Hello?
Oz?

And again, one tick. Two ticks. Blue.

Oz is online, he just isn't answering Sunny.

I'm getting iced by everyone? Pa, and now you too?

Not very becoming, you know? Sunny types quickly, before his cousin vanishes again. He's been emailing, texting, even tried FaceTiming Oz, at the risk of burning up his pa's international roaming package, and he hasn't answered Sunny in months. But Oz is getting his shit. Here he is, reading his messages.

It's starting to feel deliberate, you know?

Abandoning a brother at war? Not cool, Oz. Where you been? You got something better to do than be here with your brothers all of a sudden?

One grey tick, then two. Then blue.

Answer me.

It burns. It burns Sunny to be sitting out here, bruised and bleeding, running his body ragged with training. Did Abu Khalid make any of the other brothers pull that Captain America shit when they joined up? Weapons-smuggling in his second week, moving a transport of RPG-29s out of the Mosul Sheraton, ferrying letters from the commander to some bird in Baghdad. Having the life kicked out of him with shock training – which he knows, from talking to Sam, that no one else in their camp had to do. Eating shit, facing death all day long.

Sam claims they did it to him, too, but Sunny never saw no cigarette burns on his skinny-ass arms. He didn't see no bits of pink scalp and flaky skin from where they ripped his hair out. He didn't see no bedbug scabs all over Sam's legs and chest and arms, from sleeping out in the rough. So yeah, just Sunny then, and he passed, too. Everything they threw at him, he aced. And Oz just vanishes? Just like that?

What's with this quote of yours?

Sunny's is poetry. Frank is a poet, like Faiz, like Ali. Like all those men who loved and fought and suffered and had enough terror left in them to throw some shrapnel down on the page. But Oz's? That junk has no flow, no metre.

You know what? He's stabbing his phone now. *You ain't no Muslim, bruv.*

Oz is reading Sunny's messages, all of them. And he's not replying. Online, it says under Oz's name. But Online ain't typing back.

Do you even know what's happening out here? HERE, OZ. Where YOU sent me. You remember that? 'Islam is a battlefield, bro. We at war with the world, Cuz. We live or we die, Sunny.' You forgot all that shit you said?

What's Oz doing, posting selfies coming out of the shower, farting around on a beach? Where's he been?

It isn't hard enough for us? Muslim, brown, second gen but still getting called Paki all the time, day and night, day and night, living in migrant central, homes no bigger than jungle camps?

It isn't enough being a liberated man of colour and having to stand up to the world?

Men who understand the codes of being, codes by which you reclaim your RIGHTFUL place, your HONOUR, RESPECT, codes by which you soar or you drown, you DIE – that's who we were raised to be.

Sunny's heart is pounding. He tastes bile in his mouth whenever he thinks of Oz reading his messages and ignoring him. He feels like screaming whenever he thinks of how Oz dropped him. Just like that. Like Sunny meant nothing. Like he was invisible. Standing there while Abu Khalid and that rich kid romanced each other about Pakistan.

Monty

Back in Karachi, before the desert, before Iraq, Layla wriggled her toes in the sand, a shimmering blackish-silver.

'It's oil,' Monty said, still wearing his leather sandals, stepping away from the approaching tide.

'Don't be silly,' she replied. 'It's dirt.'

Monty arched his eyebrows high.

'It is,' Layla insisted. 'Exhaust fumes, ash, the husks of corn burned over charcoal.' She grabbed the air with her fingers. 'It's all this,' she said softly, rubbing the pads of her fingertips together. 'One day of the city, that's all.'

Monty ran his hand through her wet hair.

Layla pulled up her torn jeans and sat down in the sand. 'Monty,' she said, 'Monty, sit down.'

Monty turned and looked back at the road. Tano, his driver, was standing by the car, watching them. He must have been in his early forties, but his fair skin and light-green eyes weathered his face. Tano wore sandals with the metal buckle open at his ankles, always dragging on the floor. The soles of his shoes were cut from old tyres. He held the keys of the car, collected on a simple silver ring, in the palm of his hand and waited patiently, circling the car, guarding it with his presence.

Monty noticed how his face drained of colour whenever he saw Layla. Tano would have driven looking at the floor, if only he could, shrinking into his seat to avoid catching her eyes in the rear-view mirror. Monty kicked the empty Frooti-juice boxes and wisps of broken plastic bags away with his sandalled feet and squatted down.

'Sit,' Layla said, nestling her hand under the sand, digging it under the silver grains of dirt and ash. 'Sit down with me.'

She had begged him to bring her here. To Monty, accustomed to the beaches of Phuket and Ko Samui, it was an ugly strip of the city surrounded by naked construction sites, shopping malls and filth. But to Layla, two hours away from her home on a good day, the beach was the sum of the world.

'You see that?' she pointed a long finger at a brown tanker floating in the middle of the quiet sea. 'That's from Greece. Greece, Monty. Thousands of miles away, look how it's sitting there, waiting, on *our* shore.'

Her hair was a mess, tangled and hanging in waves down her back.

Monty held the hand that Layla had buried under the sand, squeezing her palm into his, so no one, especially Tano, would see.

'And there,' Layla turned her body to face Monty's, but her eyes were following an emaciated camel. 'Our camels are the fastest in the world, my dear Mustafa. Arab princes buy these camels for lakhs.' She kissed the pursed fingers of her outstretched hand. 'They race them in their deserts, with children as jockeys so that their speed isn't slowed down by the weight of an adult. Our camels, Monty: they gamble millions on them. But here, at the beach, they're yours for a ride – thirty rupees only.'

Her brother had clients, Layla said, Arab sheikhs who

came to shoot houbara bustards in the desert. He facilitated their permits, arranged their travel, provided them with guides, *charas* and entertainment. That's how she knew about the camels, Karachi's secret assets, she smiled.

The camel looked as though he would collapse under the brutality of Karachi's summer humidity, but Layla observed him proudly.

'Monty, look at me,' she dug her bare feet closer to his, adjusting her body so that, in one slight move, she could have curled into his lap. Monty looked over his shoulder once more. Tano was still there, watching them, his face shaded with anxiety, like the pregnant monsoon clouds. 'Monty.' Layla lifted her hand out of his and turned Monty's face back towards her own, leaving grains of cool sand on his chin. She was breathing slowly. 'Do you love me?'

Ahead of them, a dark man with a creased pair of trousers rolled to his sinewy thighs pulled fish in from the Arabian Sea. All around him barefoot boys screamed, rushing to pluck silver fish out of his net. The fisherman pulled the grey tulle out of the murky brown water with all his strength, wiping a film of sweat away from his eyes with his arm, so as not to drop his hand and lose his catch. *The best day ever*, his torn shirt read in faded script.

'More than anything,' Monty replied, searching for Layla's hand, buried under the sand.

'Monty,' Layla spoke softly, gently, 'Monty, you shouldn't.'

That night, Monty sat with his parents at the dinner table. Papa had ordered sushi from Fujiyama, and Angelise unpacked the white-and-blue takeaway boxes, preparing and arranging food she would not eat herself. Barefoot,

Angelise moved deftly, setting down bowls of pink pickled ginger and soy sauce.

Khadija had long since been fired, Khadija and a roster of young girls whom Zahra Ahmed had first demoted to downstairs, working in the kitchen, then purged. Angelise had survived by keeping her head down and adapting to all of Zahra's increasingly strict dictates. Behind each member of the Ahmed family, she broke open a pair of chopsticks and briskly rubbed the sticks against each other, like a chef sharpening a knife, freeing blond splinters of wood into the air, before gently setting them down next to each plate.

'Mix the wasabi and soy sauce *together*,' Zahra scolded the maid. She adjusted the printed silk *dupatta* that had fallen to her shoulders, lifting it back up and draping it casually across her head. 'Angelise, how many times do I have to tell you? Mix the wasabi *in* the sauce. In it, in it.' Zahra mimed stirring an imaginary bowl with one hand; the other lay hidden from view, under the table.

Yes, Ma'am, Angelise nodded, filling three glasses with Nestlé bottled water.

Monty's father drank his miso soup from an earthen mug with no handle, just like they had at the restaurant. 'Will you turn that racket off?' he moaned, gesturing at the TV, tuned to Nayar's evening sermon.

Zahra ignored her husband, who she suspected had been drinking before dinner. She could smell the faintly antiseptic whiff of whisky on his breath, though Akbar knew very well how she felt about alcohol in the house. Zahra reached for her son's hand across the table. 'Darling, why were you so late to dinner?'

Monty watched the soggy tempura being lifted out of the Avari boxes and arranged in a basket – exactly as they served it in the actual Fujiyama – and let his hand be held. 'I was at the beach,' he replied.

'The beach?' Zahra wrinkled her nose. 'Why?'

Monty could see his mother's lips tremble ever so faintly. He narrowed his gaze. Was she upset?

'You know it's not safe, all kinds of car-jackers and thieves operate out there.'

'Will you shut that bloody nonsense off?' Papa picked up his iPhone and slipped a thin pair of reading glasses onto the bridge of his nose. He picked up a tuna roll and soaked it in the shallow bowl of wasabi soy sauce, turning his chopsticks left and right, before popping the blackened morsel into his mouth.

Zahra squeezed Monty's hand, her lips still moving with the most delicate of tremors. 'Especially at night, *beta*. We can make a trip to the Hawkesbay hut one weekend if you like, but avoid that area, please.'

'Zahra,' Akbar peered over his glasses, 'turn that crackpot off.' He motioned at the TV with his phone, as though it were a remote. Zahra lifted her hand off her lap as though to stop him, and Monty saw that she had been holding a *tasbeeh*.

She had been praying along with the TV host, mouthing all the words he recited, counting off the emerald-coloured beads one stone at a time.

'He's a good man,' Zahra muttered to her husband, not looking at him, 'it doesn't do to speak of him like that.'

Sunny

The desert late at night is quiet and dark, the only light coming from a small fire Sunny built and the glow of his phone. Sunny taps his Tumblr open and tries to upload a photo: a tabby, curled up near his Rita.

He found the little kitty on her own, in the middle of nowhere. Soon as she saw Sunny, she came and rubbed her ragged body against his leg. *#jihadtourism #catsofjihad. Come to Iraq, see the world, ha-ha.* But he's straining against this shit EDGE network, Iraq's Internet connection like Chinese water torture.

Sunny refreshes the page, refreshes the page, refreshes the page.

In the time it's taken him to get back to Tumblr, four minutes later, his photo's got reblogged and the Like button is lit. One note, then five, then eight. Only thing he has going for him, since coming out here, is that his socials have been ablaze. Whatever dead nerve-endings Sunny has, whichever bits of him have gone numb, just got defibrillated and resuscitated. Resurrected. He was about to become an influencer.

Sunny clicks on the notes.

Man, wish I was a warrior out there too, fighting the crimes against my people.

Inshallah, brother, you should make the journey, he types back, feeling fresh and generous.

Bismillah, a bunch of girls write, presumably about the cat, loads of smiley faces with hearts popping out of their eyes.

Yr photos are sick! LUV THEM, LUV JIHAD SUBHAN ALLAH!

Thanks, bruv, all is thanks to Him. Sunny adds a smiley face with sunglasses as an afterthought.

I think what you are doing is great work, writes some nerd, *but how can a true Muslim movement equip its fighters with Kalashnikovs – weapons invented by the biggest atheists on earth?*

Fuck off, Sunny types and then deletes. He sits up to think of a proper reply; lots of people checking into his feed now, he has to sound right, sound woke, be an inspiration to his fans, bless them, but he's still unsettled, disturbed by that flow with Oz on WhatsApp last night. Oz still hasn't written back, though Sunny knows he read all his messages.

Maybe one of Oz's mates was playing a nasty on him, maybe it was some kind of mistake? But he hasn't come back to fight, like he promised. Sunny checks his email every ten minutes, but not a smoke signal from Ozzy anywhere.

He picks at a tin of tuna with a plastic fork. Monty's lying down, a shirt over his face for shade, out for the count.

Brother, Sunny types, a smear of sunflower oil on his fingers, **when you crawl out of your suburban living room, let me know and we can discuss the matter further.**

Inspired, he moves closer to the fire for some crucial atmospheric light, taps the Record button on his Snapchat, props Rita up next to him and holds his phone out in front of him. *People be wondering about me, wanting to know who I am and what I do — gotta get the balance right between show and tell. Bit of lessons, bit of learning about life out here, dose of jihadsplaining and then, at crucial intervals: me.*

Sunny licks his palm and smoothes his hair down, checking his reflection in the camera, before winking and sticking his tongue out. *Automatova Kalashnikova selfie for all you jihad peeping toms what what #AKLife #ritadiaries.*

Fuck knows how Snapchat works, Sunny speaks into his bronzed reflection on the phone, *but I only just opened my account and already have 150 followers — getting my holla back not from my blood, but from this legion of strangers. Imma make a name for myself out here,* he switches the phone to his left hand and thumps the closed fist of his right hand against his chest, *one that'll live, that will crest over the bodies of them that fought me, that put me down, till long after I'm gone, sent to Paradise, crowned with flowers and laid into the earth alongside my brothers, martyrs and kings.*

Sunny repositions his automatic weapon and takes a photo, editing the picture to lighten the frame and do away with the shadows between Rita and him.

But he can do better.

'Monty,' Sunny calls out. 'Give me your AK a second.'

Monty is lying on his side, watching Sunny. He rolls his eyes. 'Sunny, come on.'

'Come on nothing.' Sunny stands up and looks for something to lean against, a rock or something. 'It's part of the battle, Monty, just grow up already and give me the AK.'

Monty trudges towards Sunny and slips his machine gun off his shoulder. 'How are selfies part of the battle?' he asks wearily.

Sunny straps Rita over his left shoulder and hitches Monty's AK onto his right. Ever heard of propaganda, Monty?

'Could we go one hot minute without you complaining?'

Monty turns away, as though he's giving Sunny space to do his thing, pretending like he hasn't heard him.

Sunny rests the butts of the machine guns on his hips and holds the magazines in his hands, tilting his chin up.

'Shoot me standing,' Sunny says, scowling. 'Hold your phone up with the flashlight on, so we don't gotta use the flash.'

Monty bends down and picks up Sunny's phone. He clicks a photo.

'Again. Take a close-up.' Sunny scrunches his nose and clenches his teeth, so it looks like he's growling.

Monty turns the camera phone sideways and half-heartedly clicks another shot.

Sunny thinks about uploading the AK photo onto Facebook for a moment, just to add some new followers, just to show Oz how he's thriving, how he's flying out here.

But still, it burns. That FB post. Maybe it was a smoke-screen, just a bit of camo, bait and switching attention while he recruits more boys and cash for the cause. Maybe they'd clocked him – maybe he had to slip under the radar a while?

But still, something doesn't sit right.

Sunny closes the app and returns to Tumblr. Before Monty starts moaning in his sleep again, Rita and he have another forty-five likes.

Monty

The next morning, after hours under the sun, struggling to make up some kilometres, feet burning, throats rasping, they finally reached the Mosul dam. The vast plain of sand and desert nothingness was finally broken by the awesome machinery and architecture of the dam, but the dam itself was deserted, empty, cleared out. The water was still and quiet. There was no one on guard duty, no brothers on patrol, none of the movement's flags fluttered in the distance, there was no sign of life anywhere. The dam was the Ummah Movement's second-biggest capture after Mosul and it was already deserted. Had the brothers stationed there been captured by Iraqi military? Or, worse – killed by local militias? Did the commander know?

Monty dropped his bag to the floor and unzipped it hurriedly, rifling through his clothes. In training they had been taught to react decisively, every second in a hostile environment was an advantage. They had to alert the commander, their brothers moving across the desert, anyone. They had to tell someone they might be in danger. Monty focused on his hands, his bag – everything, over his mounting sense of dread – until he found what he was looking for.

Sunny eyed the Thuraya in Monty's hand. 'What's that?'

Monty breathed deeply, trying to stem the panic snaking through his body. Nothing, he mumbled, suddenly self-conscious, just a phone.

The structure was too large, too vast for the two of them to search it on their own without causing a serious delay to their schedule. Monty lifted a hand over his eyes, looking, searching for fellow soldiers. How could there be no one here?

'A satellite phone? Nah, bro, you kidding me?' Sunny had clearly never seen one of those things before, but still claimed with certainty that they were a bad idea. 'Seriously, Monty? You know that shit can pinpoint a location down to your exacts? Hello?'

Monty was turning round in a circle, trying to move out of the sun's glare. But it was everywhere, suffocating him, blinding him, making it impossible to see.

Were they in danger? Was Layla?

Oh God. Layla.

Monty tried hopelessly to turn on the machine, stabbing the buttons repeatedly. Tano, his driver, had taken him to buy it in Saddar. He had a cousin who smuggled electronics and said he would give Monty a good price. Monty had felt so proud, holding the sat phone against his chest as he made his way through the mobs of people, squeezing against hawkers and sellers and hundreds of busy shoppers, all rushing through the unlit *gullies* of Saddar. He had found and bought the phone by himself, he hadn't asked his father for help or for the use of his connections. Monty tried to recall that feeling now, as he held the phone in his hands, feeling so stupid for thinking that Sunny would be impressed by the Thuraya.

'What,' Sunny smirked, 'did your dad give it to you when you told him you were joining up?'

The Thuraya's tiny screen lit up and then just as quickly

blinked away. Monty didn't dare face Sunny, he felt humiliated enough already. He pressed the buttons again and again, praying the phone would turn on.

The sun was blazing, blurring everything ahead of them. Monty pushed his chin-length hair out of his face and rubbed his eyes. His skin was parched, his hair felt like straw, his sinuses and the inside of his mouth were dry and irritated. He tried to clear his throat, but it felt as though he had swallowed hundreds of burning-hot grains of sand. What if this was it – the end? He'd come all this way, ripped apart his life to travel to the end of the world looking for Layla, only to die here? His skin crawled with sweat, all across his weary, bruised body.

He bent down, held his knees and heaved dry air.

Sunny groaned audibly, 'Excellent timing, Monty.' He cocked his AK-47, holding the bolt with his index finger, pulling it back and releasing fast. The metal loading rang out in the empty desert. It was a dazzlingly cold sound.

'Sunny,' Monty whimpered as he held his stomach and retched. 'Sunny, don't.'

'Shut up, Monty.' Sunny held the assault rifle against his shoulder and, training his eye through the rear sight, started to move around the dam's perimeter.

Monty wiped the acidic vomit from his mouth with the back of his hand. He could barely stand up without feeling dizzy. He closed his eyes for a second, pulling his hand along the nape of his neck. His skin sloughed off in small rolls of black grime and dirt.

'Sunny.' Monty tripped over his shoes as he rushed to stand up. His head was spinning furiously. 'We have to lie low. We can't draw attention to ourselves.' He slunk back down to the sand, careful not to land in the mess of his vomit.

'Imma take care of this,' Sunny, who was stalking the circumference of the gates like a deer-hunter, shouted over his shoulder. 'Monty *sahib*, you rest.' His laughter echoed in the empty desert surrounding them.

Monty breathed slowly through his nostrils to avoid the sour taste in his mouth. They were in trouble. The dam was deserted. There was no one on patrol. Did Sunny understand that he was a beacon, that Monty and he alone were the advance light of the movement, its warning signal not just to their brothers back at base camp, but to the infidels ahead?

'Sunny,' Monty called weakly. 'It's dangerous here, we have to move.'

In his hands, the pale light of the Thuraya's screen flickered back to life. Off and on, on and off, briefly resuscitating, before dying.

Sunny

All of this here struggle, it means something. God's got a plan, God knows the path and, if no one else does, at least he knows what the fuck it means to have the Mosul dam deserted. He knows why it was emptied clean out, he knows why that phone of Monty's had to die right then – the only time they might actually have needed it – and he knows why their communications were strictly limited to couriers who would carry important messages by hand and mouth. Twenty-first century and all that, but the Ummah Movement's victory was going to be won analogue.

Sunny left Monty lying in a heap a safe distance from the dam. They had walked as quickly as they could, Sunny holding Monty upright, dragging his cold, sweaty body against his own. The only cover for kilometres was an old toll plaza, windows broken, springs pulled out of the chairs, no cars anywhere. Monty tried to protest, his eyes darting wildly around, looking for God knows what – soldiers, enemies, toll-booth attendants – but his body was too weak to do any bidding for the old boy. Sunny dropped him onto one of the springy, skeleton-looking chairs and left him his water bottle. Sit here and wait, he instructed Monty. Don't move.

Sunny walked back to the dam, retracing his steps without the aid of Monty's maps. There had to be an answer somewhere, it couldn't be for nothing that the dam was a dead zone. He would go back and see, just to be sure. It was the only thing that had actually happened on this depressing slog so far. First sign of any proper action.

Without the extra weight to carry and the non-stop *rat-a-tat-tat* of Monty's nagging, the distance didn't seem too daunting. Sunny walked comfortably, slowly, a hand over his eyes as protection against the blazing sun. Delicate wildflowers, thick sprays of skinny white blossoms, sprouted along the earth as Sunny neared the path towards the dam. They shouldn't still have been walking this close to noon, but now Sunny had to make sure everything was all right. What if they hadn't hit the dam till night – would they have noticed anything?

Sunny trusted. Everything was going to be fine. Unlike Monty, he wasn't slowed down by fear. Almost shat himself over the dam; Sunny had to get him to calm down and reboot, before leaving him in the booth. 'We all got troubles, son.'

Brother was grabbing his hand, trying to stop him from leaving, begging him not to go and just google it from his phone. Sunny swatted him away.

'Buck up, Monty,' he grumbled. 'You don't hear me crying about being dehydrated, about getting trachoma, 'bout being weak and alone and feeling a trembling in my stomach every night we lie down to sleep. You can't fight a low-intensity guerrilla war on Google, boss.' Fucking rich kid.

Sunny climbed the elevated guard posts of the deserted dam, eerily silent. Only the wind made any noise, whistling through doors, not fully closed, as they pulsed gently against the breeze. He entered the post and ran his hand along the guard's desk, searching for signs. His fingers picked up a coat of dust – no one had sat here for some time. He picked up a dusty beige telephone, the line was dead. He stood for a moment looking out at the dam. He'd never seen anything like it, so monstrous and industrial.

He went down the stairs, searching the steps for blood, glass, anything. But aside from a film of dirt covering the floor thick as paint, the staircase was clean. Just as he reached the bottom, the sound of a loud bang pierced the silence and Sunny stumbled, almost falling to the floor, his heart pounding before he realized it was nothing – just the door upstairs slamming. He stood up and dusted himself off. The dam was abandoned and he couldn't understand why.

But it didn't matter.

Everything meant something – Sunny didn't need to know what, he entrusted that to the Almighty. He thought of that line of Muhammad Ali's: *Just remember, you don't have to be what they want you to be.* He had fought being what they wanted his whole life, every single day, until coming here. Now Sunny was a soldier, he was brought out here for something special. He knew that. He quickened his steps away from the dam and back towards Monty, passed out at the toll booth. He would trust and he would be patient, it would all be revealed soon.

Monty

Monty pulled at the straps of his bag, wishing he wasn't carrying so much stuff. His body was damp with sour-smelling sweat, and his boots – a size too large – chafed and slid against the back of his heels with every step. Sunny said they should keep moving, regardless of the sun. If they walked fast enough, maybe they would get to the courier they were scheduled to meet in Tal Afar earlier? It was a long shot, the courier was timed to meet them just before Nineveh, but still it was something to work towards, though most of the time it seemed they were operating with no real plan, no real sense of time or organization. Monty didn't want to fight with Sunny, so he didn't say anything, but every day seemed more haphazard than the last.

They would keep moving, no exceptions, Sunny said gruffly after they left the toll plaza. They had enough water to last them till the evening, or till they came across a petrol pump or a shop somewhere. No break, Sunny insisted, not today.

Monty hobbled, quickening his gait as he tried to keep up with Sunny. 'Sunny?' he called out, hoping to slow him down slightly.

A white pickup truck barrelled down the empty highway beside them. It was the first car they'd seen all afternoon. A young boy sat in the open back, his knees bent up to his chest, shaking his shoulders and snapping his fingers, dancing and clapping to the loud Arabic pop music that tumbled out of the driver's windows. Sunny stopped and watched the truck go by. He lifted his phone out of his pocket and stretched his arm out before him, framing the truck and the boy. He clicked a picture and then brought the phone under his nose, inspecting it seriously. Only once the pickup truck had disappeared into a thick cloud of dust did he turn round.

'Kadim al Saher,' Sunny said, jerking his head towards the white truck. 'Abu Khalid made me take a load of his CDs to Baghdad.'

Monty struggled to understand.

'Must have been some sort of code,' Sunny supposed as he waited for Monty, watching him drag himself along the desert highway. He hesitated a moment and then spoke. 'You need help carrying that?'

Monty gestured to his bag. 'This? No, no, I'm okay.'

Sunny looked at him pityingly and Monty, catching the look, stood up a little straighter and walked as purposefully as he could, setting his heels down painfully into the earth instead of hopping on the balls of his feet.

'I'm fine, really,' he wiped the sweat from his brow with the back of his arm. 'I think my boots are a little big, that's all.'

Sunny looked down at Monty's Caterpillars, brand-new, hardly dirtied save for a skid of mud here and there. 'Okay,' he nodded, unconcerned, and turned back to the road. He pulled his phone out of his pocket again and tapped his finger against the screen, as though he was searching for something. He walked and searched like this for a while, before sighing and tucking his phone away once more.

In the middle of the highway lay the flattened body of an animal, grey fur and blood matted together. The wine-dark stains of its innards splattered on the road were fresh, it must have got run over this afternoon. Monty looked away from the corpse and quickened his pace slightly. 'Sunny?' He tried to keep the worry out of his voice.

Sunny stopped and waited for Monty to speak. 'What?'

'Do you think the dam was attacked?'

Sunny shrugged. He carried on walking.

If he concentrated, Monty could still hear the echo of the Iraqi music, even though the white pickup truck had long disappeared out of sight.

'I got it myself, you know,' Monty blurted out.

Sunny paused, exasperated. 'What?'

'The sat phone – I got it myself.'

A wan smile spread over Sunny's face.

Monty almost told him how Tano had taken him through Saddar's airless arcades, how he'd handed the shopkeeper 80,000 rupees, bargaining the price down from a lakh, but he knew Sunny would bristle at the mention of Tano. He wouldn't understand that everyone in Karachi had drivers; it wasn't like England.

Tano was a refugee from the north, a Pathan from Charsadda. Monty's family had helped him by hiring him, they had basically saved him and given him and his family another chance at life, but Sunny wouldn't get it.

'My dad didn't give it to me,' Monty continued, hoping this was clear. 'He didn't approve of me coming out here.'

'Okay, cool.' Sunny didn't even bother turning round.

Monty felt his admission – rather than adding an

iota of respect to Sunny's low store of feeling for his companion – had detracted what little might have existed. Was Sunny more irritated with Monty now? 'But anyway, it doesn't work, so . . .'

It occurred to Monty only then, at that moment, that Tano and his shopkeeper cousin had cheated him, selling him a broken Thuraya.

'But the dam thing is weird, don't you think?'

Sunny shrugged his broad shoulders again. Even from a small distance, even with his black shirt dusty and dirty, Monty could still make out the volume of Sunny's strength. 'Let's see,' Sunny said non-committally. Again he pulled his phone out of his pocket, unlocked it and scanned through it.

Sunny had seemed so eager to be a part of the march back in Mosul, so enthusiastic and pumped, but since they'd been walking he had reacted with a glazed indifference to everything Monty said and suggested.

Monty walked quietly for a moment, trying to piece the right words together. 'Do you think we could use your data to check the news? I mean, if you haven't already? No point fighting blind . . . right?' he ventured hopefully, echoing Sunny's own words.

Five minutes, that's all he needed, just long enough to check Layla's videos and see if she had uploaded anything new.

The highway road was deserted, not even birds circled the vast canvas of the blue sky. He waited for Sunny to answer him, but Sunny kept walking, saying nothing. Only the sound of Monty's heavy boots hitting the asphalt broke the silence between them.

'Not now,' Sunny finally said, picking up speed in his gait and walking further and further away.

*

Monty turned his throbbing head towards Sunny, squatting twenty metres away, a roll of toilet paper by his side. During the debacle at the dam, they had eaten something rancid, an expired can of tuna that Sunny had in his bag, and it had put Monty down with deadly effect. They didn't have time to look for food, Sunny said, they'd lost too much today already. He had bought the tuna before coming here, but tins don't age, he said. You can eat tuna years past the expiry date.

Monty didn't want to seem spoilt, so he ate his half of the tin without complaint. He was only just starting to recover when Sunny got hit.

They had walked less than a kilometre since then. It was early evening and the sun had begun its majestic disappearance, hiding behind the palette of the desert sky – blue and orange and pink – before it all vanished into black.

'I'm not used to water,' Sunny said, sounding defensive for the first time, when he saw that Monty had noticed the trail of toilet paper that Sunny had bought at Boots before leaving Gatwick. 'I come from the first world, Cuz.' He knew what the hadiths said, he knew that water was the only way to wash a body clean. 'But still, blood,' Sunny carried on speaking from behind the rocks, 'I don't feel like a shower every time I have to wipe my ass.'

Monty had grown tired of speaking about Sunny's bathroom habits, but if this was going to be their only meeting point of ideas, he was hardly in a position to refuse it. He had only just recovered from his own bad stomach and hoped that this would give them something to connect over.

'There's worms in my shit,' Sunny groaned.

Monty pulled out the iPhone he was using as a compass and opened the TomTom. They had only walked sixty-five kilometres so far. There were just under a hundred to go. He closed his eyes and wondered if he should tell Sunny that he was carrying antibiotics. He had brought a whole strip of Augmentin from Kausar Medico, just in case.

'Man, that's rough,' Monty said instead.

Sunny

How long is the road to the promised land? How full of stones and thunder? How many liars and thieves must I cross along the way? I'm a fighter, truth. I don't care how difficult the journey or how dangerous. Imma blaze through every obstacle my enemies throw at me. Imma build a cathedral out of this suffering, Imma grow an ocean of disciples around me.

Finally pausing for a late-afternoon break near a home pockmarked with bullet holes, Sunny turns on his roaming and edits a new Facebook post. The home must have belonged to the dam – some office or official residence. The door was bolted shut, so they sat outside against the cool cement and tried not to think too much about whether the burn marks were recent or old. Monty took a picture on his phone for the record.

Sunny had made clear that break time was private time and, keeping to his own rule, he watched Monty quietly without asking what the fuck he was doing, so as not to get drawn into a conversation. Monty walked around the structure, looking for evidence of a firefight, but aside from the burn marks, there was nothing save the splintered skeleton of a small animal, its bones bleached by the desert sun. He combed through the warm earth with his hands, bending down to inter the bones carefully, and then kicked the sand over the small, unmarked grave.

Sunny's inbox is on fire. One, two, three notifications leap out at him. At first he thinks it might be Oz, thinks he's finally summoned the courage to answer all of Sunny's emails. Must have been him explaining that the whole thing was a laugh, a mistake or something.

But it isn't him. It's Pa.

Sunny clicks away from the Tumblr post he was drafting in his notes, his hands shaking, just seeing his father's name in his inbox. Did he finally get a call from O2 about all the extra data charges? Sunny can't be cut off now, not now when he's knee-deep in building a community of followers. But it's not just Pa who's written. It's Pa and, like, five of their neighbours and friends. All with the same subject line: *Davos.*

Sunny, Pa's email begins. He hasn't written to Sunny since the week he left, more than five months ago, when it was all rage and fury, all guilt and emotional terror. Sunny never answered those emails. Didn't have the heart to. *Where have you gone?* Pa wrote in every one of those early, heartbreak letters. *Why have you left me?* Like a noose around Sunny's neck, every time he read those words. *What will I do here alone?*

And then he cut his son off. Clean slice – gone. When Sunny finally built up the courage to write to him, Pa made sure to treat his boy to some seriously cold silence.

Sunny, Pa writes now, in a good mood. *Have you seen your cousin? Looks like Oz has finally done well for himself. About time, darling. Hope you are good, though I can't pretend I don't wish you were back here with your brave cousin, instead of doing God knows what out there. Love, Papa. PS Have you been getting any job offers? I signed you up to a website, so you have options when you come back. Maybe Ozair can introduce you to some of his new contacts also?*

Huh?

Sunny clicks the link at the bottom of the email and it takes him to a CNN page. There, right onstage in front of a bright-blue backdrop, with a white broken circle that looks like a beat-up globe, is Oz, dressed up in a cream-coloured suit, pocket square, vest and a pair of brogues, buffed so you could have eaten your dinner off them. He's sat there in the middle of the stage with a microphone glued to his ear.

The video stalls, buffering. Sunny waits for it to resume, clapping his hands against his thighs. Waiting, nothing. Waiting, buffering. Ahhhh.

He pauses the video and watches for the grey bar at the bottom of the screen to creep out, so he can watch more than three seconds of the clip at a time.

Next to Oz was some brother, Farhad Zaki. Sunny googles his name as he waits for the video to load. *Desi* – Indian like them, but calls himself American now. For a second, Sunny's all excited. Oh my lord, he mumbles to himself. I don't believe it.

Oz is taking their shit global. Bringing their message out to the world. Sunny was wrong to doubt him. It was a mistake. All of it was a mistake.

For a second, he doesn't even remember Facebook and those WhatsApp messages, and he forgives his cousin. I was wrong to fight you, I forgive you, my brother, Oz.

And then Sunny hits Play:

Zaki leaning forward, looking serious: *Ozair, you've had an incredible journey.*

Oz nodding, looking tight like what. Properly dressed up for once.

Zaki: *You've gone from Britain to Syria and back again, from hate to acceptance, from radical fundamentalist – one might even say terrorist – to reformer. Your story is inspirational: in the span of one year you've run the gamut of history. First, advocating violent war against the West – the very culture you were born and raised in – and then taking up arms, recruiting vulnerable men into your religious war and playing a leading role in what you have since called 'petty religious brainwashing' – your words, not mine! Ha-ha.*

Oz leans back in his chair and buttons up his suit jacket, smiling.

Zaki: *And now you're here at Davos, joining the most influential thought leaders of our times, to talk about what you've since called your 'rebirth'.*

Oz clears his throat and shifts in his seat to face the audience, turning his knees away from Zaki: *Yes, that's right, Farhad. I call it a rebirth because my life up until this point had been crippled, morally stunted, by the religion of my birth. Turn on any television channel anywhere in the world, and all you'll see from Washington to London are Muslim apologists—*

The fuck?

The video cuts and a black screen falls over Oz's face as it stalls, coming back to life in freeze-frames: Oz leaning forward in his chair, and the words *Terror Done in the Name of Islam* scrolling in caps at the bottom of the screen; Oz smiling, reclining in his chair, *ex-Muslim warriors* in quotations, *LGBT-QIAPK Rights*, *Pro-Women*, *Anti-Sexual Apartheid Manifesto*.

Sunny can't believe his eyes.

He forwards the video to the end, dragging his finger along the bar. He catches eight seconds. Behind Oz, the beat-up globe is gone and the words *#fightbackfightextremism* fill the blue screen. *I want to invite everyone here at Davos today to join me and my think tank, Reforming—*

The connection drops. Sunny's heart aches with every word that comes out of Oz's mouth. He strains, with everything in his body Sunny strains to follow what his boy is saying. But he can't. The globe is back, the camera tight on Oz's face.

Muslims hate us—

Sunny pulls the Beats earbuds out of his ears. His head's spinning. He looks at the date of the video: it's two days old. He opens YouTube and searches for Oz's name. The video has over two million views.

Oz was his reference here. He vouched for Sunny.

How has no one in the Ummah Movement seen this?

Sunny pulls up an email and writes to his pa, the first he's written in a long time. His heart trembles as he types:

Pa, you listening to what he's saying? You were right about Oz, he's not all there. It's blasphemous! Pa, did you hear a word he said? It shames us all. It's a disgrace. He's fighting for gay rights now. Did you hear that? Pa, it's disgusting. It's wrong what he's done, Pa. It's so wrong.

Sunny looks over at Monty, searching furiously through their maps. All of them – even this duffer – came out here to die. To fight for a world on fire. And Oz is sitting on a stage, sponsored by the World Bank, bringing his people down? Speaking in hashtags like a fourteen-year-old? Dragging hundreds of brave young boys through the mud, like none of it meant anything, like he wasn't one of them, beaten down and alone.

Sunny shuts his phone, powering it off. He doesn't want to look at it. It feels like he's bleeding inside. It hurts in a place he doesn't know how to find. He puts his phone in his cargo pocket. He doesn't want it staining his fucking hands.

*

'Do you know how old this is?'

Aloush held the *tar* in his hand between fingers coiled around a cigarette. It was almost three in the morning, and small Pakistani men, wearing shapeless *shalwar kameez* and cheap plastic slippers, their eyes downcast, were sweeping the sticky floors of the small basement café.

Aloush asked one of the boys in the kitchen to brew some Turkish coffee as he sat on the edge of the DJ stage, showing Sunny the drums in his arsenal.

'Looks pretty old.'

Aloush smiled. He nudged Sunny, briefly resting his body against his. The DJ hit the tambourine against his knee. 'We made music like this for centuries. The *tar* is one of the oldest instruments in the world. Arabs have been playing this for thousands of years before the birth of Christ.' Aloush flicked his hand against it, as though he were opening a fan. The *tar* chimed like coins falling on a plate. He took a slow drag of the cigarette, almost burning his fingertips. 'You play it with one hand, okay? The other hand plays the *darbuka*.' He put the cigarette out on the heel of his boot. His arms, even there in wet, rainy Portsmouth, were golden-brown, as though he had been born under the sun.

Sunny took a sip of the coffee, thick like actual tar. It left the taste of cardamom on his tongue.

'Look,' Aloush squeezed the extinguished cigarette with his fingers, making sure it was out, before he slipped the butt into his pocket. 'Watch.'

Sunny rubbed his eyes, irritated from all the smoke in the tiny club, and leaned closer to the DJ.

Aloush ran his fingers over the skin of the *darbuka* gently, delicately, like a man slipping a hand through the open buttons of a shirt. His shoulders hunched over the *darbuka* as he played, straightening only when the arm at his side lifted to make the *tar* sing like falling metal. Even with less than three hours' sleep – he'd been up late last night watching the final season of *The Wire* – Sunny felt his body open, alive to the music, until he was moving, his body dancing as he sat on the edge of the step.

Allah allah, Aloush called, shaking his head to the music. *Allah allah*.

Sunny drummed his hands against his legs, the coffee growing cold, resting by his feet.

'Pick up the *mazhar*,' Aloush pointed to a large, round frame-drum. 'Hold it on your lap or lift it up near your ear – check the sounds.'

Sunny did both, but when he held the thin calfskin drum near his ear, he lost the ability to hear Aloush's music as separate from his own. In that moment, somehow, they played in tandem, in sync, breathing against each other.

'Do you feel me?' Aloush asked, as Sunny threw himself into the music pouring out of the Egyptian drum. 'Do you feel me, Sunny?'

Sunny felt Aloush, he saw him. And in that moment he understood that, for the first time, he too had been seen.

Monty

'Sunny, get off the phone.'

'Say what now?'

'I just meant maybe you shouldn't be on it right now? You know?'

Sunny turned round slowly, lifting his eyes off his iPhone but not lowering his hands an inch. His eyes were burning, glittering. 'You ordering me around?'

If Monty stood still, closing his eyes and breathing deeply, the scent of wild honey wafted in from the dried leaves and small flowers hidden in the desert's sparse shrubbery. But it was so faint it might not have been there at all. What he did know was that there was no smoke, no burning, no acrid smell of rubber, no metallic smell of gunfire in the air.

Monty looked over his shoulder to make sure no one had followed them. They had another forty kilometres before they reached the location where a courier would meet them, to relay anything essential before the big operation. Another forty kilometres of marching and watching the desert for signs of danger, observing the emptiness for clues and threats. The earth was lit up by a million blinding rays of sunlight. Behind them, the road wobbled hazily. Everything was distorted. Monty could be sure of nothing.

'We're totally exposed out here alone.' His voice was tense with exhaustion. 'We don't know what's happening. We're in the middle of a war, don't you think we should get moving?'

The heat of the tar rose up around them, hissing like steam escaping a valve.

Sunny stared at Monty, deadpan. 'Do I look stupid to you?'

Why was Sunny so agitated all of a sudden? Yesterday they'd been chatting and shooting the breeze as Sunny shat his guts out behind the rocks, like they were the best of friends, and now Sunny was angry that Monty dared speak to him while he was on his phone? Had something happened?

Frowning, Sunny lowered his head and went back to tapping on his phone.

Monty had woken up twice last night and heard Sunny sitting in total darkness, drumming his fingers on his thighs, as though he were playing music, like he were giving himself a private concert. Sunny didn't struggle the way Monty did, everything out here was so easy for him.

Monty envied Sunny deeply and wished he had the same confidence in himself, the same lack of fear. But the dam was deserted, they were sitting in the middle of literally nowhere and Monty was starting to feel nervous.

He looked away from Sunny. 'I just think we should be extra-careful,' he mumbled, 'that's all.'

'Extra-careful?' Sunny laughed bitterly, his voice rising. 'Who the fuck do you think you are? James Bond?' He stood up as he locked his phone with his thumb and slipped it into the pocket of his cargo trousers. He pulled up the sleeves of his black shirt. 'The fuck makes you think you can tell me what to do?'

'Sunny.' Monty shook his head, blinking as sweat dripped down his forehead and into his eyes. 'Dude, chill out. Don't swear like that.'

Sunny shrugged his backpack's straps off his shoulders, dumping it on the shallow grave Monty had just dug. 'Do you have a clue about anything happening out here?' He clenched his teeth and stepped right up to Monty, almost pressing his own nose into Monty's, breathing heavily.

What was happening? All he'd said was that they should proceed cautiously. Monty edged away from Sunny, stumbling slightly. He'd never been in a fight before.

'Don't tell me what to do and what not to do, you rich fuck. Don't tell me how this organization works, brother. I've studied. I didn't come here to get over some fucking heartbreak.'

Monty kept quiet. His heart pounded hard against his ribcage. He searched Sunny's face. His whole body stung with fear. If anyone in the Ummah Movement knew about Layla, she would be dead.

'Nah, mush. I studied. I watched the horizon. You think I came here because I had nothing else to do?' Sunny hit his chest with his hand, his voice climbing with anger. 'There are more of us Britons here than there are Muslims in the British army. You think that's a mistake? You think we stumbled into this piece of shit country because we came from one? Na, brother. I'm not from Pakistan. I don't come from a random ass country. I came here to defend the Shariah. I didn't come here to become a Muslim, I came here because I *am* a Muslim. So don't you think I'm waiting for you' – Sunny spat at the space between them – 'of all people, to teach me what's allowed and what's not.'

He turned round and picked up his bag, running his hand angrily across the canvas fabric, wiping it clean of dust before slipping it onto his shoulder.

Monty stood in his place. His ears were ringing from Sunny shouting so close to his face.

Sunny

*I'm a man out on his own in the desert, a man in the wild, and there's
some ex-brothers, sitting at home, in enemy territory . . .*

*. . . running back to the world we left to fight, to destroy, to bring to
its fucking knees.*

I'm out here creating, devastating, and what're U doing?

*Wasting valuable kinetic energy, running our struggles into the
ground, LETTING OUR people DOWN.*

Sunny tweets without editing, without pause. The desert
is bathed in darkness. He didn't light a fire, didn't do his
usual routine of gathering small twigs and dry fauna. They
have no light, no warmth. It must be late, twelve, twelve-
thirty, but Sunny doesn't want to set up camp for the
night; they'll walk another two hours at least. This is just
a break, he needs time to process Oz's shit, needs five
minutes to absorb all this hurting. The midnight breeze
carries with it the smell of smoke, of something burning
in the distance, a disturbance in the atmosphere that
reminds you no matter how desolate the desert feels, you
are never truly alone. Sunny grinds his teeth; he wants to
tag Oz, but it's too risky. He can't have anyone out here
clock what's happened. Not now, not before he has some
way of protecting himself against his cousin's betrayal,
some feather in his cap, some proof of loyalty.

Where's his apology? Where's his refund on belief, on

trust? Oz sent him out here with promises tinted in gold, and Sunny believed him. Not once did Oz stop to think about his cousin. About what Sunny was going through, about the danger he was in. Oz just abandoned him. Like he never knew Sunny at all. Like he never even cared.

Sunny opens his in-box. *Downloading 1 out of 10 emails*, it says. EDGE drops. For a second he gets GPRS. Then nothing. No service.

He goes into Settings and does the acrobatics of un-selecting his mobile carrier, then reselecting it. Airplane mode on, then off. The little wheel spins furiously, spitting the first email out at him.

Pa.

The dread Sunny used to feel at not seeing his father's name in his in-box now slithers down his spine when he does. Sunny opens the email, his heart heavy.

Darling, don't be silly. Your cousin isn't gay. It's just what people say these days to get attention. Good of you to finally write your old man. When are you coming home? Love, Papa.

Never, Pa.

I'm never coming back.

Sunny hears the whoosh of his outgoing mail at the same time as O2 – worst fucking roaming on earth – downloads the other nine incoming. And there it is.

Sunny knew it.

Of course Oz would write. First email after Pa's is from him. Finally. Oz can't dodge Sunny forever, hiding like he don't know who Oz is.

Sunny knows Oz. He knows Oz like nobody does. He's his shadow, his spirit animal, his true self. Sunny sees all that shit of Oz's and he knows he's playing like he is because he's afraid. Because this life is a lonely passage, because to fight is to change forever the chemistry of one's existence. It's an act. Sunny sees it.

But Oz hasn't written from his usual email address, but a new one: ozair@reformingradicals.co.uk, and the subject line reads *'Great News'*:

Reforming Radicals — Newsletter 1, January 2017

A Rebirth!

Dear Subscriber,

Welcome to our first newsletter! We have great news to share (and it's only the beginning!). Fresh off my inspirational talk at Davos, I've been invited to speak at TED 2017. We will send you behind-the-scenes photos and exclusive videos, but make sure to subscribe to our Instagram, Snapchat, Twitter and Facebook!

I will be speaking to the Oxford Union this week (check our Facebook for tickets – they're almost sold out!) so watch this space.

Peace,

Ozair, Founder and CEO, Reforming Radicals

Is someone you know a radical?

It can happen to anyone. Muslims have been brainwashed for centuries. Young men and women are easy prey for radicals. Check out our Facebook for the ten signs to watch out for, and if you suspect anyone you love has been radicalized, call our joint Reforming Radicals–Scotland Yard hotline **0800 442 890**. We can protect you.

Suppressed by patriarchy

Next week, Lina, abused and disempowered by her Muslim family for years, will be taking over our Instagram page and posting a few of her favourite things. Follow us at @Reformingradicals to learn more about Lina and how we help brave women like her to escape the crushing effects of Muslim male privilege.

Our mantra!

I renounce religion. I reject their propaganda. I am ready to reform my heart.

Unsubscribe

It's one thing to turn your back on your brothers, and another to go out in public and trash your religion, your people, your history and side with the oppressor, just cos he invited you to some nerdfest in Switzerland, but then to sign up the *very* people whose lives you destroyed by leading them out into battle before dumping them? What makes you think we want to read your mutinous newsletter? That was cold. Even for Oz.

Sunny pulls at the hair along his face. He's started getting fungus in his beard. When he scratches at the skin underneath his hair, small yellowish flakes peel off into his nails.

Sunny taps open Oz's Instagram. No pictures of Oz in bath towels that he can see, as the posts load slowly, four grey boxes out of fifteen, but homeboy has 40K followers. He goes into Twitter and types in 'Ozair Reforming Radicals' – and there he is, a new account and all. Sunny clicks on it. Revolutionary, Oz's name comes up even though his handle is @CEOreformrads.

Sell-out.

He wants to google Oz, to check his Facebook, to see if anyone has clocked onto his game from out here, but he just can't. Sunny doesn't have the heart to see if Oz is dirtying up the only thing he ever believed in, egged on by tens of thousands of followers.

This is the struggle our men are destined to face and fight until we win. Our horizons go further than Iraq.

Sunny is back on his Twitter:

This here's just a pit-stop, a battle run till our real jihad, our true war — reclaiming the world for our wounded people.

Punishing + destroying the infidels within our tribe.

He deletes the newsletter and starts erasing the rest of the emails. There's one from Aunty and Uncle, another from the university, another from Ben. Sunny can't deal with what he has to say about this nonsense. Guess Pa didn't tell anyone he was out here. He wasn't proud of Sunny, not the way he is of Oz.

Sunny opens up an email and types in Oz's old address.

It's not enough to always have to stare these racists down, but like all the time?

The whole world's eyes are on them — watching, judging, condemning. No one knows that more than Oz. What you playing at, Oz? What about our struggle? What about the war we were supposed to be waging for our wounded, battered pride?

Fuck you, Oz, Sunny types, his hands shaking. *Fuck you, you fucking faggot.*

*

What's your name, really?

Aloush.

Is that a Muslim name?

He laughed. What a question. But when he saw Sunny's face fall in embarrassment, he answered. Ali, he said, that was his name. He'd left Damascus after the Spring, after the euphoria and the tear gas cleared and friends started leaving, running away. His mother said it wasn't safe any more, no one knew what was happening, no one knew who to trust. Damascus was falling, she said, her voice caught in her throat. But Ali refused to leave.

Damascus could never fall. Damascus would never fall and Ali would never leave, but eventually, just as the sun rose in the east and set in the west, Ali would slip out of the only city he had ever loved. With a promise to return in weeks, he travelled first to Beirut. Then to Dubai. Then Athens. Then here, to England, another constellation away. Home was all he thought about, Aloush said, it was woven into all the strands and languages of his dreams.

Why do you go by 'Aloush'?

Why are you asking, Sunny?

Sunny laughed.

Because no one at school could pronounce my name; called me Sal-mon, like the fish, till I was eleven.

Aloush drank his second cup of *qahwa*. That's what they called the coffee whose grains ground against your teeth if you drank it to the bottom of the cup.

My mother, she always called me Aloush.

Sunny lowered his head and nodded. It's beautiful, he said so softly that Ali, whose ears were permanently drumming with blood from the loud music, couldn't hear.

Monty

Monty and Layla spoke every night till three or four in the morning.

'All my life I had to fight,' she told Monty on the phone late one night, unexpectedly revealing details he had barely suspected. It hadn't been easy for her family, living in the shadow of Karachi's big families, a city that for all its riches and openness had never given the Yusufs any space and never, ever let them in, no matter how smart, how hard-working they were. Till the American School, Layla hadn't imagined this sort of inclusion was possible; she had spent her childhood being looked down at by Karachi's finest, acknowledged only with disdain.

It really messed with her brother, Layla said. He never got over being cast out, never forgave the humiliation he suffered at the hands of the rich who worked their family down to their bones.

Monty held his phone away from his face, listening to Layla on speaker. He suddenly felt miserable. He had only thought of her so far as she existed for him – Layla who was born of his love, and lived within the exclusive borders of their relationship.

Sitting up, leaning against the headboard of his bed, the black silk sheets gathered at his feet, listening to Layla's voice echo in his air-conditioned bedroom, Monty saw Layla for the first time outside the safety of his imagination, returned to this ravaged city, held against this background of torment and inequality.

Her brother, in recent years, had used all his anger, all his fury, against the world. He had taken his lifetime of struggle and pain and imposed it on others. This was his due, he felt. He used whatever he needed to get ahead – the cost didn't matter. It was how the world worked, he told his sister, how the rich suffocated the poor and the wanting, since the beginning of time. His ambition took on the shape of cruelty at times, of single-minded ruthless focus, Layla said, but their family was set, finally. His Arab clients paid well and they had connected him to all their local associates and business partners. They trusted him and, for his part, Layla's brother was always coming up with new schemes to entice them.

She loved her brother, though. It was thanks to him that her family now lived in a two-bedroom flat, that she could go to the American School, that they had – for the first time in their lives – some savings. Sure, he was controlling and difficult, but who else did she have? You know what they say?

'What?' Monty asked.

'A friend loves at all times, and a brother is born for adversity.'

'Who said that?' Monty sat up on his elbow and typed Layla's quote into an email for himself, so he would always remember it.

'It doesn't matter. Family is family; you don't tear ties with blood.'

'You don't have to fight any more,' Monty promised Layla, clicking out of his email, turning the phone off speaker and returning it to his face. 'You have me. I'm here now.'

But Layla didn't say thank you, she didn't sound relieved.

Later that week, after Monty and his father tied a game of tennis at the Sindh Club and were sitting on the verandah, drinking cold Murree beer, Monty turned to Akbar Ahmed for a favour.

'Papa?'

'Hmm?' Akbar, who had been on his phone, his eyebrows furrowed in concentration, stood up quickly, springing up from his wicker chair as a gentleman in tight white sports-shorts called out his name. The uncle *salam*'ed and shook hands with Papa and enquired after his tennis score. Monty thought he saw his father's face contort when he heard the man in the snug shorts, which rode up his hairy thighs, announce the results of his afternoon game.

'Who does he think he is? Boris Becker *ka bacha*,' Akbar Ahmed winced as he sat back down in his chair. His phone beeped and he reached for it, unlocking the home screen with his thumb.

'Papa,' Monty began again. 'I've got this friend.'

But his father was jabbing his phone with one finger. 'Bloody keyboard . . .'

'He's a bit older, Papa. Last name, Yusuf. He's quite hard-working and entrepreneurial. His name—'

'Don't know how anyone gets anything done on these things.' Akbar Ahmed lifted his chilled glass and took a swig of beer. 'Why BlackBerry went under, I'll never understand.'

Monty, sitting with his arms crossed at his knees and feeling suddenly exposed in his Nike tennis shorts and T-shirt, leaned forward. His father wasn't typing an email, he was on some Bollywood news site. His screen was magnified and in a blank search bar he typed, with one crooked finger, D E E P I K

'Papa?' Monty lifted the legs of his own cane chair and edged closer to his father, who paused his search, as though only just made aware of his son's presence.

'*Arre* what?'

'My friend, Papa, do you think he could work for you? Or somewhere in the company?'

Akbar Ahmed looked at his son with concern.

'Who is this fellow?'

'A friend,' Monty replied casually, wondering how he would tell Layla's brother of this new job opportunity, without him knowing about Monty and his sister. Layla would have to tell him herself. She would be so happy. Monty smiled to himself; already he was taking care of her. Already he was helping her change her life.

But Monty's father put down his phone, not bothering to lock it. His website loaded, pixelated images of Deepika Padukone in a tight black tracksuit playing tennis with Roger Federer, holding onto the tennis great and laughing, popped up across the screen.

'How old is he?'

Akbar picked up the beer he had poured for his son. A ring of condensation circled the glass table where the ice-cold beverage had been.

Monty shrugged. 'Must be twenty-four, twenty-five.'

Akbar snapped his fingers for one of the passing Sindh

Club bearers, an old man with long drooping ears. He placed the beer on the old servant's tray. *Nikalo*, he ordered, before turning back to his son. 'An alumnus?'

No, Monty shook his head. 'No, Papa, he lives in Gulshan.'

Gulshan? Akbar repeated carefully.

Gulshan, Monty confirmed.

Two uncles holding folded copies of *Dawn* walked by, stopping to pay their respects to Akbar Ahmed, CEO of Kingdom Realty, largest land developers in Pakistan. But Monty's father stayed seated in his cane chair, acknowledging them, but not standing up to meet their hands.

Monty lifted his elbows off his knees and rose to his feet. He *salam*'ed the uncles who, unhappy with his father's snub, merely nodded and carried on their way.

'Gulshan,' Akbar Ahmed muttered, turning in his seat to signal for the bill. 'What kind of people are you associating with?'

The bearer with the long Buddha-lobes returned with a leather billfold, which he placed before Akbar. 'Sir,' he exhaled, so as not to interrupt or intrude.

Akbar snapped open the leather book. 'I spend a fortune on that school, just so you can pick up leeches from God knows where.' He scratched his signature onto the tab and handed it back to the old waiter.

Monty said nothing as his father stood up, put his phone into his pocket and bent down to pick up his racket. 'You should keep your distance from those sorts of people, Mustafa.'

Akbar strode off towards the parking lot, leaving Monty sitting in his cane chair, the weave from the wicker tattooing the backs of his thighs.

As he sat next to Tano in the Audi, as the Pathan drove them back home, Monty tried to speak to his father. 'It was just a thought,' he mumbled, 'I don't know him that well . . .'

But Akbar Ahmed said nothing. He put on his reading glasses and poked his touchscreen phone with his index finger. Monty turned back in his seat and faced the road. As they drove back to Clifton, Tano's eyes shifted to Monty's thighs and Monty pulled at his Nike shorts, trying to cover the red stripes of skin imprinted by the cane chair.

In the mornings Layla came to school with her *kajal* from the night before not properly washed off and her hair not properly brushed. It hung loosely down her back in greasy waves, smelling faintly of cigarettes.

Layla stashed in her locker every morning the *dupatta* that her brother packed her off with, but when she was in the mood, she took it out during lunchtime and draped it over Monty's lap in the lounge.

Once, while watching MTV, she unbuttoned Monty's jeans with one hand and touched him. 'Quiet,' Layla said, her face turned away from him and towards the television, 'or I'll stop.' But Monty already knew he didn't need that. He only wanted to be near her, to hold her, to kiss the mole beneath her lips, to touch his lips to her eyes, left first, then right.

'Layla,' Monty would say gently, 'you don't have to do that.'

He cared that people would see and that they would think badly of her, of the girl he loved. And Monty loved

her, so much that he would have paid any price, any sacrifice, to preserve what was pure and noble about Layla.

'Shhh,' Layla would reply, not even looking into his
eyes, reaching her hand into his jeans somewhat force-
fully. 'You'll ruin it.'

One time, a freshman walked into the lounge's TV
room, a short boy with scraggly hair. He had forgotten his
bag inside and had come to get it, but standing by the
door, he saw Layla and Monty. Monty had his head back
against the sofa and was breathing deeply. Layla had laid
the *dupatta* across him and was leaning close against him,
speaking to him, whispering into his ear, trying, unsuc-
cessfully, to make him hard.

The bell had already rung and everyone had gone back
to class, except the two of them. The freshman just stood
there and watched. He couldn't believe what they were
doing. He watched for a good minute before Layla saw
him. But when she did, she didn't stop. She smiled. Layla
smiled, withdrew her hand from Monty's trousers and
blew the freshman a kiss.

It was a miracle the boy didn't tell the principal. It was
a miracle that Layla, with her soft face free of make-up,
except the smudges of eyeliner across her eyes and a small
mole underneath her pink, unlined lips, got away with
murder like she did.

Monty's world was so much simpler before Layla. But it
was also empty, that was true.

It was easy, too easy.

One spring afternoon, waking up late and fiddling with
the Nespresso machine in the upstairs kitchen, Monty

heard shouting coming from his mother's room. He walked towards the noise, pulling up his boxer shorts as he shuffled into his mother's walk-in closet, where he found her, hair uncovered and undone, shouting at the maid. Angelise was sniffling and wiping her face with the balled-up end of a *dupatta* that Zahra insisted she wore around the house.

'Calm down, Mummy,' Monty tried to pacify his mother. But Zahra was enraged. The maid had left the laundry in the sun and something had got ruined.

Angelise had apologized, Zahra said, but it wasn't going to fix the damage. 'These Christians say sorry all the time, they don't mean anything they say. Nayar *sahib* was right about them. I should have fired her months ago.'

Monty was seventeen, but it was the first time he'd ever noticed his mother's unkindness – the way her face reddened from the exhaustion of shouting, the way her wiry black hair had started to grow grey at the roots – and it made him sad.

'She's sorry, Ma.' Monty gestured for the maid to leave the room. 'She's made a mistake, she's crying, maybe you could apologize, too?'

It was a compassionate thing to suggest, he thought. A big-person way to defuse the situation, befitting their standing and education, but his mother's full, chocolate eyes narrowed.

'You want me to say sorry to my servant?' Zahra's lip pinched and her face contorted with disgust. Monty hadn't noticed how brittle his mother's long hair had become, since she stopped going to the salon for her colour and blow-dries. 'My servant!' Zahra laughed harshly, throwing her head back, forgetting briefly about the transgressions of the small, frightened Filipina.

When he mentioned the incident to Layla, later that night on the phone, she held her breath.

'What?' Monty asked.

'Your mother is oppressive,' Layla said in a quiet voice. 'I mean, I'm sorry, but your mother is the very condition that this country needs to fight.'

Monty fell quiet, but Layla did not seem to notice.

'Your mother, Monty? All her "charity" and do-gooding? It's just vanity.'

Before he could mount a feeble defence of his mother, Layla drew a long breath. 'Truly they speak, only those who have seen the truth.'

He could hear the pity in her words.

Life before Layla had been easier; Zahra was not an oppressor then, not a condition, not a 'confused construct of post-colonial anxiety', whatever that meant. She was difficult and demanding, but Monty assumed that only he could see that. Until Layla, it had simply not occurred to him that all lives were lived in glass houses. And one's duty as a conscious man was to be a stone-thrower.

Once he understood that the Ahmeds and their genesis of the nation dream were false, things would never be easy again. Layla pulled all Monty's edifices down. Without her, he would have known nothing – especially what was painful – about the world.

Sunny

Sunny stands still and listens for animals scavenging for food in the moonless night. Monty's behind him, maintaining a careful distance and waiting. Without Monty's map-reading, Sunny can't tell how much they've walked, but he knows it isn't enough. They're behind schedule for the Tal Afar courier, for Nineveh, for everything.

Sunny heard brothers back in Mosul speak of jackals, wild cats, even caracals. But so far they've been lucky, they haven't come across any beasts on the march.

'Sunny?'

Sunny grits his teeth and ignores Monty. It's been at least 5K without a squeak from him but Monty can't hold it in any longer.

'Should we stop for the night and set up camp?'

Sunny turns his face away when he sees Monty hesitate, unsure whether to approach him or not. He hasn't spoken to Monty for hours, not since he spat at his shoes.

'Do whatever you want.' He walks on.

Nobody hurt Oz for nothing. He came back from Syria a glorious man, a fighter. He was happy. Sunny saw it. He didn't imagine it.

He walks as far as his feet will take him, but his bones are tired and his spirit fatigued. He makes it maybe another two kilometres before he sets his bag down in the sand. Sunny can hear Monty wheezing behind him.

He bends down and sits on his knees, combing his fingers through the desert floor. The sand is golden and, even in the dark, Sunny sees the grains of sand shimmer. He bends his face down to the dry earth and breathes in deeply. It smells like moisture, fresh like the falling rain, like sage.

This is all Sunny has in the world.

He feels the warmth of the dirt and the rocks against his forehead. The smell of burnt, old grass climbs his nostrils. He doesn't want to stand. Sunny doesn't want to rise.

He could take Oz's newsletter, his video, his Twitter to Abu Khalid, but Oz was his guarantor here. If they know what Oz is saying, if they know what he's done, they'll turn on Sunny. He would have to prove himself in Nineveh, once and for all, without a doubt.

He keeps his eyes closed and although Monty's been smart enough to keep away from him, Sunny senses his closeness. He can feel Monty staring at him, afraid.

Beads of sweat collect on the bridge of Sunny's nose, behind his ears, falling slowly down his neck. Not even the night breeze soothes him. Nothing can calm Sunny now.

He feels wounded, bare. That's the thing with betrayal — it's always the people you love.

It's never the serpents hiding in the rose bush, never the users or the liars. They hit you in the front. Only your family, your blood, come at you from behind.

Sunny lifts himself up and, feeling for small twigs and dead wood in the dark, starts a small fire.

He gave up everything; he turned his back on something true for Oz.

Sunny lights the wood, it takes a moment to catch. He sits on his haunches and presses his fists into his eyes.

Monty clears his throat softly.

Sunny shakes off the defeat curling into his bones, hunching his shoulders, feeling him old. Why am I here babysitting this kid, this nobody?

He opens his bag and takes out two tins of Spam and holds one out. Monty hesitates, like he's afraid to touch Sunny. Like he's poison.

'You don't wanna eat now?'

Monty nods quickly, too quickly, and grabs the tin, pulling the lid back and eating the cold, pink meat with his fingers.

Sunny bought the grub at a shop – before the dam, before Oz – while charging his phone. It feels like another time, another world he wanted to be connected to, plugged into. He glances at the blue tin. Everything except SPAM is written in Arabic. It's glutinous and salty, and Sunny can't taste a thing.

He chews quietly, putting down the half-eaten tin.

It's a wound he doesn't know how to explain. Sunny unclips the tanto on his belt and leans back against his bag, tracing patterns in the sand with the blade.

Monty scrapes the tin with his fingernails, sucking the meat and licking his skin.

Oz, if I could tear your throat out with my bare hands, just to show you a dusting of the pain I feel right now, I'd climb the world to find you.

Sunny rolls down onto his side and stares at the Whats-App message for a moment before deleting it, the Tanto still in his hands, and closes his eyes.

Monty

Monty tiptoed around his bag in the dark, careful not to make any noise. He held his breath as he moved, as though the slightest exhalation would rattle the earth. He walked like this, feeling his way for a minute or two. The night was as dark as he'd ever seen it, like coal. Not a star shone in the distance.

The leather of his boots tightened around his already bloated skin. He had watery blisters all over his heels and toes and he felt the discomfort in his nerves now, clipping him with a searing pain.

He held his hands out in front of him, making sure there were no shrubs or skeletal trees in his path. He kicked the dry soil gently with his boots – there were no large rocks before him. He was far enough away.

But still he looked over his shoulder, checking for the glow of the small fire Sunny had lit.

The desert was quiet, except for the feeble crack of the fire. He unzipped his trousers and relieved himself. His stomach hurt as he urinated. Monty leaned his body back, careful not to dirty his boots, opening his legs a step wider. He waited a second and winced at a sharp pain in his side. He urinated a bit more, sighing softly as a trickle of dark liquid hit the sand.

Zipping up his trousers, he walked back to their small camp, careful not to wake Sunny. He slept curled into a foetal position, his hands tucked between his legs. He had been wearing the same black shirt and cargo trousers since they left Mosul. Sunny smelled terrible, a peppery, pungent odour that clogged Monty's nose when he stood near him. 'Sunny,' Monty had spoken to the back of his head earlier, 'should we set up camp for the night?' It made no sense what they were doing – stopping in the middle of the desert for no reason, sitting there while Sunny tapped on his phone, then getting up and walking another two hours. What kind of schedule was that?

He could barely make out the shape of Sunny's dark curls hanging loosely down the nape of his neck, but he watched his words travel, suspended in the darkening gloaming between them and, if he had not seen them land and seen Sunny flinch, as though crawling with disgust, he would have thought the desert was playing tricks on him. How had Sunny known about Monty's heartbreak? How had Sunny seen through him – seen through all his sadness and weakness and worry? Was he that pathetic?

Gingerly, Monty sat back down on the desert floor and opened his bag, removing a sweater. At night a cold chill whipped through the air. What he really should have brought was a scarf, something to cover his ears with as he lay down to sleep, but he hadn't thought of that. It must have been two in the morning, but Monty's mind was racing with worry. If the dam had been attacked, then local militia forces could be on their way to Nineveh right now, headed towards Layla.

As his eyes adjusted to the spray of light from the fire, Monty observed Sunny carefully. Why had he crouched down to sniff the earth earlier – for what? Wolves? Monty had watched Sunny nervously from several metres away.

He didn't understand what had happened, why Sunny was so angry at him.

After they ate, Sunny had unclipped the knife he wore on the belt of his cargo trousers, and Monty felt his body go cold with anxiety. But then Sunny just sat there, biting his lip as he shaded etchings in the sand with the tip of his blade.

Monty looked at Sunny now, his eyes fluttering, as though sand had got trapped in his lashes, fast asleep.

He sprang to his feet again and tiptoed towards Sunny's bag. And there, just as he expected it to be, tucked underneath his bag, was Sunny's phone. Its screen was shattered, like it had been dropped, the sides scuffed and scratched. Slowly, so slowly that he couldn't be sure if his hand was moving at all, Monty extracted the silver iPhone from beneath Sunny's bag.

With the cold phone in his hand, Monty silently retraced his steps away from the fire. His boots felt the earth for rocks, while his fingers clicked the volume off and typed in the password he had seen Sunny use: 786.

It was shorthand for *bismillah*. Monty knew that, from listening to his mother's televangelist. Nayar *sahib* said every good Muslim should write the numbers on the top of every letter, email and Facebook post. Zahra even scribbled it at the top of her Agha's shopping lists.

Sunny had dozens of folders on his phone. Monty was tempted to look through them, just to see what Sunny busied himself with all the time on that phone, but he was too nervous about Layla to check any of them.

After swiping past pages and pages of folders, Monty found YouTube and typed in Layla's name. Even though he was protected by the vast darkness of the awesome night sky, he shielded the phone with his hand, careful to protect the little boxes of Layla collecting on the screen.

There she was.

Layla sitting at a desk, assault rifle laid out in front of her.

Layla standing in front of captured territory.

Layla hugging children in khaki fatigues.

Layla, Layla, Layla.

He swept through the videos until he found what he was looking for and clicked the volume back on, low:

'This is civilization – what you are witnessing here. You were born with this knowledge when your father whispered the azan *in your ear before you heard the sound of any other human voice: I bear witness that there is no God except God.'*

The camera panned away from the soft contours of Layla's noble face, untouched by the darkness of the sun, until one could barely see the mole under her lip. She was paler than Monty remembered; even the black circles that lined her eyes in the mornings were gone. Maybe she had even stopped smoking.

Back in Karachi, when she got home every day after school, Layla texted Monty on her secret phone to tell him she had reached home. The city was so unsafe, he always wanted to know she was okay. He had never noticed Karachi's dangers before, he had nothing to protect then.

Papa had contacts in the police, and an armed constable sat beside Tano whenever Monty left his house. Private security guards were stationed outside their Clifton home. The Ahmeds had a three-tonne generator in their garage and never felt Karachi's constant power cuts, even when the electricity flickered on and off in the rest of the city.

'I bet God even protects you from the rain,' Layla said sadly, as she sat behind Monty's driver in his white uniform, bulletproof sheeting on the windows and the police officer unenthusiastically scanning the street, the one time Monty snuck her home in his car. Tano looked nervously at her in the rear-view mirror, his eyes dancing back to the road whenever Monty noticed his gaze falling on Layla.

His parents were in Dubai, and Layla wanted to get high. She showed Monty the small ball of *charas* she had taken from her brother. All they had to do was empty the tobacco out of her cigarettes and crumble the sweet-smelling hashish in with the leaves. She had enough for three cigarettes.

Monty didn't do drugs, but Layla smiled at him, that smile of hers that was empty and suggestive at the same time, and promised it would be worth it. You'll feel good, she assured him. Everything felt good on *charas*. It drowns all your sorrows, Layla said, it feels like Paradise.

'Don't tell my parents,' Monty said to Tano as they got out of the car in the driveway. The older Pathan, who had stood to open Monty's door, lowered his head and said nothing. 'Okay?' Monty repeated. 'Don't say anything?' But Tano didn't speak, he didn't answer yes or no in his shy, faltering Urdu. He kept his eyes trained on his feet, on the metal buckle of his black sandals that dragged on the floor.

At the time, Monty laughed at Layla's throwaway comment – what else could he do? – but months later, driving home during the monsoons, he noticed the boys in the thin *banyans*, *shalwars* hiked up to their knees, sitting in the middle of the flooded roads, soaked to the bone.

Monty watched those dark, skinny boys, drenched with no promise of shelter over their heads, and knew that Layla, in her sadness, had been right.

Monty looked at the time stamp under the video – yesterday. He focused on the date, making totally sure. He had to be 100 per cent certain Layla was safe.

She was in Nineveh. Ninawa. Nothing had happened to the operation.

Monty looked up at Sunny, checking that he hadn't felt for his phone and woken up. He watched him for a moment, making sure Sunny hadn't heard Layla's voice. But he lay with his knees curled against his chest, dead to the world. Monty turned back to Layla, beautiful Layla, standing at the gates of Nineveh. Ninawa. Whatever.

'While we were mapping the stars, Europeans were living in the dark. While Muslims were measuring the revolutions of the earth around the sun and charting the rebirth of the moon every twenty-eight days, those barbarians were trapped in caves, dying of the plague. Of course they fear death, they know nothing of the divine.'

It had 10,000 views already and hundreds of comments.

Monty clicked the tab shut. He had to be careful and quick, putting the phone back before Sunny heard him and woke up. But his finger hovered: would it be so wrong if he looked to see what Sunny had been doing on his phone earlier? Would he even know? Monty glanced up at Sunny, his eyes quivering in REM sleep. He wouldn't suspect a thing.

But Sunny's history had already been scrubbed – everything except Monty's one search.

PART THREE

Truly They Speak, Only Those Who Have Seen the Truth

2016–17

Anita Rose

Karachi, 2016

They sat on the worn weave of Osama's forgotten *charpai*, the heat of the slum oppressive without the distraction of *jiyala* anthems playing on neighbourhood radios. The power was out again; it had been days and days with no electricity. Without the twinkling of the small shop lights, it was as though they had been cut off from the city itself.

Anita snuck out of home and travelled in the dark to come and sit with her comrade and keep him company as he drank into the night. It had been weeks since he'd seen her – she had disappeared, busy with her new life since her brother had packed them off to Gulshan.

Osama said that before – before Machar Colony had become a rotting slum – there had been a water tank up here and he used to climb up and bathe on the roof, drying his skin under the sultry Karachi sun.

He held his glass in his hands, kept his fingers wrapped around it still, after all these years, shielding it from Anita. But she could smell the spirit, strong like rubbing alcohol, suffocating the air between them. He had drunk more than Anita Rose had ever seen before; this was his sixth glass and he moved like a shadow of himself now.

'Comrade,' Osama began, bending his body down to pick up the opaque plastic bottle resting by his feet. He swayed uncertainly for a moment and then twisted open the blue cap and filled his glass to the top. It hadn't been empty.

Anita tried to read the label on the bottle, but Osama turned it away from her.

'Anita Rose,' he exhaled. His eyes were sleepy. 'Anita, you don't belong in this jungle.'

They had been discussing a black writer. The only way to look at powerful societies was through the people they excluded, Osama said. The blacks encapsulated all the sorrow of their history in art – in music, in literature, in dance. The way the Sindhis or Baloch did here. Even as they suffered, the blacks sang to the world of beauty and terror.

'I don't belong anywhere,' she said.

'Ezra's dreams are not yours,' he asked, or concluded, Anita couldn't be sure. She said nothing at the mention of her brother's forgotten name. Osama twirled the warm glass in his hands.

No, she assured her older friend, though she had little idea what her own dreams might be. No, she assured him, because she knew that was what he wanted to hear. Feroze had got her admission to a new, private school, through one of his contacts. It was Feroze who would have to pay the gargantuan tuition fees, through loans and debts and promises. He was changing her life, her brother promised. Before she knew it, all this – the wanting, the poverty, the disguises they were forced to wear through life – would be a distant memory.

Feroze didn't like Anita coming over here, to their radical neighbour's house. You have to keep your head down, Feroze told his sister, don't draw unnecessary attention to yourself.

But why did Anita Rose have to hide, while Feroze's horizons grew and grew? Theirs was a life that operated only in the shadows, he said. They had to lie low if they were going to live outside the rules. Feroze was constantly lecturing Anita, constantly reprimanding her. He was working on something big – really big – like he always was. It was just a matter of being patient, of being accommodating. Didn't she trust him? Hadn't he always taken care of her?

'I think you're ready, my little lion,' Osama smiled as they sat on the roof of his building in the warm summer night.

The monsoons had come late that year and while August had been dry and lonesome, September had been rich with rain. All the colony streets below were flooded with oily water. Even in the dark, up on the roof, Anita could hear people splashing through the puddles as they walked down the dim lanes.

'I think you're ready to have this all to yourself.' Osama had been teaching her about Habib Jalib for some weeks, not just his poetry, but the impact of his words on martyrs, fighters and men. And now he gifted her the dusty book. 'I am a poor man, but this, my dear, is the greatest inheritance I can give you.'

Anita looked at the stains on the black-and-red cover, a cheap bazaar reproduction, and wet her fingertips with her tongue. She ran her index finger around the old glass stains, rubbing away the darkened spots of dried wine, hoping Osama would not notice that she had seen the marks.

Confiscate the fields from the landowners, take away the mills from robbers, redeem the country from its dark hours ... What does Pakistan mean? There is no God ...

Anita paused, her finger hovering over the book, hesitating.

Should she have taken this? Without being fully aware of what she was doing, she lifted the Jalib from her lap and placed it down on the floor. As soon as it landed, Osama picked it up and placed it back in her arms.

'Don't be afraid,' he said gently, understanding before Anita could speak. It was that new school of hers; fitting in, blending into the crowds, had made her afraid of her own shadow. He could see her hesitate now, about everything. 'There's nothing blasphemous in it.' Osama patted the book lightly, setting off a cloud of powdery dust.

Anita Rose felt her stomach twist. She had snuck out of her home to come here; her brother was still out and her mother never noticed she was gone. The air was perfumed with the smell of *champa* flowers, thick like honey. The monsoons hadn't come; the night air was heavy and swollen with the promise of rain. But now all she wanted to do was run back and curl up on the floor next to her mother's warm body. Anita lowered her eyes.

'What is it?' Osama leaned closer to her.

'Ezra's changed his name,' Anita said, without looking up at her friend.

'His what?'

'He's calling himself Feroze now. He says it's the only way for our people to survive here.'

Osama shook his head angrily. 'He's a fool, your brother. The only way for anyone to survive here is to fight.' The old comrade ran his hands through his silver hair. 'Everyone has to fight here. What does he think: they just hand you a life? Just give you what you want without a struggle? Damn fool.' he repeated.

Anita Rose lifted her gaze. 'But he's right,' she said softly.

'*What?*' Osama looked at Anita. She was wearing a thin cotton *shalwar kameez* a size too large on her slim frame. Her wrist was flecked with ink, and even though her eyebrows were unplucked and her limbs gangly, with her full lips and the mole on her chin she almost looked like a woman instead of the teenager she was.

'I don't want to be hidden. I don't want to be afraid to carry a book or read a poem.'

'But Anita, my brave girl, who can scare you?'

Anita straightened her posture. 'Call me Layla.'

'Layla?'

'It's who I am now.'

'What nonsense.' Osama stood up angrily and paced the small crawl of his roof, but Anita sat calmly.

'You don't know what it's like,' she said defiantly, the first sign of her teenage years that Osama had witnessed.

Osama had worried this would happen, once her brother forced her into that bloody school. She would lose sight of the horizon, of the future, of the very value of truth – all in exchange for what? Acceptance? Friendship? The crumbs of those rich children. He turned to look at her sitting on the *charpai*, her arms crossed over her chest. 'Anita, I don't know what it's like?'

'Layla,' she corrected him. 'It's Layla.'

'Layla, Anita, Layla Rose, Miss Joseph, what nonsense are you talking?'

'I want to be seen, like you are.'

Osama held his head in his hands and shook it softly.

'I don't want a name that marks me.'

At that Osama laughed out loud.

'I want to be free, like you.'

'This city, Anita, it will take your heart if you let it. Do you hear me? It will eat you alive. You don't fight in retreat; you fight by standing exactly where you are. If you bend, even slightly, out of fear, it will destroy you.'

'How do I stop it? How do I stop this city from eating my heart?'

Osama sat back down in his chair and lifted his glass of *sharab* from the floor. He drank from the smudged glass and then placed it on his knee, leaning forward to meet Anita's eyes. 'You fight. You take *theirs* first. Don't you remember what Jalib said? Don't you remember anything I've taught you?'

Anita remembered everything, but she kept quiet.

'It doesn't matter what you call yourself. It matters how you resist, how bravely you are willing to stand against an onslaught, how faithfully you hold on to the truth.'

She ground her teeth. This wasn't a mistake, this was a matter of survival. This camouflage – being Layla – *was* her way of fighting.

Osama shook his head sadly.

'*This, then, is the basic thing: for the people, let freedom's bell ring. From the rope, let the plunderer swing. Truly they speak, only those who have seen the truth. Pakistan* ka matlab kya? La illaha illallah . . .'

Sunny

Mosul, January 2017

'Wake up!' Sunny throws his wristband at Monty. 'Wake up wake up wake up!'

'What's your problem?' Monty pushes the sweaty band away from his face. The sun isn't out yet, it is dark and cold, except for a pale-blue light that you only ever see in the desert. It rises up in the horizon, like the soft fire of a gas lamp. They were a day away, at least, from the courier, two days from Nineveh. Hours and hours of endless marching ahead of them.

'Me?' Sunny stands up and wipes his clothes down. He learned the hard way to pat himself security-guard-style every morning. 'Me? That's rich, Monty. It's YOU that's moaning all night long and talking to some bitch in your sleep.'

At that, Monty's beady little eyes narrow. 'Why don't you drag yourself somewhere else, if it bothers you so much?'

'Oh. Oh, I see. Someone's grown a pair of balls suddenly.'

Every single night since they've been out here, Monty has woken Sunny up with his sad howling. Sunny'd been having a dream about his old man back in Portsmouth. He'd gone home, bag in hand, and walked into their semi on Britannia to find his pa sat at the kitchen counter with another kid – Sunny's age, height, colour, the works, wearing *his* threads. Who's this? he'd asked, tired and worn out from his global travels. My son, Pa replied. This here is my real son. My one true boy.

Sunny tried as hard as he could to go back to sleep, tried like crazy to zone Monty out, but he was on rapid fire: Layla this, Layla that. Layla, Layla, Layla.

He lay on his back, his eyes on the stars, tweeting and trying to sleep:

> *I can't sit here in this desert any longer.*
> *I got to get moving, to get doing.*
> *Take myself onwards, upwards to the promised land.*

He kept waking up, all through the night. Sunny was feeling something low after that dream. He rubbed his eyes, gritty from the sand and dry heat. That shit is everywhere, everywhere. You can't wash this high-grade desert sand off. It just clings to you.

He leaned on his elbow and pulled out his phone to check the time. Four in the morning. Every hour in Iraq felt like four in the morning. Every night, as he lay down to sleep, Sunny thought they were closer to the end, but then he woke up and Nineveh seemed even further away.

He waited for his eyes to adjust to the navy of the night sky, but they didn't. Sunny blinked, searching for light, but never found any. He cleared his throat, spitting onto the floor, before lying back down, resting his head on his bag for a second before getting up. It felt so heavy, Sunny's head.

He bends down now to finish packing his bag. He can feel Monty agitated, pacing behind him.

'Why didn't you, huh?' Monty finally spits out, his anger bubbling heavily. 'Why didn't you just move away from me, if you were so bothered?'

'Cos.'

'Cos what?'

Sunny spins round and, in a move Monty doesn't have time to blink and see, picks up Monty's Bobble water bottle and shoves it hard against his chest.

Monty falls to the ground, right on his ass, with a big thud. His face is a web of shock. Sunny turns back to his bag, zero left to pack – he came out here with nothing.

Imma leave this earth with nothing, go to the kingdom of God carrying only the weight of my sins. No satellite phone's going to save me from that.

After that attack in France, an old woman in curlers spat at Sunny on the bus. I didn't fucking do it, he wanted to tell her, burning with shame. The conductor saw the whole thing in his mirror and smiled at Sunny sympathetically. 'Don't mind her,' he said, 'mad as a sack of frogs, that one. She thinks I did 9/11. Spits at everyone.'

But the conductor was a brother, like Sunny. Brown as brown can be.

The old woman looked at Sunny like she knew him. Like she knew who he was and hated him for it.

'We should go soon,' Monty mutters behind him now. He looks rattled, wiping the dirt off his backside and trying to pretend Sunny hasn't just slammed him to the ground. 'I think we should move, Sunny.'

Right now, Monty reminds Sunny of everything he hates. Of Pa and his delusional, unreachable expectations. Of the school that had no place for Sunny – no one who looked like him in their books, no teacher that spoke his language or understood his place in the world.

This is Europe, the headmistress at St Thomas's told Sunny, after he got called in for smashing Ben's jaw into the table. He tried to tell her that Ben had drawn a swastika on that Jewish kid's bag. That it was racist and hurtful. That he'd humiliated Sunny for *years*, saying he should pack his shit and go back to Pakistan – where Sunny was not even from, *Ben* was the Paki – and stop sucking England dry. Why was that not European? The fuck was Europe about, then?

But she wouldn't listen.

I was born here, Sunny told the headmistress. I'm not a migrant.

'This is Europe,' she sneered like she couldn't hear him. 'We are civilized here, we are educated. We do not assault people over an insult.' Ben lost four teeth, she said. He'd been taken away for stitches across his gums and lips. The damage could have been much worse, had they been on another kind of table.

'I'm not a migrant,' Sunny repeated. 'This is my home. *I was born here.*'

'Well then, Mr Jamil,' the headmistress replied slowly, 'you ought to know how civilized people behave.'

If Pa hadn't come into the office, if he hadn't walked in – suited and booted, Sunny could just tell he'd put on his best tie for the occasion – looking all sheepish and apologizing breathlessly before he'd even asked if his son had done anything wrong, Sunny would have slammed her head into the table, too.

Monty

Monty rubbed his back as he studied the map on his phone. His hip hurt from where he had fallen and he tried to massage the spot gingerly, so that Sunny wouldn't know he had injured him. The rattle of gunfire and thud of the mortars in the distance, which shook the earth for miles, disturbed him. He had started to hear the noises all the time now, even in the middle of the desert. The walking, the paranoia, his heart hurting when he woke up from his dreams – how would he survive it all? Wasn't it too much for one man to carry?

So what if Sunny thought that Monty was getting over a girl? He didn't know whom. He didn't know it was Layla. For all Sunny imagined, it could be anyone. If he asked, Monty would make up some story about Sarya. He'd reinvent Angelise as his girlfriend. That would impress Sunny, if he thought Monty had a working girl, a foreigner like Angelise as a girlfriend.

Monty scratched his thin beard and held his head in his hands for a moment.

Maybe they sent Sunny with him because of Layla? Because Abu Khalid suspected something? And Sunny's only assignment – which would explain why he refused to befriend Monty and was wary and suspicious of him, watching his every move – was to flush out a confession? Monty shook the thought from his mind. Sunny might

269

think he was some hotshot commander, but he clearly had no idea what was going on here; he didn't know any more than Monty about the dam, about the courier they were never going to reach, about what anything out here meant. The two of them were the same, they were both lost, trampling over the dead earth of the desert, avoiding roadkill – which, thankfully, they hadn't had to eat so far – and counting the minutes till the end of the march.

Being here had given Monty the first chance in his life to do things properly: to be organized, responsible, like someone with real agency, real value. But sometimes it was too much.

He shook the sand out of his boots and put them back on, wincing as he crammed his toes into the tight black leather and laced them up. There was something ulterior and menacing about Sunny, he could see that now. Though Monty couldn't be sure what.

'We should go soon,' he mumbled to Sunny.

Was he a sentinel, too?

Layla

Two young men carried a heavy table, each of them holding one side. 'Adam, you're walking too fast,' the green-eyed one wheezed, *'amahlak.'*

'Boss said we only have an hour.' Adam's muscles strained under the weight of the long table, its blond wood polished and shined. They had to have a long table for Layla to spread her weapon across. It had become what Abu Khalid called her 'signature style'. It was a part of the branding of the videos, he'd said; it's why they couldn't use any old table. It's why they also used a real camera now, no longer an iPhone, to film the videos; why they had someone to edit the clips, subtitle them and filter a rousing soundtrack over the opening and closing shots. People were watching, millions of people. The world's eyes were upon them, Abu Khalid said, upon *her.* All the alienated, lost and angry – they were all watching Layla.

That's why Abu Khalid said he contacted her, he told her that on their very first Skype call. He had seen her videos; imagine that, they had reached him all the way in Iraq. Was she ready to take her message to the battlefields? To be reborn, recast, in a pure and certain fight? The commander sensed that she was, he said that the very first day they spoke, and he could give her that. But what do you want from me? Layla had asked, impressed and

271

concerned at how quickly they had found her and made contact. What did she have to do in return? This, Abu Khalid had replied. Your voice, that's what I want. Your struggle.

Layla stood with her back towards the boys, staring out the window of an abandoned building. The light chill of the winter air filtered into the room through a crack in the window. She closed her eyes and exhaled deeply, imagining the late-afternoon sun on her skin, even though she knew it could not reach her. The glass was cloudy with fingerprints and dirt. Layla looked out to the desert through the smudged glass and wondered when she would be allowed outside. How far she had travelled, only to find herself back behind closed doors, locked inside, waiting for news of the outside world.

'Put it here.' The green-eyed boy dropped the table.

'No, it's not in the centre.' Adam tried to push his end of the blond table.

'*Shoo?* Styled one video and you're a designer now?' The one with the light eyes spat at the floor. Adam's small face turned red and the veins in his stout arms seemed to pulse, travelling in a throbbing purple rivulet up to his neck and temples.

'Boys,' Layla turned away from the window, 'we don't have time for this.'

It was getting dark outside; soon they would lose the natural light. It was four, maybe even later, four-thirty. They had taken away her phone, for her own safety. So many people were tuning into the videos now, Abu Khalid explained, that sooner or later their enemies would come looking for her and they would find her, just as he had.

The commander promised that he was arranging a new, secure phone, with Internet and everything, but she would get it after Nineveh. Everything was after Nineveh.

Layla walked slowly, her voluminous black *abaya* sweeping the grime off the floor as she moved, lifting a wave of fine dust and setting it free into the air.

She sat down in front of the desk and leaned back into the chair. 'Set the camera up.'

The colour of Adam's face softened to a light puce and he cleared his throat as he lifted the tripod off the floor. The other one, Layla could never remember his name – he made a racket every time she'd seen him, slamming doors and arguing with the brothers – wiped his hands together, cleaning them roughly as he stepped aside. He looked at Layla as he made his way towards the door, closing it to keep the sound out, with something that felt like malice.

Layla looked away from him and down at her notes. They had to film the video and leave the building within the next hour. She had to keep moving; Abu Khalid insisted that she did not stay in one place for too long, not until the operation was secure. Not until the movement had encircled Nineveh.

She had been moving for weeks now, never sleeping in the same place, travelling with security – four or five brothers guarding her at all times. How they were securing anything besides her was a mystery; top command didn't tell her anything about how the operation to storm Nineveh was progressing. They just put her in rooms like this and filmed videos, jazzing them up later in editing. Layla spent her hours writing in her notebook, remembering and regretting, regretting and remembering, until all her days blurred into one long, painful commemoration.

Earlier, as she waited in the abandoned room, robbed of her phone and portal to the outside world, she thought she heard someone playing Eric Clapton down the corridor. Layla's heart froze. Could someone finally have found it, her earliest video? She listened for five minutes, convinced she could hear the '90s melody of soft guitar strings, before she stood up and followed the sound. But it wasn't Clapton. It wasn't her. It was an ice-cream cart, pushed by a white-haired man down an empty street.

Layla exhaled and tried to remember her lines, closing her eyes and rubbing her eyelids gently with her fingers, careful not to smudge her make-up. She had been lucky so far, but she felt distracted, unsettled by how closely she was being watched and disturbed by the memories that haunted all her waking thoughts.

Adam bent slightly, to peer through the camera viewfinder. 'Wide-shot?' he asked. None of the brothers looked at her when they spoke; most of them trained their eyes to the floor, narrowing in on their sandalled toes. Only some of them looked at her; all this time, only three or four brothers had dared to catch her eye. And they all wore the same uneasy look, something between hunger and contempt.

Layla glanced at the boy standing near the door, still watching her. 'Close-up,' she replied to Adam, not moving her eyes off the green-eyed boy.

Is that why they looked?

Did they know?

Sunny

The only time Sunny went to Apollo in the day was the time he took Pa there. Sunny only knew the reddish glow of the stairs at midnight, and the smell of strawberry-and-mint *sheesha* that climbed the basement walls late, late at night when the boys in the harem pants swung red-hot charcoals from a small *mankal* carried off their shoulders.

Walking down the steps with his pa in the dead of afternoon, Sunny was unprepared for how ugly the place looked, how shabby.

'The food here is incredible,' he promised Pa, who walked down the narrow steps lifting his trousers with pinched fingers, so they wouldn't touch the floor.

As they turned into the room at the bottom of the stairs, Sunny scanned the space hopefully, though he knew Aloush wouldn't be there. He slept in the afternoon, after spinning all night.

'*Ajeeb hai, beta*,' Sulaiman Jamil scrunched his nose as he wiped down the seat of a metal chair with his hanky. 'So many new places on this road, why come here?'

Because they're good people, Sunny replied. Because they're my friends here.

But he'd never seen the black fellow with the acne standing at the kitchen door laughing on his phone, and there wasn't anyone else he recognized.

'Ey,' Sunny called the boy, smiling like they were old

mates. 'Can we get two *qahwe*?' But the boy just stared at Sunny, forcing him to lift his hand and mime a tipping coffee cup. 'Make sure my old man's has a proper face!' Sunny turned to his pa. 'That's what they call the foam on the top. These nuts are crazy for coffee done right.'

But Sulaiman Jamil didn't look impressed; he looked anxiously at his watch, as though he had somewhere else to be.

Sunny ran a hand through his hair, making sure it was all in place. He'd never introduced anyone to his pa before.

Aloush said he might pass by around three, if he woke up by then, for a late lunch. Sunny brought his pa early; it was only two. Aloush wouldn't be here. But Sunny was still nervous. Why was it so important to be here, at Apollo, with Pa? What did he care if his father met Aloush? He didn't need his pa's validation and he didn't need Oz's. What did he care what either of them thought?

'Darling,' Sulaiman Jamil held the thimble of Turkish coffee in his hands daintily, '*yeh kya bakwas hai?*' His face puckered in a sour scowl.

'It's something new,' Sunny muttered. 'Why you never wanna try anything new?'

'New *kya*?' Sulaiman Jamil asked, putting the delicate cup down carelessly, spilling a slick of black liquid in his saucer. 'All my life all I've done is new! New new new, all the time. This isn't new, it's low-standard, *beta*, not a clean place.'

Sunny felt his blood rise. He shook his head, trying to blink it all back, blink it down. What wasn't new was the hanky and the suit and matching trousers his father insisted on wearing everywhere, aping that rubbish he read in *GQ*, crisp accents like he was born speaking that way. That was the *past* – who did Pa think he was fooling? That was just him bowing down to the Empire all his life like a servant.

'You never had the balls to try *anything* different,' Sunny spat at his old father. 'Look at you! What are you trying to be?'

Climbing down Apollo's basement stairs a night back, Sunny had tripped and grazed his knuckles against the wall as he struggled not to fall. He rocked his scuffed-up knuckles, the skin still raw, against the table now, reminding himself of the light, tingling pain of his almost-fall. He didn't fall. He wouldn't fall.

Sunny didn't want Aloush to see his father, he didn't want him to meet Pa and think that some of him was in Sunny. He wasn't Pa. He would never be like him.

'Look at you!' Sunny shouted at his father, pushing the table, kicking his chair away. His hands were shaking, resting on the bare metal table in the space between him and his pa. He couldn't control anything: not his wanting or his longing, not his pa, not his lack of place in the world, not even the flutter of his shaking hands. 'Look at you – you're pathetic.'

Sulaiman Jamil held the small coffee cup in the palm of his hand and looked at his son, sadly.

'You're a joke, Pa.' Sunny stood up to leave. 'This life here? That hanky? That accent of yours? It's a fucking joke!'

It was an oblivion worse than death to be no one but Sulaiman Jamil's son. A nothing. A nobody whose life was marked only by its unremarkability.

Sunny threw a five-pound note on the table, grateful that Aloush wasn't here, that the two Pakistanis whose shift began at one in the morning, sweeping the floors, weren't here. Sunny didn't want anyone to see his father, suited and booted, tie cut like an English gentleman's ascot, copied from the pages of a third-rate magazine, making a face when he tasted the resinous aroma of cardamom in the coffee, pinching his trousers so they wouldn't touch the floor, like he was too good for the place. He didn't want anyone to see him with a fake, a phoney. A fraud.

Layla

'Hello, Madam! Would you like to try our new-flabour yoghurt? It's passionfruit and mint, sugar-pree.'

A small brown woman with large eyes and freckles across the bridge of her nose, possibly from the Philippines, held a round tray in the palm of her hands. Tiny plastic cups, with pink spoons poking out of them, sat untouched on the tray.

The detail Layla remembered most strongly from her trip to Dubai was the woman's white-and-green uniform. Pinkberry, her apron read. But Layla didn't have any dirhams to spare; Feroze had given her 250 AED, worth more than 5,000 rupees, an amount larger than her brother had ever given her – in any currency.

'Really, *bhaiya*?' Layla had squealed when Feroze handed her the money in their small Sharjah hotel room.

'Just relax, *yaar.*' Feroze folded away a handful of falcon-embossed beige-and-pink notes into his leather wallet, before checking his phone. 'Enjoy the city, but don't get too tired. We need you in good form later.'

She was looking for the bookshop in the mall. Kinokuniya, the African security guard told her it was called. She had already spent 15 AED on the bus into Dubai, and more still on the metro to the glistening, air-conditioned mall, which struck Layla as spacious and modern as the airport. She calculated another 15–25 for the way back, maybe another 40

AED for some lunch. Her 250 AED had seemed like an exorbitant amount back at the hotel, but now, having seen the prices of Pinkberry's sugar-free yoghurt on the stand behind the young lady in the apron, Layla wasn't so sure it was very much at all.

Feroze and Layla had flown to Dubai on Emirates Airlines; his ticket was business-class – his clients had booked it that way, he apologized – while Layla's was economy. But she didn't care. She sat in her window seat, face pressed against the grazed plastic oval window, for the entire flight. She had never been on an aeroplane before, never seen how small and breakable Karachi looked from the sky.

Layla held her breath as she watched the dry, dusty expanse and the clusters of grey dots disappear, as the plane retreated into the clouds. Karachi always felt so crowded, so suffocating. Where had they hidden all this space? Who did it belong to?

The middle seat next to her was empty and a man in slippers and turquoise *shalwar kameez* sat in the aisle. Layla had helped him read his boarding pass: 32C. The man never looked her in the eyes, never thanked her. He folded into his seat and turned his body away from her, praying underneath his breath for the duration of the flight.

Layla pulled her shawl across her body and turned away from him too, facing the clouds.

Later, before the pilot announced that they would shortly be landing, Layla unbuckled her seatbelt and walked down the aisle to the bathroom. The light outside was green, but when she tried to open the door, someone inside pushed it shut against her, as though holding it with their body. A passing stewardess, carrying a pile of blankets, noticed and stopped to knock on the bathroom door. 'Excuse me?' she rapped. 'Excuse me, hello?' Her nails were painted a deep burgundy that Layla had only seen on models in fashion magazines.

When the door opened, it was the man in the sea-green *shalwar kameez* from 32C.

He stepped past the women sideways, so as not to touch them, a look of hatred in his downcast, humiliated eyes. The floor of the toilet was wet, covered in water. 'Oh God,' the stewardess with the burgundy nails exhaled, 'I'm so tired of these people.'

Layla didn't say anything.

She didn't want the stewardess to know she was one of those people, more like the man in turquoise than she would ever be like the elegant, exhausted stewardess. She returned to her seat and watched Dubai rise out of the desert, a fantasy of metal and glass, skyscrapers and highways, glittering against the ochre sand.

'They want me to come, too?' Layla asked, after Feroze handed her the Emirates economy ticket and told her of the invitation to spend a weekend in Dubai, paid for by his wealthy clients. 'Me?'

'Yes,' he said, but softly, so their mother wouldn't hear. 'Why not?'

'But why?'

Feroze was texting on his phone, and he paused the shuffle of his thumbs across his Huawei keyboard to look up at his sister, standing in the doorframe of their kitchen in Gulshan. She was wearing ripped jeans, threads cut at the knees, and a loose shirt, a size too large for her and woven from fine Chinese silk. 'You're a beautiful girl, why not?'

He dropped his eyes back to his phone.

Layla lifted her shoulder from the frame and stood a little taller. 'Really?'

Really, Feroze nodded, pressing Send.

He turned to leave, but his sister stopped him, touching his shoulder.

'But what do I have to do?'

'Nothing,' Feroze replied, not looking at her. 'Nothing you don't want to.'

They had checked into their Best Western hotel room and called Zenobia to tell her everything was fine and that they had landed. She was so happy to see her children on the small screen of the WhatsApp video in such a smart room, guests of such important and generous clients. *Jeete raho*, she said before Feroze cut the call – live long. God bless.

They hadn't told anyone else they were travelling, people ask too many questions, Feroze said. It's a lot of information no one needs to have.

Layla understood.

Lie low. Don't draw unnecessary attention to yourself.

Nothing you don't want to do.

Layla had become good at keeping her head down and balancing multiple lives in the shadows. But still, something made her uncomfortable. The way Feroze chose her clothes for the trip: modern *shalwar kameez* cut with halternecks and spaghetti straps, which she had copied at the tailor's since joining the American School, but hadn't worn yet; the way he had taken her to the parlour the day before their flight and told the aunty at the door to spare no expense.

The aunty who took Layla behind a small partition and asked her to disrobe and put on a shapeless purple smock seemed to know Feroze, as though he came often with this sort of request.

One by one, salon girls filed into the colourless partitioned room, which looked nothing like the parlours Layla had watched in TV dramas as a child. One smeared a stinging bleach paste across Layla's face; another massaged hot sesame oil into her long hair, while two others poured burning sugar onto her legs, ripping her skin clean of black hair. No one in the parlour smiled at her, no one brought her cubes of sugar for her tea, no one even looked her in the eyes.

They were powerful men, his clients. They couldn't just turn up looking as though they were not grateful for this opportunity, Feroze said. He had never been out of the country for a meeting before; it was Feroze's first time to be invited to the United Arab Emirates. 'Don't cost me this,' he warned his sister as a taxi drove them to the airport. Feroze sat in front with the window open, a warm Karachi breeze blowing into the yellow cab. He turned to look at Layla, his body contorting over the ripped brown leather of the seat. 'If it goes well, if they're happy, you'll see . . .'

Layla thought Feroze had tears in his eyes, which seemed a little bloodshot.

'Set, we'll be set, Layla. All of us. Forever . . .'

Feroze turned back and rolled up the window, struggling with the broken handle.

But maybe it wasn't tears, maybe it was just the wind in his eyes.

Layla didn't think about it too much; she had never been on a plane, never left the city, never been somewhere new, like the kids in her elite school, who travelled the world with boredom and ease.

After clearing customs and finding their way to Sharjah, where one could stay in a room for a quarter of Dubai's price, Feroze gave Layla some money and extracted the promise that she would be back by three to shower and get ready for the evening. She noticed that he had already pulled out the black *kameez* with the thin, beaded straps from their luggage and draped it across the bed.

Layla left, eager to be alone, to see Dubai free from the watchful eye of her brother. He had been especially twitchy, checking his phone constantly, looking at her anxiously as though she would bolt, as though she would run away and leave him in this rich oasis, holding only the broken promise of a beautiful girl on a night out with his clients.

On the metro Layla tried not to think about why Feroze had brought her here and why he was so nervous. Monty was calling her constantly, FaceTime Audio ringing every time she connected her phone to Wi-Fi. She replied to all his calls with an auto-message, 'Can I call you later?', but he didn't get the hint. He never did. First, she ignored his calls and messages, then she cut them mid-ring, and finally she just switched her phone onto airplane mode.

Sitting on the air-conditioned metro, Layla read the Arabic of the subway signs, scribbled a few lines in her red notebook to describe the smell of roasted coffee beans and the cedar notes of *oudh* that wafted through the carriage. She took photos with her iPhone – of the skyscrapers teetering close to the metro rails, the billboards of girls with cherry-red lips and blonde hair extensions advertising Dubai's annual shopping festival, the rangy men in flowing *thobes* sitting next to sunburnt foreigners in shorts and fanny-packs (even the skin on their ears, on their knees, in the creases of their elbows was pink and peeling), but deleted all of them. She would keep the memories of this trip behind the closed shutters of her eyes; they would be safer there.

'Madam,' the Pinkberry saleswoman sang. 'No extra calories, you want to try?'

Layla smiled half-heartedly. 'I'm sorry,' she said, patting her pockets and wondering if this girl too had been brought to Dubai because she was beautiful. Because she was young and wanting, and naïve. 'I don't have any change.'

The Filipina laughed, wrinkling her eyes and exposing her crooked teeth wrapped in silver wire with tiny, pink bands criss-crossed over the braces. 'Madam!' She lifted one of the white plastic cups and handed it to Layla. 'It's a pree sample. Take some, try, try.'

Layla accepted the passionfruit-with-mint cup, wishing she had never agreed to any of this – her brother's invitation to Dubai, the economy-class ticket, the dirhams, the slowly melting sludge of yoghurt; Layla the name, Layla the idea.

'Thank you,' she whispered to the Pinkberry girl, but she had already turned away from her, offering her tray of passionfruit to a new stranger.

'Hello, sir, would you like to try our new-flabour yoghurt . . .'

285

Monty

That night, asleep on the rocky desert floor, Monty dreamed of Layla, her hair rising up like a corona of stars, which fell one by one at her feet every time she opened her mouth to speak.

What are you doing? Monty asked, his voice hollow. Where are you going?

That night he dreamed of Layla leaving, but also of what she had done. As in life, as in his dreams, he could only bear to think of her betrayal in flashes – a green light, a low rumbling of noise, Layla's legs.

Layla's long legs moving slowly in the dark, stretching out across a hotel bed.

Go on, Layla had said, as they stood in the ASK stairway behind the psychology classroom, leaning against the cool brick wall. 'Give me a few lines.'

And Monty would sing to her from her Eric Clapton song.

She always asked Monty to sing, always when they were alone. 'I like the sound of "Layla" on your tongue,' Layla said, kissing Monty slowly, pressing her lips against his. Her breath smelled of cigarettes. 'I like the way your voice changes when you say my name.'

They spent hours together after school, sometimes till five or six, evading Feroze, whose calls Layla rejected, and hiding from the teachers who stayed late, grading papers in their classrooms. Sometimes she vanished on the weekends, not answering her phone or taking hours to reply to a message. But after school, most days, she was all his.

Layla taught Monty how to kiss, sitting in the dark stairwell, how to move his tongue against her own, how to slow his breathing in tandem with hers, how to make the kiss soft and how to make it rough.

He even signed up for after-school sports, just to spend a couple more hours on campus with her. Once, when he caught a ball mid-air, breaking up what looked to be a fearsome partnership during a home game – a coup for un-sporty cricket novice Monty – all his teammates erupted in cheers. His friends Kashif and Shavez lifted him on their shoulders and ran around the field, but Monty spun left and right looking for her, for Layla. And there she was, sitting on the grass in her ripped Zainab Market jeans, not jumping up and down, not moving at all.

Layla sat perfectly still, her legs crossed and her back upright, looking right at him. Monty, she sounded silently, because she knew he couldn't hear her from that distance, rounding out the letters of his name with her mouth.

Monty, Layla said quietly, her eyes squeezed shut and her mouth opened wide as though she was screaming. Only once he saw her did she start pounding her fists in the air.

Layla, he sounded back to her, but she didn't see him. Her eyes were still shut tight.

There was no way to describe how Monty loved Layla, no language in which to speak of how his body tensed at her touch, how words spoken only in mime – whispered in the air – hit him straight in the ribs, shattering blood, tissue, bone.

Layla wanted to change her nose-ring, the silver wire had begun to bore her, so Monty took her to Sarwana's, where she picked out a delicate little diamond. When the jeweller finished the piercing, Layla handed him her old ring. 'Throw this away,' she said, placing the thin silver in the old man's palm. 'I don't want it any more.'

Monty used his father's credit card to order her a Kindle and Essie nail polish off Amazon, and when he brought the brown boxes to school, Layla complained about the late delivery.

But she was right. It had taken weeks.

'Why do you like me?' he asked her that day as he sat on the steps, singing to Layla from her Eric Clapton song.

She picked up her bag, weighed down by books and that red notebook she carried with her everywhere. She never let anyone see what she wrote inside it, not even Monty. 'Why do you like me?'

'Because you're different,' Monty said, reaching up and stroking her hair. Brave, angry Layla.

But Layla just chewed on the yellowing skin around her fingernails. 'No, I'm just like all the others, you'll see.'

In the dreams, she looked like she did then, in the beginning. Like a sparrow, her brown eyes smudged with kohl and her lips pink, like she had just been kissed.

Monty always woke up sweating after the dreams. But tonight, in the middle of the desert, he woke up with his body coated in perspiration and his heart beating wildly against his chest.

He sat up slowly, feeling the darkness around him. He

had laid his bag near an ant mound and hundreds of black insects crawled over the canvas fabric. Monty felt an ant bite his neck and he wiped himself quickly, his skin shuddering. He was awake, but somehow he could still hear her. Somehow he could hear Layla, whose voice lingered outside his dreams. It was as though she were near Monty, Layla drifting through the desert all this time, following him.

It was dark and it took Monty's eyes a moment to adjust to the pale glow of light coming from Sunny's phone. He was lying on his back, an arm outstretched in front of his face, no earphones connected to the device.

Sunny shifted and Monty lay back down and shut his eyes quickly, so Sunny wouldn't see that he was awake.

Layla.

Monty felt a cold dread in the pit of his stomach. She was on Sunny's phone.

Was he talking to her? Monty's heart beat so fiercely against his ribs that he struggled to hear what was being said. He held his breath and listened. Layla's voice started and then stopped. Started and then stopped.

It was a video.

Monty squeezed his eyes shut and tried to breathe normally. Why was Sunny watching her in the middle of the night? He could hear her beautiful, soft voice, floating towards him as Sunny rolled over onto his side.

'The world is in a state of advanced moral collapse,' Layla intoned, her voice thin with warning. 'There are forces planning against us now. They want to destroy us, to wipe our people from the earth. Rise, sisters. It is the duty of all Muslim women to stand up and

*empower themselves by forming a vanguard. We, my sisters, are
soldiers, too.'*

Was he dreaming?

Monty flicked one eye open.

No, he was awake and Sunny was watching Layla,
whose voice filled the ghostly wilderness.

Monty didn't move, he couldn't look – he didn't want
Sunny to know he was awake. He didn't want Sunny to
stop the video. He just wanted to hear Layla, to know that
she was safe, that somewhere in the world she existed and
maybe, just maybe, was waiting for him. Her voice started
and then stopped, stalled and then started, hanging suspended in the chill of the desert night.

With every day he was getting closer to her. Monty
wished Layla could know all that he was enduring to find
her. But why was Sunny watching her? He wasn't wearing
his earphones. Did he want Monty to know he was watching her? Was he sending him a message?

Monty shivered. Did Sunny want Layla? Is that why he
had been so eager to volunteer for the march, waving his
hands wildly in the air until Abu Khalid called his name?
Monty felt a sickening curdling in the hollows of his
stomach. Did Sunny know Layla already? Is that why
Sunny hated him?

*'Freedom is not what you wear, it's not blue jeans. It's not showing
your hair. Sisters, will you compromise everything for your comfort?
Free yourself from the lies of Westoxification. Freedom is this.*
Layla's voice rose sharply. *It's what we are building here, it is
our fight against decay, against the occupiers of our land, against the*

degradation capitalism has imposed upon us. We are many, they are few. The day is coming that we will be in power. Rise, my sisters, like lions after slumber in unvanquishable number. Step up, sisters, step out from your shadows and come to fight.'

Monty listened to Layla quietly, the volume of her voice rising and falling as Sunny squirmed in the dark. Monty listened to the anger that reverberated in her every word and wondered if Layla had ever really loved him.

Sunny

Where do you go? Where you been the last two nights?

Sunny had been at Apollo every night the past week, every night on the small stage with Aloush, only enough space for the two of them. Aloush behind the decks, Sunny sitting on the bar stool, holding the *darbuka* against his thigh.

He'd left his phone at home over the weekend. Oz had rung. Sunny had missed too many calls.

'Nowhere,' Sunny mumbled, defensive.

'Karim says he saw you on Guildhall Walk, six in the morning—'

'What was Karim doing on Guildhall?' Sunny interrupted. 'Don't drag me into his shit, I don't know what he's up to—'

'He was coming back from prayers,' Oz corrected. '*Namaz*, Sunny. You remember that?'

Sunny was quiet for a minute. They were sitting at the Starbucks window. He twisted open the cap of his water bottle and closed it again. Sunny opened and closed the plastic top.

'Your pa called me, too, said he was worried about you. Didn't understand what you were doing these days.'

'I play at a café down there sometimes,' he said, not looking up at his cousin.

Oz lowered his head so he could look into Sunny's eyes. 'You play music?'

'Yeah,' Sunny shrugged, still not meeting his cousin's stare.

Oz pressed his curled fists against his closed eyes and shook his head. He snorted. It sounded to Sunny as though his cousin was laughing at him. 'Why am I wasting my time trying to help you, when you don't care?' Oz finally spoke. 'There's plenty of other people who take what I say seriously, I'd rather help them. There's plenty of soldiers, real guns, ready to die for our cause. Why am I burning my efforts on you?'

But he needed Oz's help, Sunny promised, he did care.

It doesn't work like that, Oz replied. You want to be a son of a new world? You want to be radical and profound? You want to be someone? Then you have to make a choice. This or that. Comfort or sacrifice. Sex, rock-and-roll or solitude. Which do you have the courage to choose?

Sacrifice, Sunny swore. I choose God. I choose the future.

Oz pushed his stool away from the counter and stood up to leave.

'I don't do nothing,' Sunny spoke quickly, his words crashing against each other. 'They don't serve or anything, promise, Cuz. I just go for the beats.' He jumped off his seat, speaking to the back of his cousin's head, the black roots peeking out through the blond bleach. 'It's just a hobby . . . it's nothing, really. Just a way to kill time.'

Sunny's heart beat quickly; why was he explaining himself? Why did he have to say anything at all? It wasn't wrong — it was something real to him. Why couldn't Apollo be a part of his future? Why couldn't what he felt there be part of imagining a radical new world?

But Oz didn't turn round, just shook his head. 'I thought you were serious,' he said over his shoulder. 'I thought you were serious about becoming a new kind of man.'

Layla

Layla sat on her knees on the cool sand and watched the seagulls hover over Seaview in mid-flight. When she touched her fingers to her nose they smelled of sulphur.

In the distance a couple walked along the beach, holding hands. A long-haired camel decorated in beads and pink embroidery flapped its gums, paying no notice to the girl hunched over a red notebook in the sand.

With her finger, Layla drew in the sand, spelling the solitary letters of someone's name:

L

A

Y

L

A

She traced the letters over and over, trying to stop herself from crying. A scrawny teenage boy in ripped jeans revved a buggy, its handlebars festooned with glowing red lights and feathery silver tinsel. He hit the accelerator and the buggy roared, tearing down the beach.

Baby, her mother whispered to her as she curled into herself like a wounded animal at the foot of her mother's thin bed. Zenobia initially insisted on sleeping on the floor of her Gulshan bedroom, her body was used to the hard floor. She didn't feel comfortable on a bed; she was born of resistance, she said. The comfort she understood didn't come from mattresses and down pillows, it came from the warmth of nestling her face in the crook of an elbow, the bruising of a hipbone against the cold concrete until it ground itself into the right position, the security of being heart-to-heart with the earth.

But Zenobia slept on a simple bed now, because her son had worked so hard for this flat, for these comforts and this new life. She used her old *ralli* as a mattress and a thin, scratchy sheet for a cover, but her elbow remained her preferred station over a pillow.

When Layla came back from Dubai, she stood quietly behind her brother as he opened duty-free bag after duty-free bag for their mother: Cadbury's chocolates, Nivea cold cream, Chinese Tiger Balm for her aching hands and PG Tips imported tea. Zenobia clapped and praised God with thanks for each gift, forgetting the pain in her joints momentarily. Not once did she ask what it cost. Not once did she ask Feroze what he sold for those gifts.

Everything made Layla feel sick – ordinary thoughts, food, the sound of her brother's voice, the citrus smell of the hotel shower-gel she carried back in her small suitcase. It had been a week since she washed her hair. A week since she stood in the dark shower and poured lukewarm water from a *balti* over her dry skin. She hadn't been to see Osama. How could she face him now? When she came home from school, Layla went into her mother's room and closed the door behind her. She lay on the foot of the thin bed, drifting between tears and sleep, waiting for her mother – for anyone – to understand: she was not well.

'Did something happen between you two?' Layla heard

her mother ask her older brother one evening, after she refused to eat with them again.

'You know her,' Feroze mumbled, his mouth filled with *roti*, 'always in a mood.' They hadn't spoken since the flight home, Feroze hadn't said a word to Layla since that night. *Its 4 yr future*, he had texted her. Just one line, days after they returned to Karachi. Layla, for her part, read her brother's message and then blocked his number from her phone.

Listening to her brother and mother whisper about her, Layla coiled into herself like a shedding snake and lay on her mother's bed, waiting.

Zenobia had never had Cadbury's before and she relished the milky chocolate, rationing her limited supply. Finishing her dinner, she wiped her hands on the edge of her *dupatta*, opened a duty-free bag and carefully broke two squares of the chocolate. Walking to her bedroom, Zenobia placed the pieces of chocolate one by one on her tongue, sucking them like a lozenge until they melted. As she brought her face close to her daughter's, it was the scent of cocoa on her breath that Layla recoiled from.

Baby, her mother whispered, baby, what's happened to you?

Layla dropped her head to her knees, her hair falling like a canopy around her legs, and, covered by the loud grumble of the beach buggy's engine, screamed until her throat was dry, until she could hear only the echo of the dune-buggy flying down Seaview's dark shore.

When she looked up, the letters of her name had been erased, buried by the tracks of the buggy's jagged tyres. All that was left was the L – L for Layla.

Layla the lion.

Sunny

Monty and Sunny were pretending nothing had happened. They had finally reached Tal Afar without further incident. There had been no patronizing lecture – Monty. No aggressive sit-up demonstrations – Sunny. No bitching and moaning and whingeing – Monty. No nightmares, no sulking, no crying over spilt milk – Monty, Monty, Monty.

A man wheels a wooden cart fitted out with a silver pan warming over coals, calling out the name of something in Arabic. He trudges past the boys. Whatever's in the pan smells sweet, but Sunny's too distressed to eat.

Monty runs after the cart. 'It's corn!' he shouts at Sunny, like he'd discovered nuclear fission, but the man doesn't stop for him. Even with Monty holding out money and asking for a couple of cobs, the man pushes past him as though he were invisible.

Tal Afar is where a courier would finally come and collect their intelligence. A top-level guy sent to meet the brothers marching from Mosul. It was the last chance to alert the brothers to any problems before Nineveh, but they'd been standing in the middle of dusty nowhere for close to two hours and no one had come. They waited by the bus depot, a sad, forgotten place in the shadow of apartment blocks that looked like council estates. All the balconies were strung with drying laundry and the windows guarded by metal grilles. Monty kept pacing by

298

the phone box, stepping inside, lifting the receiver and holding it to his ear – careful not to touch his pretty face with it – and then putting it back.

'Now what are you doing?'

'Just checking for a dial tone,' he replies defensively.

Sunny shakes his head. 'He's not calling us, you fool.' At some point, people break. And Monty's cracked up good. It's a new bag he's trying on: hero. Can't say it suits him.

Sunny unclips the dagger on his belt and drags it across the dirt collected on a bench.

He traces shapes in the dust with the tip of the blade. SJ, he writes, erasing his initials after a moment, just in case. This whole exercise felt like a waste. What were they doing? No one from the Ummah Movement had bothered to check on them, no one debriefed them, no one even seemed to know they were out here.

Monty stops his pacing and stands in front of Sunny as he draws petals on the bench.

'What do you have on that thing?' he asks bitterly.

Sunny barely glances up at him. 'My blade?'

'No, not your blade – your phone.' Monty's voice is thick with irritation. 'Why are you always on it?'

'What's it to you, boss?' Lately, whenever Sunny charges his phone, jamming it into an adaptor and squatting near an outlet in a petrol pump or outside some deserted guard post, a shop, whatever, he feels as though he ought to guard his device from Monty's prying eyes. He's vibing hard, circling it, wanting it. Why?

'It's something,' Monty huffs petulantly, though Sunny feels him hesitate, measuring his puny bravery. 'It's something when you're always on it – night and day, morning, afternoon, twenty-four hours non-stop. I have a right to know.'

'No,' Sunny says slowly as he cleans his dagger with his shirt, wiping the blade carefully. 'You don't.'

He steps back to admire the AK that he drew on the ground – Rita, if she was longer and thinner. Monty is all but hyperventilating, sucking in air through the small gap between his front teeth, checking the time on his watch.

Sunny sits back down on the kerb and hits the heels of his palms and his fingertips on the pavement, remembering a beat. He's tired of listening to this shit every day. It's been rough out here, especially with one bombshell after the other from Oz. First his cousin ditches him here, then he cuts Sunny deep with his treachery. Sometimes, in the small hours of the night, when he's alone, lost in thought, Sunny wonders if it's him. If he got it all wrong; and he thinks back to that last day in Apollo, that last chance to be brave, to be real.

He runs the knife along the ground, sharpening his blade. The lyrics from 'Swim Good' come at him like revelation and he hums the song softly. He hasn't thought of Frank's lyrics in weeks, hasn't played no music since he's been out here, no drums, no nothing. Sunny's old life has washed over him.

He thinks of the Sheikh Awlaki quote Oz had shown him back home, before he turned out to be an Uncle Taimoor, backstabbing traitor. 'The one who insults Allah is like the one who looks directly up at the sun and spits at it – his spit falls back on his face.'

He stands up to stretch his legs.

Sunny doesn't question his luck too much. Things

will change. Whatever Oz thought he had gained, he would lose.

He rests his tanto on the asphalt and taps open his phone, going straight into Tumblr. He doesn't look at the notes, doesn't click to see how his followers have grown. Monty hovers somewhere in the background, Sunny can't hear him any more.

I'm a wolf, I don't need no one, just me alone, crying at the moon. I'll make it out of this, more feral, wilder, more ferocious. I don't have much out here, but watch me, watch me burn this house down and come out from the ashes, pulled out by that simple power: faith.

Monty

As part of the run-up to their six-month anniversary Monty wanted to take Layla to Okra. He asked his father to call and make sure they got the best table, by the door, the first one anyone entering the small restaurant would see as they walked in. Layla had never been. She was going to love it. Monty told her all about the molten-chocolate lava cake on the drive there. Love it, he promised – everyone did.

'*Sahib*,' Tano held Monty's door open for him. 'Can we go eat?'

It was nine forty-five, the only table Monty could get, with the added promise that they would leave by eleven, extracted by Okra's artful maître d'.

Tano had been out with him since eight-thirty. Monty checked his watch, not wanting to stand on the street and lose any of their precious dining time. 'No,' he replied, calling behind to Tano and the police officer as he led Layla up the low white steps, 'just wait.' Showing Layla the sign by the door: no cigars, no drugs, no firearms, Monty caught a glimpse of Tano's crestfallen face. There was a flicker of something, spied from the corner of Monty's eye – disappointment? Or something more? Loathing, even.

The table next to their hotly valued one by the door was occupied by four men, smoking Cuban cigars and clinking glasses every ten minutes, in one toast after another. Monty recognized one of the younger-looking uncles, he played tennis with Papa at the club sometimes. He nodded hello to Monty and, seeing Layla, winked at him. Monty noticed the uncle looked at Layla a few seconds too long.

Upstairs, in the small balcony seating area, a family with children terrorized the placid calm of Okra. One could barely hear Harry Belafonte playing softly through the speakers, as a baby cried unremittingly and two small children ran up and down the stairs squealing and shrieking, while their parents issued vague threats, shouting from the bannister upstairs. Carlos, the maître d', stood helplessly by, unable to intervene.

Through their expensive meal – red snapper that melted against the roof of your mouth, Wagyu so tender, its blood sweetened with garlic and sage – Layla kept her eyes on the stained-glass windows facing the street.

'Don't worry,' Monty said, leaning across their blue wooden table, placing his hand on hers, 'no one can see you through that.'

But Layla didn't say anything; she just pulled her hand out from under Monty's, rubbing her skin as though he had hurt her. She kept her eyes steadfastly on the blue-and-yellow glass, hardly eating a thing. She pushed the snapper across her plate with her fork, which she held uncomfortably, curled in the palm of her hand like an ice-pick. She brought it down unkindly on the fish, lancing the flaky white meat. Monty wondered if Layla preferred to eat with her hands, but didn't suggest it. It would look weird, especially with Papa's friends sitting nearby.

He noticed the uncle staring at Layla throughout the evening, almost as if he knew her and was trying to catch her eye. Layla, for her part, seemed intent on ignoring him.

Layla lightly sipped the red wine Monty had smuggled in, in a Harrods carrier bag. It was the only thing she consumed at the 3,000-rupee-a-head restaurant, and still the imported Jacob's Creek Merlot did little to alter her mood.

'Let's go,' she said, before Monty could order the molten cake.

'But the chocolate lava?' He tilted his body to call a waiter, but Layla stood up.

'I want to go.'

When the waiter came, Layla pointed at the food she hadn't touched. 'Pack it all, please,' she asked, handing him the bread basket and the bowl of fresh vegetables served with salt and a dash of sweet vinegar. 'Could I have a large bottle of water?' she asked the waiter. 'Room-temperature?'

Monty was surprised to hear her use the expression, though he still had to point out that's not how they did things here. He said it to her softly, embarrassed. He'd never seen anyone order drinks to go. 'This isn't McDonald's, Layla.'

But Layla ignored him, shifting away from him, flinching ever so slightly from his words.

When their foil-wrapped doggy bag arrived, Layla didn't bother waiting for Monty to pay the bill, she pushed her seat away and walked to the car. Monty paid by credit card and thanked Carlos, the maître d'. It was only ten-thirty.

He stepped outside, 7,200 rupees lighter, and held his breath. There was Layla, lifting the foil to explain to his illiterate Pathan driver that Wagyu was just *gosht* and that the fish had no oil, but that's what these people liked. Tano and the off-duty policeman, who held his gun like a walking stick between his legs in the front seat and whose name Monty hadn't yet learned, bowed their heads and thanked Layla. Monty watched quietly from the top of the steps.

Layla didn't say a word to him on the drive back to school, where she would catch a rickshaw home.

She didn't answer his call that night or reply to his messages the next morning.

Finally, after a typical spell of silence, Layla called Monty. It was two in the morning.

'I can't sleep.'

'Me neither.'

She was quiet for a moment. And then, 'Do you think we'll work, Monty?'

Monty held his breath. 'What do you mean?'

'I mean us. Do you think we'll make it?'

Of course, of course, of course. But he said it only once and said it carefully, so she would believe him.

'You think so?' Layla asked. Monty could hear her holding back.

'I'm always going to be here to protect you,' Monty said, trying to pacify Layla on the phone that night.

Layla laughed. 'What makes you think I need protecting?'

Monty was used to her acting tough; he saw how high she kept her guard, how fiercely she defended her space. She had become so sullen, so withdrawn lately. But she was vulnerable, he saw that. 'It's my job to protect you,' he replied.

'Monty,' Layla said, a distinct coldness in her voice. 'You are the last person I need to protect me.'

He felt the sting of her words immediately. All he had done was take care of her, why was she so angry?

'Of course I think we'll make it.' He didn't like the tone of this conversation, he didn't like it at all. 'Don't you?'

Layla was silent. Monty held the phone tight against his ear and waited for Layla to speak. At first he thought he could hear a rustle on the other end of the line. At first Monty thought she might be crying. But she was only lighting a cigarette.

'No,' Layla exhaled. 'I don't think so, Monty.'

In Monty's dreams, there was only Layla.

Layla, Layla, Layla.

Come, he said, reaching for her hand as she stood on the banks of a quiet river.

Monty stood in the water, the cold current lapping against his legs.

Layla, he beckoned softly, lovingly, let's leave.

But Layla's eyes were blank and unyielding as she searched the forest behind him. She stepped away from the moss-covered stones, retreating away from the river bank.

As though the current were dragging them apart, Monty felt Layla pulling away from him. He saw her feet lift off the earth and her body fall backwards, in slow motion, into the dark shadows.

Layla? Monty called his beloved, but she would not answer him.

He took a step towards her, but froze, afraid. And just as he wavered, his foot hovering above the gentle water, out of the darkness appeared a figure.

Sunny.

Layla surrendered herself to Sunny, falling against him and letting him hold her, resting her head upon his broad shoulder.

Sunny, Layla mumbled, her lips grazing his ears. *Sunny, I've been waiting for you.*

Layla

'Do you know who you are?'

'Who?'

'You're no one.' Osama waited for her to understand. But he saw her eyes fall, he saw her look at her feet, understanding the wrong thing. That they had been right, that she had no place in this heaving, bursting city. That she made no difference to anyone's lives at all.

'You're no one, my lion – you're everyone.'

'Everyone?'

Yes, he nodded. 'Do you understand, Layla? You don't exist. Yet you are the sum of the world.'

Layla told Osama how she used to sneak up to the laundry room of the big Clifton house. How her mother used to massage the wife of a powerful man. And how, as a child, she had found a staircase in the kitchen quarters that led to the main house, which no one could see because it was designed for the servants, built so they could enter and leave without disturbing the family, who were beautiful and so clean. Their home smelled of double *roti*, Layla told Osama, her voice lifting with the words, like warm, freshly baked and sliced white bread.

She had watched them a long time before they saw her. In the years when Zenobia started taking alternate Sundays off, Layla had not gone as often as she wanted to the beautiful Clifton house. On her last visit, she hid behind the doorframe of the laundry room, as though she had never left. They hadn't known Layla was there, like a lizard hanging off a ceiling fan, hadn't even suspected that there was a creature, breathing their air, growing tall listening to their secrets, wanting their life. But when the family, the lucky family – so lovely they had seemed to a young Layla the true embodiment of the sanctity of television, that they alone translated the glossy hopefulness and practised comfort of her favourite dramas into the real world – saw Layla peeping out of the laundry room, they hadn't greeted her with any mutual tenderness or fascination.

The son, now a chubby teenager with the blurry shadow of a moustache spreading thoughtlessly across his upper lip, had startled, as though Layla was a thief. *Oh my God*, he said, pressing a button on the remote for his video game, which cut the sound of cars racing and replaced it with fast, pumping music. *What's she doing here?*

As salam alaikum, Layla had said, opening the door wider, thinking Rahim might ask her inside the warm and lovely home to sit with him. She wanted to introduce herself and finally tell him her name; she knew his already, and knew also that this game with the cars was his favourite and that he had improved his remote driving over the past few months. But Rahim, no longer a boy, waved his remote at her. *Go, go, close the door.*

Layla had frozen, unsure of what he meant. Come in and close the door? She boldly stepped into the house, holding the boy in her eyes. But he had already turned away from her. *Rima!* he called to his older sister, his eyes blankly glued to the television screen. *That poor girl is here again. Can you make her go away?*

They had known she was there all the time, Layla told

309

Osama. It wasn't that they didn't know; they knew and they didn't want her. That cold knowledge – more than their unkindness, more than their rudeness – had hurt her the most.

'I want to leave.' Layla pressed the heels of her palms against her eyes, her body burning with the memory. 'I want to go away from here, I don't want to spend another day in this life. I don't want to remember any of this. None of it, not even one day.' She dragged her tongue across the words, as though stressing them would somehow make them true.

Osama had listened sympathetically, too kind to tell Layla what he had all those months ago: that the name was never going to change anything for her. Anita Rose by any other name was still as sad, still as lonely. He silently measured what he wished to say: Anita Rose, Miss Joseph. Listen to me. I will not be here forever. When will you listen to what I have been trying to teach you?

But Layla felt the words, she felt his warning travel between them, even as Osama shook his head and told her that running away was not the answer.

It had taken all her courage to come back here, to return to her comrade after everything she had done. After everything that had happened. Feroze wanted to go back to Dubai and asked his sister if she could come. His clients really wanted to see her, he said they'd even fly her business-class this time. But Layla fobbed him off; she had exams, she lied, she couldn't. But Feroze was insistent.

'Where would you go?'

'It doesn't matter, anywhere.'

'Why?'

'Because I'm heartsick – not for home. Not for anyone, no human soul. Heartsick for the promise of a new world.'

'*Arre vah.* Someone is a poet now?'

Layla didn't laugh. Osama didn't know what she had seen, he had no idea what she had been through. 'I'm serious, comrade.'

'So am I. *Kya style hai.*'

'One thousand kilometres, five hundred, three: those are footsteps. Do you hear me? I'll go. I don't care where. I can't stay here any more. I can't live like this – always watching over my shoulder, having no protection, depending on others for everything.'

'Anita, you stay right here—'

'Layla, call me Layla.'

The name sickened her, but still she clung to it. It was another person, all of this – everything that had happened – belonged to someone else, not her.

'Layla Rose, Anita Yusuf, Madam: stay here and fight. It's not an option for you to leave, your battle here has already begun. Be brave now. Stay here and see it through, like the rest of us.'

Layla shook her head, no. No more. 'I will walk it on my hands and knees.'

Osama waved her anger away, swatting it down like summer's bloated dengue mosquitoes. 'People like us, lion,' he took a sip from his glass, smudged with the whorls of his fingertips, 'break dreams.' Layla noticed that Osama called her lion more and more these days, avoiding her new name. He had called her Anita until she stopped answering to it. Even now, he didn't like to say her name. When he had to use it, it was always with the heaviness of disapproval. Layla, laden with disappointment. Layla, always uttered at the end of a sigh. But now she knew that she was not the first lion, not the most special, not even the original lion, and to hear this second-hand nickname wounded her a little.

Osama tilted the glass back and drank all the silvery liquid.

'We break dreams, my lion. Or else we are broken by them.'

'I will leave,' Layla insisted. 'The sea will carry me some distance, un-gently. It will carry me not because it wants to, not out of love; it will carry me because it has to. I will enter its waters and will not drown. I will pull through its currents like seaweed, floating sickly on the surface of its foaming, angry waves, wetted with salt and burned by the sun. Trucks. Lorries. Tankers. Some distance I will drive or be driven – not in a nice car. Not the kind with leather that smells of a man's cologne, of tobacco and expensive cigarettes, but the kind we have here: broken seats, smelling of sweat, engine leaking oil and fluid and ruined—'

'Layla,' Osama interrupted her with a hand placed over her own. 'Stop. People like that family in the Clifton house, they live lives of total fear,' he explained. 'They build fortresses around their fragile selves. Can you see that? Can you see how you would terrify them?'

'How could I terrify anyone?'

'Because you, unlike them, have no self. You are everything and nothing at once. You move invisibly through the world.'

Layla was not sure this was true.

'So?'

'That means you have no price – nothing to protect or lose.'

'Why is that frightening?'

'Oh, my lion, that is a truly terrifying quality.'

Monty

Monty and Layla sat at Espresso, an oceanic distance between them. The coffee shop didn't allow nannies or servants to sit at their glossy tables and, as Monty looked around, he saw only replicas of himself. Well-dressed boys with gelled hair, cigarettes and smartphones decorating their tables.

'Layla,' Monty asked, 'is everything okay?'

But Layla hadn't lifted her eyes to the room. She was holding her red notebook, her fingers splayed between its pages. Her eyes were puffy and red, as though she had been crying. Even in the dark light of the coffee shop, Monty could see the red cover shine, a spray of light every time Layla moved her hands. She pressed a pen against her lips and wrote in the notebook quietly.

When he called her, several times a day, she no longer answered the phone. Her grandfather, she said, was unwell. She had been looking after him. Is he alone? Monty asked, a question formulated only out of concern, but Layla bristled all the same. No, she snapped. He's not.

'Layla?'

Nothing.

'Are you upset?'

But then Layla looked up from her notebook and answered him with fatigue. 'Monty,' she sighed, 'do you need answers to everything? All the time?'

When he stood up to go to the bathroom, squeezing behind Layla's chair, Monty looked over her shoulder. Layla the lion. Those were the only words, right there on the first page of her secret notebook, that he managed to spy. Underneath it, in faded script, she had written and erased – and erased and erased, though the echo of the words remained: I am a lioness.

Returning, Monty noticed that Layla had brought her knees up, resting her feet on the walnut table, pulling her notebook even closer to her body, so no one in the small café could see what she was writing. He picked up his iced affogato, the hips of the cold glass bathed in chocolate sauce, and drank from his broken straw.

Monty could feel Layla slipping away from him, even after school when she took him down the unlit stairwells and corridors of their school and showed him how to touch her, guiding his hand, speaking slowly into his ear as she held him close, but then falling silent, her eyes drifting away in thought as Monty slipped his hands down her jeans, just as she'd instructed him. Layla, he would whisper in her ear, do you like this? But Layla, her body tensing under his touch, was silent and remote. Monty never got much further than that, intimidated and unmanned by Layla as he was.

That week, finally the day of their six-month anniversary, Monty had brought flowers to school. He hid the bouquet, scented with *ittar*, the perfume glistening on the petals, in his locker until lunchtime. All his books would smell of the cloying, putrid smell of roses for weeks afterwards. It would cling to Monty's things, reminding him of Layla and his inability to please her.

He took the flowers, bought at Boat Basin that morning on the way to school, to the lounge at noon, but didn't find Layla in front of the TV or by the counter. He knocked on the nurse's office, but Layla wasn't there, either. She wasn't in the stairway behind the psychology room, not on the football field by elementary. The roses were wilting with the heat and Monty, standing in the empty parking lot, was almost sick from the smell when he realized he hadn't looked in the library.

He pushed open the wooden doors, which swung creakily behind him. A bunch of friendless seventh-graders, who used the cover of a business society to disguise their unpopularity, sat on the armchairs in the entrance reading the financial papers. Monty knew where Layla would be and walked briskly to the Urdu section.

As he neared the last room in the musty high-school library, he heard the soft pat of books falling. And there was Layla, yanking books off the metal stands, grunting with the effort it took her to climb the shelves, pulling the books down by hooking her fingers under their spines.

'Layla?' Monty bent down to place the red roses on the carpeted floor.

'I can't find it,' she wailed, 'I can't find it anywhere.'

Her hair was strung all around her face. She had kicked off her brown *chappals* and stood barefoot on the library's blue carpet, breathing heavily, her eyes scanning the shelves manically. She lunged forward and pulled another set of books to the floor. As Monty moved to set his flowers somewhere safer, Layla turned and saw them. With her eyes flashing, sparkling with anger, she turned and kicked them, kicking the perfumed petals from their

315

buds with her feet, stepping on them, rubbing their soft colours into the skin of her heels.

'Layla, what are you doing!' Monty cried, but just then Mrs Sethi, the gentle librarian, came into the room.

'Dear girl,' she cooed, her blue eyes surveying the damage, 'what's the matter?'

'Habib Jalib,' Layla mumbled breathlessly, shaking her head, shaking it so hard the room began to spin and she couldn't see anything. Mrs Sethi held Layla in her arms and stroked her messy hair. Layla clung to the sleeves of the librarian's lawn *kameez*. 'I can't find him,' she repeated, her voice broken in so many places. 'He's gone.'

'There, there,' the librarian comforted her. 'He can't be far.'

Layla crumpled into tears and Mrs Sethi rocked her softly for a moment, but Layla was sobbing, and the tissue Mrs Sethi normally folded into the gold bangle on her wrist had got used that morning, mopping up some tipped-over tea. She turned to guide Layla, who was crying painfully into her shoulder, towards the librarian's desk, where a tissue box rested next to an old intercom telephone.

Mrs Sethi stepped over Monty's bruised roses. 'Pick those up, would you, dear?' she said as they left the room.

'We can go another five kilometres,' Monty said, his voice thin with exhaustion, 'just one more hour.' The desert road was sunk in darkness; they had been walking with no light ahead of them for at least an hour. The sand rustled underneath their feet, the quiet of the path ahead of them hung heavily in the air. No one had come to meet them in Tal Afar, no one came to relay their news back to the command centre. They had been forgotten. Now, all that was left was to get to Nineveh in time for the assault on the town – if it was still on. Monty didn't want to think anything negative, he didn't want to think the operation had been endangered, that he wouldn't be reunited with Layla. He hadn't come this far only to turn back.

He stumbled over his feet and nearly fell. Sunny paused and listened to the laboured sound of Monty's breathing as he picked himself up, flicking shards of stones and dirt off his hands. He didn't move to help him.

'We should keep going,' Monty insisted.

In the distance, someone was screaming.

'Another hour, then we can stop.'

'Can you hear that noise?' Sunny dropped his bag and cocked his head towards the sound.

'No, no, pick it up,' Monty stooped down and lifted Sunny's bag. They had to keep moving. They were so, so close. 'It's nothing – animals fighting or something. Let's keep moving.'

'It sounds like someone's dying,' Sunny stood perfectly still and unclipped the dagger on his belt.

'We can't stop yet,' Monty could barely feel his arms; he couldn't carry one more thing, not even Sunny's half-empty bag. 'We have to keep moving.' He raised his voice and pretended he couldn't hear the noise, even as the howling grew more savage. In his exhaustion, he could feel the painful tremor of the screams as they rang louder and closer.

They had picked up some food after leaving the meeting point, hungry and confused. Monty wanted to know what had happened – had the dam been attacked? Was it still ours? Had the Iraqis taken it back? But no courier came, no one called on the pay phone. Monty and Sunny shouldered their weapons and bags and walked on, weighed down by discomfort and exhaustion. How could Abu Khalid have forgotten them? All of the Nineveh operation depended on their march, didn't it?

'Let's walk another five K and then we can stop and eat,' Monty said to Sunny over the crying. The noise, as they neared it, sounded dry and haggard and Monty wondered if there were wolves out here in the desert. 'I bought us pickles.'

'Sorry, what?' Sunny raised an eyebrow, returning his knife to its holster. 'You bought us pickles?'

'Yeah' – bright-pink turnips and long green chillies. The man in the shop hadn't charged him for the roll of soft Arabic bread and pickles when he noticed how Monty was dressed. He knew who they were, the food was theirs – the shopkeeper shook his head and hands. No money, he said, no money and pointed to his empty till. Blease go – no money.

'Let me get this straight,' Sunny turned to face Monty. 'While we're trooping through this dry, dusty desert, at our one stop for food for the next three days you bought us food – no, *condiments* – soaked in salt and vinegar?'

'Yeah, so?'

Monty heard the crack of a pistol in the distance.

It wasn't animals fighting. It was people. And they had guns.

'So what?'

He heard it again. Another burst of noise. He wasn't imagining it. A shot like a pistol being fired and then a long, terrified howl.

Sunny shook his head. 'It's like sometimes you don't even think. You ever actually bought groceries before?' He squinted, trying to see Monty's face in the dark. 'You ever actually had to feed yourself, you spoilt shit?'

'That's it!' Monty screamed, throwing his bag down. 'I've had it with your misbehaving.'

'My *what*?' Sunny's eyes widened.

'You heard me,' Monty shouted. 'I don't care where you came from. You think just because your life was hard, you get to be an asshole all the time?'

'What do you know about hard?' Sunny's eyes shone in the darkness. 'You spend every night crying in your sleep.'

'At least I don't walk around all day feeling sorry for myself.' Monty stepped closer to Sunny, who held his ground.

Sunny's lips curled in a smirk. 'Oh, yeah? Who's Layla then?'

Monty felt his stomach lurch.

How had Sunny found out her name? What else did he know?

'I don't moan non-stop about how no one gets me, and how brown I am, and how cruel the world is,' Monty threw down. 'Be a man already.' He was surprised at himself as he blurted out the words, his heart racing with adrenaline.

Out of nowhere, Sunny threw his fist dead-centre into Monty's face. Monty felt a flash bulb go off right between his eyes. Before he could understand what was happening, Sunny slammed his body against him, grabbing Monty's waist with both his arms, ramming his head against his side until he had thrown Monty to the ground.

Monty's heart was beating wildly, but he didn't care. All he could think about was Layla and reaching her in

Nineveh and getting away from this moment. He hoped that Sunny hadn't seen the fear in his eyes when he heard him say Layla's name.

Sunny pinned Monty to the floor, lying on top of him chest-to-chest, so Monty couldn't move, couldn't twist his hands an inch to free himself or punch back.

'I am a man,' Sunny yelled, spit gathering at the corner of his mouth. He sat up and jammed his knee against Monty's neck, leaning over his face. 'I don't get all worked up because some bitch dumped me. I *am* a man.' He lifted his arm and brought his elbow down hard against Monty's chin.

'Please . . .' Monty wailed, unable to move his head to save himself from Sunny's blows. But Sunny hit him again, sweating, furious, until they heard the noise again.

Someone was firing a pistol.

A glow switched on up ahead, far enough away that Sunny couldn't make out what was happening, but close enough to cast a faint shadow of light over them. He paused and lifted his knee off Monty's neck.

Monty's head was spinning, he felt cold and dizzy. All he could hear was dogs barking. 'It's kids,' he mumbled, sitting up as quickly as he could, so Sunny couldn't attack him again. He touched his neck softly; it hurt him to breathe. 'We have to keep moving.' His chin was raw and his face throbbed with every gesture – blinking, swallowing, speaking. He winced as he stood up. He felt like he would collapse from the pain.

'What are kids doing out in the desert at night?' Sunny started walking towards the light with single-minded focus, striding ahead as though he hadn't been strangling Monty just a minute earlier.

'Wait,' Monty begged. His heart was pounding against his ribcage and his hands were shaking. As much as Sunny terrified him at that moment, he didn't want to get any closer to those gunshots. He walked slowly behind Sunny, his steps unsteady and unsure. His face was going to be bruised something awful, and he ran his tongue along the inside of his mouth, feeling for his teeth, making sure they were all there.

'*As salam alaikum,*' Sunny called loudly as they approached the figures. They were brothers, Monty could see that now. Four of them, Kalashnikovs slung across their shoulders.

The brothers were standing in a circle and, when they broke apart, Monty saw that one of them was holding a stray dog by the scruff of its neck. Monty could only see their eyes, they were wearing masks over their faces. There were three dead dogs by their feet, bleeding heavily on the desert floor.

'Welcome, brother!' the first man shouted, raising his hands and gesturing for them to come closer. He spoke with an accent, but Monty couldn't tell what kind. The man lifted his balaclava over his mouth. 'Where are you coming from?'

'Mosul,' Monty replied hesitantly.

'*Mashallah,*' the man nodded, searching his battered face. 'You all right, brother?'

'What are you doing?' Sunny interrupted, holding his AK tight.

The first man laughed and pointed to the brother crouched down on the sand, holding the remaining dog. 'Brad over here was showing us a LiveLeak video of these two American soldiers – you had to see it. Flung these puppies off a cliff.'

The dog whimpered, its eyes darting between Monty and Sunny as though they might help it.

Brad laughed. 'Hilarious. A bunch of puppies, seeing which one would land the furthest, fall the fastest, cry the loudest. But we don't have any cliffs and guard duty is long, know what I mean?'

'No. What do you mean?' Sunny's voice was brittle and hostile.

The third brother was filming everything on his phone. Monty turned away from him, wishing he had a balaclava to hide his own bashed-up face. He didn't want his mother to see him on some CNN news story, torturing animals.

'Nothing, man,' Brad laughed, 'just a bit of fun. We're trying to see if we can get more hits than that other video. Go a bit viral, you know?'

The fourth brother just stood there, a pistol in his hand.

Monty touched Sunny's arm. 'Let's go, Sunny.'

Sunny shrugged him off.

'Sunny, we have a long way to go. Let's leave.'

But Sunny didn't move. 'What are you going to do to the dog?' he asked Brad.

The brother jerked the dog's head up, and the small animal cried in pain.

'We got tired of shooting them,' Brad stood up, still holding the dog, and slapped Sunny on the back, 'want to fuck it?'

They walked for another forty minutes, their legs aching and their soles burning. 'Let's keep going,' Monty repeated mindlessly, like a mantra. 'Let's keep going.'

They walked far enough to create a gulf of distance

between them and their comrades killing the dogs. Monty and Sunny walked until the desert was quiet again and only the sound of their boots shuffling through the cooling sand trailed behind them.

I am a sentinel. I am a beacon. I am a sentinel. I am a beacon. Monty recited the words silently over and over in his head as he marched through the cold desert, but they gave him no comfort, no solace. The wind whipped through the sand. He closed his eyes against the grains that swirled in the air, disturbing everything.

Why hadn't Sunny done anything? Why hadn't he fought those men? Monty ran his tongue along the inside of his mouth. He could still taste the blood from the blows to his face. Had Sunny been afraid of them?

Monty could hear Sunny's shallow breathing as he jogged ahead of him at a slow trot. Was he crying?

When they stopped, Sunny built an altar of fire. Monty hung his head in his hands and tried to breathe through the pain that coursed through his body. 'This is all our movement is,' Monty said softly, running his tired fingers through the sand. He tried not to think of what had happened to the dog. Shadows danced through the naked flames, imprinting themselves on the sand around the boys.

'Nah.' Sunny took off his shoes and settled his head down on his bag. 'This *was* Iraq, but it's ours now.'

'Iraq will hold.' Monty stared up at the cloudless black night. Maybe he wasn't among an army of sentinels. They were crucifiers and killers and, although he couldn't even understand how, dog rapists.

'It will break,' Sunny replied. 'It's already broken. Don't you see? We're fighting a war against nationalism, against borders. Some idiots torturing an animal late at night doesn't change what we're doing, Monty. Every army has its lowlifes. Hello? Remember Abu Ghraib?'

Sunny checked his phone before tucking it under his bag and rolling onto his side. It was midnight. 'Don't be down,' he mumbled, his concentration fading. He hadn't charged his phone since Tal Afar, and even his backup battery pack was drained. He hadn't been near any sockets and was seriously trying to conserve some battery.

He wanted nothing more than to zone out with a bit of scrolling through his Facebook, playing around on his socials. He didn't have the energy to do anything else. He didn't want to think about the day, didn't want to think about those brothers, about Oz. Sunny didn't want to think, even for a second, that coming here had been a mistake.

He just wanted to watch some Snaps, check in with his followers, who expected things from him now. He was out here, fighting a holy war. He was allowed his small privacies.

But with only 30 per cent of his battery remaining, he might as well just go to sleep.

'It was just a dog,' Sunny said out loud, almost to himself.

Monty nodded.

It was just a dog.

Layla

Back then, in the early morning, Karachi's sky hung over the city, a bluish-grey slate. The glittering green domes of mosques were set upon by an unkindness of ravens, ambushing the minarets and dipping their beaks into the shallow ponds of water under the courtyard taps. Layla stood on an empty street in Saddar and waited to cross the road, listening to the rip of shutters being pulled up. She had been out walking since dawn and had seen the sky skip all the colours of the sunrise.

She walked quietly, her head down, her eyes turned away from the wallpaper of political posters peeling off the walls, listening for the birds. But that early in the morning, surrounded by Saddar's weary stones, all Layla could hear was the mad symphony of traffic: scooters without any exhaust; the cry of rickshaws, sputtering against a stream of speeding, honking cars; bells on cycles; the wail of bus conductors calling passengers to jump on buses that had no time to stop.

Layla entered the cathedral, pausing to kneel at the entrance of St Patrick's sandstone arches, just as her mother had taught her. She touched her knee to the cold floor and bowed before the blessed sacrament, crossing her fingers in a star, from her forehead to her heart, to her left and then her right shoulders.

She raised herself and walked towards the echoes of

the priest as he read a decade of the rosary before the congregation.

She slipped into a pew near the back, making sure she was alone and that there was no one in the row behind her. There were only five people seated for morning mass. Two ladies with the *palu* of their saris wrapped around their waist to keep their stomachs warm in the draughty cathedral, an elderly gentleman with his white-haired wife, and a young woman on her knees in a plain blue skirt, bowed in prayer. Layla watched her for a moment; her back was shaking, as though she were performing a secret dance, wiggling her shoulders and tapping her out-stretched feet, left and right, to the cold floor. As the woman twirled and danced, she turned round and smiled at Layla. Eunice D'Silva.

Layla looked away quickly, hoping Eunice hadn't seen her. She squeezed her eyes shut and listened to the call of the rosary.

'I believe in the Holy Ghost,' she repeated, her voice merging with that of the thin congregation, 'in the Holy Catholic Church, the communion of Saints, the forgive-ness of sinners—'

Pssst.

Layla kept her eyes closed. She should have gone to a Protestant church; all she wanted was to be alone, where no one would know her and no one would watch her. But she had come here, to her childhood church. It felt impor-tant, necessary, to be here, to run her hands in the holy water one more time, to sit on the rock-hard pews, to light one more candle, to stand before the statue of Our Mother and recite the sorrowful prayers that brought solace to lost souls. 'I believe in the resurrection of the body, and the life everlasting. Amen.'

Pssssssssst, Eunice hissed, moving her lips along every letter as though she was whistling. She rounded her lips and flattened them, gulping in a breath of air before continuing, *sssssssSSSSSSsssssssssssstttt*.

The priest at the altar began to recite 'Our Father'. Layla opened her eyes as he mumbled her favourite lines and looked at Eunice smiling broadly, waving her hand in the air.

How are you? Eunice mouthed.

Layla returned her toothy smile. *Very fine.*

Mummy kahan hai?

Busy hai. Layla eased herself gently onto the unpadded kneeler. She didn't think anyone would be here for the early-morning mass, but she should have expected Eunice. She breathed deeply as the priest's voice merged with the congregation's, reciting the rosary solemnly, hopefully.

Pssssssst.

Her mother said Eunice was a little slow, that she had been dropped as a child, that she had no family to speak of and no love to heal her. That was why one had to be charitable to her, extra-kind. That was why she was always at church, Zenobia said, because it was a sanctuary for those alone in the world. Eunice sang in the choir, she passed around the collection plate after mass, she handed out rice at weddings and sugared almonds at baptisms. Feroze called her Younis, the church pet.

Aneeeeta, Eunice giggled.

Aneeeee-taaaaa.

It had been so long since anyone called her name.

As the priest and his flock spoke the rosary dutifully, their sad voices growing dull with repetition, someone shuffled into the pew behind Layla, slapping their *shalwar kameez* as though dusting it off, before sitting down. She closed her eyes and lowered her head back to her clenched palms, checking quickly before she did so that Eunice wasn't watching her. Eunice was facing the altar, shouting the rosary louder than anyone else.

Layla exhaled and repeated the longings of her people. 'Forgive our sins, save us from the fires of hell and lead all souls into heaven, especially those most in need of your mercy.'

'Sister,' a voice travelled from the pew behind. The *shalwar kameez* rustled with movement as a man copied Layla's pose, resting his knees on the hard wooden bench.

Layla lifted her head and stared straight in front of her, at the priest counting down a decade of veneration and prayer.

'Did you have any trouble?' she asked, not looking at the man.

'No, sister.' He had a gentle voice, which Layla had not expected. She wondered if he was young – her age. He cleared his throat and spoke carefully, hesitating. 'Are you sure it's okay to be inside here?'

'This is the safest place to speak, no one is watching us here,' Layla replied.

'Some people complained, sister, they said it was *haram*.' The man relaxed slightly. 'But the commander said you are a natural fighter. You know how to hide in the earth, how to strike before anyone sees you.'

The man put his hand through the gap between them and placed an envelope on Layla's wooden pew.

'You will fly via Erbil,' he whispered. 'Our people will meet you and escort you onwards.'

Layla nodded.

'The ticket is return – you won't have any trouble at immigration. Our man at FIA will be watching you, he will make sure you get through. If you have any problems, please call the number written on the envelope.'

Layla bowed her head as though out of respect, then lifted it once more. The man continued.

'We have included bank statements and a thousand dollars in case you need it, sister.'

'I don't need it.' Layla spoke softly.

Eunice turned round from facing the altar and stuck her tongue out at Layla. The decade was almost finished. Layla ignored her. Eunice kept her tongue out, blowing a raspberry.

There was silence for a moment. Layla hoped the man hadn't seen Eunice.

'*Alhamdulilah*,' he said finally, sounding impressed as his *shalwar kameez* rustled with movement. He was standing up. Layla could feel him hovering over her. He paused for a moment. Layla couldn't see him. She had no idea whether the courier was young or old, beautiful or not, whether his hair was shaved close to the skull or grew long around his shoulders. She tried to gauge what he was looking at.

She cleared her voice. 'Anything else?'

Layla waited a moment.

'*Bhai?*' she whispered, but the man had already gone.

Sunny

Sunny sits on the broken pavement in front of a small fruit shop while he waits for his phone to charge. Empty cigarette boxes, with the health warnings written in Arabic, are crumpled and strewn across the street. Vegetable and fruit sellers are the only commerce on the road; some sell only a few metal plates of produce – two onions and a few potatoes – while others are more bountiful. The man whose outlet Sunny is using comes out of his shop with a bucket filled with banana peel and watermelon rinds, which he chucks into the gutter by the kerb.

Monty paces up and down across the narrow street, keeping his distance from Sunny. He scratches his neck, inhaling painfully through his teeth as his nails break the skin, all red and bumpy from where a mound of ants got him.

You a traitor, Ozzy, Sunny types into a blank email. *You a betrayer, a wound to your people, to your blood. If I die out here, that's on you.* He sends it to his cousin's old email address as well as that new newsletter one.

Sunny opens his Facebook, it's been a while since he was on. He uploads a picture of Rita, looking gorgeous, bless her, *#ritadiaries #automatova #thuglife,* while he thinks of the right words for his post. Two teenage boys ride a bicycle along the street, watching Monty and Sunny keenly as they cycle by slowly. Their eyes are red and, although they're kids, there is something haggard, something ghostly, about them.

Are you, or is someone you love, an apostate?

What's an apostate, you ask? A traitor. A backstabber. A Judas. A Brutus. A man who turns his back on his family and his religion. A man who blasphemes just to fit in, who will do anything to be accepted by his oppressors. A man who betrays his people and his heritage. Apostates are everywhere – no place they can't reach and no damage they can't do – eating us up from the inside, like cancer. The INSIDE, you hear? Like bone-marrow-deep, coiled into the body like a virus, like poison.

Coconuts, Westoxified brothers in Hugo Boss suits doing cartwheels for the man, 'ex-Muslims', 'Muslim reformers' – sound familiar? – they're your own blood, your own family.

What are the ten signs that someone you love is an apostate?

1. He flips sides – left to right, white to black.

2. He shits all over his past.

3. He insults his religion and the very ideas he once claimed he would die for.

You don't need seven more signs. Apostates are scum. So what do you do when someone you know is an apostate?

Ask Rita.

There's so much more Sunny wants to say, but he has to be careful now. If the brothers out here find out about Oz – before Sunny can prove to them how deep his metal runs, how firm his allegiance, how ready he is to die – they will think he's a traitor, just like his cousin. But Sunny knows how to lie low, more than any brother out here; he has true practice in bottling up all the pain he feels, taking it subterranean, deep down.

He dips into his Twitter account, a platform he's begun to use as the meta-expressions of his more substantial, political posts:

I'm a stretch of barbed wire, barbed down to the bone, my brother.

But no one follows him out there; no one really understands the depth of what Sunny feels.

No betrayal – not even Oz's – can make him drop his cover now. He has to be careful, he's just getting started here.

My final stop isn't some godforsaken Iraqi village. Hell, no. I'm going all the way to the H-O-L-Y Land, I'm flying straight on to Paradise.

How do you make a post go viral? Hashtags. But they're a pain to think of. Especially given Sunny's unique situation.
#revenge #retaliate #remove
#fuckreformingradicals #pussy #apostate #bitchceo
#askrita #hova #swag
Sunny leans over a steel plate of watermelon that the fruit seller cut up, finds the largest chunk of watermelon and eats it messily over his lap, spitting the seeds out onto the road ahead.

No retweets, no likes on Twitter, but he's got replies on Facebook already. He scans through them. But people don't seem to get what he's saying . . .

Is an atheist an apostate?

Sir, what you are meaning? You are angry with your family? Family is good blessings.

My girl was cheating on me with my best friend. Them two are apostats. #fml

Oz is on GQ and CNN and even BuzzFeed ('Ten sexiest rebels of 2017'), with literally *millions* of people lining up to agree with his shit, and Sunny can't even get a high-five on a 100-word Facebook post?

He sits tight, eating sticky chunks of sweet watermelon with his fingers.

'Tomorrow?' he asks, looking away from his phone and wiping his hands on his cargo trousers.

'Yup.' Monty is all nerves. Sunny sees him, wound super-tight. Paranoid, eyes jumping all over the place, watching everywhere for signs.

This is it, then. Tomorrow they'll reach Nineveh and he'll be done with Monty, thank God.

Sunny checks his post again. Same shit, no one gets him.

why don't you taliban bitches just go die?

He's getting shit, getting trolled while Oz is neck-deep in accolades.

Sunny closes his eyes and breathes deeply. He could break something right now. He should have slammed those brothers with the dogs into the ground. Should have broken their jaws and taken their weapons and shot them. He should have, he knows it. He feels it.

He blinks it back, trying not to think about it. He keeps his eyes closed and pushes everything far behind the gates. All the sorrow, all the pain. He doesn't think about him, about Aloush; doesn't think about Apollo Café. Sunny doesn't think of those things that didn't happen.

He doesn't think about Pa – not about being abandoned

by his only family in the world, by the only man he ever really loved. Sunny blinks it all back. That's his power, his true strength. He thinks of Oz in the car at Fratton, the morning he left. Sunny didn't tell his cousin he'd stood outside his house the night before, didn't tell him about going to Kofi's after, or where he went after all that shit went down with Naya. Didn't tell him about going home from Aloush's after sunrise, only to collect his bag and place his debit card on the kitchen countertop, his only goodbye to Pa.

'You done with this world?' Oz asked Sunny in the car as he dropped him at the station.

And Sunny nodded. He was. He was done with it all.

'You done with the girls?' Sunny nodded. 'You done with the drums and that seedy club?'

And although Oz didn't say his name – Sunny never gave him anything of Aloush, never told him anything – it ached, like Oz took a steel plank to his bones. Aloush wasn't seedy. He wasn't. He was beautiful and pure.

'Brothers go to die there,' Oz said, all lies.

Sunny ain't dead. He ain't going nowhere.

He clenches and unclenches his fists. He breathes slowly. He exhales. He clenches and unclenches. 'What's going to happen when we get there?' Sunny stands up and stretches. He has to move.

Monty looks surprised to be asked. 'I don't know . . .'

Sunny swings Rita across his chest and fires a round in the air, frightening the life out of the fruit seller, who falls to the floor. Sunny doesn't care. The bicycle boys are on foot now and they materialize from behind the corner of the street and run, their thin sneakers pounding across the concrete, shouting and whistling. They must be informers. For whom, Sunny can't even begin to guess.

'I'm just getting started out here!' Sunny shouts into the sky. 'Imma tell people my name. They're gonna be afraid of me. They better hide, they better beg God to take them out from under my fire.'

Oz is going to be reading about Sunny soon. About *me*, son.

'Automatova Kalashnikova!' Sunny screams, his ears ringing from the burst of gunfire as Monty cowers next to the shop front.

I'm going to make a name for myself out here.

Sunny's heart is pounding, beating against his breastbone.

I'm going to be someone, just like Pa wanted.

Monty crawls towards his bag, the noise of the AK filling the dead space between him and Sunny, who stands, breathing deeply, watching Monty. Why's he so jittery? He thinks it doesn't show. Monty thinks he's hiding that shit deep, but a man can see the terror in his eyes. Sunny follows Monty as he picks up his bag and dusts his trousers down. I see you, my brother. I recognize.

The fruit vendor jumps up out of nowhere, tossing Sunny's chargers at him, before slamming his shutters down.

The boys walk back to the sandy highway.

'You scared?' Sunny asks Monty, sneaking a sideways glance. Monty walks quietly, his brows furrowed and his shoulders tense. He nods softly. Sunny's not scared; he just doesn't want to die before he's done what he has to. As a teenager he had loved those lines of Tupac's, *inna lillahi wa inna illayhi raaji'oon*, back before he discovered the solace of God: 'I want to be better. You grow. We all grow.

335

We're made to grow. You either evolve or you disappear.' Sunny's not gonna disappear. He's going deeper into this thing, losing himself in it.

As he walks, he thinks about teaching Oz – who never cared about nobody, who never did anything real in his life – what it means to believe in something. To take back something glorious, to restore their people to something *true*.

Sunny rubs his eyes with the back of his fist. He wonders if Oz ever thinks about him.

He pulls his phone out and checks his email. But there's nothing.

Oz doesn't give a shit if he dies out here. Maybe he never cared about Sunny at all.

For a moment, Sunny wonders if any of it had been real.

'I'm not worried,' he says to Monty, looking up at him, his face ashy with anxiety. 'We live by the sword, we die by the sword.'

Monty shrugs. 'I've never done anything like this before.'

But Sunny sees something in his eyes.

He sees a different kind of fear, another type altogether, the kind that comes with carrying a heavy secret. Sunny knows that look. Everyone he knows wears it – Oz had it bad, Pa too, pretending to be something he wasn't all the time. Even Sunny's got it. What man doesn't have a secret or two?

But still. Monty?

What's he hiding?

Monty

After a while, it all looked the same. The dark sand, the anaemic shrubbery, the low flight of the birds, the solitary, stooped shepherd grazing a family of sheep.

Monty's hands were in his pockets and he walked slowly, his body weighed down with dread. He wished for a moment that he was out here with his mother, walking and talking like they did sometimes at Hilal Park, moving against the grain of aunties in joggers and uncles with mobile phones attached to their ears, circling the kilometre-long track. They went after *maghrib*, always when the sun sank behind the clouds and the ravens dipped in and out of the fading sky. Since her conversion, Monty had been Zahra's only real friend. He missed speaking to someone, really speaking.

He hadn't allowed himself to think of his parents very much since leaving home. His mother was the only one who supported his coming out here. Akbar Ahmed took it as a personal insult, slapping his son in front of the servants and disowning him. You are the ruin of this family, Akbar Ahmed shouted, his burgundy tie straining against his throat, his face a matching red of fury – words that Monty tried not to carry with him. He also knew that his father was worried about his business and how, as always, things would look.

He didn't mean to disown Monty, not really. His mother

would calm him down over time. Zahra liked the idea of her son working as a servant of God. Though she couldn't see that that wasn't why Monty wanted to come here. As close as she was to her son, Zahra didn't know him at all.

He tried not to think about the past; he knew if he was going to be reunited with Layla, love of his life, he had to focus.

Monty looked over at Sunny, his eyes were bright with excitement. He had come to Mosul eight, maybe nine, months ago. Monty ran the calculations in his head. That was about the same time as Layla.

'You ready for some blood?' Sunny asked him, interrupting his thoughts, turning his face up to meet Monty's, his eyes narrow and dark.

'No,' Monty frowned, digging his hands further into his pockets. Every so often, he caught a glimmer of something cruel in Sunny, something hard.

Maybe it was just the way he clenched his jaw when he was upset, or the way his face contorted when he felt you were putting him down. Sunny was difficult to read, he wore so many masks; every time Monty thought he had seen them all, a new one slid over his eyes. Monty raised his arm, blocking the sun from his eyes, to look at Sunny now, walking contentedly, a mirror of calm. 'Are you?'

Sunny turned his face to Monty and smiled. 'Baby, what else you come out here to do, if not kill some infidels?'

'I came out here to live,' Monty said, dropping his hand. I came out here to find a girl, to be with the girl I love, to be with Layla. But he didn't say that.

'I came out here to be a part of something beautiful.'

Sunny

'In Latakia, you can travel along the Mediterranean Sea at sunset.' Aloush exhaled the smoke from his cigarette in between his words. 'You float down the water on wooden boats with sails trailing endlessly like veils.'

His long eyelashes were so dark it looked like his eyes were lined in pencil.

'They're old boats, the Romans used them to navigate our waters. *Lateens*, that's what we call the sails; they skim the water, pushing against the breeze.'

It made no sense: none of what Sunny knew about the world could explain what he felt; none of the knowledge translated across oceans of history and time; none of the observations he had learned from a life lived underground, off the radar, invisible and unseen.

Why did their bodies pull towards each other when they shared the small stage at Apollo? Who could Sunny tell about the impulse he felt, when Ali's calloused fingers touched his, soft and still unbroken, as they passed the drums between each other?

When the basement swelled with people pouring whisky from hidden flasks into their teacups and the music was so loud it trembled against the walls, Aloush pulled Sunny towards him, holding the nape of his neck in the palm of his hand, and spoke into his ear. His breath always smelled of sleep, a little stale, a little strong. How could Sunny explain why in those moments he wanted to touch the DJ, to hold his calloused, hard hands, to run his own soft fingers through Aloush's dark, curly hair, to wipe a stray golden-leaf tobacco off the corner of his full lips?

When Sunny watched him, he felt Ali's body move as though it were his own. Every turn of his shoulder, every tug of his smile – Sunny felt it all.

He thought then, listening to Aloush speak of sails that caressed the sea, of the nights he had lain in his bed speaking to the ceiling in his dark bedroom. *If only somehow you could be mine*, he whispered the poem to the bricks and cement of his cold English house, *what wouldn't be possible in the world?* Sunny promised himself that some day he would know what those thick, worn hands felt like, held in the warmth of his own. Sunny promised the fine layer of neglect and dust on the blinds that he would kiss those lips, inhaling Aloush's breath, smelling of sleep, deep into his lungs. Sunny promised the dirty yellow curtains that he wouldn't close his eyes. He would keep them open and count the lashes that lined Aloush's cloudy eyes.

Sunny tried to remember now if any of it was real.

If Aloush's eyelashes really were that dark, if he really spoke to him about the sacred waters, if he had said one day Sunny should see Damascus, if he really said that Sunny should come and see his home.

'You would like it,' Aloush said – did he? – lifting the bronze *dallah* on his kitchen stove, holding it above the gas fire as the coffee bubbled to a boil, tapping it once, twice, three times, to ensure the foam collected to make a thick skin on the face of the coffee.

It was almost dawn and Sunny stood behind Aloush,

holding him in his arms, warm against his skin, his arms draped across his naked heart.

Aloush closed the flame and rested his head back against Sunny, who hadn't told him – couldn't – that in four hours he'd be on a plane.

'One day,' Sunny said, inhaling the cardamom that perfumed Aloush's skin, 'you'll show it to me.'

One day, Aloush repeated.

The words hung on his lips with hope, as though he meant every word.

One day.

Monty

There were signs. Monty just didn't know how to read them.

They had a week off school, mid-term break. *Do you want to go have coffee?* Monty texted Layla, but she didn't reply. Hours later he received only one word: *no*.

Do you want to see a movie? he texted two days later. *Caramel popcorn at Neuplex?* But again, one word, as though she wasn't even bothering to read his messages: *no*.

On the fifth day of break, Monty tried a gold card. *Do you want to go to the beach?* He saw the grey bubbles of Layla typing. They wobbled before him for a minute, lifting his spirits, and then again: *no*.

Monty had been calling her all break, with barely any answer. His iMessages were reaching her and his Whats-Apps were being read. But no matter how long he waited, Layla never replied.

When he tried her on FaceTime, always audio so that she could speak to him without her brother overhearing their conversations, she cut his calls dead. But it didn't occur to Monty that it was him. It never struck him that something was wrong with him.

He imagined it was the city – power cuts, Internet faults, maybe her mother was being difficult. So on the night before break ended, Sunday, when Layla finally called, waking him up in the middle of the night, Monty had all his defences down.

'Did you miss me?' Layla spoke in that voice she used when it was late and she wanted him.

'Yes,' Monty replied, sitting up sleepily in bed, 'very much.'

'What did you miss about me?' Layla dropped her voice to a whisper. Monty could hear noise in the background – people and some kind of noise, like a loud television playing. Layla sounded giddy, maybe even a little agitated, it was hard to tell.

'I missed all of you,' Monty said, sinking back against his pillows. 'I missed your face, your hair, your hands. What's that noise, Layla?'

'What else?'

'Are you out somewhere?'

'Go on.' Layla held the phone so close to her face, Monty could hear the shallow swell of her breathing.

'I missed you touching me.'

'Where do you want me to touch you?'

'Everywhere.'

'No,' Layla said, her voice deepening. 'Tell me where.'

'My neck,' Monty whispered. For all her openness, Monty never could go all the way with Layla. They always stopped before things escalated. He respected her, he said, he didn't need her to do those things, not yet. But the truth was, she unsettled him. 'My neck when you kiss me.'

'Where else?'

'My back.' He could hear the sudden irritation in her voice. He thought of Layla, sneaking out of a movie or a party to talk to him on the phone, and smiled. But then he looked at the time on his phone. It was past four in the morning. No cinemas were open. No one they knew would be having a party, not on Sunday before school – not at that time.

'Layla, where are you?'

'Tell me, Monty,' Layla repeated impatiently. 'Tell me something real.'

'I love you, Layla,' Monty said, sitting up, suddenly awake. He checked the time again: where was she? Who was she with? Monty listened carefully, straining to hear the noise in the background; it wasn't a party, it wasn't a TV. It was an announcement system, like a radio. It sounded and then fell silent, sounded and then fell silent.

'That's not good enough, Monty,' Layla replied, her mood suddenly dark.

He didn't want to argue with her or step on one of her landmines right now. 'What do you mean? It's all I have.'

'I meant what I said, Monty – that's not good enough. I'm a lion, do you hear me, Monty? I'm a beast. Give me something real.'

Before he could reply, before he could even think what to say – what was she talking about? – Layla walked back towards the noise. He heard the announcement system coming back to life, a voice rising and, just as quickly, ending. Was she at an airport?

'I'm going, Monty.'

That's all she said.

'I'm going now, take care.'

He looked at his phone; he wanted to see her so much, he searched for the button to turn the camera on, but when he lifted the phone, Layla was gone.

Monty tried to call her back; he messaged and called, but couldn't get through. When he called her phone number the next day in the car on the way to school, as Tano wove through traffic, dialling the number that he had given her, an automated message said the phone had been disconnected.

He hadn't eaten breakfast, had barely slept after their fight. He fumbled with the keyboard on the screen and his fingers hovered over all the wrong letters, ineptly trying to type an email to Layla.

Lalyal

Llay

'Slow down,' he grumbled at Tano, swerving past motorbikes and rickshaws. 'I can't see.'

Lyala where r u

When Monty reached school, Layla wasn't there. She had left.

'Don't you know?' Kashif asked as they sat in the lounge at lunch. 'She's no longer enrolled.'

'No longer enrolled?' Monty repeated the words, as Kashif and Shavez looked at each other uncomfortably.

'She was expelled,' Shavez said slowly, surprised at Monty's lack of knowledge about the situation. 'Everyone's talking about it. Didn't she tell you?' But Kashif shot him a look and Shavez shut up.

Layla had left school, but that was all anyone could agree on. Her mother pulled her out, she was going to a girls' convent in Murree, she had moved to Lahore to live with an aunt, she was married, she was pregnant, she was on the lam, she was in jail, she had left the country. All those rumours and more circulated around the American School. But no one would tell Monty why – why had Layla left in the first place?

Shavez took Monty aside, after watching him creep from person to person during lunch, asking when they last saw Layla. 'Dude, she was expelled,' Shavez explained patiently, 'what are you doing?'

But it couldn't be. 'There's something you're not telling me.' Monty shook his head. 'Why would she be expelled?'

Shavez held his hands up. 'Don't shoot the messenger, bro.'

Monty's heart ached. What had Layla done?

He got in his car as soon as school ended and ordered Tano to drive to Gulshan. '*Sahib*,' Tano demurred, not meeting Monty's eyes, 'I don't think we should.' Monty insisted: Gulshan, now. But where in Gulshan, Monty didn't know. He'd never driven Layla home, always dropping her off at school and handing her a hundred rupees to catch a rickshaw back. The dirty, cramped streets were alien to him, and every *gully* was teeming with apartment buildings, crowding each other for space as they rose messily into the sky. He thought Gulshan would look like his neighbourhood, tidy bungalows with nameplates outside every home. Monty had never been that far into Karachi before. He kept his eyes on the road, careful not to meet the glances of the men who bent down to peer into his silver Audi, staining the windows with their greasy fingerprints.

All the buildings, their balconies lined with laundry and covered in metal grilles like cages, looked the same to him. He thought of the boys who caught mynah birds with orange whirls around their eyes and sold them at traffic lights. You bought a bundle of three or four birds trapped in a net, out of pity, only to take them home and free them back into the sky. But the birds were trained in captivity and flew right back to the boys who, having taught them never to be free, caught and sold them again.

346

Monty drove back home to Clifton, feeling like one of those mynahs, consumed with a pain he had no mechanism to cope with.

He called Layla every day, trying to find out if any of the rumours were true. Had she really got married or become an air stewardess? Had she been arrested for drug-dealing? There was no record of her at any of the other schools he knew – not at Grammar, not Bayview, not even Lyceum. He checked her Facebook for updates, but her account had been closed. He tried asking the girls at school, but they had wiped their hands clean of Layla.

'Next time, try not to pick such an obvious disaster, Monty,' Sarya sneered as the rest of them giggled. But they were just jealous. No one cared for them the way he loved Layla.

It was a foreigner she had run away with, people said. It was a foreigner and he was white, or Indian, or older, and she was definitely married. Or pregnant. Her brother had asked for a crazy dowry, like millions – rupees, obviously: that was the gossip another week. Monty remembered Layla's stories about Feroze's Arab clients, how he entertained them and looked after their every need. Had he done the same for his sister? Had Feroze married her off for a price?

At the height of his desperation, Monty even considered calling Feroze. But as soon as he thought of it, he knew the rumours were probably true.

'Monty,' Shavez held him by the shoulders, exasperated at having to talk about Layla all the time, 'I promise you: she's not married.'

Kashif, normally keen to stay out of the whole mess, pointed out that no one had ever been expelled for getting married. But no one at their school had ever got married, Monty countered. They didn't know Layla like he did. They didn't know what she was capable of.

It hurt him to imagine her as a runaway bride, but it hurt less than the silence she had left him in. Monty needed a reason for Layla's disappearance – any reason, anything, so long as it wasn't him. She couldn't have disconnected her phone, cut him off and left school because she got bored. If it was because of something dramatic, then fine, at least it wasn't Monty.

'Do you hear yourself?' Shavez asked, scratching his arm uncomfortably. 'What kind of girl leaves school just because she's bored of her "boyfriend"?'

Kashif agreed. 'Monty, it's a bit much really . . . *chill maro yaar.*'

Monty didn't like how Shavez had said 'boyfriend': what was that supposed to mean? He didn't like how eager they were to close the topic, as though they were hiding something. He noticed how people stopped talking when he walked into the lounge, and how they smiled and bit their tongues when he asked if they had heard from Layla.

It was something bad, there were signs.

There were the missed calls, that noise he had heard on Sunday night. That call when she asked him for something real, something true. And Monty, like a child, had not understood that there was something untrue between them.

All his books and the walls of his beige locker still stank of *ittar* and rotten roses.

Irshad in the lounge insisted that Monty pay Layla's tab, showing him a register lined with Snickers and Coke and chilli chips that Layla had racked up before spring break, and her locker was handed over to a freshman

348

Monty didn't recognize. Then one afternoon, just as the bell rang and he stepped out of the library, he saw Feroze across the parking lot.

Layla's brother strode through the school, wearing a shiny leather jacket, tightly fitted, and boots that sounded across the concrete as he walked. Feroze stopped just before the gate, got into a black Toyota Corolla, started the engine and peeled out of the school. It was the latest-model Corolla, at least five times more expensive than the grey box Feroze used to drive. The gossip around school, circulated via the nurse who knew everything, was that he had come to do something about Layla's passport. Though that didn't make sense. Why would ASK have her passport?

I bet she has a boyfriend, Monty said to Kashif and Shavez as they played pool in the lounge. I bet she's with someone already.

Marriage was too far-fetched, it had taken Monty a good while to come round to that. But why would she drop out of school just because she had a new boyfriend?

His friends looked at each other and said nothing.

Monty rubbed blue chalk on his pool cue and pretended he didn't care, like he had met plenty of girls. Like he had never sobbed and begged Layla to come back to him, in hundreds of unanswered texts and emails.

'Just forget her,' Shavez said, patting Monty on the back. 'A lot's happened since break.'

'Yeah,' Monty replied, 'it's fine. I don't care', the pain building so deep in his lungs, so heavy, that he needed lies to keep it inside. 'Yeah, man, a lot's happened for me too, you know?'

'I know, man,' Shavez nodded, but couldn't help adding, 'and she didn't drop out, Monty. She was ex-pelled.'

In the afternoons, Monty sat in his room and cried. After school, he came home and locked his door. He turned on his AC and shut all his lights. He put the iPod on shuffle and the volume high, and lay under his covers and cried. He began drinking, as much as he could, enough to black out every night. It was the only rest he managed, the only respite from Layla and her disappearance.

He couldn't eat, couldn't sleep, couldn't pretend to be okay, once the school bell rang and he was forced to return to a home that was never a sanctuary.

Something was wrong, it just didn't add up. Monty could feel it in his bones.

Layla

I need my passport for school, Layla told Feroze several weeks before. He hadn't wanted to give it to her. The documents with her new name, Layla Yusuf, had been arranged by a contact of his in the police. Feroze paid him to smudge Zenobia's surname in the census records and paid extra for passports, *shenakhti* cards and driver's licences with all the correct stamps, holograms and biometric data to be issued to the whole family. When Feroze brought Layla to have her passport photo taken, his police contact met them outside the office and slipped them inside. Feroze insisted Layla cover her hair in the picture, tucking it snugly under a *dupatta*. It looked better that way, he said. More believable.

'Yusuf?' Zenobia's face had wrinkled with displeasure when her son, whom she still called Ezra, handed her her new computerized *shenakhti* card. '*Yeh Yusuf kaun hai?*'

'It's just a name, Ma,' Feroze sighed, 'something to help you.'

'How does it help me? How does it help me to lie in the face of God?' Zenobia shouted. She didn't want this *jhali* ID card, she said, and she certainly didn't want a passport – what was she ever going to do with that?

Maybe one day she might want to visit Holy Mother's house in Calcutta, or Lourdes or even Fatima, Feroze offered solicitously. But Zenobia spat down his suggestions. 'You want me to go to Lourdes as a *Mussulman*?'

He had got her a passport in case one day they needed to flee, Feroze complained to Layla later, driving her to school. (The school he found, arranged and took loans out to pay for, he reminded Layla.) 'Stupid woman, doesn't she see where she is? Doesn't she understand anything?'

Layla understood. She had learned, over the years of being seen and unseen, how to read signs for safety. Feroze was spending a lot of money – on an air conditioner for their Gulshan flat, *mithai* for Zenobia from Dacca sweets, he even paid someone to come to the house and massage Zenobia for a change. He said it was a special science, something called acupressure, said it would help her arthritis.

How much cash had he taken from his clients? In the climb to a better life, Feroze never worried about the cost. But Layla never imagined he would be willing to sacrifice her. Her brother had trained her to lie low; Osama had guided her to fight. Somewhere between the two was where Layla would survive.

'I need my passport,' she insisted, 'for school. They want it for graduation records.' And although Feroze was loath to give it – those Americans had special technology, what if they realized there was something off? – he hadn't paid thousands of dollars in tuition fees for Layla not to graduate.

In a small bag, she packed away the passport with the photo of a girl in a snug hijab, the long black *chador* and *dupatta* that she had worn in the videos, her phone – she would have to throw Monty's SIM card away before leaving – some kohl and a gold carton of Benson & Hedges cigarettes.

In the dark, tiptoeing out of the Gulshan flat, Layla

paused outside her mother's room and placed the small glossy photograph, wrinkled and torn from time, of our lord and saviour, his heart burning for the world, against the doorframe so it would be safe, untouched by hurried feet in the morning.

She had taken it from Zenobia's wall when they left their small grey home in Machar Colony years ago, but she could not carry it with her now. Layla held it in her hands for a moment, remembering another life.

In the small hours of the morning, Layla sat in a rickshaw holding on her lap her red notebook, whose pages she had erased and stapled extra sheaves of papers to over the years, distorting its shape.

The rickshaw driver wore a chequered black-and-white Palestinian scarf over his mouth, like a bandit, his eyes red and bloodshot. He pressed the pedals of his auto bare-foot, his toes – with dark henna-painted nails – curling to the shape of the slim metal accelerator. At the traffic light he turned in his seat to look back at Layla, studying her for a moment, before lifting his scarf from his lips. He smiled, running his teeth over his tongue. *'Akele hain?'*

Layla ignored him. She scanned the road for Feroze's new car, searching the hazy roads for a sign her brother was following her. She no longer knew what he was capable of.

In two hours she would be gone. If Feroze paid attention, he'd find all the videos – the ones *she* made – shortly afterwards. But by then it would be too late.

'Kahan jahraha hain?'

'Hajj,' Layla lied as she looked off to the side, out of the

rickshaw's open body at the queue of Pajeros climbing the slope towards Departures. A checkpoint of Rangers halted the traffic; armed commandos circled the cars, checking for explosives. Ahead, Jinnah International's lights sparkled like Orion, the hunter, in the night sky.

The driver's back straightened and the smile quickly disappeared from his bronzed, tired face. He lifted the scarf back up to his nose, adjusting it as he pressed his toes against the clutch. *Mashallah*, he nodded sombrely. *Mashallah*.

Monty

After a week, the American School called the Ahmed house to ask why Monty hadn't been attending his classes. Angelise answered and said that Madam was busy (it was a fasting day), but that Monty sir was in bed and unwell. He stayed in his dark room all day alone, until his mother came to his door.

'I need to go out.' Zahra adjusted the bag on her shoulder.

Monty lifted his head from his leather sofa, the fabric peeling off his face as he sat up slowly. Had his mother been standing there for five minutes or fifteen?

He felt his head throbbing and a slight burn on his cheek from the leather cushion he had fallen asleep on, drunk on a mix of gin and brandy that he found in his father's study. Akbar Ahmed kept his stash under lock and key, partly to stop the servants from nipping pegs of whisky, and partly to keep his wife from flushing bottles down the toilet. But Monty knew where the key was kept, under a pirated copy of *My Feudal Lord*, the only book his father professed to have read over the last twenty years, although the pristine spine suggested otherwise.

'Can Papa take you?' Monty hoped he wasn't slurring. He said the words as slowly and thoughtfully as he could. His tongue felt like a carpet. His heart hurt. He hadn't eaten in at least two days.

Zahra flipped on the lights. 'I'll be in the car,' she said, her voice tight. 'Put on a clean shirt.'

Monty went to the bathroom, swallowed a squeeze of mint toothpaste and put on a *shalwar kameez*, feeling uncomfortable. He only had one, reserved for Eid functions and funerals. The *kameez* was starched so severely it seemed to crack as he put it on. Monty washed his face quickly and wet his starched collars, so they wilted slightly. He sprayed XS by Paco Rabanne everywhere – under his arms, into his face and over his hair – to disguise the scent of his unwashed skin. He couldn't remember when he last had a shower.

As he put the glass bottle down, he remembered how much Layla had loved the cologne, how she had pinched one of his bottles when they first got together. He thought it was to remember him by, but she wore it to school. 'I love the scent,' she had said simply. 'Suits me, no?'

Monty picked up a washcloth and scrubbed the cologne off his neck and tucked his head under the tap, his face resting on the cool ceramic sink as he washed the alcohol out of his hair.

He sat down in the Audi and turned the radio on. As he reversed out of their gate, the *chowkidar* lifting his hand in a salute, Zahra shut off the music.

'I want to go to Abdullah Shah Ghazi,' she said. Monty looked at his mother for a second, making sure he heard right.

'The shrine?'

Zahra Ahmed nodded, tucking her hair deeper into her hijab.

'Doesn't your guru forbid people from going to Sufi shrines?'

He felt his mother bristle at the word 'guru'. On her ring finger she no longer wore a band of glittering diamonds, but a simple maroon stone that had been blessed by Nayar *sahib*'s

356

ministry. The proceeds would help train ten *hafiz* in Koranic studies. Zahra touched the ring now, turning it on her thin finger, as her son drove towards the shrine overlooking the sea.

Monty parked near the new overpass that had been built up around the saint's tomb and double-locked the car. He followed mutely behind his mother as she opened her plain black shoulder bag for a security check, beeped through the metal detector and joined the throngs of men, women and children climbing the narrow stairs to the sanctuary of the soldier Abdullah Shah Ghazi, buried on a promontory as a blessed saint, patron and guardian of Karachi.

Zahra stopped at the narrow landings and prayed at the small graves of Ghazi's disciples and followers, bending down to tie a red thread here, fasten a lock there, tapping her fingertips to touch the shrouds and then back up to graze her forehead. A solitary raven hopped along the edges of the tombs, pecking at the sugared almonds that devotees had offered to the heroes of the shrine.

'Mummy,' Monty edged away from the bird, feeling dizzy, 'I'll wait for you in the car.' But his mother caught his hand before he could leave.

'He was a warrior.' She spoke slowly, looking at her son with his starched *kameez* and unbrushed hair, the scent of despair and cologne that trailed him, mingling with the perfume of rose petals offered to the dead of Abdullah Shah Ghazi's *mazaar*. 'He came with the Arabs to conquer Sindh from the Hindu kings.'

Monty felt uneasy stopped on the stairs, as hundreds of skinny, dark bodies pushed against him in their climb to reach the saint's grave. What sounded like an orchestra of children cried and screamed, as a security guard stood in the middle of the fray, pushing people, raising his *lathi* in the air. '*Hat jao!*' he shouted at a shirtless *malang* who lay down on the floor, his dusty dreadlocked hair splayed out around him. The *malang*'s *shalwar* was pulled up to his knees, exposing thin, hairless calves and toenails black and dirty with grime. He writhed on the floor like a serpent, moaning, his long, matted hair moving rhythmically with his body.

'He was not a drifter, Monty. He was a soldier. Whatever else he was before he made his journey, Mustafa, he was a soldier.'

Zahra Ahmed held onto her son's hand, squeezing it in her own.

'He fought for Islam, for something much greater than himself. Do you see that?'

Monty nodded dumbly, turning sideways to let a family pass. But Zahra was not moved by the crowds. She stood her ground, holding onto her son's hand.

'Do you see what it means to stand for principles, Monty? Do you see what respect one man gains by fighting?'

The lights strung up on the bannister, on the roof, along the remaining trees that the overpass developers had not cut down, all came to life as the sky darkened. In the distance, the sound of a harmonium being tuned could be heard. It was Thursday and the evening's *qawwali* would begin soon. One strand of green fairy lights was lit, then another, then another, until the shrine was fully illuminated with cheap, fluorescent light inside and a thousand red brake-lights from scooters and cars circling the once-beautiful shrine outside. All along the landings, in between the hungry black ravens scavenging for sweets, oil lamps burned feverishly, fighting against the evening sea breeze.

'Monty?'

Monty closed his eyes and breathed deeply, letting his mother hold his hand, feeling un-alone for the first time in weeks.

'Yes,' Monty replied, opening his eyes and really hearing his mother for the first time that evening. She was holding his hand so tightly, her nails had begun to dig into his skin. He wanted to see it, he wanted so badly to have what his mother had developed: strength, fearlessness, focus. She no longer slept in the dark all afternoon. Now Monty was the one who retreated to his room, drew the blinds and hid from the world. He wanted to be better, he just didn't know how. He squeezed his mother's hand. 'Yes, I see it.'

Later that evening, Kashif and Shavez came over.

'Monty, this isn't cool,' Kashif said. 'You have to snap out of it.'

Shavez was holding his laptop, waiting uncomfortably while Kashif spoke.

'She's just a girl,' Kashif continued, sounding pissed.

'Whatever,' Monty replied. noticing the laptop for the first time. 'I just want to be alone.'

'I think you'll want to see this.' Kashif gestured at Shavez to fire up the Apple TV. 'I think it's time you knew.'

The video Shavez played was grainy, amateur film. Monty sat on his black leather couch in front of the flatscreen TV mounted on his bedroom wall and strained his eyes. 'What is this?' he asked, trying to make out the bodies, trying to understand what music was playing in the background.

There was a green glow to the camera filter, making the girl's brown skin look sallow. Monty couldn't see the man properly, only enough of him to see that he was older, his torso heavyset and hairy. He was kissing the girl's long legs, pawing her, straddling her and holding her arms down. Eric Clapton played in the background – that was the music.

'What is this?' Monty asked again. 'I can barely see anything.'

'Wait,' Shavez said, not taking his eyes off the TV, 'watch.'

The girl laughed, her hair falling in front of her face. She moaned in a fake, flirtatious voice, her hands moving along the man's head and neck, pulling him to her.

The man said something indecipherable and lowered his mouth onto the girl's naked stomach, running his tongue along her body. He had a beard, he must have been in his forties. He wore a gold bracelet on his wrist, which he flicked repeatedly, moving it back up his arm every time it threatened to fall.

It was gross, Kashif said, to have made a sex-tape with such an old dude. Sure, everybody made films now but, like, be respectable and make it sexy.

'Who is this?' Monty asked. 'Why do you have this? Is it local?'

Kashif kept his eyes down, focused on his shoes.

Shavez turned to Monty. 'She's a bitch, man.' He reached out and touched Monty's knee. 'You have to let her go.'

Monty frowned, he didn't understand. Let who go? And that's when he saw it. The girl moved back on the bed, crawling backwards and opening her legs. He could see her naked body, the legs, the flat stomach, the hip bones that pushed out against her tight skin, the chipped black nail polish on her toes.

Layla.

Layla

The fire lit her skin in a faint red glow and the pine crackled softly as the wind brushed against the broken logs of wood. She exhaled a tired breath and stretched her legs out, moving her body closer to the flames, inching her feet closer and closer until she felt the heat pulse against her. She closed her eyes for a moment and listened to the dying song of Nineveh's desert night, a wheezing, listless refrain.

Somewhere, an animal cried. There were wolves here, one of the boys had told her, small wolves with thin hair, like dogs. They don't howl, said the boy with the shaved head whom Layla had asked. And they live alone, never moving in packs. Nothing bigger in the wild here, only quiet, dog-like wolves. The boy's skin was nicked and small scabs of blood scarred his fuzzy, hastily shaven skull.

The strength of the pack is the wolf, Layla wanted to tell him, remembering a line from Kipling. The wolf that abides by the law of the jungle shall prosper and thrive. The wolf that breaks it must die. But he wouldn't understand. When you fight with a wolf, you must fight him alone and far.

They call me the Lion, she would have told the boy soldier in another life. I am the beast that abides by no law and belongs in no jungle, neither near nor far.

Opening her eyes, Layla ran her dry hand over her red

notebook and opened it gently, smoothing the paper with her palm. Straining to see in the darkness, she traced the lines she had been translating with the nib of a pencil lent to her. No one carried pens here, no one wrote on paper, no one remembered lists of vocabulary secretly learned, no one read poetry.

يتكلمون الحق، هم أولئك من رأو الحقيقة she wrote, whispering the Arabic words out loud.

On another page she wrote another translation: فقط من رأى الحق، يَروون الحق .

She was no longer sure which were the right words.

In the glow of the dying embers, Layla exhaled as she traced the curving letters of Arabic script over and over, careful not to press too hard into her remaining sheets of paper. Her feet burned with the warmth of the bonfire. She pulled her legs back, hugging them against her body, repeating the words to herself. She was all alone here. Like before, like always, she had no one.

يتكلمون الحق، هم أولئك من رأو الحقيقة

فقط من رأى الحق، يَروون الحق

Truly they speak, only those who have seen the truth.

PART FOUR

The Land of Milk and Honey

2017

Sunny

Nineveh, 2017

'*Bismillah.*' Sunny bends down, kissing a mouthful of sand. 'We made it.'

He jumps up and hugs Monty, wrapping him in his arms, delirious with joy. Done it, and did it right too. 'And nothing happened – we made it in one beautiful piece.'

Monty holds a hand over his eyes. 'All I can see are vultures,' he says, 'skinny vultures swooping and flying in a low circle.' He squints and cocks his head this way and that, looking at wisps of clouds, streaked through the sky.

Sunny kisses Monty hard on the forehead. 'I CAN-NOT wait to be rid of you!' he laughs.

But, like, he can feel Monty holding back, even as his AK presses into his ribs. Even with the laughter and the jokes and being metres away from the lads, from the end of their mission, he doesn't get any love back. Monty stands with his head tilted towards the sky, in a trance.

Sunny nods his head slowly. 'I see how it is – no gratitude, no thank you for protecting me all this way, no thanks for not letting those dog-killers rape me, no "I couldn't have done this without you".' What else is new?

But just then he sees the movement's red flag in the

distance. Sunny drops his bag on the desert sand and runs ahead, cradling Rita in his arms.

'*Ahlayn.*' Sam sits in the open back of a technical, thumbing through a dog-eared book. *Ahlayn*, one of the words Sunny picked up at Apollo. *Ahlayn*, welcome. *Qahwa*, coffee, the kind brewed thick and bubbly black, the face of the foam unbroken, even when poured into a small cup. *Allah allah*, how Aloush used to sing God's name in love and ecstasy.

Sunny blinks it back, he blinks it back.

Sam puts the book down and hops off the pickup truck, giving Sunny a grand slap on the back. 'God delivered you safely,' he says, holding Sunny's neck in his hands. He might not see Sunny, not yet, he can't see him truly, but he knows his value; Sunny can hear a new respect in Sam's voice.

'What's up, baby?' Sunny steps back to look at the weapon lying on the floor of the Toyota.

'9K38 Igla,' Sam pats the steel. 'We're going in heavy. How was it?' He gestures at Monty, raising his eyebrows as he watches Monty lugging their bags in the distance.

'Fine.' Sunny doesn't complain about the blisters on his feet, the rash that's turning his armpits a prickly pink, the dehydration, the parasites in his shit.

He realizes – on seeing Sam and the brothers – what they've done here, the enormity of what they have achieved. No matter Oz and the sting of his betrayal, Sunny done made it to the promised land, he done walked to the end of the world. He slides Oz off him like dust. And Pa, his pa, who never bothered to write to his son until Oz, his wonderful nephew, made the news. Pa, whose lack of faith hurts Sunny most of all.

He closes his eyes and there he is. Like nothing ever happened. Pa, in a brown gabardine suit, lifting Sunny over a birthday cake, his lips pursed behind his ears, helping him blow out the candles. Sunny's winking, just like Pa taught him, one eye squeezed shut, and his smile is like sunlight, burning up the sepia paper of the photograph. Was it all just a dream?

Sunny doesn't care now; he doesn't care about any of them – not Oz, not Pa. He doesn't have a family no more.

'No hassle?'

'Nah, we're all clear.'

'*Mashallah*,' Sam nods, waving some of the brothers over to them. 'That's why I love jihad – you commit, and Allah clears the way.' He pulls a small plastic bag out of his pocket, the same kind one of the brothers had slipped Abu Khalid. Sunny watches Sam quietly. He supposed Sam, because of his seniority amongst the brothers, was given the stuff to take the pain away, just like the commander, while the rest of them grunts had no choice but to struggle through it. Suffer, struggle, survive.

'Big day today.' Sam shakes his head as he pinches a tiny corner of opium out of the bag and places it on his tongue. He doesn't offer Sunny none, like he hadn't just walked across a fucking desert for the past week, like he isn't even there. 'Big day.'

Sunny shrugs. 'Yeah.'

At the end of it all, Sunny made it. He's here. He walked through the desert, walked out of one life and into the next, with only God able to see the weight of his soul.

He's here. And the end of the road doesn't mean anything. Sam couldn't hack one day of what he'd just done.

He gave it all up. Aloush — everything. Sunny gave it all up, and still no one can see him. Invisible.

No one will ever know Sunny Jamil suffered, no one will ever see the lost glory, the tortures Sunny Jamil endured, how he struggled to be someone. No one will ever know he was here.

Sunny blinks it back.

He blinks all of it back.

Monty

'You just leave me with everything?' Monty shouts, exhausted, the weight of two bags pulling at his arms. He throws Sunny's bag across the desert floor, kicking sand at him with what little strength he has left.

'Keep it down, you fool,' Sunny hisses.

Monty looks up at the sky, drawing a palm over his forehead. The white rays of sunlight peep through his fingers, blinding him. But he can still see them: ten, maybe fifteen vultures, falling in and out of the blue sky. For the last five kilometres, every time Monty lifted his eyes to the sky, he saw a committee of vultures gliding low, following him.

There's a commotion as men run past the parked technicals, following Abu Khalid. Only then does Monty notice the number of soldiers – twice as many as had been at their Mosul camp. So many of them, more than a hundred bearded young men, machine guns slung across their backs, jostling for the commander's attention. But Abu Khalid's on the phone, buried in his hand and held against his ear. The commander hasn't welcomed him and Sunny back yet, but he would want to be debriefed immediately.

Monty can see Abu Khalid speaking quickly, angrily, as though he's shouting. The brothers stand respectfully apart from him and wait, but their excitement is impossible to hide. In the distance, swirls of dust and dirt are

369

mushrooming into the atmosphere, trailing behind a convoy of speeding Hiluxes.

The commander rubs his temple; he's concentrating on something much closer than the vehicles. He lowers the hand holding the phone and walks briskly towards a tall, slender figure cloaked in black, standing right in the middle of all the *tamasha*. Monty holds his breath as he looks straight ahead, past the hundreds of brothers dotted around the desert like ants.

'What?' Sunny's head spins left and right. 'What's everyone looking at?'

'Her,' Monty says, softly.

There she is, Layla.

The lone woman in a desert filled with men.

She stands deathly still, her chin raised, watching a convoy of soft-skin Humvees and Hiluxes coming from the direction of Nineveh, barrelling across the desert at high speed. The vehicles are driving right at her, but Layla doesn't move.

The Hilux at the front of the fleet brakes, just before touching her.

Abu Khalid moves past Layla to greet the technicals, limping slowly through the crowds of men. The commander hits the door of the Hilux with his fist, and a line of men, dirty and cowed, some in jeans and T-shirts and others in long *jellabiye*, file out of the open back. Dust rises up into the air and, though he tries to see through it, for a moment Monty is blinded by the delicate particles of sand swirling around everywhere.

He's found her. There she is, his Layla.

Monty is light-headed with joy, with relief, with pure and total happiness.

Standing in the desert, he remembers the night he left home, the night he ended his life for the woman he loves, as though it were yesterday. No time has passed, no terror can mar the longing of his search, his secret journey.

Monty had paced the dark residential lane behind his home, stopping under the dim glow of an orange street lamp to open his Tumi bag on the narrow pavement and check one more time that he had everything. He hadn't slept since the night before, not since he had decided. He had spent the morning in Saddar, buying supplies. Just an hour earlier he tried to book his ticket online, but couldn't get Kayak to reserve it. Expedia's website didn't work and he had to spend half an hour with one of their Indian customer-service agents on the phone, wasting precious time.

Mosul, he stressed impatiently, I want to book a flight to Mosul. Her last video had been filmed there. Layla had uploaded it the day before. If he hurried, Monty might catch her. He let himself dream: if he left then, right then, immediately, he could be with Layla by the morning.

Monty smiles at the memory.

He had sat on his bed, holding the phone against his ear with his shoulder as he opened browser after browser on his computer:

Layla + Mosul + date
Mosul + Ummah Movement + contact
Karachi Mosul flight time
Layla + location + YouTube
Layla + training + jihad

Where? The customer-service agent kept asking, where do you want to go?

Mosul, Monty repeated, Mosul, Iraq. He considered that his name might be uploaded onto a database of some kind – just like Layla's must have been, after she ran away to fight in Iraq – and the thought gave him courage.

Monty had been on the street behind his house for at least ten minutes, walking up and down the narrow footpath, trying hard to be inconspicuous. He pulled his jacket collar up and the brim of his navy baseball cap down over his forehead, as he waited for the Careem that he had booked on his iPhone.

His heart beat madly against his chest. His flight was in an hour and a half. If Papa didn't check his text messages, he wouldn't receive the credit-card notification till it was too late for him to cancel the payment. By then Monty would already be in his Turkish Airlines seat, 5A by the window, looking down on Karachi, the city of lights, for the last time.

A white Corolla with its high beams on turned into the lane. The car drove slowly, stopping in front of Monty as the driver rolled down his window. 'Mr Akbar?' the driver asked uncertainly. He had thick black hair, gelled back against his head, and wore a black thread woven through his ear, hanging loosely like an earring. 'Akbar Ahmed, sir?'

'*Ji*,' Monty nodded. He opened the door and threw his Tumi bag in, climbing into the back seat. He had booked the plane ticket in his father's name, too, an inspired last-minute decision and an ingenious way round being listed on the database. No one at Jinnah International would check, and it would no doubt make Papa all the more furious when he found out. But Monty didn't care. If he was going to find Layla in a desert halfway across the world, he would need a little magic along the way.

He slunk down in his seat and checked the view from the windows quickly. Monty had thought maybe his mother would have noticed he'd gone missing and would have sent Tano out to look for him, but no one ever came.

Monty pulled at his baseball cap, shielding himself. His face stung from where Papa had slapped him and he touched his cheek softly.

'Sir?' The Careem driver, a young man in a thin button-down shirt, had turned round in his seat, watching Monty. Monty dropped his hand, embarrassed, and cleared his throat, searching the Hindu driver's face for a moment. They were roughly the same age, but the boy deferred to Monty, lowering his gaze when Monty looked up at him. Besides the black thread in his ear, he wore delicate *rakhi*, red strands looped round and round his skinny wristbone. He had a light-blue tattoo of a trident, the colour faded against his skin, on the nape of his neck.

He was sweating. He must have only turned on the AC when Monty got in the car.

The driver noticed Monty's eyes and tugged at his shirt collar uncomfortably.

Monty checked his phone one more time. He would make his flight. The trident was a good sign, an omen of what was to come. A symbol of the sea, which Layla loved; the weapon of a warrior, which Monty was to become. Monty closed his eyes and remembered the first words Layla had ever spoken to him: What do you know about the world?

Nothing, he had replied.

At midnight, Monty heard the familiar whistle of the night watchman, the old man on his rusted bicycle. He opened his eyes and smiled at the Careem driver. It was a second good sign. All he needed now was a third.

'Airport,' he ordered the driver, brimming with confidence, 'let's go.'

Everything – every memory Monty has of the past – is coloured by this moment, by the light in the desert, the heaviness of the heat and the hope he has carried all this way; by Layla now, right here, in front of him, slipping into a swell of fighters.

Abu Khalid lifts his AK-47 and fires at the earth.

Monty feels that familiar ache in his heart again, a rolling pain that drums with every inhale. He looks for Layla, but can't see her clearly. Even after all the torment she has caused him – first by her love, which she gave without qualification, and then by her cruelty, when she withdrew it – Monty harbours no anger. What can he do but forgive her?

As the brothers part from their celebration and the dust floats back down to the ground, Monty sees Layla standing beside the commander, smiling regally at the brothers who pass before her. None of the young men acknowledge her directly; they are too shy. At most, the brothers nod in her direction, before respectfully returning their gaze to the ground.

Has she seen him yet?

Monty doesn't dare move.

A shrieking, shrill noise shatters the sky. The vultures

circle the convoy of vehicles, their wings spread wide and their long, crooked necks hunched low, watching the brothers.

Up ahead, someone is screaming.

Monty's eyes fall back on the men, as Abu Khalid slams the butt of his Kalashnikov into one of the prisoner's necks as he tries to run past the Hilux, escaping the chain gang of captives. The weapon connects with the man's body with a loud crack and the prisoner, balding at the top of his crown and wearing a thin cotton jacket over his clothes, stumbles from the blow, before falling to his knees.

Monty flinches at the noise but doesn't look away. Layla stands at the front of the circle, watching the beating, her back perfectly straight. The vultures compete with the chaos, swooping down closer to the gathered men.

The birds are wailing, long, anguished cries.

The number of vultures has grown and, although Monty can't be sure, it seems like they're flying lower, grazing the brothers, dipping in and out of the band of fighters. Some are padding in between the men, hopping across the hot desert sand, smelling the earth for flesh.

Monty can't tell, from where he stands, but here, unlike in the YouTube videos, it seems as though Layla *is* wearing make-up. Her lips, just above her mole, are a dusty rose and the thread of her lash-line looks distinctly feline. Is she wearing eyeliner?

A brother with a large camera mounted on his shoulder, his eye glued to the viewfinder, walks backwards, turning slowly in circles to capture the scene. Monty tries to keep his face hidden, moving closer to Sunny for cover.

Abu Khalid says something to the men that Monty can't hear, and the bald captive lifts his hands and places them at the back of his head. Sam approaches the other prisoners, seven in total, and ties their wrists together.

'Who are they?' Sunny whispers, even though they're not close enough to be heard by anyone.

Monty shakes his head. 'I don't know.'

The pattern of the birds contracts and expands in the sky. The committee of vultures, with their stooped posture and enormous wingspan, twirl and dance in the bright blue of the desert morning.

Abu Khalid shouts something at the men in Arabic, his Kalashnikov pointed at the captives the whole time. One by one, the prisoners lean forward, open their mouths and bite onto the shirt of the man in front of them.

Erdo laughs loudly. All the new boys are filming on their camera phones.

'*Ya shabab*,' Sam calls, scooping the air with his hands, gesturing for the brothers to gather around. Sunny runs ahead, like a dog being called home, leaving Monty behind.

Monty combs his fingers through his hair and tries to tidy himself up a little. He doesn't want Layla to see him as a face in the crowd. He wants to be brought to her, he wants her to see him for what he has become – a vanguard, a front-line defender of the tribe, a sentinel.

Maybe Abu Khalid will present Monty in front of everyone as the soldier who has marched across the desert to secure this very mission.

Maybe Abu Khalid has spoken of him already?

Maybe the commander will say a few words about their

mission, praising Sunny and Monty in front of all the brothers, and Layla will turn towards Monty, not connecting the dots, not understanding which Mustafa has been a lion amongst men.

And then Layla will see him and she will know it was her Mustafa, her man, who was a leader amongst this flock of followers, and her eyes will widen with pride. Monty will see the shock on her face, but he'll stand tall, not blinking, not smiling, like the soldier that he is. Abu Khalid will embrace him. *Mustafa has walked across the desert*, the commander will say, *he has cleared the path of our enemies.*

We take Nineveh on the back of his sacrifice.

We fight because Mustafa, our sentinel, has paved the way.

Monty looks over at Sunny, fishing black watermelon seeds out of his teeth with his tongue, and smiles. Layla will see that he is a warrior. She will finally understand what kind of man Monty is.

He thought about what he might say, if the brothers demand a little speech. He runs his fingers through his hair and wipes the dirt off his chest. Slowly, as though his palms were a flat brush, he smoothes down his beard.

The Iraqi prisoners stand in a row, their eyes downcast. Only once all the brothers have gathered in a semicircle does Layla, possessing an elegant, balletic beauty, shift and take her place at the front of all the men.

Aside from the bald man, whose neck is bowed and bleeding, all the rest of the captives are young, in their twenties or thirties. Two don't look older than teenagers. No man cries or begs, they just stand there, biting onto each other's shirts with their teeth, like animals.

Monty hopes Abu Khalid has seen him and Sunny; he

won't be able to include them in his speech unless he knows they're back. A momentary panic rises in the pit of Monty's stomach, but just as it climbs through his body, it falls away. Of course the commander knows they're here – the mission to Nineveh can't begin without them. He was rallying the troops with those prisoners. Nothing could be bigger than the invasion of Nineveh itself, the conquest whose very existence relied on Monty and Sunny alone.

But when Abu Khalid moves to the front of the circle to address all the brothers, quickly glancing at his phone once again, he doesn't call Monty or Sunny to join him. He doesn't even notice them.

'Today we take Ninawa,' the commander says, in a low voice that Monty strains to hear. 'For our men to move freely between our land, we must cleanse Ninawa of the resistance, who have been fighting us since we began our march across Iraq.'

The brothers raise their weapons and cheer, but Abu Khalid holds out a hand for silence.

'By Sunday we will execute the last of Ninawa's traitors at the gates of the city.'

At that, one of the young men in the chain gang breaks down. He drops his face, leaving the fabric between his teeth, and sobs.

Abu Khalid's face darkens with anger at being inter-rupted. Sam unclips his Soviet Makarov pistol from his military webbing, walks towards the crying boy and shoots him in the throat.

The boy's knees buckle, like they had snapped, and he falls to the dirt.

The brothers are silent for the briefest of moments and then someone – a lone voice, who? – shouts in cheer. Once that first voice rings out in celebration, all the others follow loudly, whistling and jeering and clapping. Several brothers lift their Kalashnikovs and fire a round of bullets at the sky.

Monty feels the ground underneath him spin, tilting him against the earth. He closes his eyes and tries to breathe slowly, but he can smell blood, a warm ferric scent, from where he stands.

'Oh my God,' Sunny leans towards Monty. 'What a shot!'

Monty opens his eyes and looks at him. Has Sunny not just seen what has happened? There, right in front of Layla, is the bent and broken body of that boy, his blood soaking into the hot sand.

Monty closes his eyes again, trying not to feel sick. But he can hear her, he's sure of it. He hears Layla's voice rising above the cries and clamour of the brothers. His eyes twitch open.

Layla.

She must be terrified.

He listens for the sound of her voice, one note that soars over the men's. But Monty can't make out what she's saying.

Monty stands on his toes and looks for Layla. She's right next to the body, her palms clasped together in front of her face. Her hair is pulled back tight under her hijab. Maybe it isn't eyeliner; maybe it's just the curve of her high, crescent-moon eyes. Monty has to be with Layla now, to hold her, to shield her and remove her from all this.

He starts moving slowly against the grain of the gathered brothers, edging closer to his beloved's side.

'This man,' Abu Khalid silences the crowd as he pulls the bald man towards him by his elbow, 'is the mayor of Ninawa.'

The mayor's hands are still folded against the back of his head.

'He is the leader of the men attacking our brothers. They call themselves freedom fighters.' The commander laughs bitterly. 'I have warned him: convert and declare yourself a servant of our cause. Join our forces and free Iraq. Fight our war or be fought by us.'

The mayor looks at his sons, unable to speak to them through the rag bound across his mouth.

'But he has refused.'

In the expectant silence, the low vibrations of a phone buzzing can be heard. Abu Khalid speaks slowly, scanning the faces of his men.

'Who here wishes to kill their first freedom fighter?'

All the brothers heave forward, jostling and pushing their comrades out of the way in order to be selected. Monty keeps his head down and moves quietly against the thrum of people, inching discreetly towards Layla. She remains in her place, watching the commander intently. The closer Monty moves towards her, the more he can smell the blood, growing stronger and more fetid under the afternoon sun.

'Me.' Sunny, who has elbowed his way to the front of the crowd, calls out to the commander. 'Commander, please. Me.'

Monty tries to catch Sunny's eye, while still trying to keep his head down and remain inconspicuous – he is so close to Layla – but Sunny has already jogged too far away to see him. Monty breathes deeply, a burning sensation creeping along the back of his throat as though he were about to vomit. What is Sunny doing?

The sun is shining into Monty's eyes and he blinks once, then twice, counting how far he is from Layla – five men, maybe six. She still hasn't noticed him as everyone around her pushes and shoves, a sea of bodies heaving, trying to get a better view.

Sunny takes the mayor's hand, like a shepherd leading a lamb, and walks him towards one of the technicals, acknowledging the hoots and applause coming from his brothers with a proud fist raised in the air.

Sunny runs his eyes across the gathered men, calling them to witness him, like a boxer stalking the ring before a fight. He looks over at Monty and winks, blowing him a kiss.

Monty breathes through his nose. His tongue feels heavy in his mouth. He swallows the saliva gathering at the back of his jaw and takes a step forward, looking up as Sunny leans in to the mayor and whispers into his ear.

Sunny places a hand on the mayor's shoulder and gently lowers him to his knees. When the mayor is on the ground, Sunny brings his lips to the man's ear and whispers into it once more.

He straightens up, dusting off his cargo trousers before handing his phone to Sam, who points it at them. Sunny unsheathes the dagger from his belt and stands behind the mayor, holding what thinning hair the man has left in his closed fist, jerking the mayor's face upwards.

Sunny closes his eyes for a second and takes a deep

breath, exhaling slowly. He opens his eyes and nods at Sam, who hits the phone and starts filming.

Monty moves closer to Layla, squeezing past bodies dressed in black, bands of bullets strung across their backs.

Sam holds the phone at Sunny, who speaks into the lens, his British accent stronger than Monty has ever heard it.

My name is Salman Jamil and I am a soldier of Jerusalem, destined for Paradise.

For a moment, it looks as though Sunny has done nothing at all, only drawn the tip of his blade across the man's throat, tracing an invisible line, the way he has done so many nights in the sand. Monty thinks back to the flowers Sunny shaded during their journey, squatting over patterns with his dagger, the way a painter handles a brush.

Monty watches Sunny now, slitting the man's throat, severing his tendons with an artistry he has kept secret all this time, and wonders how he has travelled so far with a man he doesn't even know.

Sunny, the executioner.

The mayor's body jerks into shock, a gargle of blood spilling out of his torn windpipe as he wheezes and coughs, gasping for air. In the movies, a man dies quietly, falling into a heap as soon as his neck is cut. But the mayor struggles. Wordlessly, he fights to breathe.

Monty has to get to Layla *now*. He closes his eyes and pushes past the men between them, reaching Layla just as she lifts a hand over her mouth. He wants to hold her, to comfort her before she cries, but as he nears her, close enough to smell the faint whiff of tobacco that still lingers in her hair, she tilts her head back and howls at the sun, her tongue dancing across the roof of her mouth.

'God is the greatest,' Sunny shouts in a language that is not his own.

Layla lifts her face to the sky and ululates loudly, like a bride.

Monty stands behind her, breathing deeply as his heart pounds against his chest. 'Layla,' he calls softly.

But her tongue continues its battle cry.

She isn't afraid, she is celebrating.

'Layla,' Monty says, speaking into the back of her hair as he had once done, back when she was a different woman, back when she was still a girl. But she doesn't hear him.

Monty touches her gently. Immediately he sees her shoulders rise and her body flinch.

Layla spins round angrily.

'Don't you dare lay a finger on me,' she spits at Monty, glaring at him as though he were a stranger.

'Layla,' Monty stammers; doesn't she recognize him? He has grown a beard since she saw him last and he is a little tanned from the sun, a little leaner, but that's all. 'It's me.'

She pulls her long black *abaya* tightly around her and turns away from him.

'I came here for you, Layla,' Monty continues softly. 'I'm a soldier now.'

The brothers all around them are shouting. Some fire in the air, others clap their hands loudly, mimicking the hollow beat of a drum. No one has seen Layla shout at Monty.

Layla turns her face only a fraction, enough for Monty to see her lips move, and speaks to him over her shoulder.

'If you don't stop bothering me, Monty, I will have some-one remove you.'

It is the first time she has said his name.

'Go home, Monty. Leave me alone.'

Takbeer, the brothers shout, not really knowing what it means. *Takbeer*.

Sunny

I have never felt so good. Never never, not ever.
Hand me a crown, I'm about to be King.

Sunny lies on his back on the sand, cooing to his Kalashnikov. The desert is aglow with bright comets of light, phosphorescent green-and-gold tails bursting outwards into glittering rays. It is four in the morning and the thud of mortars shakes the earth.

'I am a new man, Monty.' Sunny bites his lip and nods slowly. 'Took that mayor's life and sucked his soul into mine, you hear? You know what it's like to execute a man?' Sunny holds Monty's eyes, watching him so intently he can *feel* Monty tremble inside him. His tiny, precious heart pounds across Sunny's ribcage, rattling Sunny's bones. His whole being is animated by Monty's fear. It sounds like some crazy necromancy, but it's true. All those doubts, all that pain, Sunny blinked it away. Blinked it dead.

It's gone, all of it. Nothing holding Sunny back now, reborn.

'I got two spirits, Monty. Mine and his. His power, his strength, his fear, his anger – all of it came into me. I felt it coursing through my veins when I cut his throat. I inherited his world when I spilled that filthy blood of his, Monty. He's mine now. Everything that man was, I am.'

Monty holds his breath and listens to Sunny.

I killed a man, I ate his soul.

Ain't no way out of the fire now, boss. It's who we are. Born by fire, son. Born by blood.

Monty doesn't know what to say. Sunny can see it on him – he's paralysed.

Things change, Monty mumbles softly, this is over now. We did it. We made it. Aren't we finished?

'Oh no, son.' Sunny shakes his head. 'This is only the beginning.' He moves closer to Monty, dragging his body towards him through the cool night sand. 'You can put them out, Monty, but the fires will keep coming.'

Monty

Monty hasn't slept all night. He'd been too afraid to close his eyes, knowing that Sunny lay beside him. Of all the things Monty suspected Sunny of – lying, spying, anger – he had never once imagined he was a killer. How had he not seen it in him?

The Nineveh offensive was launched after midnight. While the locals scrambled, the Ummah Movement bombarded the town. Even now, hours later, heavy machine-gun fire cracks in the distance.

Monty looks up at the night sky. It's light, he tells himself. Fireworks, stars, that's all. Only light.

Layla doesn't want him. Worse, she hates him. Monty thought she missed something of her old life, that she was alone – like he was – even in this army of people.

Maybe she lashed out at him because of the others, because she didn't want anyone to see them together. Maybe Layla thought Monty would expose her? But he would never do that. He thought of the fury in her voice, the bitterness with which she spoke to him. Was she happy here, without him, making propaganda videos and motivating beheaders and murderers?

Monty turns on his side and watches the trail of detonative golden lights streaking the navy of the sky. He thinks of Layla, her hair falling over her face as she ran her long hands through Karachi's polluted shore, how she had held his face with her fingers, leaving grains of silver pebbly sand on his chin and the corner of his lips, how she had moved closer and closer to him until her shoulder was square with his heart. Monty, she had whispered, the air thick with salt and smoke, Monty, do you love me?

His heart swells with the memory.

But that was another life ago. That was another woman.

And Sunny. Who is Sunny?

Monty sits up and watches the various fire teams getting their gear together. Distance-bombing had begun two hours ago, while Nineveh slept. They had already hit the town's water supply and telephone exchange.

The brothers scurry around their temporary camp now, passing news back and forth, boasting of body counts. The local militia has only just started to mount any defence, but it's too late. Artillery rounds fall on Nineveh like rain.

Monty glances over at Sunny, looking as calm as he's ever seen him, cooing to his Kalashnikov. 'Who's a darling girl? Who's ready for a big, big day?'

Yesterday he cut a man's throat, and now he gazes upon the dying stars and sings to his Kalashnikov.

'Who's a pretty little thing?' Sunny turns on his side, resting his head on his arm as he strokes his weapon. 'You are. Yes, you are.'

Sunny

All night Sunny watched Monty twitching and tossing and turning. He didn't sleep a wink, kept his eyes on Sunny at all times, checking constantly that he was still there. Like he was afraid Sunny'd leave him.

Now, as the brothers eat a small breakfast of fava beans and bread, shovelling the food quickly before they are all called to duty, Monty sneaks up off the floor and tries to tiptoe away, out of range somewhere. But he doesn't see Sunny watching him.

'It's too late now, Monty.'

He stops dead in his tracks.

'We're going to crumble Nineveh like dust. No one leaves the city till we say so.' Sunny looks for the whites of Monty's eyes in the faint glow of light that bursts and then expires after every explosion. 'Not even you.'

'What do you mean? Who said I want to leave?'

Sunny sits up slowly and laces his boots. 'I can smell it on you, Monty. You're terrified.'

Monty shakes his head, panicked. 'It's just ... I've never seen anything like this before.'

Heard it all before, mate. I'm just biding my time, lying low under the radar, 'recruiting some more boys'. Code for I'm a coward and just want to stay at home, playing Fifa. Same shit, Monty, different smell.

Sunny carries on collecting his things. 'You ain't fooling

me, Monty. I can tell. I've been baptized, got all sorts of new powers now.'

The whistle of artillery shells is followed by a shattering, crushing thunder. Monty bends his head, holding it in his hands. Sunny can see him shaking.

Sam calls out to them – he needs Sunny at the back of the Hilux, positioned to fire the Dushka.

Sunny jogs over and jumps up on the back of the truck, inspecting the mounted machine gun. It looks like a piece of tank ripped off and slammed onto the technical.

He runs his fingers along the Dushka.

'You see this?' Sunny shouts over to Monty. 'This baby fires six hundred rounds a minute. *A minute*, you hear?'

Monty nods, his eyes downcast.

Sunny can see the terror in him. Whatever it is, Sunny knows this – it's a big secret that Monty's guarding, and it's got some mad energy to it now. Boy has no skills to hide the terror he's feeling.

'Why are you here, Monty?'

Monty shifts his weight uncomfortably.

Sunny jumps off the Hilux and walks over to him. 'You don't give a shit about the weapons. You don't want to conquer and kill – at least, not from that queasy look on your face.'

He circles Monty as he speaks.

'And you don't know nothing about the mission, or the fighters we out here to observe and protect. So, why are you here?'

Monty turns his eyes back to his boots.

'If it's a secret, Monty,' Sunny whispers into his ear,

standing so close Monty can smell his rancid morning breath, 'I'll find out.'

Yalla ya shabab! Sam shouts from the top of the Hilux. There's twenty or so technicals lined up, all mounted with light machine guns, ZZU-32 anti-aircraft guns and sweetheart Dushkas.

The men get into formation, one brother driving, one brother navigating, one shooting, one prepped for ammo runs. Sam pulls up one of the prisoners from the chain gang, one of the mayor's sons. Must be fifteen or sixteen, just a kid. His hands are still bound behind his back and his face is covered in dirt, except for track lines on his cheeks.

'Get in the truck.' Sunny kicks the boy as he struggles to climb onto the back of the Hilux without the use of his hands. 'I don't care no more.' Sunny folds his arms across his chest, refusing to help. 'I. Don't. Care.'

Sam, who's holding the prisoner's T-shirt, pulling him up onto the truck, laughs and drops him. The kid's face kisses the floor of the Hilux. *Slam!* Sam crushes the kid's neck with the heel of his boot, pushing down on him till he chokes.

Sunny leans against the Hilux, level with Sam's boot and the mayor's kid, and hands Monty his phone for a selfie. 'Take it, Monty.'

Monty snaps the picture without a word.

Sunny sits down on the floor of the Hilux and starts editing the picture right then, heightening the colour, adjusting the structure.

'Boys,' Sam unclips the walkie-talkie from his webbing and holds it to his ear for a minute. 'You have to get down.'

'What?' Sunny looks up from his phone. 'Why?'

Sam shrugs. 'Abu Khalid's at base camp.' He points the hand holding the walkie-talkie in a death grip towards an apartment block that looks like a council flat.

'Ain't we going in?'

'No, they want you there now.'

Sunny shakes his head. 'Shame, really.' He snaps his fingers and looks at Monty with something that resembles pride. 'All kinds of darkness hidden in this one.'

Sunny keeps his eyes on him.

'Full of secrets, our Monty.'

Monty doesn't look at him, but Sunny can see him exhale, relieved as anything.

The carnage ahead of them is some extreme shit. The soft-skin Hummers are stationed outside key points around Nineveh, and brothers have already started lining up resistance fighters to be shot. Tanks are on guard outside the hospital, post office, telephone exchange and all major roundabouts and markets.

Sunny feels his body towering now, his courage flying. With his laurels and guerrilla cred on point, how can Oz fight him now? Oz is a pygmy. Sunny's a giant. Oz is an ant, crushed beneath the weight of his colony. Sunny's a firefly, rising and falling, but always carrying light.

He puts the photo, all filtered and freshened up, into an email to his cousin. Subject line: *Are you, or is someone you know, a revolutionary?*

#fuckyou #naturalbornkillerz #swag

Monty

Monty sits in the back of the technical as Karimov drives wildly towards an apartment block on the outskirts of Nineveh. It was strange that Abu Khalid hadn't spoken to him and Sunny yet. He hadn't spent the night with the brothers camping out in the desert, and hadn't sent a lieutenant to debrief them the night before. No one has asked them anything – not Abu Khalid, not one of his deputies. Sam asked if they had fun. Erdo wanted to see pictures, but that was all.

They had walked more than 150 kilometres across one of the world's most dangerous countries, for nothing. Monty had been sent to cross the desert, alone and unprotected, for no apparent reason. No one here wants him here, no one needs him.

He could have died. Monty holds his throbbing head in his hands and considers what a waste all of this has been. He could die out here.

And for what?

Was it worth it to have made it here, only to be spat on by Layla?

He closes his eyes and tries to calm the panic rising in his chest. It's fine. It's going to be fine. Abu Khalid isn't part of the cadres attacking Nineveh, he isn't anywhere close to the fighting. He never is.

The long veil of night hasn't lifted and the streets of Nineveh are bathed in a soft orange-blue glow. It's a light Monty has only ever seen in the desert before, a luminescent wisp of colour streaking through the sky. He thought of the scraps of paper that burned with a garish halo of colours for a brief second before extinguishing, failing to light any fires.

Nineveh's electrical plant and power mains have already been hit. The town has been fighting by candlelight for hours now. As their technical drives past decrepit, bullet-ridden buildings, Monty tries to peer through the windows, but they're dark and cold and the Hilux moves too fast for him to see anything.

He exhales deeply. Nineveh is hours from falling. They'll debrief Abu Khalid and he'll find a way out of this. But a feeling of dread rises in his stomach and, for a second, Monty thinks he's going to be sick.

He wants to close his eyes again, to shut them for a moment and rest until they reach their destination, but someone is watching him. He looks up and there's Sunny, sitting across from him on the floor of the Hilux, a thin smile spreading across his face.

*

Monty opens his eyes slowly, a gentle melody ringing in his ears. It's a song he has heard before, though caught in the foggy limbo of dreams, he can't remember where until he opens his eyes to the sight of Abu Khalid standing over him, lifting his mobile phone to his face. *I said not now*, the commander barks into his phone in a clipped voice. *Do you have any sense of what I'm doing here? Of what's going on around me?* But whoever's on the other line hangs up, and Abu Khalid slams the phone against his leg, cursing in Arabic. Monty quickly shuts his eyes.

He hears the commander shuffle towards him, dragging his bad leg. Abu Khalid rests a heavy hand on Monty's shoulder. '*Ya* Mustafa,' he shakes him, sniffling. 'Mustafa?'

Monty pantomimes waking up, opening one eye at a time, making sure to frown, as though the only thing he'd heard was his name. The commander's pupils are dilated and his nostrils rimmed with dry skin and redness.

Monty sits up quickly, running a hand through his hair and across his cheek. They had been taken off the Hilux and brought to an apartment on the outskirts of Nineveh. But the commander hadn't been there to receive them. Instead, Monty and Sunny had been taken to an empty room and told to wait.

When had he fallen asleep? How long had they been waiting?

Monty's eyes sweep the room for Sunny, but he isn't there. A warm light floods the room, it's still morning. Monty is alone on the cold floor of the room, his back pressed against the wall.

'I'm sorry,' he stammers, 'I was so tired.'

Monty flicks a finger along the inside of his eyes, wiping his lashes of the crust that gathered in his sleep. Abu Khalid is holding two cups of tea in his hand, and he passes one to Monty as an aide brings him a chair.

Monty drinks a sip of the too-sweet tea, the sugar coating his throat.

'You did well, *ya* Mustafa,' Abu Khalid congratulates him, settling himself down. 'You have proved yourself and it has not gone unnoticed.' The commander nods and takes a swig from his cup, before placing it on the ground. 'But Sunny tells me you are disturbed?'

Monty feels his stomach churn.

'He says you are a little unbalanced by what you have seen?' Abu Khalid leans closer to Monty. 'We have cemented our presence here,' he waves his hand across the abandoned room. 'We are conquerors, *ya* Mustafa. We are soldiers. This is our moment. You are a sentinel – what can be greater for a man?'

Monty doesn't want to speak if Sunny is nearby, but he's too weak to stand and he can't see outside the door from where he sits.

'But, Abu Khalid,' Monty starts, unsure of how to say it, 'the march was very dangerous . . . there were moments when I wasn't sure we would survive . . .'

The commander lifts his cup of tea from the floor. 'Mustafa, do you know how we bury martyrs? Do you know how we return boys to the earth before they become men?'

Monty shakes his head. Abu Khalid's tea, he notices, isn't black. It's a pale amber, like honey.

'We carry their *kaffans* dancing, we walk behind their bodies like a *barat*, taking a groom to his bride.'

Abu Khalid drinks slowly from his cup.

'Our women follow the body to its grave singing, we wash their bodies with rose petals, *ya* Mustafa. We do not fear death.'

Monty understands that this is why he's unhappy, this is why Layla haunts him in his dreams. He had risked his life to prove to Layla, travelling through the desert, guided only by the mood of the stars, that he was another kind of man. And she doesn't want him, no matter what kind of man he tries to be.

'But how does it end?' Monty's heart beats with worry. Where is Sunny?

The commander's eyes are glittering, you can no longer see the whites. Suddenly Monty wonders if that's why he never fights, why they never see him in the field, why after his pep talks he always whispers to his lieutenants and disappears into his tent.

Is he high?

'When the Mongols captured the Silk Road, no one could stop them.'

Monty listens carefully. His head hurts. He has no idea how long they'll have to stay here in this deserted apartment building before he can leave.

'No one,' Abu Khalid repeats.

'Then how did the Mongol Empire end?'

'It didn't.' The commander stands up, wiping the creases from his neatly pressed trousers.

Is that whisky in his teacup?

Monty looks up at Abu Khalid questioningly.

'The Mongols run China, Uzbekistan, Tajikistan, Kazakhstan.' Abu Khalid hits his chest with his closed fist. 'We are the Mongols.'

Monty feels fear rising at the back of his neck. He doesn't want to die here, not for these people, not for a girl who doesn't love him, who hates him – not for this.

'You, on the other hand.' Abu Khalid tucks his pistol into the back of his trousers. Monty can't remember him removing the Glock. Is he seeing things? The commander slaps Monty on the shoulder with his free hand. 'The Mongols would have hung you upside down and fed you to the wolves, *ya* Mustafa.'

Sunny

Sunny's about to bounce out of this rundown, depressing Josef Fritzl building and fly back to the boys. He doesn't want to waste this energy coursing through him, not an ounce. But just before he gets out, skipping down a dark flight of stairs, his email pings. And then it pings again. And again. And again.

Sunny opens his in-box and, lo and behold, there's one from Oz, and two from Oz, and three from Oz.

He must have had ten emails, downloading slowly, all from Oz, all with the same subject line: *A Rebirth?*

Sunny's heart beats like a flutter of wings.

He knew Oz would write. Sunny knew Oz would come back. Oz saw Sunny, he saw the look of battle in his eyes. Oz can't fool him no more. One of them is coming out of this thing on top, and it isn't going to be Oz. Sunny's been seen. He's been heard.

Sunny's no sheep, not any more. He won't be guilted, moved this way and that by Oz and Pa. Sunny's his own man now. He's been seen. Sunny's been heard. He's got his own gospel now, a language to call the world in. Oz must have seen that photo and been terrified. Oz must have seen it in Sunny – the fire, the truth, the power.

And then he opens the email:

A Rebirth?

Renounce • Reject • Reform

Patriarchy + Religion = FRAUDS

Ozair here, back with our second newsletter. Wow! Thanks to all 100,000 of you who signed up! Keep spreading the word, we have centuries of backwardness to fight!!

Which brings me to my next point: anyone with the Internet will have seen Layla. They call her the nightingale of war, the princess of jihad. Sound familiar?

Layla, a young woman, has become an emblem for radical hatred, fundamentalism and violence and is the quasi leader of a crazy (trust me, I know) militant group in Iraq.

Layla is working to erase the West from the map, conquer the Middle East, and convert the world away from atheism. But did you also know she has a secret past as a different kind of video star?

This week Reforming Radicals brings you an exclusive investigation into the hypocrisy, lies and secret past of one of the world's most vocal supporters of terror. For the first time

Why does religion produce liars?

The constant judgement of religion creates the necessity for lies. No one is more affected by this than women, who are never central enough to influence religions but are included enough to be traumatized by its rules.

Are sex-tapes un-Islamic?

In a word, yes. They are also anti-Christian, anti-Jewish, anti-Hindu, anti-Buddhist, anti-Jain, anti-Sikh, anti-fun basically. Morally and ethically, so long as you and your partner have discussed consent, the global connectivity of the Internet, and fluidity of gender constructs and respect, then they're fine by us!

Lunch with BHL!

No one understands the oppression of women more than Bernard-Henri Lévy, global feminist and humanist icon. Tune into our YouTube page to see clips from our CEO's lunch with the legendary philosophe and his thoughts on Islam, terror and the great cafés of Paris.

Monty

'Do you remember?' Sunny stands over Monty.

Monty looks up at Sunny, leaning against the door-frame. He must just have come in. Monty has been alone for hours, sitting on the floor, by a cold radiator, lost in his worries, waiting for the commander to send word that they can leave. *I am a sentinel*, Monty repeated the words to himself over and over again. *I am a sentinel. I am a sentinel. I am a sentinel.* He recited the words like a prayer.

'Do you remember what we're doing here?' Sunny's voice slithers into his thoughts like smoke. Monty can see every word as it travels towards him. He rubs his eyes, unsure how to stop Sunny from entering his mind.

'Of course.'

Monty remembered what they were doing here. No to democracy, yes to Shariah. Our law above all. Protecting the world from the dangers of national identity, greed, secularism, infidels, corruption and decay. Layla. Being with Layla, finding her, bringing her home. The girl he loved. That's what he was doing here.

But he doesn't understand why they're still here in this desolate room, sitting by the rusted silver radiator.

'You?' Monty asks Sunny. 'Do you remember?'

Sunny smiles. 'Get up.' He moves towards the door and peers outside. 'Abu Khalid wants to talk to us.'

Monty sits up, noticing only then that Sunny has changed.

He wears khaki camo like the commander now, his shirt tucked into his trousers, his dagger clipped to his belt.

He looks up at Sunny. Sunny who has more selves than he does. Sunny who knows how to navigate this jungle, because he possesses the perfect balance of violence and charm. Sunny, his only friend in the desert.

Sunny stands in the doorway, watching the hallway. Daylight is slowly fading and, from where he sits on the floor, Monty can see a shard of sunlight fall across Sunny's face, illuminating it.

'He has a mission for us.' Sunny turns away from the corridor and glances at Monty, curled up on the floor. He looks radiant. Monty has never seen Sunny look so at peace. 'A mission for you, really.'

'Another one?' Monty asks.

Oh yes, Sunny replies. His face is filled with joy.

'We have failed,' Abu Khalid sighs as he sits on a metal chair in the room functioning as his makeshift office. He folds his hands decisively and rests them in his lap. 'We are fighting a losing war.'

'But, Abu Khalid,' Monty begins hesitantly, 'we won.' He can't imagine one more day fighting, not another week spent marching. He can't do it again. They had won. He has seen men die and be reborn as killers. He's finished here. What happened to the Mongols? That was only this morning. Wasn't it?

Monty looks at Sunny, standing perfectly erect, no sign of emotion on his face.

'No, Mustafa,' Abu Khalid shakes his head slowly. 'We cannot win anything while we are rotten from the inside.'

The Iraqi rises from his seat, steadying himself the way a much older man would, resting his palms against his thighs. 'We have been misled.'

Abu Khalid glares at both Monty and Sunny.

'We have been deceived.'

Monty holds his breath and sneaks a sideways glance at Sunny, who doesn't return his look.

'Abu Ninawa,' Abu Khalid addresses Sunny. 'Show Mustafa the video.'

Abu Ninawa? Father of Ninawa? Monty stares at Sunny. Since when?

Sunny turns to Monty for the first time since the commander walked into the room and winks.

What video?

From his pocket Sunny extracts his shattered iPhone and opens a LiveLeak page. It takes a moment for the small black square to load and, when it finally does, Monty doesn't know what he's looking at. He leans against Sunny to get a better view, so close that he can smell the fresh soap on his skin. When had Sunny bathed? Where?

The video is grainy and Monty squints, trying to make out what's happening through a green filter of light. And then he hears the music.

Eric Clapton.

'She has dishonoured us.' Abu Khalid limps slowly in front of the boys. 'With this video, she has brought shame to our brothers, to our organization and to our cause.'

Layla. Oh, Layla.

Abu Khalid's voice trembles with anger. 'She has insulted our beliefs. She has ridiculed our people. What kind of future do we have now?'

Monty covers Sunny's screen with his hand, pushing the phone away just as the man crawls over Layla's legs.

They don't know anything, they don't know that the man who made the tape owned a TV station; someone found it on his work computer and leaked it. They don't know that Feroze had threatened him with a Hudood case, warning that he would drag him, his company, his reputation through the courts if he didn't pay the family to compensate their lost honour, and it was this – this *very* thing – that had baptized Layla in fire and driven her to the Ummah Movement, to Iraq.

In under three minutes, they had tried to destroy her. But days later, in another video, she had shown them that she was unbreakable. No man could destroy Layla. Layla the lion. Layla the beast.

I hold in me the legacy of millions. I am born of the Night of Power, she said in that first video, her hair newly covered behind a black hijab. She wore no make-up and her nails had been scrubbed clean. There was a light in Layla's eyes that Monty had never seen before. Something victorious and brave, something pure.

She began her broadcast with a religious recitation, delivered in perfect Arabic, her eyes lowered as she read from a paper on her desk. Once it was over, Layla raised her head and stared at the camera. *There is no God but God, the Rab al Alameen. All you depressed, downtrodden daughters of men, come forward and claim your anger. Rise, my sisters. Rise like lions after slumber. Pick up your weapons. We come this time to fight.*

What did Abu Khalid and his men know about Layla's injustice, about the unfairness of the world against her?

The peculiar isolation of the educated poor, reduced to watching life from the outside, from the gates of big houses they were not permitted inside? What did Abu Khalid and his men know about the hunger with which she consumed the world, one library book at a time? They don't know anything about Layla, nothing. It's a miracle it took them this long to find it, but Monty feared they would eventually, no matter the web of lies Layla had spun.

'I don't want to see this,' Monty says. He feels his hands shake, he hopes Sunny doesn't notice.

'It's too late,' Abu Khalid snorts. 'People have seen it. The moment our brothers understand that we are unable to cleanse the Ummah from corruption, we will have lost *everything* we have been fighting to build.' He paces the small, empty room, his fists clenched at his side.

'It can be removed . . .' Monty starts, looking at Sunny for confirmation. He knows more about the Internet than Monty does; he's on his phone all the time, he knows how to do these things.

But Sunny shakes his head.

'It can't.'

He scrolls down the page and points to a small number in grey. 'You see this? Thousands of views already. People have downloaded the clip, copied it and shared it. You can't un-see it now.'

'You can try to put them out, *ya* Mustafa.' Abu Khalid waves his hand in the air, his voice heavy with disgust. 'But the fires will keep coming.'

Monty's heart sinks.

Sunny.

It was Sunny all this time.

'Karimov!' Abu Khalid barks at the door. The Ingush pops his head into the room, a small envious look in his eyes as he sees Sunny and Monty at attention before the commander. 'Bring me the notebook.'

Abu Khalid has his back towards them, stalking the perimeter of the room. 'We've interrogated her, studied her papers – none of it makes sense. We don't know who sent her here or who she is working for.' The door creaks open as Karimov carries in Layla's red notebook between the palms of his hands. The commander snatches it from him and slaps at the pages, turning them angrily, pages and pages of illiterate poetry and ramblings. Some verses are written in English, some in Urdu, other pages are filled with long, gloomy quotes. Abu Khalid pauses on one of Layla's lists of English words, written in neat columns, with their grammatical tenses and definitions carefully inscribed in red ink.

He used to make lists like that when he was translating for the Americans. He used to have a diary of words just like this.

'She's a liar,' the commander shouts, flinging the notebook against the wall. Monty watches it hit the floor, its pages exposed to the world.

'And she has been under our noses, right here, watching us, deceiving us, all this time.'

Abu Khalid breathes deeply, the betrayal settling into his lungs.

'And it is because you two have proven yourself, conducting yourself with the righteousness and honour of your people, that I have chosen you.' Abu Khalid circles the two of them, standing behind Monty and Sunny, speaking into the gap between their bodies. 'Today you are soldiers for something much larger than our movement. Today you have been chosen to purify our tribe.'

'It's an honour,' Sunny bows his head. 'Thank you, Abu Khalid.'

'Chosen for what?' Monty asks, but the commander has already walked back to the metal chair and sat down, folding his hands into his lap.

Abu Khalid rests his head against the back of the chair, looking up at the ceiling, as though exhausted from his circuit around the room.

Sunny walks towards the door and Monty follows mutely behind him. Looking back at Abu Khalid, whose eyes are still closed, Monty bends to the floor and picks up Layla's red notebook, tucking it quickly into his trousers.

As soon as they are past the brothers standing guard outside the room, Monty grabs Sunny by the neck, pulling him into his chest. 'It was you?'

Sunny laughs and slaps a hand against Monty's back. 'What a vault you are.'

Monty holds onto Sunny and for a second he feels him bristle. 'You brought it to him?'

But Sunny doesn't release himself from Monty; he just readjusts himself, lifting his body out of Monty's chokehold. 'Thought you were dead weight, Monty *sahib*, but there's a bit of juice in you yet.'

Sunny raises himself up, freeing himself of Monty's arm and grabbing him, holding Monty much tighter than he had been held himself.

'You dirty, dirty dog,' Sunny speaks into his ear. 'You

didn't tell me you had a stash of naughties? Moaning about Layla every night – I should have known really.' Sunny snapped his fingers together. 'I should have known.'

Monty doesn't understand where they are going. Looking over his shoulder, he sees that they are being escorted by several of Abu Khalid's bodyguards, walking behind them. He pulls his shirt over the top of his trousers, making sure no one can see the red notebook in the waistband of his trousers.

Sunny bounds down the steps of the abandoned building. 'No skin off my back, Mush. You wanna play it coy?' He pauses in his flight and brings his mouth so close to his friend that his breath tickles Monty's ears as he whispers, 'I'm happy to take the credit.'

Monty pulls away and rubs his warm, clammy ear. 'Credit for what?'

'For the kill, baby. That's what.'

Monty holds the bannister of the stairway. He feels his heart stop. 'What do you mean?'

'Your girlfriend with the sex-tape, blood,' Sunny says. 'She's curtains.'

Layla

There are monsoons and narrow gullies filled with rain-water and somewhere there are small, sandalled feet running through the puddles, racing to the thin gunmetal door on the top of the *chawl*.

Is she laughing?

There's the rush of the waves, the long stretch of unbroken silver sea pressing itself up against the muddy shore before retreating. It rushes up and then it vanishes, as though pulled back to the centre of the earth. Rushes and vanishes, rushes and vanishes. The rippled shells, broken, all of them, buried under the sand like a secret mosaic. Hundreds of thousands of sea crabs with gel-atinous, transparent skin, scurrying over her toes and fingers, which she digs into the beach, burrowing deeper and deeper. All day her skin will smell like petrol.

The memory is painful.

She can see it all, everything, with every shallow breath, every desperate inhale. Machar Colony, the dark clouds over Seaview, her comrade's soft, wrinkled hands as he brings a book off a shelf, a glass of *sharab* to his lips.

Layla screams.

'Shut up,' one of them yells. The boy, the one with the light eyes. It was him. He knew. How did he know? Had he always?

She screams until her throat burns.

'Shut up!' the boy shouts and strikes her harder, much harder than he had when he stormed into her room a moment ago. Bound, Layla's sense of balance is gone. She falls, her body pulled to the concrete floor by the force of the boy's slap and the heaviness of the chair they have tied her to, like an anchor strapped to her bones.

Layla's eyes flicker shut.

The girl in the memory is laughing. She has a dark fringe and short, shoulder-length hair and, though she didn't know it then, she had been happy. So happy.

The men around her scream at her in Arabic. Layla can hear three voices, maybe two, rising in fury.

But all at once, there it is again:

The gas cooker, her mother's heavy thigh draped over her body as they slept together on the cement floor of her childhood home, the mynahs, the motorcycles with no exhaust, Ezra crying, his face coated with tears, lost in the jungle garden of that beautiful, beautiful Clifton house, pages and pages of discoloured *Soviet Life*. *You will hear thunder and remember me.* Layla heard Osama's voice, dry and rattled with age. *And think: she wanted storms.* His white hair was long like a lion's mane. She could see the pages of her notebook bruised with ink. All the words, conversations, arguments, poems – everything blended together. Layla felt her head spin. Anita Rose, never as sweet. A name by any other means. *The rim of the sky will be the colour of hard crimson. And your heart, as it was then, will be on fire.*

Her cheek tingled with cold as though she was there, at home, sleeping with her tired mother, on the floor. And then the boys, two of them, she couldn't see properly, leaned over her as she lay between dreams and dirt and brought their feet against her, kicking her and cursing, shouting, screaming.

But Layla could see him, even as she struggled to keep her eyes open, she could see his kind, smiling face and the warm brown of his eyes.

Comrade, promise me?

I promise.

Carry these words with you always.

Always, pukee baat.

Monty

Somehow Monty is moving. Though every step feels belaboured and heavy, he puts one foot in front of the other until he reaches the ground floor.

There's a chill in the stairwell, but nothing masks the smell of the men, like dogs in heat, trailing behind him and Sunny.

The brothers hold their weapons across their chest, defensively. Monty looks at Sunny in his starched khaki camouflage, bouncing off the walls in excitement, his feet dancing in an elegant boxer's shuffle.

Sunny jerks his head towards the darkened parking lot. 'Brothers already have her in there, tied up.'

Monty tries to steady himself, exhaling deeply. Everything has gone wrong. Everything he planned – coming here, finding Layla, all of it – has gone so terribly wrong.

Sunny

Okay okay okay. Sunny shuffles left. He shuffles right. Sparring and getting into the groove.

'Get lost, guys,' he snaps at the guards who stalked them down the stairs, dismissing them with a flick of the wrist. 'We got this.'

Not even three days into nation-capturing and he was going to clock two substantial kills – the mayor, one. Layla the phoney hypocrite, two.

Sunny digs his hands into his pocket and brings out a tiny plastic bag. He takes a small pinch of the sticky paste Abu Khalid gave him and rolls it in the palm of his hand. Promoted baby. 'Bout time.

'Please imagine how many sick fans of hers are going to tune into our shit now. We're going to be *fay-muss*, bro.'

It's like there's music in him. Sunny can feel it swimming through his veins, coursing through his body.

'Picture it, Monty: Classic Jihadi Videos. The towers falling, number one. Then, the beheading series – but only the big ones, Daniel Pearl, Iraq circa 2005,/2006.' He rolls the paste into a pea-sized ball and places it under his tongue. Sunny sucks down on it; it tastes sweet and smoky and bitter at the same time. 'Then there's the Abu Ghraib shots.' Sunny considers this for a moment while rolling a third little pat of raw opium. 'Maybe not those . . .'

This shit makes him sharper, catching all these errors like autocorrect.

'Then us – you and me, Cuz, killing this charlatan bitch. You and me.'

He holds out the tiny ball of brown paste to Monty, although he knows he won't take it, fucking nerd.

Monty shakes his head, even after Sunny tells him Abu K says it helps. Sam takes it too, on the regular. But nothing. He's standing there all hyper-vigilant, chest puffed out, body on high alert, turning his head every time he hears the brothers slap Layla out in the garage.

The sound of skin being flayed like that is a pretty slick sound. Like jungle beats in drum and bass. Sunny thinks of the drums now, of the music he peeled off those drums stretched tight against the palm of his hand. But that's gone. Gone, gone, gone.

It's not the opium. He barely had a bite. But you get that beat under your blood and it fuels the flame, you know? It stays with you, stakes a claim on your spirit. Sunny doesn't think of the drums now. He blinks it back, blinks it gone.

The slapping keeps going and going. He can't hear her screaming, though – brothers must have gagged her.

Monty turns and starts walking into the garage. Whattup, Monty! Always a surprise. Raring to go, for once.

'Let's go, baby,' Sunny shouts behind him, popping the rejected opium into his mouth. 'Let's do this.'

He high-fives the guards coming out of the garage, whom Monty must have booted out – savage today, my brother – and saunters into the parking lot.

Let's do this.

Monty

As he walks closer towards the single metal chair at the end of the empty parking lot, Monty sees her.

He sees Layla's eyes widen as she makes him out in the darkened garage, terrified. It's the first time he has ever seen her look afraid.

They have torn off her black *abaya* and bound her to the chair. Even though the brothers tied a gag around her, Monty can see that Layla's mouth, just above her mole, is cut. Her lips are red and swollen, like she has just been hit. As though she has been kissed too hard. Monty can't tell which.

Her face is a map of bruises and welts, one of her eyes is ringed in broken skin and sealed shut. Her hair is wild and uncovered and he can see patches of scalp, as though some of her long, black hair has been ripped out.

When she sees him, her chest expands with air and she screams as loud as she can, a muffled sound caught behind the rag in her mouth.

Sunny unclips the tanto from his belt as he swaggers towards Layla. He waves his blade in front of her face. 'Someone's made a fool of us.' He whistles loudly.

Layla's head rolls backwards and she moans painfully.

'Hello, sister.' Sunny bends down so he's eye level with Layla. 'This thing you've done? You ever played with fire before? You ever played with fire, girl? You ever got burned?'

414

Layla's eyes dart between Monty and Sunny.

Monty looks away from her.

'I have.' Sunny speaks in a taunting, teasing voice, stepping away from Layla and walking behind her. 'We all do. Who doesn't play with fire, when handed a lit box of matches? Whose eyes don't spark at the idea of destroying everything they love, everyone they care for? I played with fire, sister, my whole life, that's how I know.'

Layla struggles against the ropes that hold her to the chair. She shakes her head furiously as though she's biting down on the gag in her mouth, trying to spit it out. Her one unruptured eye is brimming with tears.

Sunny wipes the blade along the outside of his thigh and steps closer to Layla's chair.

Layla strains against her binds. As she bucks and pushes hysterically against the ropes, Monty watches the skin around her collarbone redden.

'What's happening is this, darling.' Sunny squats down in front of Layla, placing his body between her knees. 'You were a bad girl and you're about to get done for it.'

All the colour drains out of Layla's face and she drops her head to her chest and begins to sob, her whole body shaking with fear.

Sunny lifts her face with his hand, moving himself deeper between her legs. He looks at her longingly, turning her face left and right, studying her. The opium is slowing him down slightly.

Layla whimpers and tries to free her face, recoiling from Sunny's hands. She screams as loud as she can, but with the cloth tied tight against her mouth, she barely makes a sound.

'Don't want me to touch you, princess?' Sunny laughs. 'Why not? Everyone else has.'

Layla jerks madly against her chair, rocking backwards to tip it over. Sunny grabs the back of the frame and, as he does so, Layla head-butts him squarely in the face.

Sunny's head snaps back with the force of the blow and he hits the floor, stumbling backwards as he falls.

Monty rushes to help Sunny up off the ground, but he pushes him away, springing up and lungeing at Layla.

Sunny slaps her so hard there's a cracking sound. 'Trying to attack me? *Me?* Your reign here is over, Layla. The fuck you doing dirtying up our good name?'

He is screaming, spittle flying out of his mouth. 'Do you even know who I am? I'm a *soldier.*' His face is flushed with that same radiance Monty had seen earlier. 'I'm a soldier. I don't sit in an air-conditioned room reading out speeches on the Internet. I don't write newsletters for cowards. I don't insult the soil I come from. I defend it. I protect it. I fight for the truth. I go out and I wage *war.*'

Sunny's eyes are bright and his voice rings loud and clear.

'I didn't make my name off the back of others doing the hard work. *I* worked. *I* have blood on these hands.' Sunny hits his chest with the hand that holds the knife, thumping his breastbone. 'I'm here. I been seen. *Seen,* you hear me? You will treat me with respect.'

Layla slumps back in her chair. Her tangled hair falls over her face as her head rolls back down, so low that her chin seems to rest against her neck.

'You will treat me with the respect that I deserve.' Sunny moves his face right to Layla's, touching his nose to hers before he straightens up and, looking down at her, runs the tip of his blade along her clavicle.

'You treat me and my boy Monty here with the proper fucking decorum and we'll make it quick for you.' He turns to Monty. 'Won't we, my brother?'

Layla lifts her head and looks straight at Monty. And though he has been watching her all this time, though he has seen and heard it all, though he has seen Sunny slap her and run his knife across Layla's soft, white skin, he can't be sure if right then, under the constraints of her gag, she opens her mouth and speaks quietly, only to him.

Monty.

Monty, he thinks Layla whispers.

His hand reaches to his waistband, anxiously checking for her notebook.

Monty – rounding out the letters of his name.

Sunny

'Cleopatra, Cleopatra. What sort of subtle power you think you can play out here?'

Sunny thrusts his fists into his eyes. Oz has a newsletter that 100,000 idiots read and he can't get one random person to grasp a basic concept: apostasy.

The voices coming at him, rushing up like the ocean in a shell pushed hard against his ear, he speaks to them all now. Sunny speaks to every single one of them – Pa, Oz, her, Him, Him. Him.

'I've been seen. You hear? The hunt is over, the queen is dead.'

He lifts the truth over his head like a sword. All that poetry is in him, all those songs, all those verses written by dead Kashmiri men, they swell and break inside him. *Cashmere, Qashmir, Cashmir. We shall meet again in Srinagar.*

Pa, I been seen. Do you love me now? Do you?

Did you ever?

'You reap, you sow,' Sunny snarls at Layla. That's the way the world works, doesn't matter if it's ours or theirs.

'Women, am I rite, Monty?' He runs his hands through his hair. He hopes he looks okay, hasn't seen a mirror anywhere. Sunny adjusts the band of bullets along his chest. Gotta look fly for the video. 'They never know what they want.'

'True,' Monty says, piping up. First time he's ever agreed with Sunny. *Que pasa*, Monty?

418

Sunny sniffs, rubbing the back of his hand against his face. His mind is sharp, blade-sharp and clear. He feels nothing. No pain, no sadness, nothing. Like there's a clock going on in his chest and his life's passing him by, but he don't feel it cos he don't believe in time. Sunny closes and opens his eyes, so he knows he's not dreaming. He feels none of it. It feels still in his heart, for the very first time.

'They never know what they want,' Monty echoes, moving closer to Sunny.

Sunny licks his palm and smoothes down his beard. He's going to send this clip to Oz right away.

Reform this, Ozzy: Traitor + sellout = your sorry ass.

Liar + fuckface = you.

Sunny flicks through his phone with one hand, opening the camera. Oz will be able to tell right away from his threads and war name that he's been promoted. Then, after he emails Oz, Sunny's putting this straight onto the World Wide Web with a direct message for his cousin: I'm coming for you, Oz. You're next, Cuz.

His *#automatovakalashnikova* series is picking up good. He readies himself with a new one: *#cleopatra*.

'Monty,' Sunny calls, giving him his phone, 'hold this.'

Monty

Monty shakes his head and holds out his hand.

'No,' he says. 'I'll do it. You film.'

Sunny raises an eyebrow, impressed.

Outside, mortars fall on Nineveh like a scattered shower. The earth shudders with every explosion, but far enough away that eventually your body stops trembling from the shock and, in time, you no longer feel afraid.

Nearby, a lonesome dog barks.

It's a strange thing, bravery. So long as he follows his thoughts, observing them as they come to him, Monty finds he can turn them any way he wants. He pushes away the sound of the bombs and concentrates on the barking, a growl deep enough to have come from a bigger, more dangerous animal than a dog. Maybe there were wolves here. Maybe.

Anything is possible now.

He runs his hand across his waistband, feeling for the notebook.

'All right, Monty.' Sunny drops the blade into his friend's open palm. 'Didn't know we were playing it like that.' He blows a kiss to Layla. 'Sorry, darling, I'd have liked to do it myself, but my boy here is a dark fucking horse.' Sunny holds up the phone, ready to capture the moment, *#killtime*.

Layla looks at Monty, her body heaving, truly shaking,

as she cries. She shakes her head slowly, slowly, like the hands of a clock brushing delicately against the seconds of time.

'Let's go, Monty.' Sunny nods, watching Layla through his smartphone camera. 'Let's do this.'

'Ready?' Monty asks.

'Baby, I was born ready.' Sunny doesn't take his eyes off the screen.

Monty holds the knife in his hand for a second or two and directs his thoughts. He breathes deeply and forbids himself to second-guess himself or regret what he is about to do. He is a soldier. This is the only way.

Monty spins on his heel and strikes the knife with all of his strength.

After he pulls the blade out of Sunny's ribs, Monty closes his eyes and listens to the helicopters flying low over the walled city of Nineveh.

It doesn't sound like it does in the movies, where helicopter blades merely whistle, soft as the hum of birds in a thicket of trees. Here, it's a deep, rumbling staccato of thuds, like blood rushing against the ear, like jet engines in a tunnel.

Monty listens to the dog, the one outside the parking lot, howling into the night. He breathes deeply and tries not to listen to Layla, screaming and crying in her chair, her face wet with tears.

He is a sentinel, a beacon.

This is why he was sent here, why he walked to Nineveh through the desert, why he is a vanguard of this army. He's a sentinel, a watchman. This much is true.

'The fuck?' Sunny takes his eyes off Monty's face to look down at the warm, crimson blood pooling around his body. He tries to move his feet before his boots are stained by the dark-red blood, but he can't. Sunny can't move at all.

He looks back up at Monty.

And at that moment Sunny thought Monty – whose face was slightly tanned, the bridge of his nose burnt from the sun – was somehow more beautiful than when they had first met.

Acknowledgements

My deepest gratitude to:

Carl Bromley, Pankaj Mishra, Mary Mount, Karolina Sutton, Binky Urban, Molly Atlas, Lucy Morris, Caroline Issa and Masoud Golsorkhi, Muwafak Ghazal for his poetry translations, Rosanna Forte, Mandy Greenfield, Natalie Wall, Meru Gokhale, Gaurav Shrinagesh, Gunjan Ahlawat, Varun Talwar, Ambar Chatterjee and Katy Loftus who saw this through many drafts with enthusiasm and rigour.

My precious C.

Allegra, Ortensia, Cyril, Megha, Sophie and P. for their friendship, which I treasure.

Adrian Gill, who was excited about this book all those years ago and offered several completely inappropriate titles. He is always missed.

Frank Ocean, whose music was a balm for me too.

Baba, without whom nothing, none of this, would have happened. Baba, who will always be the greatest gift life has ever, and will ever, give me. Thank you most of all, my beloved Baba.

He just wanted a decent book to read ...

Not too much to ask, is it? It was in 1935 when Allen Lane, Managing Director of Bodley Head Publishers, stood on a platform at Exeter railway station looking for something good to read on his journey back to London. His choice was limited to popular magazines and poor-quality paperbacks – the same choice faced every day by the vast majority of readers, few of whom could afford hardbacks. Lane's disappointment and subsequent anger at the range of books generally available led him to found a company – and change the world.

'We believed in the existence in this country of a vast reading public for intelligent books at a low price, and staked everything on it'
Sir Allen Lane, 1902–1970, founder of Penguin Books

The quality paperback had arrived – and not just in bookshops. Lane was adamant that his Penguins should appear in chain stores and tobacconists, and should cost no more than a packet of cigarettes.

Reading habits (and cigarette prices) have changed since 1935, but Penguin still believes in publishing the best books for everybody to enjoy. We still believe that good design costs no more than bad design, and we still believe that quality books published passionately and responsibly make the world a better place.

So wherever you see the little bird – whether it's on a piece of prize-winning literary fiction or a celebrity autobiography, political tour de force or historical masterpiece, a serial-killer thriller, reference book, world classic or a piece of pure escapism – you can bet that it represents the very best that the genre has to offer.

Whatever you like to read – trust Penguin.